Critics praise novel
by Nobel Prize winner Pearl Buck

"THE TIME IS NOON has some of the most poignant
pages in modern writing."
—*Chicago Tribune*

"The story is told with honesty and
steady narrative drive."
—*Time* Magazine

"Pearl Buck's name on a novel always assures fine
reading. But this has something more: passion.
It will be read with a lump in every throat and a
tear behind each eyelid."
—*Boston Herald*

"Genuinely moving..."
—*Detroit News*

"A beautiful and stimulating novel..."
—*Sacramento Bee*

The Time Is Noon was originally published by
The John Day Company, Inc.

Pearl S. BUCK

The Time Is Noon

A POCKET BOOK EDITION published by
Simon & Schuster of Canada, Ltd. • Richmond Hill, Ontario, Canada
Registered User of the Trademark

THE TIME IS NOON

John Day edition published February, 1967
POCKET BOOK edition published March, 1968
4th printing........October, 1971

This POCKET BOOK edition includes every word contained in
the original, higher-priced edition. It is printed from
brand-new plates made from completely reset, clear, easy-to-read type.

POCKET BOOK editions are published by Simon & Schuster of
Canada, Ltd., Richmond Hill, Ontario.

Trademarks registered in the United States and other countries.

The Time Is Noon

I

It was Sunday morning. The year was 1920, the place was Middlehope in eastern Pennsylvania, in the United States of America. Joan Richards, lying softly relaxed and asleep in her bed, opened her eyes quietly and fully to see the sunshine of June streaming into her window. The light illuminated every touch of blue in her blue and ivory room and fell upon the delicately faded cornflowers in the wallpaper. A small summery wind stirred the cream-colored ruffled curtains at the windows. The room was alive with wind and sunlight.

A rush of strong joy swept through her. She was home at last, home to stay. All her senior year of college she was conscious of being through with her girlhood, impatient to begin her woman's life. All during the last months she had been breaking away, bit by bit, from things which in the years before had absorbed her. Now even the final promises cried out across the campus, to write, to visit, never to forget, were tinged with unreality. In the life to come would she want to keep what she had? Who would stay—what friend fit her need now? She wanted everything as it came, to the full, packed, running over. She was confident of the years, reckless with plenty of time in her long life, plenty of vigor in her big body, plenty of everything needful for whatever she wanted to do. There was such plenty in her that for this hour she could push

1

aside even her own plenty and lie in a happy pause. Later, when life came rushing at her, she would choose this and this. Today she would not choose—only enjoy.

She yawned and stretched herself and smiled. When she stretched, her head and feet touched the ends of the bed. She was always too big for her bed. She was always outgrowing everything—everything except home! She was glad her first morning at home was Sunday. She loved Sunday mornings in this old manse where they had lived since she was born, although on Sundays it was not really theirs. It belonged to the Presbyterian Brick Church, which belonged to the people of Middlehope, except those who were Baptists and Methodists. But these were not many. Middlehope was the Presbyterians, and perhaps the Episcopalians, like the Kinneys, who were too few to have a church of their own and so came to the Brick Church. Once a month her father held a special service for them, and read the Evening or Morning Prayer. She liked it. She liked the slight sense of pomp it introduced into the white-painted old church. She liked the robe her father wore. On other Sundays he wore his frock coat, buttoned tightly about his tall and slender body. There were a few people, like Mrs. Winters and Mr. Parson, who stayed away on Episcopal Sundays, but her father always did what he thought was right, anyway.

A clock struck somewhere in the house and echoed mellowly through the long hall to her room. She counted the slow musical notes. Eight. It was time to get up. In the minister's house on Sunday, breakfast must be over by nine. She sat up in bed, and then in the mirror facing her bed she saw herself, too big, always too big, but still surprisingly pretty.

She wanted desperately to be pretty. She so loved pretty people. In college she had often wondered if she could be called pretty. But perhaps she was really too tall. Perhaps at best she was only good-looking. There were even a few months in her sophomore year when she wore shirtwaists and mannish ties with success. Then she had revolted against them. She secretly loved wearing very feminine things, like the nightgown she had on. Above its pink lacy ruffles her head rose nobly, her long golden-brown braid over her shoulder. She admired herself a moment, her very clear blue-green eyes, her rather large red mouth, her smooth pale skin. Then she was guilty with her vanity. "Pretty is as pretty does," her mother always said. Curious how her mother's little moralities had lain so heavily on her when she was a child—could lie so heavily on her now if she let them! She would not let them. Nothing in life should ever make her sad—nothing, nothing! She wanted only pleasant things, pleasant thoughts, safety from suffering.

She lay back and savored deeply and with joy the fresh wind, the pretty color of the room, herself, her freedom. She was young and strong and free. Intensity flowed in and about her. She put herself wholly into this moment, into this instant of sunshine, at this hour on a quiet morning, in this house of peace. She felt an exquisite sharpening of every sense. Here it was quiet. Here it was safe. Here she was little again, a happy little child for an hour, waking as she had waked so many mornings of her life to the security of the walls about her, to food hot and delicious upon the table, to her mother's face on the right of her at breakfast and her father on the left, and across from her Francis and Rose, her brother and sister. They made a warm circle of intimacy and safety about her. She loved them ardently.

And beyond the garden gate was Middlehope, almost as near as her own family. Faces sprang into her mind—Mrs. Winters, Miss Kinney, old Mr. Parker—they would all be in church today, all eager to see her. She was richly surrounded by them all, waiting to love her because she was young and beautiful. Surely she was beautiful? In the quiet of the house, on this June morning, she lay waiting, waiting, sure of everything, about to begin richly but prolongingly the delicious childlike hour.

Then through the intense Sunday stillness she heard a murmur, a dual murmur, a clear full voice sharply subdued, a lower steadier insistence. She could not catch the words, she had never been able to catch the words. This murmur she had heard at times all her life, coming from behind the closed doors of her parents' bedroom next to hers. As a child she had listened, sensitive to every atmosphere in her world, and hence troubled. Was it possible her father and mother were quarreling? But her mother always came out of the closed door with her usual brisk cheerful step.

"Now then, Joan darling," she would say pleasantly, "are you ready for breakfast?"

It could not be quarreling. At the table as a little girl she paused over her porridge and looked from one face to the other searchingly. But there was no new thing to see. Her mother's dark rosy face was cheerful, the eyes snapping and brown, her curly brown hair rising like a ruff from her forehead. Her father's pale serene face held its habitual high look. She was relieved. These two who were her childhood gods sat undisturbed upon their thrones. She forgot them and was at ease again. They were all happy. Everything was pleasant.

Yet in this moment she paused. The old sense of childish foreboding fell upon her once more. Were they not quarreling? Had it been quarreling all these years? She turned on her side and listened. She heard her mother's voice rise swiftly almost into articulateness and then stop. What was that muffled throb? Was her mother sobbing? She had a moment's panic, the panic of a child who sees an adult weep, and is struck to the heart, since if these weep, too, none are safe from trouble.

But soon, even as she listened, there was a knock, quick and firm, and the door opened and her mother came in, very fresh in her lavender print frock. The brown ruff above her forehead was waved with white now, and she was a little stout and compact. She spoke in her clear warm thrushy voice, and her face changed into a lighting smile. A smile made a great change in her mother's resolute face. "Still a-bed, lazy bones?" Her swift bright eyes darted about the room and she picked up a pair of stockings and laid them straightened across the back of a chair and her rich voice flowed on in tolerance, "Stay in bed if you like, dear. Father won't mind if you miss church this once." How silly to imagine this sure and comforting woman sobbing behind a closed door! She leaped out of bed and wrapped her mother about in long eager young arms and bent from her height and kissed her. "I don't want to miss anything!" she cried.

Her mother's cheeks flushed darkly. She received the embrace warmly but with shyness.

"You've grown so I hardly know you. You take after Paul's family, growing so—" she said, half-embarrassed. "When I think of you I still think of a little girl about twelve with two pigtails and suddenly there you are, taller by a head than I am!" She looked up into her daughter's eyes. "I'm almost afraid of you," she said. Her face sobered and the two looked at each other in an instant's gravity. There was strangeness between them. The girl could not bear it.

"I'm the same!" she whispered, frightened, looking down,

her head drooping. The undertone of a lost child was in her voice, and her mother recognized it and knew her again.

"Of course you are," she replied quickly. "Now, dear, *if* you are coming—then don't be too late."

So her mother was herself, practical, able, managing. Under the familiar dominion things were right again. She was happy and safe once more. She began to brush out her hair, humming the tune they would perhaps be singing later in the Brick Church, since it was her father's favorite: "How firm a foundation, ye saints of the Lord." The sunshine brightened gloriously with the mounting day. Out of what had been the silence of dawn now sounds arose, the clack of the latch at the gate, her father's quiet measured step down the stairs, Hannah's quick dump of coal into the kitchen range, her brother's shout for a clean shirt, the tinkle of the piano. Rose was playing a hymn gently. Everything had begun in the house.

She came into the breakfast room a little late but sure of their love. She was the eldest daughter in the home, the dearly beloved, the young queen. She caught the fond look in her mother's eyes and smiled regally. Though with her lips her mother might say "Pretty is as pretty does," her eyes were proud upon her daughter.

"I do like that green dress," she said. "I'm glad we got it instead of the white one. It won't show soil so much, either. And you can wear those ruffles real well—though you are so big."

Thus her lips spoke staidly and with composure. But in her mother's eyes the girl saw other words. "Joan is lovely—Joan is what I dreamed I might be—she is big and lovely and strong. She will do everything I have not been able to do." All this was clear in her mother's eyes before she turned away and began to pour out the coffee. Then she subdued her pride decently. Rose cried out, "Oh, Joan, you are lovely!" But the mother said quietly, "Sit down, dear. Father is waiting to say grace."

At this Joan looked penitently at her father, waiting to give thanks before he could eat. She wanted to please him, too. She cried out eagerly, "I'm sorry, Father dear!" He did not reply, but waited mildly. By his peaceful remote look she knew he could never see that her dress was green and ruffled and her hair shining in its large soft mass at her neck. He was a man of God. Her mother was warm and quick and human and she knew her children's bodies intimately and loved them with secret passion, secret because she was afraid of showing herself out, lest something, lest somebody, have a hold whereby to thrust and injure her heart through her children. If anyone praised them she answered tranquilly, "They're good children and that is enough." But her very tone showed that it was not really enough. They were a great deal more and she knew it and rejoiced in it.

But the father knew nothing about his children except that they had souls to be saved. He painfully hoped and believed they were saved. He could not forbear, even in his thanks to God for daily food, to slip in a petition that was really for them, since he knew his own soul of course was safe. "Save us, O Lord, we beseech Thee, and if this day be the day of death for any of us, accept our souls and let us live with Thee to all eternity. Amen."

Death and eternity—these two words took shape and meaning when he spoke of them in his deep grave way. God also lived for the brief moment of his address. This man could call upon God, and out of the sureness of his belief God was summoned and lived. But when his voice ceased and all their eyes were opened again, God and Death and Eternity returned to their shadows and were no more.

Instead there was life, this life in this room, the painted yellow walls, the fluttering white curtains, the worn brown carpet, the books overflowing from the rest of the house, books everybody had read and were done with, but which could not be thrown away because they were books. Upon the shining table were the very means of life, fruit and milk and bread and butter and eggs and bacon and a glass pot of marmalade which caught and held the sun deeply—so deeply that when Rose reached for it Joan said, "Put it back in the sunbeam, Rose. It's ambrosia in the sun."

Rose smiled and set it back, ready to please her sister. But she was silent, for she seldom spoke if she were not questioned.

Then the door opened with a burst and Francis came in. He looked at his mother first and she looked at him and the pride she took in her children blazed in her look.

"Come here, son," she said. "Let me tie your tie again."

"Can't ever get a bow right," he said, smiling wryly. He folded his long legs and dropped before her, kneeling, and leaned his arms upon her lap and gazed into her face confidently. She pulled the ends of his red tie loose and set it again with neat compact movements. She had bought the tie and chosen it red because her son was as brown as she was and she loved red secretly, although she felt it now a color unbecoming to her age and she would not wear it except as an edge to a collar or as a seldom seen lining. When she was young she had always a red dress among her others. But now instead she loved her son's round dark chin above a red tie, and she liked to put a red rose in his buttonhole. The blackness of his hair and eyes were richer for red. Now as she finished he clasped his arms about her waist and pressed his face into her bosom.

"You smell nice, Mom," he murmured.

She patted him on the cheek and straightened a lock of his hair. There was no embarrassment in her when her son made his love to her. She was not shy of him as she was of her daughters.

"Go and eat your breakfast before it is cold," she said, and to the maid Hannah she said, "Bring in fresh rolls for Francis." The boy rose and moving with the lazy grace of his too swiftly growing youth, he dropped into his chair and began to eat. But now his father saw him and spoke to him. "Are you not going to give thanks to God?" he asked.

The boy looked at him coldly, unwillingly. Then meeting that clear solemn priestly look he wavered and bent his head an instant and moved his lips, and so placated the man of God who was his father. But he did not summon God.

So the early morning life went on with energy in this room. Hannah brought in fresh bread and fresh coffee, and they all ate robustly except the father, who took his food sparingly. But to this they were all accustomed. Until he had delivered himself to his people of what he had learned newly about God he would not eat heartily.

For his hungry body was his temptation. He loved food. When he was a child he grew fast and he was always hungry, always eating so much that his brothers laughed at him. Then, after he was converted by the missionary in his thirteenth year, he began to know that he must fight to subdue his big body. For how could a man save his soul if his body were master? He had sat at his mother's dinner table on that cold November Sunday, among all his vigorous brothers and sisters, and had let his piled plate stand before him. "I will take one-third of everything—no more," he promised God. The rich smell of the chicken gravy moved in his nostrils. The fragrance of baked potatoes, of golden mashed turnips, of hot biscuit, made him faint. There was the sharp sweetness of honey, the spice of the pickled peaches and the heavy intoxicating perfume of hot mince pies. Across the table the missionary ate delicately, refusing much.

"You don't eat, Mr. Barnes!" his mother cried, despair on her round face. What could be done with anybody who did not eat? In this great farmhouse everybody ate.

The missionary had smiled thinly and a little sadly at her. "I have eaten poorly for so long that now my stomach will not feast. It has the habit of poverty and prefers it."

Then he also would so teach his own body. His mother saw his plate taken away and was frightened. "Paul, you're sick! I never knew you not to eat!" He smiled sickly, the palms of his hands wet with the strength of his hunger. But he had not eaten. In a fire of blushing and shyness he had withstood his brothers' teasing. "Well, if Paul's not eating, he's sick enough to die." Even his father had smiled dryly. "I always say it keeps Paul poor just carrying all his food." But they had not known how hungry he was all the time.

Even now, after all these years, he never sat down at the table and smelled the food without that voracious faintness in his belly. But no one knew this. He would have been ashamed even for Mary, his wife, to know. So he had early made it his rule to deny himself before he went before God for his people. At night he would eat hungrily and sleep soon, spent, his soul emptied. But now he sat silent and brooding, his eyes shining and strange and his mind not in his body, his ears deaf unless his name were called.

The children were used to this also. They accepted him among them, let him be as it seemed he must be, and turned toward their mother. She was their sun and they turned toward her and told her everything, or nearly everything except the secret core of themselves which without knowing it they kept from her and from everybody.

And she gave to them joyously in turn. Each had what he needed of her. As she had given them her milk when they were born, now she gave them the food of her brain and her thoughts and everything she knew. Sometimes it was not enough, but she did not know it and they did not tell her, if indeed they knew it. She gave them so much that it seemed enough.

Sitting among them on this Sabbath morning she was at her best and richest. She knew her house was warm and comfortable about her children. She was feeding them the best she had, feeding their bodies with milk and bread and meat and fruit, feeding richness into their blood and their flesh, making the mother's eternal mystic transubstantiation. Soon their souls too would be fed. She did not wholly understand how, but in the house of God they sat and received for their souls bread and wine, and their father's hands gave it to them. They were safe. Body and soul they were safe. She smiled peacefully and gave them bits of her love.

"Joan, is your egg as you like it? You used to like it coddled that way, but if you want it different—people do change! ... Rose, I've put a fresh cover on your bed. I didn't like that one. I decided you might as well have the pink one. It suits your room so well. ... Frank, darling, here is more bacon—crisp, just as you like it."

In all this she did not forget the man. But she spoke to him most often through the children.

"Pass his cup, dear," she said to her son. "He's let it get cold. I'll change it—"

She lifted her voice slightly higher and said clearly, "Here's some hot coffee, Paul. Now drink it before it chills again."

He looked at her vaguely and took the cup and drank a little of it and then rose.

"I'm going to the vestry," he said quietly, and seemed, with his gentle and silent step, to drift from the room.

They knew that in the hour before they were all gathered in the pews he would be praying. He would pray so long and intensely that he would come out to them transfigured, the skin of his face shining and his body holy. They did not understand it. Francis begrudged his father the exaltation. Thinking of it now he said aloud, "I can't see what he prays about so long. Gee, I'd run out of anything to say long before church time!"

But this even his mother could not endure.

"He is not saying anything," she said quietly. "He is waiting before the Lord."

He knew by her voice that now she would not let him have his way, not even him, not in this one thing, this thing between man and God. He dropped his head, pouting his red lips, and piled the golden marmalade recklessly upon his bread and swallowed it in great mouthfuls. Rose was playing with a small heap of dry crumbs, dreaming, absorbed into herself.

But Joan caught the words from her mother and sat gazing across the table into the garden, smiling. Waiting before the Lord! Waiting—waiting—before the Lord! The words marched through the air, shining, sonorous and caught to themselves other words. She was waiting, waiting and radiant—Lift up your heads, O ye gates, and be ye lifted up, ye everlasting doors, and the King of Glory shall come in. Who is this King of Glory? . . . Lift up—lift up your head—and wait!

She followed her mother into the church proudly, her head high on her straight neck. Years ago her mother had said to her, "You're tall, so be as tall as you can." After that, however she hated sometimes to have her head above all others, she remembered, and made herself as tall as she could.

Behind them came Rose alone, small and composed. Francis would come when he chose, or if he were rebellious enough he would not come, if the day were too fair and enticing by the river. But his mother's wish was still compelling upon him. All her wishes were heavy upon him because of her love for him, and he did not feel her love too heavy since as yet he had no other.

But he resisted her a little now. When she said to him today, her eyes guarded, her voice determined to be pleasant, "Are you ready for church, son?" he looked up at her from the hammock on the porch where he had thrown himself. "I'll be along," he said, staring into the rose vines. "Don't wait," he said when she waited.

She looked at him, locking her tongue behind her set teeth, keeping her smile on her lips. A year before she would have said to him sharply and naturally, sure that because she loved him she knew best for him, "Go at once and get your hat and coat and come with me." But now the instinct in her, always alive and fluttering toward her children and especially to this son, warned her that he was very near the moment when he would refuse her utterly. Some morning he would say, "I hate church. I won't come with you again." She was afraid of the moment and week by week she pushed it off, and he knew it, and was arrogant with her, lordly because of his youth.

So she had left him alone to come when he would, and she

led her two daughters into the church. Joan sat beside her mother and Rose beside Joan. To them this was an air as familiar as home. This place, too, was a sort of home. Years full of Sabbaths Joan had sat in this same front pew beside her mother and Francis's place was on the other side. Between these two strong lively children the mother sat, dividing them, quieting them, compelling them to their father, that he might compel them to God. Rose was obedient and she did naturally, or seemed to do, those things which she should do.

Yet today they were not complete as they had been for so long. Joan could feel her mother's unease until Francis came into his place. Her mother prayed quickly, her hand over her eyes, and then sat back waiting for Francis, wanting him to come. Before the congregation she wanted her children assembled, still around her, still faithful. Many parents came alone. The church was full of old people alone, whose children were gone from the small village, or if they were not gone, they were grown and sat willfully at home or went out for amusement. But she was here with her children about her. Joan knew and could smile at her mother's pride and humor her in it when after the service she would lead her children down the aisle through the people.

She turned her head slightly and looked about. It was early and the people were gathering. All her life she had come early with her family, to be, as her mother said, an example. The sun was streaming through the church in long bright metallic bars and the light, faintly colored by the stained-glass windows, shone upon the silvery heads of a few aged men and women who were early also. She caught old Mr. Parker's eye and threw him her smile and felt her heart warm toward him. He had taught her music and from him she had learned how to write down the tunes that sang so easily into her head. He kept the little music store in the village by which he could not have lived unless he had tuned pianos and taught classes in singing in the district school. He taught faithfully, regularly, so that at the end he might sometime have a small pension. He could not sing much anymore, although once he had had a mild sweet baritone voice. But these days he could do little more than clear his throat and hum a note for the younger voices to catch from him.

notes caught and held strongly. Joan turned her face toward

Now the organ began to sound, deeply and quietly, the

the music and listened carefully. She could see a man's back, straight and slenderly shaped. She knew him, at least she knew him like this in the church, sitting with his back to her, reaching and plucking music out of the organ. She knew his back better than his face, his music better than his voice. At other times no one knew him very well, though he lived in the village and had been a child here. He had a law business of his own in the city to which he came and went almost daily. At night he slept in his mother's house in the village where he had always slept except for the two years he had been away at the war. He was an only son, whose father had died when the son was a child. To the villagers he seemed to have no other life than this one in the village, to care for his mother, to walk sedately with her in their garden, to remark upon the flowers. She said to him, "I believe the lilac will be in bloom by tomorrow." He replied, "I think it will, Mother." She said to her neighbors, "Martin is all I have to live for." So she clung to him that she might have something for which to live, and for him she kept the square red brick house rigidly dustless and ordered. He entered every night into the clean shadowy hall and moved in silence about the clean shadowy rooms.

Yet every morning he went away to Philadelphia and did his work and so well that he gathered a little fame about himself as a lawyer, a fame of which the villagers heard remotely and always with doubt and wonder, because they had known him since he was born. They had always said, "His father was no great shakes—he had big ideas about that shirt factory in South End, but he couldn't keep it going—a good man, but not very bright." So it was hard to believe in the son. "If Martin had come into the factory and helped me, things would have been different." But Martin had gone early to his own life, and as soon as his father died he had sold the factory to Peter Weeks.

Of himself Martin Bradley never spoke. Silently, smiling a little to everyone, he came every Sunday morning to play the organ as he had begun to do when he was eighteen years old. On his first Sunday home from the war he was at the organ again. No one asked him what had happened between and he said nothing and soon it was forgotten that he had ever been away.

Now while Joan listened and looked at his straight back and narrow dark head, upon which the hair was beginning to turn gray, he played a Bach fugue meticulously and perfectly, making each note round and complete and valued. The choir door opened and four people came in irregularly as they chose and a little apologetically, as though they felt that everyone knew them in other guise than this. There were two women and two men, Mr. Winters and Mrs. Parsons and Mr. Weeks and Miss Kinney. They took their seats and stared earnestly and self-consciously in front of them, except Miss Kinney, who had once been a missionary in Africa. She smiled continually and her eyes darted here and there, as restless as pale blue butterflies.

Then the vestry door opened and the music softened. Joan's father came in, a priest newly come from the presence of God to his people. Through thirty years this had never become stale in him or usual. He would not come unless from God. Once in her little childhood Joan remembered a delay. The people waited for him, at first patiently and then in surprise, their eyes fixed on the vestry door. Moments passed and the organ rolled on and on and wandered into bypaths of variation, but ready at any instant to come through to the final major note. She was only six years old, but she caught her mother's wonder and then her anxiety. She heard her mother whisper, "I shall have to go and see what is wrong." She felt her mother gather herself to rise.

Then the door opened as though on the wings of a wind, strongly and swiftly, and her father strode in with triumph and his voice rang out to his people, "Let us praise the Lord by singing—"

Later when her mother cried, "Paul, where were you? We were all waiting!" he said simply, "I could not get God's blessing and I could not go to my pulpit until I did."

But now, in the beginning of his age, his temper stilled, it seemed he had always God's blessing. He moved tranquil and serene, tall, a little bowed, but his eyes were clear and blue and guileless as a child's eyes are. He stood before his people and paused. The organ fell silent and the people looked at him, waiting. But before he could speak there was a sound at the door, a step in the aisle and a movement. It was Francis, come to sit beside his mother once again. His father waited for him.

They were complete now. The father was set above them in the pulpit and the mother and the three children were in their accustomed places. Their faces were turned to him, waiting for what they were about to receive.

So they received their food from God. The people rose in the bars of many colored sunshine, and were for the moment caught and held in the brightness. They sang together, and Joan sang, above them all, her big young voice soaring above their feeble old voices, carrying them along, gathering them in its full stream. Then they sat back comfortably and gave thanks and heard the reading of Scripture. They gave too at the due moment small bits of silver that tinkled into the old pewter plates.

In the choir loft Mrs. Parsons rose tall and gaunt, yet with sweetness in her disappointed eyes, and sang, "But the Lord is mindful of His own." She sang it a little too slowly, clinging to the favorite words, and her voice faded upon the high notes, but she still sang with a touching hopefulness. What she longed for might yet be. So she sang, believing wistfully in what she had not received. She loved these moments of singing, when she could lose herself in vague hoping about the story she was writing.

Emily was so much like her father, so impatient of her mother's "scribbling" as they called it. Edward had always been hard on her about it. When he came home and found things not quite ready for dinner because she had been writing, he was so hard. And now Emily, although she was only fifteen, was hard too. "You write such silly stuff, Mother!" Her voice was cold and she rattled the dishes in the sink. But Ned—dear boy—he was older than Emily but still he listened to her stories, and his eyes would grow wet. "Neddie, it's only a story," she said to him time and again. He helped her to keep on hoping. Some day someone would want her stories. One of the letters would not be a rejection, and Edward would say, "Well, well, Florrie—you were right and I was wrong." Edward would say what he never had said about anything. "Forgive me, Florrie." She would just be patient and keep on writing as nicely as she could.

"But the Lord is mindful, is mindful of His own. He will not—" she crooned tenderly, slowly, her eyes misted, her voice thick and soft in her throat. She sat down, strengthened, and began to plan a new story—the best. It was so easy to plan stories in church, in the quite while the sermon was going on. She drifted happily away.

So the sermon began. Because of this sermon the children had gone quietly every Saturday of their lives, though the day was a holiday. In the bare study they knew their father sat and searched the Scriptures for them all. They could not go in there for any cause. They tiptoed through the house with their small friends following them, their goal the cookie jar in the kitchen. With their hands full of cookies they burst out of the silent house, and ran down to the end of the street, released and joyful and screaming with glee. About them were trees and meadows and under their feet the grass green, thickly green, and the day was holiday.

Their voices sang and shouted and they played with desperate pleasure and at times fell into quarreling. But even the quarreling was sweet and intense. They gave no thought to their father in his study, searching the Book to find food for their souls, even as they gave no thought to their mother cooking and baking for them in her kitchen and making and mending for them. All this was of course; it all made the foundation of their life safe, and for them it was forever.

Of God they knew nothing except what they were told. They believed, or thought they did, what their father told them. They trusted him about God. When he said God was a kind father who did not let even a sparrow in the garden suffer, they believed him. Besides it seemed true because all the sparrows they saw were plump and busy. When he told them the very hairs of their head were numbered they believed him, for they were used to love. They would not have thought it strange if their mother numbered their hairs, because she so loved them, and it was not strange in God. They were important and complacent and sure of God, believing He loved them and cared for them.

There was also Jesus Christ who died for their sins, and the Holy Ghost. But the Holy Ghost was a shadow and without substance or shape, and they left it at that. But Jesus was real, "Gentle Jesus, meek and mild." He was touching and real, though more real before his resurrection than afterwards. Afterwards he became arrogant and proud. He said, "Touch me not." But before, when he was a man, he said "Come unto me," and "suffer the little children." Then they understood him. They would have rushed to him, laughing and shouting if they had been near him, because he was real to them, though dead.

But when he hung on the cross for their sins they were uncomfortable and guilty about themselves although they did not know why. They only knew they were sinful and everybody was sinful. They were "conceived and born in sin." Long ago Joan had used to wonder what "conceived in sin" was. She asked her mother one day, "Was I conceived in sin, too?" Her mother's eyes opened in surprise and her dark cheeks flushed and she said quickly, "When you are older I will explain everything. Would you like to take Francis and go and play with Netta Weeks? You can take a couple of cookies so she can give one to little Jackie."

Still she never did quite explain. But after a while Joan knew it could not be a thing for which she alone was to blame. If everybody was so conceived it was a common sin and so she forgot it because there was so much else to think of in the crowding seasons. There was so much to enjoy and she wanted never to think of unpleasant things. She chose to be happy and to laugh.

But Rose could not forget. Once Rose asked her miserably, her lips suddenly dry, "Joan, do you—do you understand about being conceived in sin?"

Joan was shocked by the question. She knew by then how life began inside a woman's body, out of a man's body, but it was secret knowledge. She had learned it secretly at school, guiltily against her will. She had listened, surprised, and had shouted angrily, "I don't believe it." But she was compelled to believe it. "I know," said Netta Weeks. "How do you know?" Joan demanded loudly. But Netta only smiled foolishly. Joan felt sickness rush over her. She went away but she could not forget. It was a long time before she could forget when she looked at her father and mother. But she made herself forget at last, so that she could escape from it.

But she could not bear to speak of it even to Rose. Indeed between them, spoken, it would be the more shameful. Her healthy flesh crawled at the thought, outraged. "I don't know anything about it," she said shortly. She ran out into the garden and picked a great handful of her mother's red roses.

So Rose asked no more. She grew inwardly toward herself. She read her Bible every night even in winter, however cold her bedroom was. She never hurried at her prayers. If she felt tempted to hurry and to get into her warm bed she punished herself and prayed more slowly. Rose was ready always to go to church, to dream, to take the bread and wine, the tears filling her eyes easily as she thought of him who died for her sins. She felt herself full of sin. She saved every separate sin and remembered it when the bread was crumbling upon her tongue and when the wine burned her lips delicately, because it was so sweet to feel herself washed clean by Jesus's blood. It was almost sweet to sin that she might be washed clean. But that again was sin, to want to sin, and so she prayed in ecstasy, to be forgiven again and again.

This intense and secret life Rose kept within herself and because she lived inwardly, outwardly she seemed always mild and gentle and obedient and her blue eyes were saintly in their mildness. The villagers said often, "She is an angelic child—so *good*." And hearing it she felt pleasure, a strange pleasure, tingling in all her body. She planned fresh goodness, a set number of kind deeds every day. She took flowers to old Mrs. Mark who lay in her little stone house, at the edge of the village, bedridden with creeping paralysis. She took flowers until Mrs. Mark said plainly, "I haven't any more vases, child. Anyways, roses bring on my hay fever. There—I know you mean well enough, but I'll take the will for the deed."

"Yes, Mrs. Mark," said Rose, shrinking away from the harsh fretting old woman. But still she could not give up her goodness. By the time she reached home she remembered that she must not mind being persecuted for her goodness. So she still went to see Mrs. Mark and took her apples and a jar of jelly she had coaxed from her mother, and she welcomed her bitterness. Once when the old woman railed against her useless legs she said gently, "God has a meaning in it, dear Mrs. Mark. He sends us suffering to fit us for heaven." She had heard Mrs. Parsons say that when little Emma Winters died.

Then the old woman rose up against her. She braced herself against her cottony pillows and shouted at her, "Get out—don't you dare talk such stuff and nonsense to me! I'd like to know what sense there is in God's keeping me on my back like this— I could have been a useful woman with my legs. Don't talk to me! You don't know anything—you palaver like your father. Go on out and play where you belong."

Rose gathered up her books gently and went away. At first she was angry and hurt and then she remembered Jesus and exultant righteousness filled her. She had been like Jesus. She had answered nothing. When her enemies persecuted her she was like him, a lamb, innocent, led to the slaughter. But she gave up going to see Mrs. Mark and prayed for her instead, at night, safely in her own room.

Now in the church she sat quietly before her father, her face upturned to his, her spirit subject to his. She loved the hours when he rose to preach, dominating her, telling her what to believe. He was not her father now. He was her priest, her savior. She loved him passionately. He stood for Jesus to her, Jesus who died for her. Now she would be washed, from head to foot, made clean and new. She cried out in her heart, "Wash me and I shall be whiter than snow." She sat waiting to be cleansed, cleansed and filled anew with love—love—love. Her eyes shone, her lips parted, her breath came soft and quick. She forgot everything except her savior, her beloved savior.

Her quickened breathing sounded fluttering at Joan's ear. She turned and looked at Rose curiously, small strange silent Rose. Rose's hands were folded in her lap, little white immaculate hands which she washed many times a day, soft pale hands, full in the palm, pointed in the fingers. Sometimes it seemed as if she and Rose were not sisters. She could not understand Rose's patience. She was resigned as old people are resigned, ready to suffer. It seemed to Joan that Rose even liked to suffer.

One day in a spring cleaning her mother had flown at her for being so slow and dreaming. "Rose, I declare, we'll never get cleaned up in the sitting room if you keep stopping for nothing." And Rose had turned her face to her mother, smiling, drinking in her anger. "I'm wicked," she had answered in a strange passionate whisper. "I know I ought to be beaten, Mother."

Her mother, shocked, paused in her sweeping and stared at Rose straightly. "I've never beaten any child of mine," she said, outraged.

"No—no," Rose urged. "But I really ought to be!"

And yet she was so small and childlike, her little figure so roundly childish, her face as pure as a child's face, her voice gentle, her leaf-brown eyes sweet. She had no wants, she never asked for anything. She wore uncomplainingly Joan's quickly outgrown garments. This very hour she had on Joan's last summer's dress, a blue voile, now a little faded. Joan felt a rush of love come over her. She must see that Rose had something new. The next new dress should be for Rose. Some day she would buy Rose new things from head to foot. She wanted Rose to be happy. It was so pleasant when everybody was happy.

Her father's voice came earnestly into her ears, "So let us take thought before it is too late what God is to each one of us. He is not far from any of us—"

His voice faded again as the question caught itself into her thoughts. What was God to her? She did not know. It did not matter to her now if he were near or far. She did not believe or disbelieve in God. It was not important. God was like these old people in the church, these loving old people who were kind to her and had known her from her birth and cared for her and would always care for her. He was doubtless there to be called upon if it were needful. But she needed nothing. She had everything. Here was her youth. Here was her beauty. That is, if she were really beautiful?

But she was beginning now to believe secretly and often in her own beauty. She treasured every small affirmation of it that she heard about her. "Joan's growing prettier as she grows older." "I believe Joan's going to be the beauty of the family, though she's so tall." "Joan's eyes are lovely," and at Commencement there was Mary Robey's teasing whisper, "Do you know what my brother Tom said, Joan? He said he'd like to kiss your mouth!"

Her lips burned. She had never yet been kissed by any man. Once a shy boy had drawn near at a dance and after a walk in the moonlight he had drawn very near. But she drew back. Her body cried to lean toward him but her heart would not. She laughed because she was so torn in her embarrassment and he drew back too, and she said, half laughing and half crying, "Let's go back to the others—to the light—"

Yet somewhere the kiss was waiting. She believed in love waiting for her. He would come to meet her, tall and strong, taller even than she was, and she to meet him. She wanted it all, all of love, love waiting for marriage and growing into children, many children. She wanted her house full of children, conceived not in sin but in love. She wanted to work for them, to cook and bake for them, to mend for them, to play with them, to sing to them, to love them passionately, to build about them walls of home and of love and make them safe. Among them she would live safely, too, safe and surrounded by them even as she surrounded them and made them safe. "Miss Joan Richards was married today to—to—" Whom would she marry? "The church was decorated in ferns and June roses. The bride was lovely in white satin and she wore her mother's wedding veil of lace caught up with orange blossoms."

Up the aisle she came, under the flowery arches. Rose walked beside her in a new dress of palest shell-pink. She paused a moment to plan Rose's dress. Then she swept on. Her father stood waiting to perform the ceremony. Her mother was matron of honor. Her mother should have a new dress too, of silver-gray chiffon. What could Francis do? She paused, considering. She wanted them all a part of it. She looked across at him, planning, pausing. He had taken off his mother's wedding ring mischievously and was fitting it upon his own little finger. The mother was watching him anxiously and he teased her by pretending to let the ring fall.

Then like a scourge cutting across her dreams she heard her father's voice accusing the people in a solemn anger.

"I say God will not hold us guiltless—"

Her dreams were gone like a mist. She hung her head. She cringed inside her big body. Why wouldn't he stop talking about that ugly dreadful thing? It happened so long ago. The people were always displeased when he spoke of it, as sober good people are, if their one madness is remembered. It had been so pleasant in the church until he began to talk about it. She could feel the people stirring under his words. There was a dry cough here and there. Only Mrs. Parsons was still smiling her vague misty smile. Out of the corner of her eye she saw Mr. Weeks in the choir loft reach for a hymnbook and begin to read ostentatiously. Everybody knew Mr. Weeks had gone to Mr. Bradley that time, years ago, when they were all small, and had told him what his little daughter Netta had said. . . . And Mr. Bradley had said she was a damned little liar with a dirty mind and that no boy from South End could have been in the village all day because it was workday in the factory. And then Mr. Weeks, raging, had taken Netta with him to South End to find the Negro boy who she said had put his hand on her. And afterwards when Mr. Bradley failed, Mr. Weeks had bought the factory.

South End had been full of bad blood anyway, what with the white workers on strike against Mr. Bradley because he had brought in the Negroes. He had started with all white workers and then times got bad. Men stopped wearing so many stiff starched collars, for instance, just about the time he had bought a new lot of machinery for making stiff collars. So he had lowered wages and then when the whites struck, he put in Negroes.

Netta had told all the little girls at school that a Negro boy had stopped her on her way to school when she was alone in the lane. "See, he did this to me!" She pulled up her skirt and put her hand inside her thin thigh. "And my father took me right over to South End and we hunted and I knew him right away. He wasn't so awful black—kind of yellowish." Over and over she had told it. But then, Netta was a liar. They had listened to her, half unbelieving. Even so, afterwards the boy was whipped by a gang of whites in South End. Men and women had run from Middlehope to watch. Netta shivered when she told of it.

. . . In the church after all these eight years her father's voice was scourging them still. He never let them forget.

"God will inquire of us that we do nothing for these people. We have shed blood unlawfully, it may even be innocently—and the stain remains upon us still if we do not remove it by our prayers and good works."

He was going to ask them again for money for his mission in South End and they did not want to give it. They wanted to forget about South End. The church was suddenly filled with silent strife between the people and her father. She could scarcely breathe. She saw her mother's head droop, her hands fold tightly together. Only Rose did not mind. Rose was smiling a little, listening. In the choir Mrs. Parsons did not mind, for she was not listening.

But Francis was staring directly at his father, his face a stone. He had put the ring back on his mother's hand and he was staring at his father, hating him. What good did it do to go and preach to those people? Preaching was no good. If his father knew anything, any of the things other men knew, he'd see how silly it was to think preaching would save anybody in South End.

At last it was over. Joan lifted her head to breathe the old atmosphere of peace in the church. It was so pleasant to have peace in which to dream. Where was she? She was walking down the aisle, satin-clad, her long white train—But now her father broke ringingly into conclusion: "Let us live therefore victorious to the end, triumphant, knowing in whom we have believed. And now unto God who is abundantly able—"

The organ crashed joyfully into dismissal. The people rose eager and relieved, waiting to talk to each other, to saunter out into the sunshine, to make plans for meetings in the week. Her mother gathered the children together and led them down the aisle, her hand upon her son's arm, and he straightened himself and dropped his childishness and took on the gravity of a young man, and she looked on him with pride shining on her face. She tried to cover her pride decently, but it shone out of her eyes and glittered in her smile and rang out of her voice. On the other side Joan walked, smiling, the sweetness of her dream still alive in her face. They all greeted her with love, with welcome. She was their child, too, the daughter of the village.

"Well, Joan, I see in the paper you took a lot of honors." "Joan'll be famous some day—" "Won't we be proud to have known her—"

"Shucks," said Mr. Billings loudly, "somebody'll marry her long before that! She'll have babies instead, and a sight better, too."

Joan's mother held her head a little higher. "Come, Joan," she said coldly, because she thought Mr. Billings very coarse. He was after all nothing but the butcher and it was a common trade. Then she remembered he gave the parsonage every week a roast of lamb or beef and he was a member of the church and his profession made him coarse, doubtless, so she said, "Good morning, Mr. Billings. It's a fine day." But her voice was polite and ladylike, and she turned at once to Mrs. Winters, whose husband was an elder, besides being in the choir, and asked after her peonies. Joan smiled apologetically at Mr. Billings, but he did not mind at all. He winked one of his small merry black eyes at her and his big red face crinkled under his scattered eyebrows. "I sent a tenderloin this week," he whispered loudly, "specially for you. I thought it would be more kind of suitable, you know, than a plain pot roast."

"Thank you," she said, dimpling at him. She accepted the gift, too, of the admiration in his eyes. He was an old fat man, coarse and ignorant, but even so it was worth taking his look which lingered a moment upon her face. Everything was worth having, every least bit of love, all admiration. She wanted flowers strewn to walk upon. She turned from one to the other,

laughing, greeting, taking everything. It was all lovely. She
lavished her promises richly. "Yes, of course I'll come!" "Oh,
picnics are fun—I'll make a chocolate cake—I make grand
cake!" She forgot her mother and Francis who was pulling
them impatiently along. "Gee, I'm starved, Moms," he was
muttering behind his grave grown-up face. "Church always
makes me hungry—" She forgot Rose stealing softly along
behind them. She was full of herself, a queen returned to her
kingdom, a woman returned lovely and young.

For it was excitement to see dreams and yearnings even in
old faces. She knew she made them remember again, love
again, because she was so living and so young. The few young
people were timid of her, she was so confident and so gay.
There was Netta Weeks, who hadn't gone to college after all.
"Father says he can't spend the money now until the factory
pays," Netta had said everywhere. Now she clutched at Joan,
and whispered, "I want to see you—I want to have a real
old-fashioned talk like we used to have—" "Of course, Netta,"
Joan answered quickly. Poor Netta—she understood her—she
understood everybody—she pitied them all—she was full of
richness for them all. A young man nearby looked at her co-
vertly, a tall stolid young farmer, and instantly she knew it,
though she did not look at him, for he was a stranger. But she
lingered a moment, letting him look at her.

So at last they came out into the sunshine of the cloudless
day and at once Francis broke away and strode whistling
across the grass. He was glad to be out of the church. No use
remembering things. Sometimes in the sunshine like this he felt
maybe he had imagined he had seen the hanging Negro, or
made it up from talk he heard around South End. The people
talked about it still, some, on lazy afternoons around the streets
there. But at night he knew he had seen.

"Hi there," he shouted loudly to a boy across the street.
"Meet you this afternoon!"

"I'll go along and start the meat," her mother said.

"I'm coming," Joan answered. She looked about her. Everyone was scattering now, suddenly hungry and remembering
their Sunday dinners.

"I'll wait for Father," said Rose.

"Then I'll go and help Mother," she replied.

But there was one more person to come out of the church. It
was Martin Bradley. He came gracefully down the steps, his

music rolled under his arm. He always waited and came out alone. Now he lifted his hat easily. "How do you do, Miss Richards?" he said. "It is nice to have you home—I hope, to stay?"

She was surprised. He had never spoken to her so directly before and never had he called her Miss Richards. She looked into his melancholy brown eyes. He was a little shorter than she, a very little—no, they were the same height. "Why—I don't know—for a while, anyway," she stammered, suddenly taken aback. He lifted his hat again and she saw his smooth dark hair, white at the sides. He smiled slightly and pleasantly, but only with his lips, and walked away. She strolled smiling across the lawn to the manse. It was strange how when one was grown up, people seemed different. She had known Martin for years, on Sundays a part of the organ, on weekdays a face in the village. Now suddenly he took on a shape for himself; he was even rather handsome in a quiet secret oldish way.

But what his shape was she did not know and the little wonder she had now faded, at least for the moment. It was driven away by the warm noon, by the peace of the shadowy lawn, by the roses hung upon the porch and now by the smell of broiling steak and spiced apple pie. She ran up the steps and into the house. There was food upon the table, hot and delicious, ready, waiting to be eaten. She was suddenly very hungry.

On weekdays the house became itself again. It no longer belonged to the red brick church and to the village—it belonged to them. It was theirs to live in as they chose and each of them lived his own intense life, intensely alone and yet always warmly, intensely together. There were the occasions of every day when they were drawn together by a need of each other, not so much by the need of any one of them as by the need of all of them together.

In the mornings Joan drowsed in the sweetness of half-waking sleep. Her body was at once heavy and light, her mind deeply slumberous, and yet on its surface awake to the sunshine, to the angles of familiar furniture, to the smoothness of the sheets against her limbs and to the softness beneath her. There was no need to rise. There was no urgency yet to work. Life was still waiting and still holiday. Each morning her body was appeased with sleep and she was not immediately hungry.

She could sleep as long as she liked, she told herself, and eat when she liked. This was her home and she was free in it. She smiled, deeply free, deeply happy, and turned upon her pillows to sleep again.

But then her sleep would not come. Perversely her mind crept out of her languorous body. It crept downstairs and saw the others at the table together. Her place was empty. Her father hesitated before grace, as he always did if one of them were not there. He asked, "Where is Joan? Is she ill?"

"Let the child rest," her mother answered comfortably. "This is her vacation—let her be."

So they went on without her. But they missed her and she knew they did. The meal was not complete. They were not wholly fed unless they took their meal together. Her mind came creeping upstairs and into her body again. It urged her body lying inert, her eyes closed. She found herself thinking, I miss them, too. I'd rather have breakfast with them than all alone. I want to be in my place among them.

Suddenly she leaped up, wide awake, and dashed off her nightgown and darted under the shower in the bathroom. She turned it on full, a cold stinging rain against her. She whirled around and received it upon her breasts and let it rush to her feet; and turned and caught it upon her shoulders and down to her heels. She wrestled an instant with the thick towel, passing it this way and that over her body. She drew her garments over her head and buttoned the few buttons quickly and slipped into her stockings and shoes and brushed the length of her hair out and twisted it. She ran to the table laughing, the tendrils of her hair still wet.

They looked at her joyously. "I thought you were going to sleep this morning!" her mother cried gaily.

"I didn't want to miss anything," she answered. "I suddenly felt I was missing something."

"You sure would have missed these muffins," Francis shouted. "I'm seeing to it you miss as many of 'em as I can manage." He reached for a hot one as Hannah passed them, smiling and flattered.

They were all cheerful with her coming. Each one began speaking for himself and of his own thoughts except the mother, who must listen to them all. But each had needed the circle complete before which to speak. Her father ate with appetite today, pondering on the day before. He looked up in the midst of the chatter to ask his wife, troubled at a thought, "Mary, did you think there were as many out as usual yesterday?"

She answered him at once, although her eyes were still merry among her children. "Yes, I did, Paul—considering the time of the year. People like to take trips and picnics in weather like this."

But he was not wholly comforted. He murmured, "The church members ought to remember their duty. The service ought to be necessary to them—as necessary for their souls as food for their bodies."

"Oh, but, Father," Joan broke in. "Don't you think food for the soul comes in other ways, too? I know I find it in music—in beauty everywhere—"

Her father's grave face grew a little more grave. He compressed his lips into patience before he answered with certainty, "These things do not lead to the knowledge of God. There is but one Saviour, and He is the Crucified."

Now Rose lifted her secret heavy-lidded eyes and flashed them at her father and dropped them again, musing. Beyond Rose's blond young head Joan looked into the garden and there she saw the glowing newly opened roses and the summer lilies in the border. The lemon lily was wide open. She forgot what her father said. After breakfast she would go out and dip her face delicately into the lily, as the hummingbird did when he discovered it. She remembered from summer to summer the fragrance of the lemon lily; among a hundred scents and perfumes she knew that clear single sweetness. But such knowledge, her father said, was not the knowledge of God. She turned to her mother impatiently.

"Mother—" she cried.

But her mother was not ready to hear her. She was listening to her son and her face was troubled.

"I don't see why I can't, Moms," he was arguing. His dark beautiful face grew darker and somehow still more beautiful. Red rushed into his dark cheeks and he bit his lip to crimson. "All the fellows are going. Why, even Ned Parsons is going and you're always holding him up to me—Gee, I've already asked my girl."

"I don't like your going off to that dance hall," she answered stubbornly. "Your father is the minister." She paused and pressed her full lips together. They were shaped exactly as her son's were. Then she asked with constraint and in a different voice, "What girl have you asked?"

Now he was determined to punish her. "Why should I tell you if I can't take her?" he muttered. He really had not asked a girl. But he wanted to hurt her.

"Oh, Frank," she breathed, beseeching him, "don't be so— You know I want you to have good wholesome fun. But I can't think this is good for you."

"That's not the reason," he retorted. "It's because Dad is the sacred minister. Gosh, I've been hampered all my life because Dad is the sacred minister!"

But now his mother's mobile face changed. She could be angry even with her son.

"If you're half as good a man as your father, Francis—"

"I hope I'll die before that," he said between his teeth.

"Where do you want to go, son?" his father inquired. He had heard nothing, but now he looked up suddenly, aware of some discord.

"What's the use of asking anything?" the boy broke out against his mother, ignoring his father. "I ought to do like the other fellows and not tell—I'm a fool for telling!"

Now he had the victory over his mother. Above all else she wanted him to tell her everything. She dreaded the hour when there would be silence between them, the silence of trivial surface speech. She clung to him as he still was. When he was stormy and rebellious at least she knew what he was, and as long as she knew him he was still hers. But she perceived that she was holding him now only from day to day, even from hour to hour. She gave way before him, frightened lest this was the last hour.

"I'll see about it," she said.

He understood her and he grew amiable at once and turned to his father. "There's a new place to eat and swim about three miles down the south road and a bunch of us thought we'd go down tonight for supper and stay a while afterwards."

"I see," his father said vaguely. It occurred to him nowadays that he should take an interest in his son's life, now that he was sixteen—or was it seventeen? At any rate he was ceasing to be a child. When they were children it was natural that their mother should care for them. But Francis was no longer a child.

"Your—ah—studies are over?" he asked politely.

The mother broke in impatiently, half ashamed for him before the son. "Paul, don't you remember we went to the closing exercises a week ago?"

"Yes, my dear, I do," he replied mildly, looking at her with his clear blue distant gaze. "But I thought there was something said about Latin to be done this summer." He brightened suddenly and seemed to come nearer. "I might be of help there," he said with diffident eagerness.

"Or I could," said Joan, smiling mischievously.

The boy broke out into rich laughter, "Gee, I'll have to work yet with a bunch of teachers right in the family! Now don't you speak, Rose!"

"I?" said Rose, looking up out of mists. "Oh, I couldn't—Besides, I've promised Father to take a special catechism class for little girls this summer."

"I've promised him a month's vacation, Paul," the mother said. Then she beamed unexpectedly upon him. "But it's dear of you to help him—I know he'll be glad—"

"Oh, sure," said the boy gaily, satisfied, and pushing away from the table.

So the meal came to an end and they were knit together again by it. Their lives parted now and each went his way, but three times a day they were knit together again bodily. The body was their tie, the sameness of their blood and flesh. They met together and ate and drank and they renewed their flesh and their blood. They rose refreshed and ready to live apart for a while. In the search for what they wanted beyond the body they lived alone. But they would come together again and again, so they were never lost in loneliness.

What her own life alone was to be, Joan did not yet know. She rose, light and idle in her heart, and walked into the garden. The sun poured down into it like wine into a cup. The smell of the earth rose up through the grass, hot and close. It came up even between the flowers. She went to the lemon lily and bent over it and drew its fragrance into herself. She drew deep breaths until her body was filled, a vessel full of fragrance. But under its delicacy was the strong musky odor of the hot earth.

She straightened herself and walked about, unhurried and at her ease, looking at every leaf and flower. There was nothing she had to do and the garden was lovely. Between the opening buds of a white rosebush a spider had spun a web, catching delicately here the point of a leaf, there the edge of a calyx, drawing a cluster of white roses together surely and lightly into a silver net. In the center of the whiteness and the silver the spider sat small and black and still.

Beyond the garden stretched the street, leading away from the house and the garden, away from the village, into country and beyond. She gazed east and west. To the east the church was closed and silent. It had nothing to do with today. Yesterday people had gone into it and lent it life, but today they passed it by, putting their lives elsewhere. A woman passed now. It was Martin Bradley's mother, and she did not even turn her head to see where she had been yesterday. But she stopped when she saw Joan alone, for here was someone to whom she could talk and she could not resist that. She smiled at Joan cozily and sleekly. She was small and plump and satisfied with herself and her son, and her neat gray cotton dress fitted her as closely as feathers are fitted to a plump bird.

"Isn't it a nice day?" she said. "I'm on my way to the butcher's to get the sweetbreads early. Martin loves a good crumbled sweetbread for his dinner, done with a bit of bacon. I do myself. We're both fond of sweetbreads."

She nodded and smiled and went on importantly, stepping solidly on her small fat outward pointing feet. She was on her daily mission. Each morning she went early to the butcher to get the tidbit she planned that day for her son. If she got it she was triumphant for the day. If she failed, if someone was before her, the day was embittered. She carried small intense hatreds against her neighbors if they were before her.

"Sorry, Miz Bradley," Mr. Billings would roar, cheerful and bloody among his carcasses, "Miz Winter's just been and got my kidneys today. How about a bit of liver? My liver's extra fresh this morning."

But Mrs. Bradley would not be consoled by liver. "Martin doesn't like liver so well," she replied coldly and chose a chop. If she met Mrs. Winters on the way home she would be cool. She would be cool until she was successful again. If for several days she failed she grew bitter. Then she would revenge herself on Mr. Billings and Martin must bring her something from the city. She boasted among the villagers, "I declare, it's getting so I can't get anything I want at Mr. Billings'. He don't run near so good a place as he did. Martin brings home the meat from the city as often as not."

"Joan—Joan!" her mother's voice called suddenly from an upstairs window.

"Coming!" she sang back. She lingered lazily. It would be fun to see what happened today to Mrs. Bradley. But her mother would not wait. "Joan!" she called again.

So she put aside Mrs. Bradley and ran to her mother.

In the big upstairs bedroom her mother moved swiftly and competently. She had made each movement exactly the same each day of each year for many years, and now her hands knew the quickest direction, her feet the sparest step. She squared the corner of the bed tightly, the large double bed where she had slept with the children's father since the night they had come home from their homeymoon. It was all as familiar to her as her own hands and feet. She finished as Joan came in and sat down in the rocking chair. Joan was used to her there. In this chair of worn brown wood, with its strip of brown cotton quilting lining in it, her mother had always sat to darn and patch, and on the sagging carpet-covered hassock at its foot each child had sat in turn to recite the psalms and hymns and catechism they must learn by heart. It was always noisy downstairs in the family sitting room and the parlor was not to be thought of. But here was quiet. As a little girl Joan had looked out of the low window over the roofs of the village to the rolling hills where the sheep grazed, and had chanted, "The Lord is my shepherd, I shall not want," and here she had stammered over "the chief end of man is to glorify God and enjoy Him forever." How did one enjoy God? She asked her mother, and listened and never understood. Her mother never could make it clear. Here in this room, too, her mother had talked to them when they were in fault and here set upon them her rare punishments. Once, Joan remembered suddenly at this moment, she had thrown herself down upon the bed with a wail of sorrow because she had told a lie—she could not remember about what. She remembered only that she could not go to the Sunday school picnic because she had lied. Their mother could not endure lies. She might waver and delay judgment in anything else, but her voice came down as hard and bright as a sword after a lie.

"Don't tell me a lie!" she would cry. There was no patience in her then.

Now here she sat in the rocking chair and looked at her daughter straightly and shyly, with an unaccustomed pleading. "Joan," she said, "I've been waiting until you were home a few days to tell you something. I haven't wanted to spoil your graduation and coming home. But today I've got to tell you because I just don't feel equal to the missionary meeting this afternoon. Miss Kinney's going to speak on Africa and I want you to go instead of me."

"Mother!" she cried, astonished, sinking on the firm square bed. Why, her mother had never been ill! She was a little thinner, perhaps—She searched her mother's face. "Why haven't you told us?"

"I've wanted to keep up," her mother said wearily. "I've always felt I ought to keep up before the children. Trouble comes soon enough. Children oughtn't to share their parents' troubles."

She stared at her mother. "I didn't know you had any troubles," she said in a low voice.

"I didn't mean you should," her mother replied. "I wouldn't now, only I'm in pain—and yesterday morning when I went into your room, Joan, it came over me that you aren't a child anymore. You're a woman grown, so tall as you are, and I can't keep trouble from you any longer."

Joan could not answer. This was not her mother, this woman sitting slackly in an old warped chair, the smile gone from her face as though she had never smiled. She felt afraid of her.

"I'll do anything I can, of course," she said uncertainly. Had she been in the garden in the sunshine ten minutes ago?

"I have something wrong with me," her mother said vaguely. "I haven't been just right since Francis was born." She paused, embarrassed, and went on with difficulty. "He was such a big baby and I was torn somehow." She did not look at Joan, but turned her head and stared out of the window. About her hung shyness. She could not quite forget that this tall young woman had also been born of her. A slight repulsion wavered between them. Joan, filled with anxiety, felt a thread of disgust in the anxiety and instantly would not feel it. If this were only a strange woman she would have poured out quick sympathy. It was easy to be kind to strangers. But this woman was also her mother. She felt entangled in something she did not understand, entangled in a bodily repulsive way with her father, with her mother, even with Rose and with Francis. They were all bodily entangled together. She hated it and rose restlessly from the bed. She wanted to be happy all the time.

"Have you seen the doctor?" she asked. She went to the other window away from her mother and looked out. She should not have asked the question so coldly. Why was she cold to her mother now? She was afraid of something. She did not want her mother to come close like this. She wanted her mother as she had always been, cheerful and sure and surrounding them with warm pleasantness.

"Yes, I've seen Dr. Crabbe," her mother answered unwillingly.

"Dr. Crabbe!" Joan repeated. "He's nothing but an old country doctor."

"He was with me when each of you was born and he knows me," her mother replied simply.

Again she felt the throb of rushing repulsion. Her body—once it had been torn from her mother's flesh, held in old Dr. Crabbe's rough coarse hands. She knew his hands. She had felt the thick fingers pushing bluntly into her mouth when she was a child, to feel a loose tooth, to hold down her tongue when he looked at her sore throat. She remembered his peering red face coming hugely near, spotted with scars and badly shaved. He opened his mouth while he stared and his teeth were stained with tobacco and he breathed heavily through his hairy nostrils. His eyebrows were like yellow beards, and whiskers an inch long grew out of his ears. He was as short and thick as a topped tree.

"You ought to see somebody else," she said, looking steadily out of the window. Now Mrs. Parsons was going down the street. She had been to the post office again and under her arm was a bulky package—a returned manuscript, of course. If this were her mother sitting here as usual in the rocking chair, her hands busy instead of lying loosely like that in her lap, she would cry. "Mrs. Parsons has her novel back again—I wonder which one it is?" and her mother would answer kindly, "Poor soul, don't laugh at her. It's been such a curse in that family, her wanting to write novels. I declare I don't see how Ned and Emily have grown up so good. It's really poisoned Ed's life. He told me once he felt he'd never really had a wife or the children a mother. They don't mean anything to her beside those novels she writes. She measures her whole life by them. If one were accepted I don't believe she'd ask for heaven. She's been like that ever since I knew her."

But now it was trivial to speak of Mrs. Parsons. "What does Father say?" she asked.

There was no answer. She turned and saw her mother's eyes downcast, but along the edges of the lids there were tears. "Mother!" she cried. She rushed to her mother and knelt beside her and put her arms about her. Strange—strange to feel her mother's body relax in her arms! The repulsion was gone. She wrapped her arms about her mother and pressed her head down upon her shoulder. "Mother—Mother—Mother—" she said over and over. Oh, what was this disaster?

"There's no use telling your father anything," her mother said, choking. "He doesn't understand anything—he never has."

There was the closed door and the subdued passionate voices were behind it. Was this—but before she could ask the question her mother straightened herself and wiped her eyes.

"I'm a wicked woman," she said suddenly. "I don't know what came over me to say that. Your father is a wonderfully good man. I've a lot to be thankful for. I look at poor Mrs. Weeks and thank God—that awful Mr Weeks—" she pushed Joan aside and got to her feet and took the pins out of her long hair. She went to the bureau and picked up a brush and began to brush her hair swiftly. "I haven't anything to complain of," she said. "Lots of women at my time of life don't feel quite as strong as they did."

So she pushed her daughter away, and Joan stood up quickly, shy to the heart, made ridiculous. She hesitated, and then said, "What shall I do this afternoon, Mother? I want to help."

"Just go to the meeting for me, dear," her mother said calmly. She coiled her hair on top of her head and thrust the gray bone pins in swiftly. "Just make a few remarks about Miss Kinney—anything you like—you know her. If you can, dear—I think I will just rest the once. I'll be all right with an afternoon's rest. And Rose will go—she always wants to go—"

She looked into the mirror at her mother's face. Framed and in the bright light of the windows it looked whiter and more tired than it would when she turned around. "Of course I will," she said to the white face. She went to the door, and there hesitated again. After all, there had been this half hour. "Just the same, you ought to see another doctor," she said.

"Maybe I will one of these days," her mother said tranquilly, busy about her hair.

She went out and left her mother standing before the mirror.

In the afternoon before she went to the meeting she tiptoed to her mother's room. The door was open and she went in softly. Her mother lay asleep on the bed, covered by an old knitted afghan the Ladies' Aid had given her, once gay, but now faded into squares of faintly varied pallors. Above it her mother's face showed darkly pale, the mouth a little open, and ashen shadows about the nostrils and eyes. She could scarcely believe this was the same face she had watched secretly at the table, for at the noon dinner her mother had been quite herself among them. A little quiet perhaps, but then they were used to her rare stillnesses, although they loved her laughter. When they were small children and she fell into stillness they were afraid and begged her, "Mother, what's the matter? Mother, do please be funny again and laugh!" Sometimes she roused herself, but sometimes she turned her dark eyes on them in terrible gravity and said. "May I not be still sometimes in my life? I want to be still."

So she would be still and they could scarcely bear it. The whole house was gray with her stillness and they were burdened with it until even the father noticed it.

"Are you ill, Mary?"

"No, Paul," she answered serenely. "Just still."

In her stillness they clung to her in misery, not able to leave her, not able to play. When she came out of it they began to live again, and everything took on its true color once more. They ran and sang and shouted and played busily, and they could leave her and run out into the village to look for pleasure.

Now, looking down at the sleeping face, Joan felt again the old dependence on her mother's mood. Everything was wrong. She turned away frightened, and went softly from the room. The meeting suddenly became a burden to her. It would not be fun. She dreaded it—she did not like to hear sad things told, not even about people heathen and far away. She had not been to a missionary meeting for years, not since she was a little girl too small to leave at home alone. And she dreaded it because her mother had dreaded it always, too, although she made jokes about it. Still it had been one of her tasks, and when it was over she always came home sparkling and laughing and relieved. "There," she would cry, "I'm done with the heathen for another month!"

Nevertheless she had always worked steadily, since she was the minister's wife, at getting together the money the church promised. One hundred dollars each year they promised and the women planned and contrived and gave chicken suppers at which they sold bags and lace-edged handkerchiefs and embroidered towels and knit dishcloths and a score of such small things which they made and bought of each other, although they would have preferred neither to make nor to buy. Old Mrs. Mark regularly bought the same bag each year and donated it the next and bought it again, without pretense, and called it "my missionary bag." . . . Her mother, Joan perceived with surprise as she went slowly downstairs, had done many things she hated.

At the door she came upon Rose, dressed in white linen and with her wide straw hat already on her head. "Shall I go with you, Joan?" she inquired seriously.

"If you like," Joan said. She walked across the lawn beside Rose, constrained. She was somehow very constrained with Rose now. She had not thought much about her these last years. She had been too busy feeling her own growth. But Rose had been growing, too. After the summer it would be her turn to go away to school.

"What shall you do after the summer, Joan?" Rose asked suddenly, turning her large sweet eyes upon her sister. "What do you plan for your life?"

Plan? She planned everything. But she answered vaguely, "I don't know—" She could not tell Rose anything. But then it was true she did not know.

Besides, they were at the church. Miss Kinney came to them out of the side door, and she was softly anxious, her small nose trembling like a rabbit's. "I'm always nervous before I speak," she began breathlessly. "But somehow God gives me strength as I go on. I miss your dear mother. She did cheer me up always at the beginning—she always looked so interested—"

Under her arm was a portfolio of pictures. She had shown them many times, but still they were pictures of Africa and she had been there. Yes, she had walked among jungle trees and beneath swinging serpents and she had crept out of a hut on a tropical summer's night and seen the moon red behind palm trees and she had heard the throbbing beat of deep-toned distant drums. Once for five years out of her life she had escaped from this village and from her father and her mother. She said the voice of God called her. No other voice could have enticed her, not love, not lust. But when she was thirty-three, "yet not too old to learn the language," she always explained, she obeyed God's call, as she put it, and became a missionary.

Mr. and Mrs. Kinney had been shocked and deserted in their dignified old house. But they could not in decency protest against God as they had against the voices of young men. Nevertheless they delayed her. They said, "Sarah is impetuous. She decides everything so quickly." So year after year they delayed her, as they had delayed the two young men who had loved her childish ardent eyes, who came and waited and went away. Yet the parents could not drive away God. She kept him invisible but constantly beside her. "I have the call," she reiterated with more firmness than she had ever said anything in her life.

She grew quite wildly firm after a year or two, so that Dr. Crabbe said gruffly, "Let the girl have her own way for once or she'll have to be put into an asylum."

Old Mrs. Kinney wailed aloud, "But what shall we do without her? Her father's devoted to her. She's all we have—our only child!"

"You ought to have had grandchildren ten years ago," he replied with rudeness.

"Sarah's delicate," said Mrs. Kinney positively. She was old, but she was very pretty and fragile and her house was exquisite. Mrs. Kinney had inherited the house and some money with it, and neither she nor Mr. Kinney had ever needed to do anything.

So they never did anything, and Mrs. Kinney, who had always been afraid of everything, grew more afraid as the years went on. She would never, she said years ago, ride in one of these new automobiles. It was tempting God, it was suicide. She walked down the street every afternoon a little way, clinging to Mr. Kinney's arm, and on Sundays they walked the three blocks to church and back. She always explained, "We are both rather delicate. We have to take care of ourselves. Sarah inherits my delicate constitution, I'm sorry to say."

But for once Sarah was not delicate. She took ship and made the voyage breathless and arrived at the remote mission in the jungle and plunged intensely into the life. Hardship could not touch her and she was afraid of nothing, although always breathless.

After five years when she came on a furlough the old pair had her again. They clutched her with their love. They spoke piteously of their age, of their fragility. She heard her father's cough. She saw her mother's hand tremble with a palsy. Now they did not speak of her delicateness. Instead they spoke of her strength. They cried, "You are so young and strong and we will soon be gone. You will never miss a year out of your life. It will not be more than a year."

She waited year upon year. She served six years' waiting and her father died. Then her mother, trembling very much and grown as thin as a dried leaf, cried, "Sarah, can you bear to leave me alone? It will not be more than a year. I shall not live the year out."

So Sarah Kinney waited a year and two years and then five years and now she was beginning the seventh year of her waiting, and the old woman lived fretfully on, thin to her bones, trembling so that she must be fed and dressed like a child, and each day death was no nearer. Of course Miss Kinney was tender with her and never even in her heart did she allow herself to hope for anything except her mother's health. Her one self-indulgence was to remember the five years of her own life in Africa, to remember them and hope.

She stood before the two young girls now, happy because she could remember again, a narrow spare old-maidenly figure, so much taller than everyone else that she had stooped timidly since she was sixteen and first saw how she really looked in the mirror, her hair, now whiter than her mother's, flaring about her small excited face. "Five blessed years, dear friends," she began, her voice quivering. "I did God's work. The African people came to me—the dear people. They were not afraid of me at all. I loved them. When they were ill it was such joy to me—joy to minister to them, I mean—the little babies especially were so sweet. They were not afraid of me, although I know I looked strange to them. You know we do look strange and pale in a country where everybody is black."

Her gaze fluttered from one face to the other, all unbelieving because they remembered her as a small sickly child with protruding front teeth, upon Rose, sitting rapt and listening, her eyes downcast, her soft hands folded in her lap, and then she found Joan's eyes. Joan felt the beseeching eyes like lighted lamps upon her face. Staring down at her the white-haired woman hesitated, and her voice deepened and trembled. "It wasn't only the people," she said.

In the bare quiet room no one knew what she was saying, not even Rose, dreaming Rose, who turned everything into her own thoughts. No one understood except Joan, and to Joan this misty-eyed woman, whose wild white hair would not lie smooth, talked. She talked on and on, the words tumbling out of her, trying to make Joan see. Mrs. Parsons leaned over to whisper to Mrs. Winters. "Poor Sarah Kinney!" But Mrs. Winters said aloud, "Joan, I think we ought to take up the collection and adjourn. I've got company coming for supper."

Instantly Miss Kinney recalled herself. She began to gather up her pictures, her fingers shaking. Her voice quavered, shocked, apologetic, "Oh, is it late? Oh, I'm so sorry. When I get talking about my Africa—"

Joan started guiltily. Was it so late? She ought to have held the meeting better. She tore her eyes from Miss Kinney and gave a shudder of relief. She rose and said clearly as her mother might have done, "After the collection for the mission at Banpu—Rose, will you take the collection?—we will sing hymn number sixty-one and the meeting will be adjourned."

The minute bits of copper and silver tinkled the plate that Rose passed quietly and they stood to sing. The women sang heartily and quickly. They were thinking of suppers to be set upon their tables, of men and children to be fed. If food were delayed a man might growl sourly, "Better be taking care of your own family!" They sang hastily, "The Son of God goes forth to war." Joan heard their loud plain voices, slightly out of tune. She looked at their honest aging faces. No young women came to missionary meetings. It was one of her mother's problems. "How shall we get the young ones interested?" She looked from one to the other of the kind abstracted faces, at the frank open mouths, at cotton gloves being slipped surreptitiously on roughened hands. Her heart warmed to them. She was glad to be back among them. She was safe with them. How good they all were, how dear, how kind they were to care about Africa! Why should they give their pennies to sick babies in Banpu? Their own babies were often ill—a hospital in Banpu when there was none in Middlehope. But they would go on giving, go on rolling bandages and sending soap and safety pins because they were so patiently kind. Any tale of sorrow would take their pennies from them in small steady streams—sorrows of people whom they would never see.

She loved them warmly. They were so dear and warm about her. They stopped even in their hurry to say, "Joan, I'm sorry about your mother. I'll be over to see her tomorrow sure." "I'm making yeasten rolls, Joan, tell your mother, and I'll send her a pan." "I'll bring a jar of crab-apple jell. She's always been partial to my jell."—She felt comforted, so comforted that she forgot Miss Kinney until everyone was gone in the summer dusk, all except Miss Kinney and Rose and herself. Then she remembered and turned contritely to Miss Kinney.

"Oh, Miss Kinney, thank you so much. It's always so interesting to hear about your experiences in Africa. I'll tell Mother we had a good meeting."

"Did you really think so, dear?" Miss Kinney's voice came out of the twilight under the trees toned in delicate wistfulness. "I sometimes think—I'm afraid I talk—you see, it's the only thing that ever really happened to me. I still hope to return, you know, some day, when dear Mother is safe in heaven. She's eighty-two this year. Of course I couldn't leave her. But I practice the Banpu words every day so that I don't forget the language. I could pick up right where I left off."

Rose had said nothing. She had stood, a younger quiet figure behind her sister. But now she spoke, her voice soft. "You made me see everything. I saw it all just as it is."

Miss Kinney looked up at her, her face a pale emptiness in the shadows, and she gasped. She cried out, "Why—why—why—you dear child!" She began to weep a little and reached for Rose's hand and squeezed it hard and hurried away into the shadows. They walked quietly across the lawn in silence until Rose said softly again. "How wonderful it must be to have served—like *that!*"

But Joan's heart rose up. It rose against the sweetness in Rose's voice. Suddenly she hated sweetness, Rose's steady unvarying holy sweetness.

"I should hate it," she said abruptly.

"But, Joan," Rose protested with gentle reproach, "wouldn't you go—if God called?"

Her mind glimmered with dark half-formed pictures shaped out of Miss Kinney's words. She felt the heat, too fierce for health, forcing the strange dark jungles into fearful lush unnat-

ural life. She saw the black people, their eyes gleaming white-
ly through the jungles.

"No," she answered shortly, and ran into the house, into her
home. She wanted always to stay where it was safe and warm
and light. She wanted her own.

When she looked back upon that summer, months after it
was over, she saw it was more holiday than she knew at the
time. For her mother said no more of her illness. She rose as
usual in the morning and when after days Joan put a question
to her shyly, for she was still shy of flesh intimacy with her
mother, the mother wore her accustomed cheerfulness and she
answered, "I'm no worse, anyway. Don't worry, child. Go on
and have your fun this summer. I'm all right."

And because it was what she wanted to believe Joan believed it and took her pleasure, falling easily back into the old
happy dependence. They all leaned more than ever upon the
mother. The house was full of their merriment. Tall half-grown
boys stumbled up the wooden steps of the porch and shouted
for Francis, and when he came roaring to meet them they
clattered off to fish and to swim and to their own haunts by
river and road. Older youths came shyly asking for Joan, and
Rob Winters asked always for Rose. He was a tall fair grave
boy, his parents' only son, in school to be a minister, and
careful and always anxious to be right. If Rose minded that
only this one asked for her she did not show it. She met him
with her invariable quiet smile and they went away alone
together.

But Joan did not want to be alone with any of the ones who
came to find her. She welcomed anyone. She was full of
warmth, ready to live, hungry to laugh. All she did she did as
though she starved for it. A small picnic of village boys and
girls was a feast to her. She woke on the morning of a day set
for pleasure and found her heart beating with pure joy and a
song in her mouth ready. It did not matter who was to be there,
whom she would meet or what she would do in this time of her
life, this time when she waited, sure of what was to come. It
was joyful to rise, to bathe, to dress, to eat, to run out of the
house and cry out to other young who came to meet her, to run
down the quiet street and plunge into woods and clamber up
mountainsides and dive into deep cold pools. She lived in her
body only, and all the rest of her lay sleeping, shut off alone

and asleep. She scarcely read a book, or if she did it must be some easy story of summer love. For a while she was through with learning. Her body grew very beautiful. Her face rounded and the color of her skin grew dark and rich with sun and health. The hours of play made her eyes merry and her laughter quick and some nonsense was forever bubbling at her lips.

So during the short lovely summer she paid no heed to anyone while she lived for her own sake. Her father was a ghost to her. She kissed him gaily in passing and cried a greeting to him because it was a pleasure to be kind to everyone, and then he was gone from her mind. Rose she forgot except as they passed and then she laid a careless gay hand upon her sister's cheek, and Francis was nothing to her except to give and receive teasing and laughter.

One would have said she was in love and yet she was not. She was not in love with anyone or anything except with the whole world. She was in love with the morning and the sun. She was in love with rain and moonlight. But she was not deceived by any hot young voice swearing his love by the moon. She smiled and listened gladly, because she liked to listen to love, to any love while she waited, and out of what she heard she made dreams. Ned Parsons, strumming his guitar under the wisteria and staring lovesick into her eyes, could make her smile. She could not love Ned, whom she had always known and whom as a little girl she had fought and conquered many times, poor Ned to whom his mother had given with her blood her foolish romantic imagination. He did not look like Emily, dusky, stocky Emily who was like her father. Emily was going to the city to get a job. "I've got to get away from here," she told Joan tersely at picnic. "I want to make my own way." But Joan said quickly, "I'll never go away from home. I love it here in the village, with everybody always exactly the same."

"I don't," said Emily shortly.

But then Emily never laughed. And Emily was ugly, with her long hard upper lip and coarse black hair and her decided way of saying even small things such as wanting the sugar passed to her. Joan liked Ned better, though she knew even in the moonlight that his pale gray eyes were a little popped and she heard in the midst of his loving how his big bony fingers faltered upon the strings and she winced at every discord. She was not deceived by him, but in his reedy voice she heard another voice. In his gangling body bent toward her she dreamed another devotion, and so she cried softly, "I love music under the moon!" And she cried it with such ardor that he felt it next to love for him. Meanwhile, she gazed across the lawn while he sang and saw with ecstasy the tall deep shadow the church threw among the lighter shadowing trees. Someday, somewhere, in a lovelier place upon this earth, she would hear a song, a great new song. Because of this she was tender to Ned, warm even to Jackie Weeks who was still in high school, warm to every voice she heard. So she enjoyed everything, a campfire beside a lake, a canoe darting down a stream, a bird's call in the night.

And there was always about her the good steady warmth of her home. She accepted her mother's ready smile and pushed away a foreboding that her mother grew thinner or that she seemed tired. Once in the night, near the end of the summer, she woke to hear the old subdued quarrel behind the bedroom door. Or was it a quarrel? She did not know; she did not want to know. She wrapped her braid about her ears and pushed her head into the softness of her pillow and slept again deeply. When the morning came she thought she had dreamed it. Surely she had dreamed it.

Suddenly the summer ended. Her mother said one day, "It is Rose's turn now. I must see Rose through four years of college. When Rose is through and Francis, when you are all ready to begin your own lives, then I will rest—not just rest a little of an afternoon, but a long rest. I'm going to be selfish then for a long while." She smiled over a heap of flowered summery lawn she had in her lap and threaded her needle again with pink silk.

"As if you could be selfish!" Joan cried. She was still not dressed for the day, though it was nearly noon. The morning had turned gray and soft with rain and she had danced late at a party the night before and then slept far into the morning and waking very hungry had gone to find food. Now she sat in her yellow silk pajamas upon her mother's bed, a slice of bread and apple butter in her hand—she was always hungry—and her mind full of sweet leisure. But her mother was unexpectedly grave. "I could do with a rest," she said, sighing. Then she made haste to amend it. "Oh, I don't mean I don't want to work. I've always enjoyed every kind of work. When I was a girl I used to think I didn't like sweeping. But I've learned to

like it, too, now, through having to do it so much. One might as
well enjoy what one has to do. I like now to feel a room grow
clean under a strong broom. . . . There comes Mrs. Billings. I
daresay she wants me to tell her what to talk about at Ladies'
Aid tomorrow. She is a good soul—but stupid. Darling, would
you mind calling Rose and having her slip this dress on? You
have such a good eye for style, and I want her dresses to look
right when she goes away. I'll try to get rid of Mrs. Billings
quickly." Her mother was up swiftly and with energy, calling
as she went, "Rose—Rose, come and try on your dress—"

Joan, shaking out the flowery folds, waited while Rose took
off her dress. Then she dropped down the fluffy stuff over
Rose's head and over the smooth round shoulders and met
Rose's eyes in the mirror. "Oh, Rose, you're pretty," she cried in
honest praise. "I'm glad it's your turn for the new things."

The small multicolored flowers upon the pink background
suited the round pale face, the dark eyes. But Rose was composed. She smiled a little and said nothing. Joan cried at her
again. "Don't you care, Rose? Don't you want to be pretty?
When I was your age I was so frightened I'd never be pretty.
You're so much prettier than I was then. I'm too big—bony big
—and my mouth is awful. I try to think it isn't, but I know it
is."

Rose hesitated. "I don't want to think of such things," she
replied.

"But you are really pretty," Joan said laughing. "Silly little
saint!" She shook the pretty shoulders lightly. Funny Rose,
always afraid of sin! She began to sing carelessly, her mouth
full of pins, fitting the dress here and there, letting it into a
little more fullness at the breast—Rose's breasts were rounder
than her own—tightening it at the waist. She felt her sister's
body soft and warm under the lawn, a girlish shape. Here and
there her fingers touched the fine skin. She saw the little yel-
low-brown curls soft upon the bent white neck. Tenderness
flowed up in her for her sister. She did not often feel near to
Rose like this. The touch of Rose's flesh brought her near, the
service she did her brought her near. She felt warm toward the
young girl, warm as a mother might, full of generous love for
her.

"Little, little saint," she murmured and smiled intimately
and kindly into Rose's eyes in the mirror. She was so much
bigger than Rose. She would always take care of Rose.

Then abruptly one day the house was empty without Rose. Until now when each summer ended it had been she, Joan, who had gone away to fresh faces and new life; she who when she came back again made complete the family. Now she stood with her father and her mother and watched Rose's face at the train window with secret dismay. Her own safe years, years when she knew clearly what to do, were now so quickly gone. Slow in passing, now that they were gone, they were so swiftly gone.

When they walked home together in the early sunlight of a September morning she felt very grave. Her holiday was over. Even though she walked to her home and between these two who had always given her shelter, she was no longer sheltered. She must push out from between them, go out from her home. She must begin something for herself if she were to live at the pitch of delight. But she wanted and feared this independence. She wanted to live for herself, and yet she wanted this warm home about her at night.

Her mother looked at her and smiled. "I felt lost when you went away as Rose is doing today. I never get used to any of you going away. The first time you went away I went home and cried."

"Did you, Mother?" said Joan, astonished, staring. Such a thing had not occurred to her. She had gone away that first morning four years ago filled with herself and with her wonder at what was about to happen to her, and her strong cheerful mother went home and cried because the house was empty without her! She was immeasurably touched and comforted. It was lovely to be loved. Wherever she went there would be this love to which to return. She put out her hand and patted her mother's gray hair under the small brown homemade velvet toque. Her mother smiled back to her and the moment was warm and close until in mutual shyness they looked away from each other's eyes.

"I hope," said her father gently out of his own silence, "that Rose will not lose her faith, even as you did not, Joan. But I never saw a young soul with clearer conviction than hers."

A guiltiness fell upon Joan. She ought to tell her father she didn't really know what she believed. But she shrank from hurting him.

"I hope Rose has a good time," her mother said with energy and then went swiftly on. "Joan, I've been thinking that old gold-brown cashmere of mine could make Rose a pretty jumper dress, and the color would be becoming to her. The skirt's old-fashioned and it has a lot of cloth in the gathers. I believe I'll set to work on it. It helps to get to work on something."

Incredibly soon they were home and soon the house was still except for the sounds of the morning. Hannah polishing the stairs, the whir of the sewing machine from the attic where her mother sewed, her father's slippered footfall in his study. So it might have been if Rose were there. Rose who in her quietness seemed to add nothing to the noise of the house, and yet now the house seemed empty. But it was not that Rose was gone, not that Francis was in school again. It was that she, Joan, was still there, idle, when the others were busy. She must think what to do next. She must of course earn her bread. Her mother had said many times, "Stay at home a year, darling. Take your time." But she was restless now that the summer was over. It was time to work, to do something else. She wanted the next thing. The house was suddenly too small, the furniture worn and old and tiresome to her sight.

She went to her own room and closed the door and sat down by the window. Where was the mood of the summer gone? Why was she discontented? But the village was absurdly small, a crisscross of half-a-dozen streets, a little nest of poor houses, a few dull folk. She brought to her memory one after another of the houses whose interiors she knew completely, where not a chair or table had been moved since she could remember. She was weary of them. They stood dingy in the sunshine of this day. It was not enough.

I want something more, she thought resolutely. I must find the thing I can do really well. . . . Maybe music . . .

But she knew in her secret heart what she wanted to do, and what she could do well. She could love a man well and keep his house clean and make it beautiful and bear his children. It was all she secretly asked of life, that she might follow this old beaten path. But how could love find her, hidden away in a little country manse?

There was a knock at the door and Hannah thrust in her rough red head. "Miss Joan, your pa says there's a couple downstairs to be married and will you come and be a witness with your ma?"

She rose mechanically, used to the summons. But today there was acuteness in the moment. Downstairs she waited while her father drew off his study gown and put on his old frock coat. The groom was a young country fellow, a hired man, doubtless, upon some farm. His hands hung huge and misshapen and his great stooped shoulders were bursting his coat. The girl was his mate, a strong squat figure, her arms red and thick, her face broad and low-browed and burned red by the sun. They were foreign, sprung from some peasant soil in an older world. They stood awkwardly, closely together, their dull greenish eyes fixed faithfully upon the minister's face. She could hear their heavy breathing, and on the man's thick neck she saw the sweat stand out in coarse drops.

It was over in a moment, a few words, a halting promise interchanged, an instant's suspense about the ring. He fumbled at the girl's finger and she snatched the ring from him. "Here, give me it," she said loudly, forgetting where she was. He watched absorbed while she worked the thing over her knuckle, and then sighed gustily in relief.

"Now come and have some cake and coffee," her mother said with brisk kindness. It was her custom. They smiled sheepishly and followed her into the dining room with the stumbling docility of beasts. Behind them Joan saw their hands clasped, two rough knotty young hands, holding each other hard. They would go back to some house, some small wooden house in a field, and they would work and eat and sleep and make crude love and rear children together, mated. It was a life. She was suddenly very lonely. She turned abruptly and went back to her room.

In a night autumn came rushing. The wind blew cold across her sleeping and when she opened her eyes in the morning it was to find upon her bed a shower of leaves from the maple tree outside her window, dry leaves veined with yellow. She sprang up to shut out the cold and saw early frost upon the green grass. The chill woke her sharply and she did not go back to bed. She must get to work this day. As soon as breakfast was over she would work on the prelude she had begun last spring and never finished. She would go over to the church and work alone at the organ. She dressed resolutely and swiftly and ate her breakfast quickly.

Her mother worried, "Joan, you haven't eaten enough."

She answered, "I want to get to work, Mother, I must work this very day. I have an idea for my prelude."

But her mother did not hear her. She sat listening, her head lifted, her hands hovering above the coffee cups. There was a clatter on the stairs and the door burst open and Francis fell into the chair beside her.

"Say, Mom, gimme my food quick, will you? Jackie Weeks said he'd help me with my math this morning if I got there early, and I want to get it done so's I can go nutting. I'll bet the frost was hard enough last night to make 'em drop. He's a shark at math. Lord, how I hate math!"

"Perhaps Joan would help you, darling," said his mother. "Here—let me butter your muffin. I wish you wouldn't go so much with Jackie."

But she would not wait, Joan told herself. She had her own work to do. Besides, her mother had not even heard her. "I'm not good in math, I'm afraid," she said, and then hated her selfishness. "Of course I will help, Frank," she said.

"Jackie'll do it quicker," he said carelessly, and she was released.

With her music under her arm she walked across the still frosty lawn and into the quiet church. Outside the air was pungent and fresh, electric with cold, but here in the church it was warm and still and untouched by freshness. There was a faint aged odor, the odor of old people, a little sweet, a little dying. She tiptoed through the empty aisle, past the empty pulpit, and sat herself at the organ and opened it and immediately the waiting keys invited her. She was tired of idleness —work was pleasure. She spread her pages and played the first bars softly and critically. She played on and then broke off. There she had stopped writing it down last spring just before Commencement. A melody had come to her and she had written it down in haste and then left it incomplete because they had called for her, Mary Robey and Patty, her roommates.

"Joan—Joanna! Practice—practice for the senior parade!"

The senior parade was the most important thing in the world to her then. It was nothing now—less than a memory. Strange how she could hear their voices and yet she did not want to see them—not really. They were over, somehow. She wanted—she wanted—not them—someone. She set herself resolutely to the music. Slip there into a fourth, now minor it in the left hand, now repeat the theme slowly and so through the variation to the last bar—the last chord—major, minor? A fifth, perhaps. She moved her fingers tentatively over the keys, humming the air softly—so—to a minor sixth. There let it be. Though it might sound unfinished, she could not find another end.

She tried it over again from the beginning. The church, empty as a shell, echoed deeply behind her. It flung back at her her own lonely music. The melody ran through the arches and came back again to her ears and she listened, absorbed. Not quite right somehow, not quite right. The minor note was not introduced soon enough into the melody of the right hand. It began too gaily for its end. The minor note must be sounded very soon, there in the beginning. She put her pencil to her lips and dotted in a note and then tried it over softly.

"That is right," said a voice out of the church. She leaped up from the seat and turned. There beneath the pulpit in the front pew sat Martin Bradley. His hat was on his knee and in his hand was a roll of music. She remembered instantly that it was Friday morning. Of course he always practiced on Friday mornings. How could she have forgotten it when all through her childhood her Friday mornings had echoed with the strains of his music from the church? She ran quickly to the choir rail.

"Oh, I'm sorry," she gasped, looking down at him.

He rose gracefully and smiled. "Why?" he asked simply. "It's been delightful. That was a charming little thing—delicately sad. What is it?"

"I made it," she answered shyly.

His face, upturned like this, was new to her, a narrow sensitive face. He did not look old at all, even with his gray hair.

"I can't make up my mind where to introduce the fifth," she added with impulsive confidence.

"Let me see." He mounted the steps lightly, a spare, graceful figure, and came to the organ and sat down. Very precisely and clearly he began to play her prelude. Strange to hear her own music come like this from his hands! She was intensely conscious of him, his look, his presence; the church was full of his presence. Suddenly he began to vary it. "How's this—and this—" He modulated softly, plainly. "Is it your idea still?"

"Yes, yes, that's lovely," she said eagerly. "Now bear upon that sixth and repeat it in the left hand. Yes!" she cried delightedly. "Why didn't I see how to do it myself?"

He played on. The fine black hair grew smoothly upon his neck, a little silvery at the edge. She was listening to the music, thinking about the music, but she saw his brown neck with the fine short clipped hair smoothly upon it, and the white about his ears, as smooth as though the white were brushed evenly over his hair. When he turned to her, questioning, she saw the dark skin wrinkled closely about his eyes, but he was not old, not as old as she had thought he was. She liked the spare distinguished line of his shoulder. "So—to the minor end," he finished, and wheeled around and smiled at her.

"Thank you," she said with ardor, and he smiled again quickly and then she was shy and began to gather her music together.

"Don't go," he said.

"I must," she answered, and then wondered at her urgency. She did not need to go. She might linger here as long as she liked and no one would miss her. But still she was urgent to go away. What should she talk about to him? For now she did not see him at all as Mrs. Bradley's son, for whom the old woman searched out tidbits. He was a man, mysterious and able, who made his own life in a great city, and only slept in this village. Doubtless he knew many women, beautiful and clever, and she was only a girl out of school. Beside his finished slightness she felt herself too hearty and too big and hopelessly young. Then she found herself looking down into his smiling steady eyes, and she saw he thought she was pretty. She was relieved and at ease, and mischief rose in her. She smiled back at him.

"I must go and help my mother. She's making a dress for Rose."

"You look like a tall pretty boy. A boy doesn't sew!"

He was teasing her and she laughed with pleasure. "I can cook and sew and sweep and make beds and lead missionary meetings and dance and swim—"

"Surely out of so much there is something we can do together?"

She felt a heat run into all her veins. It was the first time a man had ever asked her—she dismissed with huge momentary scorn all the boys she had ever known, and looked at him, shy again. "Do you sometimes walk—on a Sunday afternoon?" he continued.

"I can," she said with gravity.

"Then Sunday—about four? If I let you go now?"

"At four," she promised, very gay.

He turned again to the organ, smiled at her, nodded, and began to play long smooth rills of notes. She walked softly away and the music followed her across the lawn and into the house. She went to her own room and opened a window and the music mounted and climbed in, muted but still clear. He was playing gloriously now, swiftly and triumphantly, clear, climactic chords. She sat down to listen, and leaned upon the window.

Strange how she had forgotten they were in the church! Something had begun for her, though she did not know what it was. But she knew that now the house was empty no more and now she had plenty to do. There were a hundred things she could do, wanted to do. Why had she felt so empty yesterday? Life was rushing again and full and deep with promise. Anything might happen to her any day now in Middlehope. She laughed and turned contentedly to her desk, and opened the pages of her music score. She would write in the notes he had given her, that muted varying fifth which introduced early the minor theme. Sunday afternoon would be here before she knew it.

"But I can't see what you find in that old man!" her mother was crying at her.

"He isn't old!" she cried back hotly.

They were in her mother's bedroom, and her mother had shut the door so that she might say what she had to say. She sat down in the rocking chair and began to rock frantically back and forth, her arms folded tightly across her bosom in the way she had when she was beside herself. Joan stood by the window, rebellious, determined, furious that her mother made her still a child.

"He's forty-five if he's a day! You're twenty-two! Why, he's old enough to be your father! You're Ned Parsons' generation!"

"Ned Parsons bores me," she answered shortly.

"I thought this summer you liked him—"

"Only to play with—"

"You'll break my heart—every one of you children seem to have your own special way to break your mother's heart—"

"It's not fair for you to try to force me by making me sorry for you," she answered hardly, shocked at her hardness.

There was silence except for the creak of the rockers. Now she remembered that sometimes in the night, when she heard the subdued quarreling voices, she heard also this same swift loud creak. But she said nothing. She stared steadily out into the gray November afternoon. The leaves were gone already from the trees and the red brick church stood tall and bare and angular, immovably large in the landscape. But it was all nothing to her. In less than ten minutes Martin would be home and the telephone would ring. She would hear his voice. She had been waiting for it all day.

"Has he proposed to you?" her mother asked in a dry voice.

"No," she replied coldly.

"He'll never marry you, that's one comfort," her mother said bitterly. "He's philandered with one girl after another. It's a joke in the village, Martin's girls. And no one knows what goes on in the city. But he'll never marry anybody—his mother wouldn't let him even if he wanted to. But he'll never want to. There's talk about him—I can't tell you—" She paused a moment and went on with difficulty. "There's something downright queer about him. I feel it."

She would not answer. What did she care what this foolish little village thought? They did not know Martin. Besides, he had been honest with her. Only yesterday he had said to her, "I won't pretend never to have loved anyone before. But, darling child, you came when I thought it was all finished. You've come like a lovely late spring into my life. And there's never been anyone like you. You're everything I've wanted—you are a sweet boy, you're a pretty lady, you—"

"I know all about him," she said to her mother, her voice very even and clear.

"Joan—Joan—Joan—" her mother cried helplessly. "You're nothing but a silly child. Don't you see what you're doing? Everybody's talking about you. And your father's the minister! Why, even Mrs. Winters—"

"Don't tell me!" she broke in, turning furiously on her mother. "I don't care—what's Mrs. Winters?"

Her mother was silent before her fury, but she did not turn away her eyes. She swallowed hard and began again, looking at her steadily, making herself calm and reasonable. "Let's talk gently, Joan. Every young girl falls in love once with an older man—"

"Listen!" she cried. The telephone rang loudly in the hall and she ran to it. There was his voice at her ear, warm and ardent and rich. He had a beautiful tender voice, not deep, but light and tender as a woman's.

"Joan?"

"Martin—Martin—"

"Meet me in ten minutes, sweet—in the same spot?"

"Yes."

She hung the receiver up softly and flung herself into her coat and ran bareheaded from the house into the dusk.

But her mother was in her still. However she might answer rebelliously, however she might run, however she might cry aloud to herself in the dusk that now she would choose her own way and have her own life, her mother had carried her in herself, now she seemed in some strange like way to be sharing her body with her mother. Once she had lain, small and curled, a stubborn part of her mother's larger being. Now in her own large strong young being her mother held a small dark stubborn part. She could not be free of her mother.

She strode on through the cold darkness and met Martin outside the station and threw herself passionately into the darkness to find his arms and lips. But though it was dark he drew back.

"Wait," he whispered. "Wait. Someone else got off the train behind me."

He stood away from her a moment and they waited in the silence. A girl's figure came by and passed at a little distance.

"Do you recognize her?" he asked in a whisper.

"No," she replied, shortly and aloud. Her mother in her made her answer shortly. Her mother in her made her go on against her will. "Why should we care? I hate sneaking about."

He answered very gently. "It's not sneaking, sweetheart—it's only being discreet." He took her arm coaxingly and she could not answer. They walked pressed closely together in the dusk along a roundabout road by the edge of fields to the other end of the village where he lived. She longed passionately for his arms. She was hungry for his touch upon her. She did not want to make him angry, because when he was angry he did not smile. He was silent then and took his arms away. If he were angry he could leave her with absolute silent suddenness. But her mother was doggedly with her.

"Why should we be discreet? We have nothing to hide."

"Sweet . . ." he began, and he reached for her hand and thrust it into his overcoat against his breast. She felt her hand there alive with a separate life. But still her mother drove her hard against him. She had not been willing to hear what her mother said, but she had heard and was saying it over again.

"What's the end of it all, anyway? Martin, aren't we ever going to tell anybody?"

Now he stopped and in the lonely black road took her in his arms and kissed her. Against his kisses the voice of her mother struggled once more. "Isn't our love ever coming to anything?" He gave her no answer except his kisses. He held her against his hot thin body and kissed her again and again and again, hard strong practiced kisses that played intolerably upon her young unused flesh. For a moment the thunder in her ears silenced her mother's voice, the thunder of her own rising rushing blood. So she was silenced. She put her head down upon his shoulder and stood trembling against him.

In her home her mother said no more. Days passed and she said no more. She moved usually about her household tasks and if she were quiet, Joan would not speak of it. She would not ask why her mother was quiet because she did not want to be shaken in her love. She would not give up her love. She worked every day upon her music, long hours alone in her room, long hours alone in the empty church, but now she was never lonely. She had conceived the idea of a love sequence in music. Each day she would put into it some meaning of her love with Martin. But she had not yet really begun to write it into a shape. As yet it was only a drift of melodies in her imagination.

For now she lived entirely in the secret life of her sudden love. To her mother she was always pleasant, always ready to be helpful, to conciliate her. There was a quick cry always ready on her lips, "Let me do it for you, Mother!" Sometimes her mother would let her take a broom or a duster from her and sometimes she would not. Sometimes she answered tranquilly, "Thank you, child." But sometimes she cried bitterly, "Go on and do something you really want to do." Out of this bitterness once she looked at Joan and said hopelessly, "I expected too much—I seem always to have expected too much from my children." Then Joan went away quickly and in silence, for she would not hear her mother speak of that one thing which now fed her.

Yet she still wanted the old family love about her and now she turned eagerly to her father, grateful for his guileless ignorance of all that went on about him. She knew her mother had not told him anything—why tell him who understood only the mysteries of God? So in the daytime, when she was waiting for the night and Martin, that she might escape her mother she went sometimes with her father along the country roads when he went to visit his people, and she sat silent in his silences or heard him talk of his far thoughts.

In the silence she thought of Martin. But it was not really thinking. It was not her brain saying words and making thoughts about him. It was only that if she were left alone for a moment without occupation, talk in her ears, tools in her hand, a task to be done, suddenly she was empty and in that emptiness there was only Martin. Nothing she could read in books, nothing she had once learned in school, had any meaning for her now. There must be something for hands and feet to do, a question to be heard and answered, or else she was empty and in the emptiness was Martin.

So when her father talked she listened, her upper surface hearing, answering what she scarcely heard. He said, not talking to her, but speaking aloud to himself as he often did riding along the country roads, speaking aloud to himself or to God, "I must enlarge the chapel at South End. I am grieved continually that in that village of several hundred souls there is no real church. People live together like savages without marriage laws and their children are not baptized. Even though they are black they are nevertheless souls in God's sight. But I need help—I need help—the people in Middlehope don't help me—"

She listened, and for a moment she heard. Black souls—she remembered Miss Kinney and Africa. South End was like Africa. The people were black. They were savage—that meant they lived together without marriage laws. At missionary meetings no one spoke about South End. But since she was born she had known that people did not like to pass that way by night. Ever since the factory closed things had been worse, quarreling and feuds between families. Peter Weeks kept saying he was going to open the factory again, but meanwhile people lingered on, waiting and quarreling and drinking.

Her father's voice continued gently and calmly.

"But if my people do not see it as I do, yet I can say as Christ said also, 'I have other sheep not of this fold.' I will tell them God has spoken to me of it. I will proceed upon God's call and leave it to God that my people will hear his voice also." He spoke as definitely as though what he had planned to do was done.

She did not answer, letting him talk. On their homeward way her father turned his small old car and they passed by South End. He drove slowly past the chapel, full of plans.

"It's an ugly place," she said, looking down the dirty broken street, the shabby people shambling out of doorways.

"It is ugly because it is full of sin," he replied tranquilly.

But now she did not want to hear him. She wanted to hurry away from South End and get home, for the afternoon was late and she must be there to meet Martin.

Yet her father had his part in her, too. If her mother had made and fed her body, here was her father, and he had fed her spirit. Day by day, week by week, by his presence, by his words, he had shaped something in her. Her mother's part in her was passionate and dark and strong and hard with good sense. "He will never marry you," her mother cried in her continually now. But her father's part in her was not weaker than her mother's. He was not in her blood. He had not shaped her bones or created her flesh. But he had breathed into her life of a sort, a life not of this world. He had informed her spirit. He said, "It is ugly because it is sinful," and she understood him.

She could not, therefore, forever live quite wholly in her body with Martin. Her soul had a hunger, too. Her father had not satisfied her soul, but he had fed it enough to keep it alive It was alive and hungering in her so that she wanted to talk to Martin, to feel his mind and hers in communion. But he did not talk to her. When she talked he listened smiling, tolerant of her as of a child, and then he took her into his arms and kissed her again and again. It was his only answer to her, and after a while she foresaw, dimly, that this would not be enough.

But as yet this was enough, or nearly enough for joy. The very strength she had from her mother's share in her being, the dark earthy strength, made her hungry for joy and Martin was the only means that had come to her. She did not see him for himself, but only as a means for joy. For it was indeed joy to have him kiss her as often as he would, because it was a man's lips upon hers. It was a joy to have his hands upon her hands, even though she was secretly ashamed because her hands were broader than his and harder in the palm. It was joy to have his touch smoothly upon her throat, delicately at her breast. She called these lips, these hands, this man's shape that stirred her,

Martin. That he could by his music also move her heart did not make the true Martin the more clear to her. He had her by the blood.

And yet he did no more than kiss her and fondle her when they were alone—no more than that. He was very guarded. She made her joy out of very little—a moment or so every day when she could meet him at the train, a half hour in the church when they were alone on Fridays. There by the organ she bent to him while he played, leaning her cheek against his hair, watching his quick supple narrow hands upon the keys. Or she waited for him, sitting quietly in a pew while he played over and over again a phrase that did not please him. And he let her wait.

For now as months went on he changed, as often as a woman might change—as she, indeed, never changed, because she did not know how. It was her being to be straight and simple and unchanging. But he was delicately hot and cold, and she did not know what to do with him, or how to shape herself to his changefulness. Sometimes he was anxious and then he forced her to leave him soon. The church, he said, was so near her parents. They might be discovered. He was afraid her mother might discover them. He was cold and hot together, a strange cold hot creature. Sometimes he kept her waiting miserably, shy because of her youth and his maturity. Sometimes he came late to practice and he said coldly and formally when he found her already there, "Good morning, Joan," as though she were a little girl, and he went directly to the organ and began to play, and did not touch her. In his aloofness he behaved as though he had never touched her. Then she did not know what to do. Once in the spring, in a fury of hurt she had run noisily out of the church and to her own room, and there she sat shivering by the window she still must open to hear him play. He played on and on steadily. Surely he did not even turn once to see if she were there. When at last he stopped she closed the window. . . . Now he missed her. Now with some excuse he would come to the door of the manse and ask for her. . . .

But he did not. She saw him walk quietly and gracefully down the street toward his mother's house. That day and the next she did not go to meet him anywhere. He did not call her and she forced herself to silence. On Sunday morning he came into the church before the people as he always did, and he did not look at her. But by now her heart was like a beaten puppy.

For her own sake she must not go to meet him again. She swore she would not meet him in the afternoon in the deep hidden spot they had, a small well-like dale between two sharp little hills, halfway to South End.

But she went. He was there before her and without a word he began to kiss her and to fondle her with his smooth expert hands. And she had not the heart to ask why two days ago he had not kissed her or wanted to touch her. She did not understand him. He was strange and not to be understood. She only said sadly and at last after long silence, "Why do you love me at all?"

"Why do I love you?" he repeated. They had risen from the log where they had sat. He looked up at her, and ardor flew into his eyes again. "You're like a lovely boy, Joan," he said. "I love you because you're so lovely—and like a boy—you've a boy's head and a boy's mouth. Look at your hands—" He held outspread on his own palm her strong spare hand. "Even your hand is like a boy's! I wish you'd cut off your long hair."

His face was dry and brown and wrinkled in the hard sunlight and for the first time he looked old to her. She saw him for one moment as himself, as Martin Bradley who had always lived in the village. Something repelled her. Was there some odor about him? It was faintly sweet, faintly vile. It was like a perfume a woman might have used upon her handkerchief yesterday.

"We'll never be married," she said suddenly.

"Darling—" he began.

"You'll never marry anybody," she said.

"Darling," he began again, and drew her toward him by the hand he held.

But now she knew he was repulsive to her. "No," she said abruptly. "I'm going to South End to meet my father at the mission." She remembered that on Sunday afternoon her father went to South End. She could go to her father. She wanted her father.

She strode off sharply and left him on the instant. She held her body straight and hard and she did not look back once to see what he did. But within herself she began to weep. Behind her straight grave face she was weeping inwardly and bitterly, and when she asked herself why, she found herself crying in her heart, "I wish it had not been he who kissed me first." But she forced her feet to go on and on, and soon she was at her father's chapel door.

In the small bare room, she sat down at the very back and watched. The room was crowded with shuffling curious people. They were dark and sullen. They were yellow and livid. They were filled with black blood and white, with blood ill-fused and cross-currented. But when they were old, their faces grew placid, aged beyond good or evil, as tranquil after evil years as Mr. Parker or Mrs. Parsons in their goodness. All the faces were upturned to her father who towered above them.

She turned her face upward to him, too, with a rushing sense of safety in his goodness. He was to be trusted because he was so good, so simply good. She lifted her face to him again.

But inside her body something beat and ached strongly. Her defrauded body, denied, drew back upon itself its own ardor. To what should touch and kiss proceed, then? her body inquired most passionately. To which her good brain answered coldly and relentlessly, "He would never have married me."

So she turned to her father and received from him hungrily another sort of food. Among all the others she sat and received certain words for food. "And Jesus Said, 'Come unto me all ye—'" Surely this was a sort of food her father gave her, too, while he gave to the others. She listened anxiously when he told of the prodigal son. She listened, groping for something from her father.

But then it seemed to her she could not, after all, bear his unearthly physical presence. While he was standing in benediction over the restless half-subdued crowd she slipped away and swung solitary down the country road toward home. She was glad for the dusk. No need to turn her head now toward that dale, no need, for he was long gone. She was clear of him now. No more—no more of his kisses! Her mother and her father had her back again. She would go back into them. Tomorrow she would humble herself and say to her mother, "I have been a fool." The prodigal son two thousand years ago in the old story had said, "I have sinned." Perhaps it was the same thing. She turned at the gate of the manse to enter.

But as she turned she saw someone standing there, waiting for her. It was not a man—not Martin. It was a woman. A trembling hand came out to her and she seized it and knew it.

"Why, Netta Weeks!" she cried. She forced heartiness into

her voice. Poor Netta, for whom she was always too busy! They had never had their talk.

"I had to come, Joan—I had to see you—"

"Yes, Netta?"

"Everybody's saying—they're all saying—" The voice choked, the twitching hand tried to free itself.

But Joan held it hard. "What are they saying?" she demanded.

"You and Martin—and I saw you once—when I got off the train—I saw him—Oh, Joan, I've never told anybody, but we used to go together—and I thought—I was sure if ever he married anybody, he'd marry me!"

Now strength came pouring into her, good scornful prideful strength. Oh, how could she ever be clean of his kisses?

"Did he?" She heard her own voice very cold and clear. "I'm sure he meant it. There's nothing between Martin Bradley and me."

"Oh, Joan!" Out of the darkness she felt Netta's head lean upon her shoulder, and she heard her weep and she felt her hand clutched again. "Oh, Joan, I'm so relieved!"

She shrank away from the leaning head, from the weak hot hand. She did not want to be touched. No one must touch her. "Nothing—nothing at all," she repeated cheerfully. "Good night." She moved away quickly toward the house.

But she never went to her mother with any confession of herself. She was saved it. For she could not speak that same night, not with the dry sterile pain she bore in her defrauded body. It was so dry a pain that she felt fevered with it. Her mouth was dry, her palms were dry, when she thought, I will never see him again—I will not. If he comes back I must remember the moment this afternoon when I hated him. I must hold fast to that hate, because he's never really loved me—never wanted to marry me. While I was loving him terribly, he was only—playing.

She scarcely saw the others in the lamplight. Beside the fire with them she was immensely alone. Far away she saw them, heard them. Her father was saying, "I had a very good meeting at the mission, Mary. I believe the Spirit is working among those people."

Francis sat in the next room at the dining table whistling as he sharpened a pencil for his homework. She knew the tune, she had heard it often during the winter, and she had sung it at a campfire, delighting in knowing that while she sang her voice rose clear as a thrush's note above every other, but she could not have spoken its name tonight. Her mother read aloud a letter from Rose, but she could not understand what it told, though her mother said contentedly as she folded the letter, "I am glad the cashmere fitted. The gold is almost the color of her eyes."

Nothing was near to her. She sat hunched deeply in the old blue chair, staring into the fire, crying to herself, "How shall I ever be clean of his kisses?" And then to her terror she made another cry. "What shall I do if he never kisses me again?" She shivered and stared into the fire, her book open on her knees. Where were they? Why did they not come near, these who were her own? Why was the fire cold? Her mother caught her look and her instinct flew awake, like a bird frightened by the chance touch of a wind, threatening storm.

"Joan, you are ill!"

"No," she answered quickly. "No, not ill. I'm tired. I'm going to bed. I'm all right."

She fled from them. She could not speak tonight, not when there were two voices clamoring in her. How could she silence one—how not speak what she did not want to tell? She must wait until she was clear, until she was sure she was glad that Martin was never to touch her again. She lay in her bed and began to sob suddenly and quietly, her face in her pillow. The door opened and she stopped her sobs instantly. She held her breath. It was her mother, driven by unease.

"Sure you're all right, child?"

She swallowed and turned her face up in the darkness. She made her voice even and careless. "Sure—only sleepy."

Her mother came over to the bed, and went to give her one of her seldom given kisses. But she did not move to meet it, and in the darkness the kiss fell upon her hair. Her mother laughed. "Where are you? There—good night, darling!" She patted the covers, waiting a little. But still Joan made her voice even and careless. "Good night, Mother."

So her mother went away and the door closed. Perhaps tomorrow she could tell. But tonight her breast was hard and cold and shut. She must weep to ease herself, weep as long as she could, so that she might sleep at last.

She was awakened by a soft uncertain knock at the door. It

was not a knock she knew. She heard it through her sleep and she seemed to come up for a long way toward it, through a long silence until she heard her own voice calling drowsily, "Yes—yes? Come in—" But she was not awake. She was not awake until the door opened and she saw her father standing there in the doorway, his gray cotton bathrobe clutched about him. He looked immensely tall and thin and out of the folds of the collar his neck rose bent and thin as a bird's neck, and his head with the high white brow looked much too large for the thin neck.

"You'd better get up, Joan," he said. "Your mother's ill this morning."

Then she was awake indeed. "I'll be there right away," she said. But even though alarm was beating in her breast she waited to leap out of bed until he had shut the door softly and carefully and until she heard his slippers pattering down the hall. He had always been shy of his body before his children. She had scarcely seen him even in his gray bathrobe except as a shadowy figure slipping in and out of the bathroom, a towel over his arm. If he met her at such times he did not speak to her. Because of him she stopped now to tie her own kimono securely about her waist and to find her slippers. But she stayed no longer. She hurried fearfully down the hall. Something was about to happen. In the early morning she felt life impending, large, looming, unknown. At her mother's door she hesitated, dreading not so much to go in as to begin upon something that was about to change. "I've got to go on," she said half-aloud, and opened the door, dreading.

Instantly her dread sharpened and focused upon her mother's face. The room was empty except for her mother's face, lying upon the pillow, turned to the door, waiting for it to open. The blankets were drawn tightly about her shoulders, tightly about her neck. Her body lay small and scarcely mounded under the covers. But the face was vivid. Withered, and strangely yellow in the hard morning light, it was vivid because of the great dark despairing eyes.

"I've got to give up, Joan," she said. "It's my legs. They won't hold me. I got up to take my bath and they gave under me like old rotten sticks."

She stared down at her mother's face, horrified at the change. Surely it had not looked like this yesterday—this was the whiteness of the pillow and the counterpane, this was the bleakness of the gray hair drawn back from the forehead. She was afraid again. "What shall I do?"

"Go downstairs for me when you are dressed." Now it was her mother deciding, and somehow she was immediately comforted. "See that everything is right for the breakfast. Let me see—It's Monday. Tell Hannah not to buy much meat—not a big roast or anything. There's enough left from yesterday—maybe have baked beans for dinner tomorrow and that hash tonight. Frank likes beans. See that your father gets his two cups of coffee—like as not he'll forget to ask. And I'd started to write to Rose. You'll find the letter in my desk. Just put a little note in saying I don't feel so well but I'll be up tomorrow and mail it so she'll get it tomorrow. Now hurry, dear—"

"Yes, Mother," she answered. She felt lighter. Listening to her mother's commands, hearing her mother's voice strong, the room was natural to her again. Her mother turned over and closed her eyes. Now she looked more herself and as she might look sleeping. Closing those great shadowy eyes made her face her own again.

"Don't you want anything to eat?" Joan asked.

"No," her mother answered drowsily. "I want only to rest. I'll be up again tomorrow. I'll just rest a little today. Such a help to have you—"

Her voice dropped off into a whisper and Joan went away. But at the door her mother's voice caught her and held her back. It came strongly and clearly, so clearly that she turned instantly and saw her mother's eyes open again. "If Hannah has boiled eggs for breakfast, and she will if you don't tell her not to, you crack Frank's for him. He minds hot things—his skin's so tender." The eyes stayed open until she answered. "Yes, I will, Mother."

In her mother's place at the table she felt strange to herself. Everything was strange because the mother was not there. It was she who bound them into one and when she was not in her own place they were each separate and desultory and critical of each other. "You have made my coffee too sweet," her father said in mild surprised rebuke.

"Oh, I'm sorry," she said, in equal surprise. He did not then, as he seemed to do, eat whatever was before him. It was that her mother always set before him what he liked. The eggs came in boiled and she cracked two in a cup for Francis, a quick irritation hot in her breast when they burned her fingers. Why should his fingers not be burned? He was late to his breakfast as usual. She should have called him. Now she remembered that each day their mother called him several times and she had forgotten this morning to call him at all. She must go—but before she could rise he was at the door.

"Say, what's the matter?" he demanded indignantly. He halted, his eyes astonished upon Joan. "Say, where's Mom?"

"She's ill," Joan answered coldly. But when she looked into his tempestuous face she felt herself beginning to feel like her mother. His cheeks were ruddy and dark and he had put on his red tie. Her voice grew milder. "I forgot she always called you. Here are your eggs. It's late—you'd better begin."

Now she could remember what her mother did for Francis. Now she knew she had always secretly noted with a small inner jealousy everything her mother had done for Francis. But she did it all too, this morning, half against her will, buttering his toast, stirring the sugar and cream into his coffee, putting the jam in his reach. Even her voice for the moment sounded like her mother's voice. "Hannah, bring in fresh toast for Francis— Frank, pass me Father's cup."

Then perversely she found a pleasure in it, the pleasure of something to do. Last night she had wept herself to sleep— yesterday she had met Martin in the dale where she would never meet him again. But this morning was another life for her. There were things she must do—a house, a family, a sick woman to be tended. When Francis had swallowed his breakfast and dashed up the stairs to see his mother, before school, when her father had wiped his lips and folded his napkin meticulously into the old silver ring that he had had since he was a child and had gone away into his study as usual, it was somehow pleasant to sit there in her mother's place. It was pleasant to answer Hannah.

"Miss Joan, I'd better be getting down to the butcher's."

"I think you needn't go today, Hannah. We'll have baked beans tomorrow—Francis likes them—and today we can have that meat left over made into hash."

"Just as you say," said Hannah, docile as she had never been before, Hannah who had once spanked her for spilling a tin of coffee into the sink. She clattered a heap of dishes together and went back into the kitchen.

Now as she sat in her mother's place the whole room began

to shape about her in a new way. It was almost like a strange room in some other house. All her life she had seen the table, the chairs, the pictures, the old carved buffet, from her own place and in a certain same composition of planes and angles. At this moment these were all changed, just as the garden was changed as she looked out of the window. She could see from the window what she had not seen before when she sat at the table—the north corner of the lawn, the two big maples, and the front of the church and the steeple, but with the top cut off. She felt the whole house gather about her strangely. Today she was something more to it than she had been yesterday. Yesterday it had looked to her mother but today it looked to her. And it was more to her, too, than it had ever been. Yesterday, only yesterday afternoon, it had been no more than a place from which to escape. In the afternoon after the heavy Sunday dinner it had been dull and close and heavy about her, and she had been impatient with its dinginess, and so she had escaped into the sunshine and then against her own will her feet went toward the dale. But this morning she did not want to escape—she must go all over the house, straightening, freshening, putting fresh flowers in the vases. It was almost her own house.

The door opened and Francis thrust his head in the crack. "You still sitting there? Say, Joan, I didn't want to wake her up. She was sound asleep and she looks awfully tired, even when she's asleep. Besides, I didn't want to tell her I'd be home late tonight—we're going down the road—a bunch of us—"

She found herself speaking for her mother anxiously. "But, Frank, your lessons—"

But to him she was nothing but herself. "That's my business," he retorted, and banged the door.

She jumped from her seat. She was furious with him for a second, a sister's fury, but her father came in helplessly, and she paused. "What is it, Father?" she asked.

"On Monday afternoon," he began, "I usually make pastoral visits, and I've mislaid my little black book. I cannot remember where I went last, and I usually mark the name. Your mother wrote down the complete list for me alphabetically in a little black book, and I can't find it."

She was needed again and so assuaged for Francis' independence. "Where did you have it, dear?" she asked. Her voice was rich with kindness, as her mother's was when any of them needed her.

He put his hand to his brow in a gesture of bewilderment. "I can't remember," he said in agitation. "Your mother—"

He was for the moment as different to her as the house. Was this simple creature the priest of God whom she saw coming out of the vestry every Sunday morning to preach to them all, radiant with assurance? She said as she would have said to console a child, "It must be in your study somewhere. I'll come and hunt for it."

She went out and he followed her hopefully. Under a heap of his papers she found it. "This it?" she said, holding it out to him and smiling.

"Yes," he answered, and laughed a small noiseless laugh and sat down at his table, instantly forgetting her. She went back to the dining room and began to clear the table. She hurried happily. There was a great deal to do.

All morning the house grew thus at once more strange and more real. She tiptoed several times to her mother's room, but each time her mother lay motionless in sleep. Heretofore her own room had been the only real part of the house to her. In her own room she had been meticulous, placing the furniture exactly, studying the effect of each picture and small ornament. But the rest of the house had been neutral, a place in which to live and share life. There were certain pictures she did not like and secretly she had wished when she came home from college that her mother would take them down from the walls. She had thought often, If ever I have the chance I'll take them down. Now she looked at them uncertainly—Hope sitting upon the world, Christ entering Jerusalem, Samuel in the temple. But, no—her mother would be up tomorrow. The house was not quite her own.

Tomorrow came and her mother was not up. When Joan entered her room this second morning already it did not seem strange to see her mother lying there. But today there was fear in her mother's dark eyes. "You'd better send for Dr. Crabbe, Joan," she said, and then, "I don't feel able to get up and wash myself. Fetch the basin here, dear."

This was no common weariness. Joan, troubled, watched her mother wash herself slowly, stopping often to rest. The skin on her face and hands shone yellowly. She lay back and closed her eyes and the lids were like shadows upon her face. Joan crept on tiptoe with the basin and towels, and set them down and ran to find her father.

At this hour, at seven o'clock in the morning, he was where he had been for thirty years. She knocked furiously upon the door of the study, for even now she would not have thought of entering otherwise. She had seen her mother there knocking. She knocked impatiently and frightened, and then without waiting she pushed into the room. He was on his knees by the worn old brown leather armchair, his head in his hand. At the sound of her entrance he looked up.

"Father," she cried, "Father, Mother is really ill this morning —you must go for Dr. Crabbe!"

He stared at her bewildered. The change was too swift for him. He had been drenched in the radiance of God, and now he was back in this drab room. "She seemed to sleep quietly all night," he protested mildly. "She scarcely moved, although sometimes I have been disturbed by her tossing. I left her still sleeping quietly this morning." He was so bewildered he forgot to rise from his knees.

Joan's eyes upon him sharply saw him absurd, upon his knees, his pale blue eyes looking up at her childish and absurd. She repeated harshly, "She's very ill now—you or Francis must go for Dr. Crabbe. . . . Francis—I'll send Francis," she went on quickly. Of course Francis would be quicker than this old man. It was the first time she had known he was really old.

"Frank—Frank!" she called, leaping up the stairs. "Frank!" She burst into his room. He was sleeping vigorously. The sun was streaming across his bed and over his face and in his sleep he was scowling a little against the strong light, his black brows drawn and his mouth pouted in determination to sleep. He was beautiful in his sleep, in the sun. Even in her haste she caught the moment of his beauty, full of youth and wildness though in sleep. She shook his shoulder.

"Frank, get up! Get dressed quickly and get Dr. Crabbe. Take the car and bring him back with you."

In the strong sun close to him she saw the faint first stubble upon his lips and his chin. They had been shaved—Francis shaving! He had said nothing. Unknown to them all he had been growing into a man. He had gone and bought a razor and secretly he had shaved. None of them knew, unless perhaps their mother.

"What?" he cried. His eyes flew open and he looked up at her, instantly clear and comprehending.

"It's Mother," she said.

"Get out of here!" he roared at her, leaping out of bed. "How can I put on my clothes unless you get out?"

She went away comforted. It was strength to feel his impatience and his haste. She had always thought of him as a boy, a child, a younger child. She remembered him as a strong impetuous baby, a frowning red-cheeked little boy. For years he had been this hobbledehoy, tumbling down the stairs, eating voraciously, demanding loudly his freedoms, absorbed in his next good time. Now he was none of these. He was the one person to whom she could turn. He had leaped from his bed, tall and a man. He was strong. Their blood was the same. . . .

Upstairs at her mother's door she listened. She heard his clattering footsteps and a moment later she heard the roar of the engine. She looked out of the end window of the hall. He was gone in a whirl of smoke and scattered gravel.

Downstairs in the sitting room Dr. Crabbe laid upon her shoulders the burden of her mother's life. The uneaten breakfast was cold in the dining room and Hannah stood sniffling and listening at the door. Her father was there, his face solemn, the eyes grave and pure and exalted. Upon his lips was the stern peace of his continuous prayer, "Is this Thy will, O God? Thy will be done." Francis stood by the window, staring out into the winter sunshine, his face turned away from them all. His hands were thrust furiously deep into his pockets. But it was to Joan Dr. Crabbe spoke, his loud voice sharp and each word a thrust of emphasis. "She should have told me long ago, Joan. I can't take the responsibility now—you'll have to get somebody in on consultation. The idea of her dragging on and on in mortal pain!"

In mortal pain! The words were an accusing sword to cut her heart in two. While she had been absorbed in her foolish love, while she had heard no voice but Martin's, seen no face but Martin's, dreamed of nothing else, and lived for nothing else, her mother had gone in mortal pain. She pushed Martin away and turned passionately to cry out, her heart strangling in her throat, "How long do you think she's been suffering?"

"Months—maybe even a year—" he answered shortly. "I can't get the truth out of her—her damned cheerfulness. She always was that way. You hadn't been born an hour until she was chirruping, 'I must get up soon, Doctor, as soon as I can. Paul's got to go to the presbytery.' And though she nearly died the last time with that great feller there by the window, it was the same thing. 'I've got to get up as soon as I can'—for something or other. Well, Joan, it'll be a long day now before she gets up, in my opinion. The thing we have to find out is whether or not she can stand the operation or whether it's too late whatever we do."

Out of the silence of doom Francis' voice came shrill and breaking. "Get the other doctor here, can't you? What are you all sitting here like this for? Just sitting and sitting—" He turned his face toward them, his face a grimace against weeping. He looked away again quickly.

Dr. Crabbe went on as though he had not heard or seen and Joan received steadily his commands upon her life. "I'll get the specialist up from the city right away—this afternoon or tomorrow. But it means days and days—maybe even years of nursing. This kind of thing goes on and on even if it's hopeless —she has a strong constitution—a lot of life—unless they decide to operate and something goes wrong."

Days and years, days and years— She gazed at Dr. Crabbe's hairy old face and did not see him. She saw her life passing steadily by—days and years—years and years made of day after day after day. She gave them up in an instant's foresight. "I will take care of her myself," she said.

Dr. Crabbe rose. "Good thing you're home, my girl—good thing you're big and strong!" he said, brusquely cheerful. "I'll be getting on after that other chap. Now brace up, the three of you. We're going to do all we can."

He was gone in a gust, slapping his thick knee, touching Joan's cheek delicately with his stubby forefinger, clapping Francis' hunched shoulders and throwing a short nod at the man.

Then they were alone, the three of them. They were alone and separate because the mother who had bound them together was not there. The mother had bound them together, pouring into each of them a part of herself and gathering them into one whole by the parts of herself. Now she had left them. She was fighting for herself alone, and only as they poured themselves into her could they be united. Each must think of something to do for her. Joan saw her father put his hand to his head in his gesture of bewilderment. His eyes were vague and fixed upon the ground. "Yes . . . yes . . . " he whispered, forgetting them. "Yes, O God!" He rose abruptly, and left the room. They heard the door of his study shut. He was in his refuge.

Francis said, "I can't go to school—I can't sit there—like any other day—" He stood as he had stood, his back to her, his sharp young shoulder blades drooping through his old coat, his hands jammed in his pockets above the wrists.

But in Joan there was a large sorrowful tranquillity. She looked at Francis' discontented face and her mother in her spoke to comfort him.

"There will be so many times I'll need you, just as I needed you to fetch Dr. Crabbe. But just now I have things to do for her that you can't do. We each have a special thing to do for her. She will want everything to go on in the house as it always has."

She looked about the room. On the wall opposite hung the Hope drooping over a gray and barren world. She had so hated it. Only yesterday she had planned secretly to take it down to make the house hers. Now she knew she would never take it down. For this house would never be hers. It was her mother's house and it would always be so. She could live in it only insofar as she took upon herself her mother's function, her mother's being.

"Guess you're right," said Francis. He turned. "Well—" he said, and sighed gustily and marched from the room. It was the first time she had ever heard him sigh. She smiled with a sad mature tenderness for him and went slowly upstairs. She climbed, gathering herself together for what was ahead of her, for all that she had never planned.

Now the mother drew her children's lives into her. She drew them by her willful dominations and by her catastrophes of weakness and by her little cheerfulnesses. Joan never could know, though she opened the door a score of times a day, what woman she would find there in the bed. She came in when Francis was gone to find her mother washed and fresh and sitting in her bed, cleaned and freshened. While they were downstairs, while Dr. Crabbe was dooming her, she had risen in sudden willful strength and put the best linen on the bed and upon herself she put an orchid-colored bed-jacket which Joan had once given her at Christmas, which she had never worn because of its delicacy of silk and cream lace, but which she had cherished. For two years it had lain in her drawer, on top, hiding by its beauty the old and mended garments beneath. She kept it there for the pleasure of seeing it whenever she opened the drawer.

Today when Joan came in she lay propped up in her bed, faint but triumphant. She was panting a little. "I'll be up tomorrow," she said. "I'll just take today to rest. Tell Dr. Crabbe. And Francis is to go to school. And you mustn't write a word to Rose, because before the letter gets to her I'll be up and around. Tell Hannah I'll have my breakfast. Don't I look lovely? It's the first chance I've had to wear this."

And Joan was gladly deceived. The orchid jacket, the bright dark smiling eyes, the neatly piled white hair, the brown strong hands upon the counterpane, nearly deceived her. She ran down and called to Hannah and then she went out into the garden to gather a handful of short-stemmed violets to put upon the tray. She bore the tray herself, entering the room with a quick gaiety. After all, they might be wrong, all of them. She would not tell Rose yet.

Her mother's eyes warmed at the violets. "You're the only one who would think to do that," she said. "Not many people know a flower on a tray seasons all the food. I never taught you, Joan. You've always known. Rose now, would be careful, but she'd forget the flowers—and of course men don't think."

She began to eat happily. "What did Dr. Crabbe say?" she asked. "Did he say I just needed a little rest? Sit down a minute, child. It's so pleasant to talk." The whole room was pleasant in the morning light, in the vigor of her mother's voice.

But on the bed, very near her mother's face, Joan was undeceived. The eyes, if they stopped their sparkle even for an instant, were sick and dulled. Her mother could make her eyes sparkle, but the impulse failed quickly and the eyes were veiled as a sick bird's eyes are veiled. She cried out suddenly, "Why didn't you tell us you were in pain? Why did you let us go on leaning on you?"

Her mother put down the bit of toast she held. "Did he say I had such pain?" she asked.

"Yes."

"It is true," her mother said slowly. "I have often such pain. I shall never be healed of it, and so I have learned to bear it."

"But you may be healed of it," Joan cried passionately,

yearning over this woman, her mother. "He is going to bring a city doctor to see you this afternoon."

Her mother stared at her, startled. She pushed the tray away. "I won't see him," she said suddenly and loudly. "Do you hear, Joan? I won't have a stranger peering into me. Dr. Crabbe was with me when all the babies came. He's different. Besides, I know myself. I know—" Her lower lip began to tremble and she looked piteously at Joan. Above the gay bed-jacket her face shrank into grayness. "Don't let me die!" she begged, in a whisper.

"No—no—no" said Joan passionately behind her clenched teeth, tears hot under her eyelids.

But in the late afternoon her mother was willful again and stubborn against the new doctor. Joan, waiting beside her, saw her grow momentarily strong with her stubbornness. She sat braced by her pillows, her hair smoothed, her gaze upon the door. Her eyes met the doctor's eyes, freshly and strongly with a shock of life.

"Mary, this is Dr. Beam—Mrs. Richards," said Dr. Crabbe.

"How do you do?" said Dr. Beam languidly. He stared perseveringly at her face and hands.

"Patient has vitality," the doctor murmured to Dr. Crabbe wearily. He was a tall drooping gentle figure, his hat and gloves still in his hand because no one had come forward to take them from him and put them down for him.

"Not physical vitality, though," grunted Dr. Crabbe. "Sit down."

"Will to live, perhaps," hinted the doctor. He held his hat on his knee, dropped it, and set it at last upon the floor beside his chair. He fixed his large vacant eyes again upon her, without noticing Joan.

"There is nothing really wrong," Joan heard her mother say, brightly. "I don't know why they got you here." She arranged the covers briskly. She looked suddenly well, her hands normal with vigor.

"Yes," murmured Dr. Beam. He rose, unexpectedly alert. "Let me see your abdomen," he demanded. His languor was gone. He was avid, keen for knowledge of her. No, not knowledge of her, for what was she to him? She was nothing. It was the thing in her body which interested him. Without it, with nothing but health, she would not have existed for him. She did not exist for him now, except as the possessor of this malignant life in her, this monster feeding upon her. He felt her abdomen with his long thin delicately probing fingers. His face grew sharper. His eyes were black and narrow and inquisitive and about his lips the skin was hard and white. He was excited by what he felt.

"Hm—hm—" he kept murmuring to himself. "Hm—hm—"

At last he knew everything. He covered her exhausted body quickly, and turned to Joan. "Where can I wash my hands?" At the door he commanded, "Fetch my hat and gloves along. I shan't need to come back. Crabbe, I'll meet you downstairs."

Downstairs with Dr. Crabbe she waited. He rumbled along of other things. "Miss Kinney's down with that queer fever she brought back with her from Africa—don't believe she'll ever get over it—old girl, her mother, sound as a dried hickory nut —never saw the beat of it—she'll outlast us all—I don't dare hope to be at her funeral myself. Mr. Parson's got bronchitis— needs outdoor life instead of clerking in an office the way he does. Where's your pa?" he asked abruptly.

"It's his afternoon for the mission."

Dr. Crabbe coughed suddenly and went out to the porch and spat in the yellow rosebush under the window.

"Well . . . yes," he said, coming back and sitting down. "Well, you can tell him when he gets in. Here's Dr. Beam."

Upon the threshold Dr. Beam stood in cultivated haste. "I need not stop, I think, Crabbe," he said. "My car's waiting. You're quite right—no use—the whole organ's hardened and everything is hopelessly involved—if you'll come along I'll talk as we go—"

"Back later, my dear," said Dr. Crabbe.

Joan at the window watched them move down the walk to the street, the tall slender stooping figure and Dr. Crabbe, short and burly and rolling along like a sailor. They were talking excitedly. She could see Dr. Beam's face now as he climbed into the motor. It was eager and animated. One long probing forefinger stabbed the air as he talked. Dr. Crabbe thrust out his square short hands. They were tossing her mother's life back and forth between them. She sank suddenly into a chair and wept bitterly.

But weeping could not endure for long. The house clamored at her now as it had clamored at her mother. Hannah, thumping in from the kitchen, dried her tears at their source. "What'll your pa relish for his supper, Miss Joan?" she asked mournfully.

Joan wrenched her mind from its torture to think of her father's appetite. She must remember there was also her father.

"He'll be tired coming in—a milk soup, and corn muffins—he likes them—"

"I have a little chicken left over—Frank likes chicken," Hannah suggested.

There was Francis, too.

"Your ma—" Hannah began.

"I'll go and ask her," Joan replied. Upon the stairs she hesitated. She was dragging her steps slowly, hating to go in. Her mother's vivid eyes would be turned on that door waiting, searching No use lying to her, no use pretending she had not heard those two words, "hopelessly involved."

She put her hand upon the knob and swallowed. Her mouth was dry. She was afraid to see her mother's eyes.

But when she went in the room was in shadow. She had not known that the sun had set in the little while she was away. Her mother's form was shrunken, a little heap. She could not discern her face.

"Mother!" she cried, moving to the bed.

"Yes," her mother said. Her voice came up small and tired.

"You frightened me," she cried in relief. "I couldn't see you. What do you want for supper, darling Mother?"

"Joan," her mother said in that small voice. "Joan, do you suppose you could do one thing for me—just one thing?"

"Why, yes—anything," she answered, surprised tender. She felt for her mother's hand and found it. It was not a small hand Awake it was shapely, beautiful and strong. Now it was asleep Without life it seemed larger than it was, inert stiff difficult to hold the fingers limp and sprawling. Out of the shadows her mother lifted her head from the pillow, suddenly intense. Her eyes came out to beseech Joan. "Don't let him come in here by me—make up the bed in the guest room. I'm too . . . tired . . ."

She dropped the stiff hand. "You mean—*Father?*"

"Yes." Her mother sank back again and Joan could not see her eyes. They were closed in the even pallor of the face vaguely outlined.

"Tell him—I'm—tired," her mother said with weak urgency.

She had sat down on the bed. Now she rose, aware again of

repulsion—that subdued quarreling in the night—was it this?
She would not think of it.

"Of course," she said resolutely, turning to the door. But her
mother was not eased yet.

"Don't let him even come in—not tonight," she said. "Tell
him I'm sleeping—tell him—"

"I'll tell him," said Joan, and shut the door behind her. She
wanted to hear no more. This was not for her to hear.

But still he must be told. How could she tell him? She
wondered, her hands busy about his solitary bed. How tell a
man who had slept with his wife for thirty years that he could
sleep beside her no more? Before she could plan she heard his
steps upon the stair, soft footfalls, the left foot dragging a little.
She ran out to meet him at the head of the stairs.

"What did the doctors say?" he asked.

"Dr. Crabbe said he was coming back, but he hasn't," she
answered, putting him off.

He hesitated, and then moved to go in. Now she must speak,
now before he went on. She stood before him, stopping him,
her blood beating in her ears. "Father," she cried above its
beating, "Don't—you mustn't go in!"

"I mustn't go in—to my own room?" he said, astonished.

"No—Father—I'll explain—"

"Did the doctors—"

"No—she did—she—she'd rather you didn't come in—she
wants to sleep—to be alone. I've made the other bed for you.
She's very, very tired."

They looked at each other, father, daughter. The daughter
cried at him in her heart, "What have you done to make her so
tired?" The father answered with his calm righteous look. His
look said, "I have done nothing that is not my right to do."

But she was stronger than he. Without a word he turned and
went downstairs.

She was not herself anymore, not Joan, not a young woman
home from college who had been waiting. She was some
strange composite creature, more than a sister to Francis, more
than a daughter to her father, less than herself. Her mother,
lying in her bed, shut into her room, was a secret life to her.
She was living secretly there. Though outwardly they called
her Joan, though outwardly she was doing the things her
mother had always done in the house, her secret, intense life

was in the room upstairs. It set a wall about her, it made all else unreal. Now the only reality was this woman, whose body was dying while her mind was full of ferocious life. There was the reality, and it removed her from everything.

It removed her even from the memory of Martin. Sometimes like an echo, far away, she heard music coming from the church, but when she heard it she went steadily on about her moment's business. She threw open no window to catch a chord or to hear the fragment of a melody. Music—even her own music—she had put aside and why should she stay her feet to listen to the echoes of his music? Nor did she ever hear his name anymore. Her mother had forgotten that the name was once a quarrel between them, and she could forget, for now she had her child back home again, completely returned. And in Joan's heart there was no name either, and if there was the faintly echoing music she passed without listening to it and went on to what was now her work.

One morning the doorbell rang and passing by on her way upstairs, she opened the door and there he stood, smiling his faint melancholy smile. For a second it was familiar as seeing her own face unexpectedly in a mirror might be familiar. He said, "I've waited—I thought surely you would give me a sign —I thought you would come back—"

His voice was known to her. Once she had heard it with ecstasy and painful desire. Now she heard it only as something once known, a voice to which she had once listened but wanted no more to hear. He leaned with both hands on his stick, his hat in his hands, his music rolled under his arm. She stared at his narrow dark aging face, the white sides of his smooth dark hair, his sad hazel eyes, his thin beautiful mouth.

"Come back to me, Joan? I am not changed—I shall never change."

Strange that his eyes, fixed deeply upon her, were no more than the eyes of a photograph, now put aside! Yes, he was not changed. He would never change. So he was not enough.

"I am busy with my mother now. She's very ill." She waited a moment. It was said rudely, like a child, and she thought an instant for something to add to it, to soften it. But when she tried to think of more, there was no more. She stared beyond him into the garden, and saw what she had not seen, that it was a sunny morning, gentle with spring. So after the moment's waiting she shut the door on him quietly and without anger, and even with a little remorse lest it be too rude. She did not even care enough now to be rude to him or to hurt him.

Then she went upstairs.

At first the village came clustering about her mother. Miss Kinney was often at the door with flowers. "A few flowers, dear Joan—and if there is anything I can do—sit with her a little if you want to go out."

"Thank you, Miss Kinney," Joan said.

Mrs. Bradley brought calf's-foot jelly. "It's toothsome," she explained. "Martin's fond of it. How is she, Joan?"

She looked into Mrs. Bradley's small stubborn gray eyes. "Thank you, Mrs. Bradley." But the jelly she would not give her mother. She threw it into the garbage when Hannah was busy in some other room.

They all came to the door, all the old people—asking for her mother, missing her. At first they came often. They came expecting to sit by her mother's bedside, and at first, because they had been middle-aged when she was a child, she thought she must let them have their way. It seemed impossible to say to Mrs. Winters, who had taken over the missionary society and the Ladies' Aid work, that she could not come in to see her mother.

"I'm sure your mother would want to know about the meeting—if she'd listen to me a minute. I won't stay but a minute."

But Joan saw her mother did not care about the missionary meeting any more or want to listen to Mrs. Winters. Her mind was turned now upon her own life. For the first time she was absorbed in what was to happen to herself. Her eyes were dull and empty, staring at Mrs. Winters. "It's very nice, I am sure," she said faintly. "I'm very pleased—so pleased—Joan, my feet are cold."

"You must get well, dear Mrs. Richards," said Mrs. Winters warmly. "We miss you very much. I can never take your place with the ladies. You have such a way with you—you keep us all laughing so nicely that it isn't so hard when the collection comes round—there, you dear soul!" She bent and kissed the sick woman, her corsets creaking over her large bosom. "Now you just listen to me!"

But after she was gone Joan saw her mother's eyes full of wonder, staring at the wall opposite her. "I'm finished with it all," she said in a half-whisper. "It's all gone far from me, all I ever used to do. I'm only in this body lying here."

So after a while Joan kept them all away and soon they forgot and went about their days only remembering sometimes to ask how she did and to murmur or cry heartily, "Oh, I'm sorry to hear that," or sometimes, on Sunday, when good deeds were natural to think of, they wrote little notes: "We remember you in our prayers, dear friend."

Prayers! Joan smiled bitterly. At first prayers had gone up from the village like smoke to heaven. Everywhere people were praying for her mother. Her father came home from Wednesday night meetings comforted by the prayers of his people. He went straight to the sick room. "Mary, I wish you could have heard Mr. Parsons' prayer for you tonight and the 'Amen' that went up from the people. It may be the Lord is going to use your illness to stir the people's souls into life again." He spoke happily and unusually quickly, his pale guileless eyes beaming. He could bear even his dear wife's illness if he saw God's will in it. He hurried downstairs to pour himself out to God gratefully. Joan, listening to his footsteps, thought to herself that one could not be sure about praying. "Do you pray, Mother?" she asked timidly. There was no physical shyness left now between them. She tended her mother's body as she did her own. But her mother's soul she had not penetrated. She dared not think of it. Did her mother know she must die?

"No, I don't pray," her mother said simply, "I don't pray anymore. I guess I began to get out of the habit when you children were little. You woke me so early in the morning and at night I was too tired. And it never seemed worth while to pray for myself."

And so it was after a while with all praying. It became tedious to pray for a woman who steadily grew weaker. It became rebellion against God finally to keep on praying when obviously she would not get well. Even the father at last prayed only thus, "Thy will be done, O God." Or he prayed, "Help us to be ready for sorrow," So the mother slipped gradually out of life and out of the minds of the people. She was not yet dead but since she was not seen or heard and since her struggle was solitary, she had no more to do with them. Only Miss Kinney still brought flowers faithfully to her door.

"I won't come in," she said, standing drooping upon the threshold, her narrow length topped by her flopping leghorn hat. "Just a nosegay for your dear mother! I love her, you know. She always understood so well about Africa. No one else will ever understand so well as she did—just as though she had been there. She used to see it all, just as it was!"

And so the spring passed, and summer came and it was the grave autumn once more, and it seemed as if her mother had always lain like this, helpless and to be cared for, as if for years she had been in her mother's place. Rose came home and the summer passed and it was autumn and Rose was gone again.

Now Joan and her mother lived quite alone together. If her father or Francis or even Dr. Crabbe came to see her mother, Joan was the gate through which they must pass. Her father was no more her mother's husband. She stood between these two, her father and her mother, at first shyly, feeling herself between them, knowing there must be some secret life she interrupted. Then she came to see there was no such secret life. She intercepted nothing, no warmth, no hidden tenderness. Twice each day her father said to her, "Would your mother like to see me?" She went in and asked her mother, "Do you want to see Father?"

Her mother always paused to consider it, bringing her mind back from afar to consider, and her mood changed. Though she had been cheerful now she would say fretfully, "I want to sleep," or she would say with suspicion, "What does he want?" or sometimes, and usually, she would say, "A little while, perhaps," and unknowingly she sighed. Then her father went in and they talked. "Well, Mary, how are you today?" "Thank you, Paul, I am about as usual." "Would you like me to read to you?" "No, thank you, Paul. Joan reads to me a good deal." He paused, searching his mind for something to tell her, and then he began again carefully, "You will be glad to hear, my dear, that at the mission at South End I have baptized—"

"Yes, dear Paul," Her eyes closed. Soon he would leave the room on tiptoe to find Joan and say, "She is asleep. She seems to sleep a great deal. It is best, perhaps."

"It's best," she answered, with pity for this unearthly man. In some sort of momentary human warmth she must have been conceived, but there was no human warmth in him now. All significance of him had passed from that room upstairs. It was as though he had never been there at all. The room was given over to her mother, now.

In the evening after supper Francis rose from the table quickly. "Mom ready for me?" She nodded, for she did not come down to supper until her mother was ready for Francis. She had brushed her mother's hair and put on her fresh bed-jacket and touched her face with rouge. For one evening her mother had asked for the mirror from the bureau. "I want to see how I look," she said. "I don't want my son to remember me ugly. I look ghastly—" She stared at herself mournfully.

Joan said playfully. "I could dress you up with a little rouge." Her mother had never worn rouge. She would have felt ashamed, as though she were aping a worldly woman. But now she looked at Joan with a gleam of the old mischief suddenly shining out of her eyes. "Why not?" she said. "It can't matter much what I do now. I have to stand or fall by what's done. A little rouge here and there won't weight the scales much."

So laughing together a little sadly, they did it. Joan fetched her rouge pot and touched with delicate faint rose her mother's wan cheeks, while her mother held the mirror. "It does look nice," her mother said with great interest. "I do believe I'm a little pretty even yet." She looked up at Joan shyly and the tears rushed into the girl's eyes. She bent to kiss her mother quickly and as she bent she caught from her mother's body that smell of death. No washing with perfumed soaps, no sprinkled scent could hide it. But her mother did not know it was there, since it was the atmosphere in which she must now live. She was sprightly for the moment.

"Don't you tell on me," she cried gaily.

So every morning the rouge was put on and every night she would have it there, peach bloom upon her deathly pallor.

But Joan did betray her a little. She coaxed Francis, "Tell Mother how pretty she looks, Frank—tell her over and over."

"Gee," he muttered, and the father looked up astonished to say in mild rebuke, "Your mother hates flattery, Joan."

"You tell her, Frank," she insisted. "Tell her and see what she says."

"Oh, sure, if it'll do her any good," he shouted back, leaping up the stairs. Ten minutes later he thrust his head into the kitchen, where she was cutting raw beef into cubes for beef tea. "Gosh, she did like it," he said. "Looked like a kid when I told her—cheeks all pinked up." He hesitated and she saw sudden tears in his eyes. He swallowed and snorted, "Wasn't any lie I told, either," and slammed the door.

And Dr. Crabbe, bursting open the front door in the mornings, shouted to her, "Joan, you got her ready for me?" Afterwards, to Joan alone, waiting in the hall, forcing his voice to low hoarseness he said, "Can't be long now—just give her whatever she wants—don't matter now except to keep her happy."

"How long, Dr. Crabbe?"

"A month—two—maybe six—she's got such a vitality—don't tell her—" He was gone in a small cyclone of speed.

Joan, running upstairs with wine, with broth, with delicately seasoned milk soups, cried to herself fiercely. "She shall have all my strength. I'm strong! I'll pour myself into her. I'll make her live months, a year, maybe two years—"

She poured her huge vitality into her mother's body. Tirelessly she washed her mother's flesh and rubbed olive oil into the wasting muscles to nourish her. She centered her heart into her hands, willing her own strength into her strong hands, into her strong palms, pressing upon her mother's flesh until she could almost believe a current passed, taking virtue out of her. She wheeled the bed to the window and uncovered her mother's body to the sunlight and to the warmth of the noonday, standing watch in hand to force the last moment she dared of sun and wind. She wanted all the power from the sun and the warm wind to pour into her mother's body. Food and sun and sweet air and her own steadily cheerful young strength she poured into her mother's body, fighting that death in her. But that living death grew, too, upon all she did.

In the night there was no sun and it was hard to laugh in the night. Then everyone lay asleep and apart and the house was silent and she was alone with her mother in the darkness. Beyond the shadowy walls of the room was the universe, waiting in endless empty space. Soon, soon her mother would escape her and be lost in those empty spaces. She lay on her little cot by her mother's bed, listening and watching for that escape. Out of the moment of her young exhausted sleep she rose instantly if her mother moved. She heard her mother whisper, "Joan, am I to die?"

Passionately she cried in a loud strong voice, "I will not let you die!"

"Touch me—let me feel you—"

She seized her mother's hand and held it, rubbing it, fondling it fiercely. From it, too, rose that faint stench. Her mother's voice came small and far away out of the darkness. "I am always half asleep—Don't let me slip away while I sleep—"

"No—no—" she said. "I have you hard—"

In the stillness she listened to her mother's breathing. If it grew too faltering she must give a stimulant, but not unless she must, because there would be greater need at the end when the pain would be so great they must give it constantly. She had asked steady questions of Dr. Crabbe. She knew how each day must go. Curled against the bed in the darkness, kneeling upon the floor, holding her mother's hand, her body strong and tense, she fought the universe.

Out of her sleep her mother woke again and again to clutch at life. She struggled against this insidious constant deathly sleeping. She forced her eyes open, frowning, thinking of something she wanted to do. "Tell Paul to come here," she commanded in a strange loud voice. Her ears were dulled so that now she spoke loudly, to hear herself. "I have something on my mind to tell Paul."

So Joan called her father and he came in timidly. He was very timid these days in the presence of this near-death. At many bedsides he had stood in triumph to speed a soul to God. But he could do nothing for this soul. This soul who knew him allowed him no special power, and without belief he had no power. He was troubled by this. Sometimes he said, "Mary, should we not speak of spiritual things? I am your pastor as well as your husband. I am responsible for you before God." But now that she had separated herself from them all she had no respect for him. She did not even remember he was father to her children. She remembered him only as a man against whom she had a grievance deeper than her soul. She was fighting off the poisonous sleep to tell him what she had to say. "Be quiet!" she said in that strange harsh voice. "There is something—a hundred dollars—"

He stared at her, astonished. A hundred dollars! She was dreaming. "What hundred dollars?" he asked.

But sleep had come down on her. She struggled against it, moving her lips, forcing her heavy eyelids, but sleep came down upon her and her face settled into empty gravity.

Again and again it was so until Joan was broken by the struggle. "Let it be, Mother," she begged. "Never mind—never mind—"

But her mother would not give up. "Tell Paul," she said, and at last one day it was told. "A hundred dollars—in the attic—in the old trunk—Joan and Rose—"

"A hundred dollars—in the attic!" he echoed. "Where did you get it?" He forgot that she was ill. A hundred dollars! When he had needed money so sorely for his mission.

"I saved housekeeping money—dollar by dollar—Joan and Rose—" She was fighting the sleep. It was almost upon her again, stiffening her lips, pressing her eyelids down. Then he helped her. Then he woke her. He woke her with a lash, with a whip. He rose and shouted at her, "You stole it!"

Her eyes flew open. Her dimmed ears caught the shout and held it. She was awake because once more she was angry. He could still make her angry. "I stole it? Slaving for you and your church all these years? Never having anything for my own— never anything—anything—anything—?" She turned to Joan piteously, her face a child's face, working with weeping. "Joan, he says—he says—"

Joan ran to her and gathered her up into her arms and soothed her. "Oh, darling, don't mind, don't mind, my darling—" She pressed her mother's head to her shoulders, murmuring to her, soothing her. But the relentless sleep was there again, now mercifully there again, silencing everything. The tears were still wet upon the sleeping face. Above it Joan flashed upon her father a look. She hated him. But he did not catch the look. He was hastening away. She heard his footsteps hastening up the attic stairs.

... In the morning, unless it was Sunday, he was a little hungry after his hour in the study. When his soul was refreshed all his bodily impulses quickened and he felt light and at ease and he knew it was because he was right with God, and he was hungry. It was pleasant to come out into the cheerful dining room and begin a hot breakfast. Coffee on a chill morning was very nice. It was nice to come into the companionship of the others. Across this comfort, across the pleasure of the sweet creamy coffee he was stirring slowly and about to drink, Joan's voice broke cruelly. He looked up, shocked at her hard voice. He was not accustomed to hardness from her. To Mary's strange unreasoning angers, yes—he had taken her unevenness to God and God had said, "Bear thy cross." So he had borne his cross, and he was rewarded, because as she grew older she had grown less stormy, less often angry with him, less demanding.

For when she was young Mary was always wanting something from him, something more. In the night he would hear her weeping because she had not something more. "What is it, Mary?" he had asked again and again patiently. At least now that she was dying he had nothing wherewith to reproach himself; he had always been patient with her. And always she had answered, "I thought there would be something more." "I do not understand," he replied, patient still. Indeed there was no understanding her, who was in so many ways a very good wife for him a minister, for the people loved her. With the people she was always pleasant and cheerful. But when he was a man with her alone, how changed and difficult a woman!

Now he said to Joan carefully, "You do not understand the circumstances. Your mother knew that for nearly a year I have been niggardly and thought that I must be robbing them of something of my services to them. And all the time your mother knew she did not need all I gave her—all the time your mother—"

"But she saved it bit by bit, out of what you gave her!" she cried at him. Her voice was like Mary's voice, crying in the night.

She heard her own voice sound suddenly like the voice she heard crying behind the closed door. What made her think of night when it was broad day and the sun was across the table, shining on the silver molasses jug, shining on the white cloth and the blue plates? Hannah came in with a plate of toast and they waited until she was gone. Then her father began to speak patiently to her, his voice tranquil, reasoning, his voice that was always quiet in the night.

"I have always put first, above all, the Lord's work. Let God's work be done and He will see that I and mine are fed. To save for ourselves is to distrust Him, the giver of every good gift. And shall we save when others have nothing, not even a house where they may go to have their souls fed?" But suddenly while she stared at him she heard his voice take on a human angry passion. His priesthood dropped from him. "Besides, Joan, it was hard of her. All this time—she knows I have not had where to turn for a little money and the work is just beginning to prosper and to let it go now would be to waste it all. She knew it—she heard me pray. At night when we prayed together she heard me ask God for money and she had all that money and she kept silence—there on her knees before God, beside me, she kept silence, knowing there was all that money in my own house—money that was really mine!"

Here was his hurt, too. She wavered, her eyes fell, and she sighed. He went on eagerly, his blue eyes pleading. "And now, what will she do with it? She has all she needs—" He had quite forgotten her mother's voice, struggling against the deathly sleep.

"Joan and Rose—Joan and Rose—" her mother had said. She could not remind him. She poured his coffee in silence and let him have his way. After all, it was not for himself—it was for God. But now it seemed somehow the same thing.

Almost every day her mother had said, "Don't tell Rose—don't spoil anything because of me—" But now they could not listen to her, although Christmas was less than a month away. Dr. Crabbe hooked his thumb at Joan as he left the bedroom and when she followed him downstairs he whispered to her hoarsely, "Better have Rose come home. I can't answer for these days. Like as not she'll slip off in this sleep. It might be a month—it might be any day. Her whole body's full of poison—everthing's giving way at once. Get Rose home—needn't tell your mother—she don't know one day from another now—let her think vacation's begun."

She nodded miserably and plodded upstairs in great weariness. It would be good to have Rose home. Maybe Rose could take a turn at night now. Dr. Crabbe had spoken of a trained nurse, but trained nurses cost a great deal and besides, the village would never understand the preacher's having a trained nurse when there were two grown girls in the family. She went into her own room and sat down at the small desk and wrote to Rose, chewing the end of her pen, thinking how to spare Rose —Rose who had not seen the change, the nearing inexorable death which no vitality could push away more than a little while. She wrote carefully.

In the evening when the letter was mailed she told them. She told her father and he looked up from his book and the gravity upon his face settled into a somber depth. "I feared she was worse," he said, and went back to his book. But he sighed again and again and soon he closed the book, putting the marker carefully in its place, and he went away.

"Does Dr. Crabbe—do they think she is going to die soon?" asked Francis as soon as his father was gone. He had said nothing at all. He had idled about the room, restless until now. But before she could speak he rushed on, "Don't tell me—I won't hear it—" and he burst into a loud sob that was like a hiccough. He coughed quickly and turned to a bookshelf and after a moment's fumbling drew out a book and opened it and stared into it. "Rose ought to get here by Thursday night," he said. "I'll go and meet her—you needn't bother."

"Thank you, Francis," Joan answered gratefully. She longed to touch him, to seize his hand, to lean on him a little, but she could feel him resisting her touch, fiercely demanding that he not be touched. He was so strange these days. But she had not time for him now, not time to think about him or even to ask him what was the matter and why he was so fierce and moody and easily angry with her and with them all. So she passed him quietly and went back to her mother.

Rose came and it was good to have her. Joan had not realized how good it would be until she came downstairs and saw her standing neat and compact in the hall, her gloves still on and her brown coat still buttoned about her. She ran down and threw her arm about her sister and put her face down into the furred collar and felt Rose's smooth cold cheek against her own hot flesh. Rose stood sturdy and still under the embrace. It was good, it was good to have the family whole again.

"Here's your bag, kid," said Francis, coming in and throwing it down. They stood there an instant, the three of them, and looked at each other in a second's silence, feeling themselves together. But it was a new sort of communion. It was without their parents, without the older ones. They were the strong ones, the able ones. The other two were old and ill. The other two were the ones to be cared for and protected. The study door opened and the father came out. He had been sleeping on the couch in his study and his thin white hair was pushed in spikes above his high brow.

"Well, Father," said Rose quietly, "how are you?" She went forward and stood on tiptoe and met his pursed lips with her own soft red mouth. He always stood stiffly and pursed his lips and kissed as though it were a thing he had newly learned to do and so it was hard for him.

"Your mother is very badly," he said directly.

"Yes, I know," she said, unbuttoning her coat. With the father's coming the moment between the children was not broken. They were tender to him secretly and embarrassed at their tenderness and a little impatient with him.

"I'll take up the bag," Francis said abruptly.

"Thank you, Frank," said Joan, and she waited a moment for him to turn the landing and said to Rose, "You wouldn't have believed how he has changed and grown up—"

"He certainly wouldn't have offered to take a bag upstairs for one of us before," Rose agreed, picking up her gloves and hat and pocketbook, and they started slowly upstairs.

Now Joan must tell Rose. Before they went into that room she must prepare Rose for the way death could look in a still living human face, and for the way death could look out of dark human eyes. In their mother's body death sat, looking out of her eyes, breathing its stenchy breath out of her nostrils. She pushed the moment off frantically. She said lightly, "No, you wouldn't know Frank at all. Why, he even cracks his own eggs at breakfast now!" She tried to laugh.

Rose was standing at the head of the stairs, her hands full of her things, looking at Joan two steps behind. She smiled a little at the idea of Frank, her small cool smile. Then she pulled the moment before them.

"Now tell me," she said.

"Come into my room first," said Joan.

Rose was strange. Rose was different from what Joan had thought. Rose did not need to be shielded, for all her soft looks and small gentle voice and mild slow ways. She looked steadily at Joan, listening. It was Joan who broke, not Rose. Joan flung her head into the pillows of her bed where they sat and Joan cried as she had not yet cried, even to herself. "She's going to die—she has to die—I've told her again and again that I won't let her die, but I've got to—we can't do a thing!" She felt Rose's smooth, very soft hand stroking her quietly. There was quiet in the touch but not warmth. So any kind stranger might touch her if she wept. She sat up abruptly and pushed back her rumpled hair. "I'm tired, I suppose—"

"Yes, of course you are," said Rose. "Now I'll help." Her

face was serious and kind, but there were no tears in her eyes. "Shall we go in?" she asked.

So they went into the mother's room and Rose went straight to the bed. Joan had dressed her mother freshly and put on a new bed-jacket of shell-pink. Her mother had many pretty bedjackets now, for Joan had said boldly to Mrs. Winters, to Miss Kinney, to Mrs. Parsons, when they asked, "If you really want to give her something, give her a pretty bed-jacket. She loves pretty things." So they made her pretty, extravagant things of lace and silk and Joan held them before her mother's half-blinded eyes and they made a variety of it for the days.

"The new pink one for Rose to see," her mother had clamored childishly. She had kept off the sleep a while, a long while, nearly fifteen minutes, when she was dressed, and Joan had plucked a pink geranium bloom from a pot in the window and put it in the snowy coil of her hair and had held a mirror for her to see it. She held the mirror high to show the lovely hair, the flower, the brow, the eyes; she held it high to hide the wasted cheeks, the withered lips.

"I look right nice," her mother said with content, her eyelids dropping.

"You look lovely," said Joan fervently.

But sleep had clutched her while she waited. She lay deeply asleep, the flower in her hair, and the two daughters stood looking at her, and Joan watching Rose. But Rose said nothing. She looked quietly at the face and said nothing, she breathed the faint vile odor and said nothing. Suddenly her mother's eyes opened and recognition came up like a light breaking through dark deep water. "It's Rose—"

"Yes, Mother dear." Rose stooped and kissed her forehead.

"I'm all dressed up," her mother began brightly. "New clothes—Joan put a flower in my hair—" She drowsed again and they stood silently while she slept.

"She's sleeping her life away," Joan whispered. "But if it were not this it would be pain, Dr. Crabbe says—better sleep than pain. Only it seems to take her so far away—already."

Rose nodded and said nothing. Joan could not endure the silence. Would Rose never speak, never cry out "Oh, Joan—Joan—Joan—," never weep? But Rose did not cry out nor weep.

"You'll want to go and unpack," said Joan at last, and Rose went docilely away.

Thus alone again Joan sat down in the old rocking chair and rocked softly to and fro while her mother slept. She looked out into the late winter's afternoon. She could see only the stark black branches of trees against a pale orange sky, a sky orange with a band of apple-green above. The sun had already set and it was the sunset's afterglow.

So after all, they were still alone together, Joan and her mother. Rose, careful, helpful, gentle Rose, could not join them. She came and went and fetched what was wanted and saved Joan in many ways, but in the end Joan must sleep by her mother and Joan must be near.

For now through the sleep came the deep waves of awaking pain and her mother cried for Joan. "Joan—Joan—where's Joan?—pain, Joan—"

She forgot all her children except Joan, and she forgot that Joan was her child. Joan was her nurse, her mother, her one to lean upon. She forgot even Francis now. Sometimes when he came in she fixed her eyes upon him, her eyes small and shrunken in her face puffed with the poison in her. She said in her hoarse loud voice, "When Frank was little I made him red suits."

"Sure, Mom," shouted Frank. "I remember them—red with an anchor on the sleeves and stars on the collars."

But she did not hear him. "Where's Joan—Joan—"

"Here, dear." She must always be there, there until the end. Dr. Crabbe said, "Got to have a trained nurse now, my dear. No reflection on you two girls, but there've got to be different hypodermics and things—"

So they had a trained nurse, but still Joan must be near, near to her mother and near to them all while they waited. Now her mother scarcely woke at all except when the father came in. However deeply she slept, she woke when he came in and cried out uneasily in her hoarse dry loud voice, "Who is it? Go away—"

"It's Paul, Mary," he said timidly. All of them could look at her and bear it, but he could not. He looked at this swollen misshapen creature and sweat stood on his white forehead. Once he forced himself and took her swollen hand in his. She cried aloud, and he dropped it. "Go away, Paul," she muttered, opening her eyes suddenly. He went away, bewildered. Why did she hate him? He had been a good husband. He was a good husband now. He went away and poured out his soul to God, forgiving her.

"Lord!" said the trained nurse, smirking at Joan as she tucked in a hot water bottle. "It's plain there wasn't much love lost between those two!"

But Joan would not answer.

No one of them could say the word death. Death was in the house; already death must be planned for, considered, but the word could not be spoken.

"What'll you bury her in, Miss Joan?" Hannah began, moaning. She paused in her sweeping to stare mournfully at Joan. "Her lavender or—"

"Don't!" said Joan sharply. "She's still here."

She went on her way upstairs. Cruel and wicked death, not to come swift and clean! Death should come clean by lightning clean and sudden by sword, or swift by sea or by accident, not this long slow planned dying. The body should be consumed by immediate death, broken to atoms, burned to ashes utterly destroyed. "I've got to get out," cried Francis desperately. He stopped her in the hall, his face pale. "I've got to go away. I can't stand this this waiting. If it's got to come why doesn't it come? I hate waiting—"

She seized him by the arm and shook him. "You'll stand what we all have to stand!" she shouted furiously. "I'm so tired I can't sit down without falling asleep. But I must go on, and so must you—"

He rushed past her, out of the house and slammed the door. He was away somewhere all the time now. She strode still furious to her mother's room. She was not anxious about him. He would fling himself off somewhere for the day, but at night he would be back.

She was so tired she was cross with Rose, willing earnest Rose, whose soft white pretty hands were so strangely clumsy, who dropped a hypodermic needle she was given to hold and grieved so much that she could not be scolded. But sometimes Joan was so tired she did scold. "Rose, how can you be so stupid!" But there was no satisfaction in it. The shallow gentle hazel eyes widened a little, and Rose said nothing But soon she slipped away to her own room to pray. Joan knew. Once, contrite, she had followed Rose and opened the door. Rose was on her knees by the bed, her face in the curve of her arm, her eyes closed, her lips moving a little. Joan closed the door abruptly. Rose did not need her contrition. Rose had her comfort. Soon she came back, her eyes placid, her lips curved in tranquillity. "Shall I fill the hot-water bottle now, Joan?" Joan, wanting to cry out at her, "Why do you ask me—why don't you feel it and find out?" said gently, "Yes, please, Rose."

"She means well," the trained nurse said, pug-nosed and cheerful, "but lots of people who mean well are all thumbs and fingers when it comes to doing something." She seized the bottle when Rose came in. "I'll put it in," she said. "You'll burn her feet—she can't feel them now."

In the end it was this stubby pug-nosed woman upon whom Joan leaned. The nurse clapped her shoulder heartily. "I'll be having you as my patient next, if you don't let down! Cheer up! When you know what's got to come, take it!"

This cheerful stranger was good for them all. She skillfully warded the father away. "Here, Reverend," she cried with much good nature, "you're not wanted here. You go back to your preaching where you'll be out of the way. Patient's sleeping. I'll tell you if you're wanted." She advised Joan in a hissing whisper while the dying woman slept, immaculate for death, "I'd let that young Frank have a rip if I were you when all this is over. Let him go away somewhere. He's hit hard by this, or something. I can't make him out. Rose is different. Nothing's going to hit her hard, nor your pa. They're all wrapped up in themselves somehow. I don't understand it, but I've seen it before. Religion's a selfish thing—they don't feel if they've got religion. You let the boy have a fling and don't worry about those two, but think of yourself for a bit. Got a feller or something to give you a little fun? This is an awful hole of a town. Can't you get away to some real place where there's something going on?"

Go away? She had forgotten there were places to which people could go. She shook her head. "I don't know—I'll have to take care of my father and the others."

The nurse rocked back and forth, considering. She was health in this place of sickness. She made the fetid air wholesome and hearty as though a wind blew cleanly through the room and Joan welcomed her. It was good to have this forthrightness, this simple decision, this humorous comprehension. Her mother stirred and moaned in her deep sleep. The pain was coming again. The nurse jumped to her feet and in a second had thrust the needle deep into the swollen arm. "There, ducky," she said cheerfully. "You always know the very minute, don't you—"

Watching the compact thick figure move amiable and competent about the bed, Joan was made conscious of life beyond this room. From death to death this woman moved, always lively, always carrying with her the atmosphere of casual, bustling, outside life. By her very comfortable casualness she put death into its place and made it part of life. Despair melted before her cheerful commonplaceness. Beyond, beyond this sorrowful room, beyond this hour, there was a strong everyday life, which, forgetting death, proceeded heartily to work and pleasure. She must be brave for death, looking beyond.

But at the end she was not brave. She and Francis were not brave. Rose was brave, and the father was brave. They were all downstairs waiting. All day the nurse had said, "Any moment now." She said, "Don't come in—I can tend to things." She ceased her joking for the day and put off for the day her ready smile. She was quiet and cool and without feeling and they all turned to her. Dr. Crabbe came and went, jamming his hat upon his head with fury and nodding at them speechlessly. "Can't do a thing," he muttered at last. "Fixed it so she won't know. Nurse'll do everything—tell you—"

So they waited, listening. But they could not wait together. When they were together the waiting grew intolerable. They must part to bear it, each knowing the other near, but not near enough to see a face. The father shut himself behind his study door and sat alone, listening, his head drooping, his hands folded upon his knees. Francis sat curled into the great old red leather chair in the sitting room, a book in his hands. He had pulled the chair to face the window and the high back hid him except for the crown of his black head and he sat listening. Rose sat quietly at their mother's desk, writing in a little diary she kept, writing steadily in her small clear compact script, pausing to think and write again, pausing to listen.

But Joan went out into the garden. It was two days before Christmas. The air was warm and still but the garden was dying, was dead. She walked about in the sunshine, listening, waiting, her footsteps rustling in the fallen leaves. They had forgotten to clear the leaves away. In other years it was always her mother who said, "This week we must rake the leaves." But this year they were not raked.

The garden was full of her mother. Here were the lemon lilies she had planted, years ago a solitary bulb, now a great undying clump. Next spring they would burst heartily into life and blossoming. Strange and sad that people alone could live but once, that human bodies alone must die and turn to dust, with only a single spring. There was a secret in those strong dark rooted bulbs living on and on to blossom every year. A belated bird called through the quiet air, and listening, Joan heard the faint monotonous cheeping of the last autumn cricket, awaking drowsily in the warmth of the winter sun.

Then the voice for which they had all been listening fell. The nurse called strongly to them all. "Now—she's ready to go—" Joan's feet ran to carry her to her mother. They ran with the habit of all those months. But her heart was frightened and crying out, "No—no—no, I don't want to see—" Running past the dining room door she heard Rose calling to Francis, "Aren't you coming, Francis?" She heard Francis crying back, his voice cracked and crying, "I can't—Gee, I can't—" He began to sob.

But she ran on. At the door she met her father and Rose. They passed her and went in together. She would follow them. Of course she would follow them. She leaned against the door frame, panting. In a moment she would follow them. Just now for this moment something blinded her—not tears. She was not weeping. Her throat was thick, her eyes fogged, her heart beating all over her body. She was afraid. She turned blindly to the window and stood looking out across to the church. Steady herself—she must steady herself, and then she would go in . . . They were coming now to decorate the church for Christmas, all the people. There they all were, laden with evergreens to make wreaths. The organ began to play. She could hear it rolling forth, deep faint enormous chords rolling out of the pipes. "Joy to the world!" the organ shouted. Joy—strange foreign word, meaningless word, false and lying word!

Rose's voice broke across the moment. "She's gone—Oh, Joan, why didn't you come in?" She turned and looked at Rose. There were tears in Rose's eyes and reproach in her voice. But Joan did not weep, not now. Relief swept through her. Now she need not go in because the moment was passed and it could never come again—never, never. Rose asked again, "Why didn't you come in?" She wiped her eyes delicately and went no, "She never waked at all—just slept until the last second, smiled, and sighed. That was all. You should have seen her smile, Joan."

But Joan cried out passionately, "I'm glad I didn't!" She rushed to her own room and flung herself upon her bed and cried over and over into her pillow, "I don't want to see her dead—I don't want to see her dead!"

Yet they would not let her have her way. No, soon they took possession of the house where her mother had lived so long. The women came out of the village, crowding into the house, friendly, kindly, eager, curious, and the house must give up all its secrets to them. Mrs. Winters, dressed in an old noisy black taffeta, pushed them firmly away. She herded them together and cried at them, "Now you all go away. We are going to do everything necessary. Mr. Blum is here waiting. The Ladies' Aid is going to see to the flowers and everything."

Behind her Mr. Blum stood, short and fat and dark, trying not to be facetious. "Sure, we'll do it all, folks," he said loudly. "That's our business, you know. I always say it may be a dead business, but—" He stopped and coughed, remembering he was in the presence of the bereaved. "Sure—" he ended weakly.

So they were together again in the sitting room. They had nowhere else to go except in this one room that had been kept for them. The house was not theirs. Even in the study there were women's coats and hats piled on the table. Hannah was crying and hurrying in the kitchen to make coffee for everybody. Past the open door went wreaths and flower pieces. There was the sudden shadow of a great black box. "Easy there, boys," Mr. Blum's voice roared, "careful of the corners!" Francis, standing by the window, turned away from them, biting his nails, and leaped and banged the door behind him and ran through the kitchen into the backyard and down the south street.

Rose sat by the desk. The little diary was open before her. She began to write in it again, weeping silently, writing down the story of her mother's death. She blotted it carefully and turned to Joan. "I wish you could have seen the smile at the end—" In the leather chair the father sat in his plum-colored sateen quilted robe. The sunshine of midafternoon shone searing across his face, withering it, making him white and old . . .

·   ·   ·

Joan sat on a stool before the wood fire Hannah had lit and stared into it. She spread out her hands to the blaze, for she was cold. Upstairs they were tending the body she had tended all these days. But all the tending had not been enough. She was tired to the heart and it was not enough. Death had not stayed for all her fighting. They were washing the flesh. Strangers were there at the end.

Her father's melancholy voice broke across her agony, reflective, mournfully surprised, "I think I am the first one of all my family to have been left a widower, Joan."

"Yes, Father?" she answered. A little clear blue flame darted out of a log and flashed slender and upright as a dagger toward the chimney.

"Yes," he continued in a sort of sad surprise. "John was younger than his wife Annie and he died before her, and Isaac never had his health after the war and he died of old wounds, and David died of typhoid, and Frederick is still living—"

"Dearies," said Mrs. Winters at the door, "come and see her! She's so sweet—I never saw her look sweeter—" Somehow she herded them all together. "Where's Francis? Oh, he'll be too late. We do want to get all this sadness over before Christmas —I do think he might have stayed with the family this last hour—I wish he had listened to—"

She was pushing them upstairs. Rose and Joan and their father. The father tripped and Mrs. Winters caught his elbow and held it firmly, guiding him. "Now, Doctor, I don't wonder you feel it, but the Lord giveth and taketh. Joan, we put on the orchid bed-jacket and a fresh— It was difficult to dress—you know—Well, she looks so sweet, her lovely hair all white and still so curly, and Mr. Blum just touched her up a little."

"I can't," gasped Joan.

"Oh, honey, she's so sweet to look at—your own mother— You'll always regret it—" She was pushed into the room. Now it was a strange room, full of strangers. Mr. Blum was there, wiping his hands on a stiff linen towel. "One thing," he whispered hoarsely. "I always ask the family, should we take off the wedding ring?"

Against her will Joan's eyes searched in terror. She saw a tall stiff doll lying in the great box, dressed and tinted into the semblance of life. The strong shapely hands were folded upon the breast, the wedding ring was shining there. For days they could not have taken away the ring if they would. But now the hideous swelling was mysteriously gone. Her mother was her own self once more, but strangely her own self dead, dead, with her hands folded upon her breast as only the hands of the dead are folded.

"Let her alone!" Joan cried, her voice bursting from her, and to her own horror she burst into loud childish weeping before all these strangers.

So she lost the body of her mother. They took her from the hour of her death and she was no more for her children. Others had her. Even at the funeral she belonged to others. Only for a moment did Joan regain her. There was the moment when she spoke for her mother to them all and so for that moment regained her. The church, they said, perturbed, was decorated for Christmas. Holly and pine wreaths and a silver star were for Christmas. They all had loved her, of course they wanted everything right for their beloved pastor's wife, but the wreaths were so hard to put up and take down.

"Leave them as they are!" she cried at them. There they were, the women of the Ladies' Aid, crowded into the sitting room, heavy-bodied, anxious, kind. "We don't want to seem lacking in respect," they said, their faces solemn. But Joan flung out her arms and cried at them, "Dont you remember how she loved Christmas? Why, on Christmas morning she used to run over to the church before breakfast to see it! She thought the church never so beautiful as on Christmas morning. Even when she'd spent days on the wreaths and even after she had hung the star herself and had seen it all the night before, she'd run over alone on Christmas morning. She wouldn't want the wreaths taken down because of her, and not the star, especially."

So, dubiously, they had left the wreaths and the great silver star shone above the chancel and they set her there under it.

But it was all strange and awry. It was strange for the father to be in the pew with them instead of the mother. He was out of place there, while the short stout Methodist minister stood in his pulpit to praise the dead.

He felt shorn and embarrassed. To hear these praises made even her memory unreal. "A good and faithful wife," a strange voice said, "a shining light in the community, a friend to us all —we shall miss her." It seemed indecent to hear his wife thus publicly commended. He shrank within himself. Mary—his mind was full of Mary, Mary going about the house at her little swift half-run, Mary at the table managing for them all, Mary —but he could not quite remember her face now. He had never been good at remembering faces. Her eyes had been brown, he knew. He remembered that because when they were alone in the night and she had got into bed first as she always did because she was so quick, she lay looking at him, her eyes strange and dark and quiet, and this look always made him uncomfortable although he did not know why. She was so strange when they were alone together—he wanted the light out because she was always less strange when he could not see her. Her warm and present body was familiar to him, but when the candle was lit her dark silent eyes made her strange again. They had argued about the candle lit in the night. She said, "Let me light the candle, Paul. I want the light. The darkness weighs me down."

But he did not answer. He held her and hurried on. It was not only that her eyes were dark and strange, but the light made him ashamed of what he wanted to do. He argued it with himself in the daytime, in the study, working on his sermon, the Bible open before him. Why should he be ashamed when it was lawful wedlock? Why should he want the darkness to hide him? But if she prevailed, and sometimes she had, then desire went out of him and he felt himself injured and helpless, and he could not see why, because to put such things into words seemed shameful to him . . .

"So He giveth His beloved sleep," the voice from the pulpit declared with unction.

But her mother did not want sleep, Joan cried passionately in her heart. She wanted to be awake, to live, to run and to work and to laugh. She begrudged even the sleep of night. She arose early every day, eager to be awake. She asked nothing except not to sleep. But God had given her only sleep, eternal sleep. A rush of anger rose up in Joan, anger against God, God was suddenly real and alive to her, a shape of force, definite and inexorable and powerful. They were all lost in that power, helpless in the reasonless tossing ocean of God's power. Tears filled her eyes, furious tears. She looked at the family. She gathered them together in her heart, her father, Rose, Francis, and each was touching. They were forlorn and deserted. God had robbed them. Her father was very pale, even his lips were suddenly dry and pale. He was not listening. He had opened a hymnbook and he was reading a psalm in the back. Rose, pretty Rose, her little sister, was sitting quietly, her hands folded, sitting so still, her tongue moistening her lips now and then. And Francis was her mother's love. She must be responsible now for Francis and for all he did. His face was twisted and set into sternness against weeping. He alone of the three was staring rigidly at what lay beneath the Christmas star.

. . . She had died, after all, his mother. Now he need never tell her. There would never come that moment when he would go into the house and see her face and know she knew. For nothing of him was hidden from her long. There was something between them so hot and close that when he tried to hide a thing from her she knew it. She caught it from him by sight and smell and touch. And he knew when she knew. He was helpless with her, loving her and hating her at the same time because she was so close. She had been too close sometimes so that he was rebellious and wanted to be free of her, flinging himself away from her, flinging himself against her will. He wanted to obey her because he wanted to please her. He was driven to disobey her because she was too close and he loved her more than he wanted to love her.

Now that she was gone, he was half dead too. He wanted her back, he wanted her close again. There was no one in him really except her. As soon as this damned preacher was done talking he'd go and find Fanny.

No, he couldn't go and find Fanny on the very day of his mother's funeral. That was worse even than he was. It had been bad enough to go when his mother was dying. But Fanny was the only one who could make him forget. He was trembling with the need to cry. Fanny was the only person to whom he could cry and not be ashamed. When he had put his head down on her breast and cried, "Fanny, she's going to die!" Fanny had hushed him in her arms and murmured over him richly. "Sweet boy, cry and ease yourself—cry and cry, sweet boy. It's no shame to cry on me—" He was trembling with the need to cry again . . .

Joan saw his hands, wet, trembling, twisting. She slipped her hand into his arm and held him. She must take care of them all now—her father, Rose, Frank. She gathered them all to her, they were hers, hers. She would care for them and defend them, comfort them and love them, protect them against everything, even against God.

The people rose and she rose too. The organ was playing quietly, "For all the saints who from their labors rest." It was nothing to her that Martin was playing, nothing that people were singing softly and sadly to his playing. She would carry on her mother's life. She would never rest. She would go on doing her mother's work, working, working, making her mother's life go on.

"Good-bye, Joan," the nurse whispered to her as the singing slid to an amen. "I'm catching the train for my next case. I almost didn't have time for the funeral. But I like to stay to the funerals if I can, especially if I get fond of the patient like I did. I'm lucky today—just got a telegram this morning there was an arthritis case waiting, and they're apt to last. Now remember what I said and look out for a little fun for yourself. She was sure a grand case, and I'm sorry she had to go. But don't sit and grieve."

"I'll be very busy," said Joan steadfastly. She grasped the thick strong hand gratefully and clung to it a little. It was something to cling to for a moment. But almost at once it was pulled heartily away and the ruddy round friendly face disappeared among the faces gathering around her. She lost the rough touch of the hand in many gentle touches of other hands. "Dear Joan, let us do anything we can." "We'll all miss her, sir." "Francis, my boy, Ned says he'll be over first thing tomorrow—wants you to go hiking if you feel like it. I said I didn't know if it was the thing—"

Against her cheek Joan felt Mr. Billings' gusty breath and he whispered windily in her ear, "She was a real lady, your mother was—never niggled over anything—bought it or didn't buy it, but no complaining like some I know. I'll be sending the meat up just the same, as nice a side of lamb as I ever had—I said to Mollie you wouldn't be wanting turkey this Christmas." There were tears in his small black eyes and they glittered on the insurmountable mounds of his cheeks, and then ran down by his ears. Joan's heart flew to him. "*Thank* you—thank you for your feelings especially," she said, and somehow for the first time was a little comforted.

Used as she was to leaping from her cot many times in a

night, it was strange to lie quietly in her own bed again in her own room, so strange that for long she could not fall asleep. When at last she did sleep it was only for a little while. She woke to find herself standing in the blackness of the night, groping for her mother's bed. "Yes, yes," she was muttering, "here I am—here—here—"

But her hand fell on nothing and instantly in the darkness she was awake and she knew what had happened. She remembered that they had put her mother in the churchyard, there on the far side of the church, away from the house. Her mother was lying now in the utter closed darkness of the earth, forever sleeping. For an instant she, too, was in that narrow buried cell. She saw the somber intensely sleeping face. Her hands flew to her breast. Her mother would not be changed yet. Oh, somehow she must get her out and away, into the air again, into life again!

Then she heard the sound of a cough from the next room, her mother's room. Her father was there. He had moved back again this very night. Into the same bed where he had been used to sleep he had gone, and now he lay alone. She listened. He was awake. She had heard him cough once more and felt a new pity for him. She forgot she had been angry with him. He was alone, too, and she must go to him. She opened the door softly, a small crack. He lay there in the bed, the candle lit beside him, the covers tucked beneath his arms. On his breast he held his large thin hands folded. He was staring ahead of him, but she was not sure he did not sleep. He had opened the windows wide and in the stir of air the candle threw a moving shadow over his face.

"Father," she said softly, tentatively. He turned and looked at her from afar off, solemnly.

"What is it?" he asked her.

"I heard you coughing—are you wanting anything?"

He hesitated. "No, nothing," he replied quietly.

She waited, but he said no more, and she closed the door and went back to her own room, her pity in her still, but now somehow cold.

Ah, but she was cold, her body cold, her feet cold! The air had changed in the night to great cold, and she huddled into her bed, suddenly forlorn and chilled to the heart. And then the pity which was in her turned upon herself and for herself she wept and wept until sleep came at last.

But it was well to weep in the night and have it done. She woke in full dawn spent, with the quietness of one spent for a time, knowing that for a while she had wept her fill. She rose quietly, subdued, with no aching necessity for any weeping, and dressed herself and went downstairs and spoke to Hannah gently. "Good morning, Hannah."

Hannah was late and untidy. She had not combed her hair and she was moving about slowly, sodden with weeping, ostentatious with grief.

"Let's try and have everything as cheerful as we can this morning, Hannah," she said quietly. "Mother would want us to."

She found a clean tablecloth and put it on the table, and out of all the flowers in the house she found some red roses Miss Kinney had brought. "I bought them," said Miss Kinney in a piercing whisper. She had not wiped away the tears running down her small withered face. But Mr. Blum had not been willing to use anything except white flowers.

She set the red roses on the table. The sun was careless and beautiful. It shone through the windows at is always did and poured empty cheerfulness into the room. She made everything ready and perfect for them all, postponing sorrow. Even Hannah's trembling lips did not bring the tears again to her own eyes. She waited while Hannah dried her eyes upon her apron and listened when Hannah asked, "Do you want I should go over your mother's things for you?"

But then she was struck with delayed remembrance. Of course there were her mother's things, her dresses—oh, no one could touch them. "Rose and I must do that—"

She could not forget it, now that Hannah had spoken, and she could not bear to have it done. She would put it off a few days. It was still good to have her mother's things in this house. Let them hang in the closets, lie in the drawers. Let as much as could be rest as her mother had left it. She clung to all of her mother.

Then one by one they came down to the breakfast table, Rose, Francis, and her father, carefully dressed, for it was his day for pastoral calls and it did not occur to him to delay duty. She took her mother's place without question now. She served them in silence, and in silence they received her service.

The next day she and Rose together opened the drawers of

the bureau in her mother's room. They opened the closets, and took away everything that was her mother's. There were not many things besides the gay bed-jackets—her few house-dresses, her brown suit, her best dress of a dark wine-brown silk, her black winter coat long worn, the brown velvet toque she had made herself. But because the garments were all long worn, because they had seen them so often, upon her, they were still part of her now.

And there were the gloves worn to the shape of her hands. And there were the shoes, mended at the heel, with here and there a small neat patch. Old Mr. Pegler, the cobbler, had used to mend them for nothing. He would not come to church, he said, for he followed Ingersoll. But he mended the shoes she had brought him and would not take payment. "Not, mind ye," he said stoutly every time, his glasses pushed up on his bald head, "because you're the minister's wife. I do it because I want to." And she, because she was proud, took him a cake now and then, for his wife was long dead and he did for himself, and he loved her dark chocolate cakes and her silvery angel food. "I can do everything for myself except the sweet stuff," he told her, crinkling his little round meaty cheeks. "It takes a woman to do the sweet stuff."

Sorting over the shoes Joan suddenly recognized among them pairs of her own, shoes she had thrown away because they were not fit to wear, or so she had thought. Her mother had said nothing. She had taken them to Mr. Pegler and he had mended them and she had worn them that she might add a little to the secretly saved money. It hurt her heart to see what her mother had done, and none of them had noticed it. She began to realize that none of them had noticed their mother. They all took from her, each took what he needed for his own life, without seeing that she also needed something from them for herself. But now it was too late—

Joan, looking at all these things, cried out to Rose, in a low voice, "What shall we do with them? I feel as if we buried her body, we should have buried these, too."

Rose looked up. She was kneeling at a drawer. "We could give them to the mission at South End," she said in her reasonable, practical way. "They would be doing good there."

"No," said Joan abruptly. "I couldn't bear it. I couldn't bear to think of her clothes, her dresses, the things she made and wore—put on that riffraff—"

She gathered them into her arms, all she could hold of her mother's garments. "I'll pack them away for now," she said. "I'll put them in that old round-topped trunk in the attic that she kept our baby things in. There will be room for these, too, there are so few—"

She mounted the attic stairs, her throat tight with tears, hugging her load. Inside her heart cried out, "Oh, Mother, Mother, Mother!" From the things came the smell of her mother. It was not scent. Her mother had never used scent. It was the odor of her mother's body as it once was, the odor of clean and healthy flesh. She knew it, she remembered it. In her childhood, sitting upon her mother's lap, wrapped in her mother's arms, there was that fresh, slight odor. She loved it then, it added its comfort to the embrace. Once, when she was very small and her mother had been away a day and left her with Hannah, in intolerable loneliness she had run to the closet and opening it, she had buried her face in her mother's dresses, and there was the odor of her mother and it comforted her.

It comforted her now. It brought back her mother's health and her old vigor. She forgot that odor of death from the sickbed, and she remembered her mother as she had been, her open smooth forehead, her clear wide dark eyes, the brown of her face mingled with the red in her cheeks. She stood at the head of the attic stairs, remembering—staring, smiling at what she remembered—

Then she saw the round-topped trunk was open. She went to it and saw the baby clothes tossed this way and that. The tray was partly full of small socks and shoes and crocheted baby jackets, all in confusion. She understood instantly. Here her mother had kept her little store of money, and from here her father had taken it. But now it mattered no more. That, too, was over. Only she was glad her mother had not known the end, glad she had slept and not heard her father's footsteps hastening up the attic stairs. She put down her load upon a chair, and lifted the tray and set it on the floor and kneeling began to sort it. Here were Francis' shoes, and here a red jacket he had had. She could remember it because her mother had made it and had loved it on him. Lifting it to fold it she saw something else—an envelope addressed to her in her mother's writing. Joan Richards. There was her name, her mother's

. writing. It was like hearing her mother's voice. She tore it open, her heart throbbing in her throat—

"Dear Joan—my darling child—" That was like her mother to begin a little formally and then to rush to warmth.

I write this to you because you are the eldest. I have worried so because I have nothing to leave my children. It is so hard to begin life with nothing at all, and because of this several years ago I began to put by a little of the housekeeping money. There are always ways to cut down for something one wants very much. It has been a joy to do this. Now today you are graduated. I have been tempted to take this money—it is nearly a hundred dollars now—and use some of it for a nice present for you—a watch. I always think a lady's gold watch is nice, perhaps because I have always wanted one. But something makes me feel I am not to live very long. I am tired much of the time. And I have nothing to leave my beloved children except this little heap of money. I leave it to you Joan, to use for yourself, for Rose, for Francis, as you must. I can trust you. You have always been a dear honest child. I shall tell your father it is for you.

Mother

So her mother spoke to her. But it was too late. She folded the letter and thrust it into her dress and went on sorting. In her bosom the letter lay like pain. Rose came upstairs, her arms full. "I think there are no more," she said. "Shall we put them into the bottom?"

"Yes," Joan answered. "Fold them and put them away."

She would not tell Rose or Frank of the letter. They would not understand. Perhaps Frank would hate his father. And they must not hate each other—none of them must hate any of the others. She could understand. She would find a way to help the others if the need came. She must find some way.

She rose and packed her mother's things steadily into the trunk, and when they were all put away she closed the lid and locked it fast. Their babyhood, their childhood, their mother's life—all were locked away now, forever. It darted across her mind that there was nothing there of the man's—nothing of their father at all. He had come and taken all he wanted and he had left nothing behind. There was no human thing he possessed which could have belonged there with the mother's garments, with the little children's garments. She turned away and looked at Rose and smiled, her heart hard with the pain of the letter.

"It is all over for her, isn't it?" she said. "Let's go now and put his things into the closets and the drawers."

II

EVERY DAY NOW AT THE MEALS
she sat in her mother's place. Her own place was gone and she
had her mother's. Without knowing it she even began to use
her mother's words and ways, to do all those things her mother
used to do. About the house she saw as her mother would have
seen. It did not occur to her to take down the pictures she had
once despised. She was so mingled with her mother that the
house, the family, became her own. She found herself watching
each one possessively, jealous for the good of each. She had no
life of her own.

Her father gave to her each week the small sum he had been
used to giving her mother and out of it she wrested fiercely
their food and clothing. And then one night in her bed, lying
awake in the light of the cold clear moon, she planned that she
would do more. She would save still more fiercely and build
again that small store of silver, bit by bit. She would do it for
her mother.

She leaped out of her bed and went to her little desk and
wrote to her mother. She wrote an answer to the letter she had
found. *Mother, I do not know if you can see this or not,* she
wrote. *But I am going to go on with the fund, and if Rose or
Francis needs it, it will be there.* She went back to bed planning where she might save a penny or two from the meat, from
the butter. Her father would not notice. The next day she put

the two letters together in a little box her mother had used for handkerchiefs, a small sandalwood box someone had once brought her from Italy, and she took out of her housekeeping money twenty-five cents. She would save it somehow during the week.

So bit by bit each week, some weeks only a penny, some weeks as much as a dollar, she added to what was in the sandalwood box, where her mother's letter lay with her own letter. She kept the box in the attic in the tray of the round-topped trunk. He would not look there again, thinking he had taken everything. It came to be a secret comfort to her, the knowledge of that small, steadily growing store, as it had been a comfort to her mother.

But it was not easy to be her mother. She had not the years it had taken to temper her mother, to make her patient. She was eager, too eager, to do for them. Her young boundless strength rushed out to do for them more than they wanted. She straightened Francis' drawers and he scowled at her. "I wish you'd leave my things alone." It hurt her amazingly. He never had minded when his mother had done the same thing. "Leave my drawers alone, will you?" he demanded again. "I can't find my things."

"I only put your clean collars—"

"I can put my own things where I want them," he said.

And there was Rose with her strange, soft obstinacy. When the long Christmas holiday was nearly over Joan said briskly, "Now we'll have to be getting you ready to go back to college. We'll need to look at your clothes." She thought of the sandalwood box warmly. If Rose needed a new hat or some little thing there'd be enough. Or she could give her something of her own. In the village she needed very little. There was a blue evening dress. She needed no evening dress here in Middlehope, where the gayest evening was to go with her father and have supper with one of the families in the church, a plain home supper. They would not have known what to make of an evening dress. They would have thought she was putting on airs. There was really no place to wear pretty clothes.

"I want you to take my blue dress back to college with you, Rose. I don't need it."

"I'm not going back to college, Joan," said Rose.

They were alone, making beds, now in Francis' room. She

paused, astonished. "Not going back?" she said stupidly, staring at Rose.

But Rose tucked in the corners carefully. She did not look up. Her face was quite composed.

"No," she said, calmly. "I have other plans."

"You've not told me, Rose," said Joan. She was hurt. She longed to reproach Rose. Rose never would come near—Rose never told anything—her only sister, just the two of them, working about the house together and Rose had never told her what she was planning.

"Rob Winters and I are going to be married," said Rose, her voice placid and certain. "He finished seminary in June and we shall be married and go as missionaries. He has been accepted for the service in China."

Joan did not move. "You didn't tell me," she said hostilely.

Rose stood erect, her eyes innocent, candid, clear. "I've only just had the call, Joan," she said. "Only yesterday I heard God's voice plainly saying, 'Go ye into all the world.' I was not sure until yesterday, when I was sewing. I was by myself in my room, thinking about Rob, and I had my call. Then I knew I was to go, with Rob."

"But—you're *marrying* him—just to be a missionary? You're a child—you don't know—"

"I'll be twenty in September," said Rose. "And don't put it that way, Joan. You've never understood—how I feel about my life. I want to obey God—I want to save souls—" She paused, and repeated softly, " 'Go ye into all the world.' "

"Do you want to marry Rob, Rose?" asked Joan. She thought of Rob, tall, thin, ascetic, his eyes alive in his set, pallid young face.

"If God tells me to," said Rose. A slight, exquisite flush crept into her creamy cheeks. She went steadily on with her work, trying to make the corners of the bed square. But she never could get them quite as square as her mother used to do.

It was so hard to talk to Joan. Joan was always wanting to probe into her and find out things, the things she told nobody, things she could not put into words, feelings not to be put into words. It was all mixed up in her, this warm sweet need for devotion. She wanted to offer herself up. She had offered herself to Jesus, giving herself up, feeling herself swept into Him, into His being. She and Rob had talked about it, Rob knew what she meant. He had looked at her with such worship that suddenly she wanted to cry. "You are a saint, Rose," he whispered. "I never knew there could be a girl like you, so pure, so . . . so holy." When he took her hand, that same familiar sweet rush of feeling had swept through her and she knew it was right for her to love him. They had kept their love so beautiful. When they had kissed each other, she said, "Let's keep our love pure and beautiful, always." And Rob kissed her gently. When she was in his arms, when he was holding her so purely, she could think about Jesus, too, in all the lovely misty warmth inside her. It made her know it was right for her to marry Rob.

Joan said shortly, "I don't understand it—I don't see what it has to do with Rob."

She fell to work again. Now they were silent. But Joan was in a turmoil of surprise and discomfort. What was the discomfort? She paused, searching. Was it that she would miss Rose? No—strange, strange, it had nothing to do with Rose. It was Martin. Here was Martin's face suddenly in her mind, the memory of his lips on hers. But surely Martin had nothing to do with marriage. She put the brief memory away again.

So it became an accepted thing that Rose was to marry, was to go to China. Her father heard it and grew unexpectedly cheerful. In the evening as they sat about the fire he told them what they had never known. "When I was a young man," he said diffidently, "I also planned to go to the foreign field. The call came to me when I had been married a year and you were an infant, Joan. It came very clearly. I remember. Dr. Peter Davidson of China had my pulpit that Sabbath evening, and I remember the congregation was very small, for even then my people were not interested as I have wished in saving souls. And while I was troubled about this, God's voice came through the preacher. He leaned over the pulpit—a great tall thin man he was, burned nearly black by eastern sun, and he pointed his finger at me and said, 'Why not you?' And I knew it was God's voice. I came home to Mary and told her." His face looked suddenly withered as he spoke. He finished very quietly. "She would not go. She said God had to call her, too. I have regretted it all my life."

He had never said so much to them before. They did not know what to answer. Francis, looking up from his book, closed it suddenly. "Going to bed," he said gruffly, and slammed the door behind him. They did not notice him. Joan was sewing, mending the pile in her mother's basket, and Rose was sitting, half dreaming, in the shadow, near the fire. Ah, but Joan must speak for her mother. "I suppose she thought of me—of us," she began. But her father did not hear. He stared into the coals.

"God has punished me," he said somberly. "I have labored here in this one small place all my years. Where I might have harvested my thousands, I have only a few score of souls saved. That is why now I turn so eagerly to the mission at South End. I did not heed God's call, and he punished me. But now he has relented. Within these last few years people have come to me, unsaved and ignorant of God's love. God is kind."

His voice quieted. In their silence he went on a little more, revealing himself wistfully to them, compelled by a lifetime's compulsion.

"All these years I have been waked in the night by the groans of those across the sea whom I never went to save. I should have gone. I have lain awake in the night, hearing them call."

Joan looked up at him across her mending. This, then, was what he thought about when she saw him lying solitary upon his bed, his hands crossed upon his breast. He was listening to voices calling to him. All these years, when they had seen him lift his head and stare away from them, it had been to listen not to them, but to those others whom they had never seen. He had moved among ghosts.

Rose was already gone. Though she moved about the house during the spring, though her hands helped here and there, pretty hands, so strangely clumsy for all their shape and smoothness, though her soft voice made its even replies—"Yes, thank you, Joan, a little more bread—the white bread, please," "The white meat, please, Father," "I'll dust the parlor clean, Hannah"—Rose was gone. She had withdrawn her life from this house, withdrawn it into waiting, into the years to come, into a life Joan could not imagine.

She could not imagine Rose's life away from Middlehope, far from everyone they had known. Together they planned Rose's clothes, the things she would need for her marriage. They said, looking at each other in sisterly, practical fashion, "There must be this, and this—" "Surely a white satin wedding dress?" said

Joan, pleading. But Rose shook her head. "What would white satin be afterwards? Brown, a brown crepe—" So Joan let it be brown crepe, though how could it be a real marriage without white satin? . . . "Miss Joan Richards was married today to—to —her gown was white satin with a train—" . . . "A thin dark dress for travel," said Rose, with pencil and paper, "a voile or two for the heat—"

But then it was not so much getting ready for a wedding as getting ready for what was after it. That Rob and Rose were to be married seemed nothing but a convenience before they went away together to be missionaries. What were missionaries? . . . Joan, standing tall and irresolute beside Rose in Mr. Winters' general store, let Rose choose the plain striped voile, the dark brown silk crepe. These were not chosen for Rose the bride. They were chosen for someone else, for Rose the helpmeet, neat, subdued, standing beside the young missionary.

Mr. Winters waited on them fussily, urging one thing and another. "Here's some pretty newfangled things," he said, hurrying from one cardboard box to another. "Doggone, where are they? I had my hand right on 'em a minute ago—costoom jewelry they call it. It looks almost real."

"No, thank you, Mr. Winters," said Rose. She did not call Rob's parents Mother and Father. She was no warmer to them than she ever had been.

They cut and sewed the stuffs together, quiet plodding sewing. It was like sewing under a gray sky. Her mother would have hated these dull colors. "Where is that flowered lawn Mother made you?" Joan asked suddenly. That day it had slipped over Rose's head like a shower of plucked flowers.

"I still have it," said Rose. "I haven't really worn it much. It wasn't a very practical dress," she added after a moment.

Joan did not answer. Rebellion against this sewing, against this marriage, this life Rob had chosen, rushed up, a heat in her body. Her hands felt stiff with unwillingness. She stood up suddenly and the stuff and the spool and the scissors fell to the floor.

"I've just remembered something I forgot," she said abruptly to Rose's calm, upturned eyes, and whirled out of the room in long-legged haste. But before she could get to her own room she heard the front door downstairs open and a voice shot clearly up to her ears. "Where's Rose? Rose—Rose!" it called loudly.

It was Mrs. Winters. But when Rose came out of her room, she cried at Joan, leaning over the balustrade, looking down. Mrs. Winters was slapping a letter she held in her right hand with her plump left hand. It was so plump her gold wedding ring was deeply imbedded in her finger. "Joan, what's this about Rob and Rose? I don't say anything about their marrying and I didn't say a word about Rob's being a minister—he'll always be poor, and I've nothing to leave him—Mr. Winters and I—but to go to China's something else! I don't believe Rob'd have thought of it by himself—it's Rose—" Her voice filled the hall, strident, sharp, rising up the stairs. In the kitchen the dishes Hannah was washing stopped rattling. Then the door of the study opened and the priest of God stayed her angry voice. He stood, sudden and tall, his hand uplifted against her to silence her. "Do you mean you are not willing for your son to follow his call?" he asked.

Across the strident heat of her voice, his voice fell like a sword of ice, silencing her. But she was not used to silence. "You're a good man," she retorted, "but you don't understand. Rob's my only boy. Rob's always been too enthusiastic—emotional—his father's emotional. If it hadn't been for me, Mr. Winters would have been here, there and everywhere. He wanted to go out on a gold rush once when he was a boy not any older than Rob is now—Why, once he wanted to throw up his good general store and go into automobiles! Rob's just like him. They hate to listen."

"Take care that you are not a hypocrite," said the priest of God with slow, deadly coldness. "You lead the missionary meetings in the church but you will not give your own son to God."

"Oh, Father, don't," cried Joan. "Please come in, Mrs. Winters—Oh, Rose, I didn't know Rob hadn't told her—"

"He's afraid of her," Rose said breathlessly. "He's always been afraid of her."

She threw reproach at Rose in a look, then ran down the stairs, trembling in her large young haste. How she hated to see people hurt, even Mrs. Winters! She seized Mrs. Winters' plump arm and drew her eagerly into the empty parlor and pushed her into a seat and closed the door. "Sit down—sit down—there—we can talk about it—not quarreling—I hate quarreling—"

She forgot how strong she was until Mrs. Winters fell into a chair under her strength. "Joan—I do declare," she exclaimed breathlessly. Then she saw Joan's moved, troubled face, and her lips trembled. "It's awfully hard," she whispered hoarsely, pulling her handkerchief from her belt. "Of course I believe in missions—I've been brought up to—I've been brought up a Christian—I can't remember when I wasn't a member of the Church. But I never thought it would happen to me. It was hard enough for my son to want to be a preacher—so poor preachers always are, and no help in the store—and Rob's a sensible boy at heart. But he doesn't listen to me—Still, I just don't believe he'd have thought of such a thing himself. Rose's always been a little queer. She's had such an influence on him." Her full purplish lips quivered beyond control and she put her handkerchief to them.

"I know," breathed Joan. She towered over her, instantly understanding. "It's terrible—it's terrible for me too, letting Rose go."

She hung over Mrs. Winters, yearning with comprehension. It would be like seeing them die on their wedding day, Rose and Rob. Her immense imagination leaped to the day, saw them upon the train, the train smaller and smaller in the distance until they were gone. In Mrs. Winters' house there would be no child left, and in this house Rose would be no more. It was terrible as death, her mother gone in death and now Rose gone into life stranger than death. It was easier to understand death. Her eyes swam in tears. People ought to stay close, close together—families ought to cling together always until death came. They could not help death but they could help choosing in life to part. "Mrs. Winters," she whispered, "Mrs. Winters, Mother wouldn't have wanted Rose to go. I'm sure she wouldn't."

"Of course she wouldn't," Mrs. Winters whispered back, her fat cheeks shaking with the sobs in her throat. "Your dear mother—Joan, I'm not a hypocrite. I—I really did mean what I said in the missionary meetings, even though Chinese always did give me the creeps. I used to see them sometimes on the streets in New York when I went with Mr. Winters to get stock. But to put a nickel in the plate or even a dime once in a while —it isn't the same thing as your only child wanting to go."

"No—no," said Joan. She knelt down and wrapped her long arms about Mrs. Winters' large encased body, and Mrs.

Winters leaned for a moment upon her shoulder and wept aloud.

"I haven't done this—not since my little girl died before Rob could talk," she gasped.

"There, there," said Joan, patting her back gently. How could Rob be afraid of his mother? Under her hand she felt a hard full ridge of flesh above a corset. But it didn't matter. She saw suddenly that this woman, this managing, bristling woman, was nothing but a child after all. Strange how nobody grew up—Her mother had died, really nothing but a little child, and she had never understood her mother wholly until she had seen she was a child. And now she would always really know Mrs. Winters. She would know her better than she did her own father, better than she did Rose, who never gave of themselves. Mrs. Winters sighed and sat up abruptly, and wiped her eyes.

"I don't know when . . ." she said feebly.

"It doesn't matter," said Joan quickly. "I understand perfectly."

"I know you do—I feel you do, though you're only a girl and I'm sure—But I'll always oppose it. Joan—so long as I draw breath. I've been a good woman and served the Lord and I oughtn't to be asked to do this besides."

Joan stood up, delicately conscious that Mrs. Winters was ashamed of her weeping.

"Yes, Mrs. Winters," she said docilely.

Mrs. Winters stood up also, and took out her side combs and combed up her pompadour and thrust the combs in again strongly on either side of the knob of hair on her crown. "But nobody listens to me," she said. She scarcely looked now as though she had wept at all. "There—I've got to go–I left a cake in the oven. I don't know what came over me. I shall write a good hot letter to Rob. And you speak to Rose, Joan. Tell her what your mother'd have told her. It's that Kinney girl that's started Rose, Joan. I'll bet—a queer unnatural baby she was from the start. She had to be took, and I shouldn't wonder if it made her a little queer. Well! I'm sure . . ." She moved toward the door and looked into the hall. It was empty.

Joan felt suddenly shy. "Good-bye," she said gently. "I shan't tell a soul how you've been feeling."

Relief crept into Mrs. Winters' small opaque gray eyes. She reached up her lips and kissed Joan under the ear. "You're a good girl," she said abruptly and went away. Joan, watching her, saw her march down the street, competent, determined. She saw her meet Francis, sauntering home from high school, swinging his books idly against the fence, and stop him a moment.

"What did she say?" Joan asked him as he came in, scorn upon his face.

"Said it wasn't any way to treat my books," he replied. "Old hen! Seems to think I'm a kid."

But Joan went back upstairs smiling. Well, there it was—people! For she could understand that to speak so to Francis made Mrs. Winters whole again.

But no more than Joan could push away with her two hands her mother's death could she push away this life Rose had chosen. Spring ended. The useful dark dresses were packed into the square trunk her mother had bought for her in college and which Rose had in turn. She had seen her mother kneeling before it—the last time to fold carefully the flowery dress. Now Joan knelt, feeling herself almost in her mother's body, folding the useful clothes. She knelt, silent, taking the garments Rose piled ready on a newspaper on the floor. Where would these garments be unpacked again? She could not see—she could only feel that Rose was going very far, forever far away. She finished and stood looking down.

Rose called from her room. "Will there be room in the tray for a few more books?"

"There is a lot of room left," Joan cried back. Yes, too much room—there was pitifully little in the trunk. Days before she had gone to the attic and taken out the few dollars she had saved to buy a wedding present for Rose. But it was so hard to give Rose a gift. She wanted nothing. "I want to buy you something pretty with it, darling," Joan had pleaded. But Rose had been her soft, obdurate self. "It wouldn't be suitable, Joan. Thank you ever so much, but it wouldn't be really suitable." So it had ended by her slipping the money into Rose's hand. "Then here, darling—sometime you might want something—even something pretty."

But now though all the little store was given, she could not close the somber trunk. She must put something in—something for her mother, if not for Rose. Her mother would not let a trunk go like that, full of nothing but useful things. Every year at college when she opened her trunk she found bits of surprise her mother had tucked in a corner, a lace-frilled sachet, a pair of silk stockings—but Rose had said no silk stockings, so they had bought lisle.

The door opened silently and her father stood there, a small, solid, leather-bound volume in his hand. "Is there room for this?" he asked. He came to the trunk and stood hesitating above it. "I bought it small not to take up much room." Joan took the book from him and put it into the tray. "It's to start their life upon," he said gravely. " 'Thy word is a lamp unto my feet.' "

But she did not answer. She left him and ran into her own room and began searching in her bottom drawer wildly, her throat tight. There she kept her few precious pretty things, the things she did not often wear, the few things she had too pretty to wear yet. There was a satin nightgown of palest peach. Mary Robey had given it to her at Commencement. "Wear it on your wedding night, Jo," she had said, teasing her. Joan had put it away with the frilly sachet, half planning. Now she seized it and ran back to the trunk. From Rose's room she heard her father's voice talking to Rose. "In time of trouble . . ." he was saying. She lifted the dark useful traveling dress and thrust the peach-colored shining garment underneath. She ran back to her room and at her desk found a bit of paper and scrawled upon it, *Wear this your wedding night, darling, darling Rose.* She ran back and pinned the note upon the lace bosom of the folded gown.

It's the prettiest thing I have, she thought, and covered it quickly with the dark dress, and suddenly she missed it intolerably.

But it was a comfort to her, even though she missed it. It was a comfort to her when the grave little wedding took place in the church. The church was full of the people gathered not so much to see the marriage as to see the leave-taking. They stared at this young man and this young woman, whom they had always known and not found worthy of wonder until now. They stared at the tall, pale, delicate-faced lad whose gray eyes seemed already too sunken in his face, and at the short, plump, composed girl beside him, brown as a wren in her plain dress. Marriage was not wonderful. But it was wonderful to stare at them and imagine them crossing seas and strange countries. Nobody in the village had crossed seas except Martin Bradley and Miss Kinney and they a long time ago. Besides, they had come back and stayed just as though they had never gone.

So from everywhere people gathered to the wedding. Let it be so, the priest of God said. Let the congregation see this dedication. God would move their hearts. Joan, entering the church with Rose, saw that everybody was there. People were here she did not know. Her eyes caught the direct stare of a tall, thick-necked, oafish young man, his eyes hot and small, fiery brown under rough red hair. She held Rose's hand hard, secretly, by her side. She mustn't cry, not until after they were gone. There was Mrs. Winters, standing stout and stiff, staring out of a window. Joan understood at once that under that stare she also was saying she must wait to cry. The wedding march sounded delicately under Martin Bradley's fingers, even perhaps a little scornful. He played it carefully, like an exercise, without expression, completing each phrase and flicking it from his fingers. She paused with Rose before their father, and Rob drew away from Francis, and Rose drew away from Joan, and Rob and Rose stood together. The father, priest of God, stood tall and solemn with his duty. But Joan, sensitive to him, could feel coming from him some force of ecstasy. It shone about him, electric in his face, in his silvery blue eyes, about his white hair. He was at sacrament. His voice rose, high and clear as light, above the two at whom he gazed. He drew them out of the world into the place where he stood and the three were alone.

He said, "We are gathered together this day before God to witness the dedication of these two . . ."

Joan looked at Rose, so staid, so sure. She doesn't look like a bride at all, she thought sadly, and turning her head a little she gazed across the aisle out of the open window into a square of clear blue sky. It was June but Rose had wanted no flowers in the church, only the lighted candles, and against her brown dress she carried nothing but a stalk of lemon lilies Joan had picked for her at the last moment—the lemon lilies. She felt vaguely as though if her mother had been here it somehow could not have been like this—not grave like this. She thought passionately, I'm glad I put in my satin gown—I'm glad, I'm glad.

If this was dedication more than marriage then perhaps tonight alone when Rose lifted the gown and put it on, and when Rob saw her, in such a pretty gown, perhaps Rose would look a bride and Rob would see her so, and so it would be a wedding after all.

It was soon over, so soon over. They marched out to the music played perfectly without joy. The people crowded about the two. Here and there a little money was pressed into their hands. "Instead of a weddin' present—" "Going so far you wouldn't want glass or dishes—" Miss Kinney darted through them all and seized Rose and thrust a large album into Rose's hands. "It's my African pictures—not quite all, but many, many. I wanted to give you what I loved best—Oh, God bless you, dears! You lucky, lucky—" She kissed Rose upon the mouth, and tears streamed upon her cheeks, and suddenly standing on tiptoe she kissed Rob, and darted away. And the crowd, after a moment's astonishment, remembered she was only Sarah Kinney and forgot her.

In the night, after it was all over, Joan woke suddenly, wide awake. What time was it? After midnight, for the setting moon hung low at her window. By now Rose would have found the gown and would have put it on. She shrank away from her sudden vision of Rose standing before Rob. What would then befall? She ought to have talked to Rose. But what could she have said? What had she to tell Rose, what did she know to tell except the few hot fruitless hours with Martin Bradley?

She remembered that as they were leaving the church she had seen Martin Bradley's mother, talking to Mrs. Winters. She heard Martin's mother say, "It's a comfort to have a son like Martin. He loves his home and his mother." Her little dried mouth had folded itself complacently. Mrs. Winters had opened her lips and closed them again. She hurried forward to Rob and Rose, forcing her face into a smile at last as they stepped into the old Ford car to go to the station. They had all gone to the station. And then Rose went away with Rob, the train growing smaller and smaller until it disappeared in the west. Joan had watched it until it seemed to enter the sky. She could almost imagine a little hole in the sky where the train was gone, dragging them with it. She and Rob's mother and father had stood waiting, gazing down the small empty hole. Then they had walked home together.

"I'm sure I don't know," Mrs. Winters had said at last, sighing. She usually talked a great deal, but she had walked in silence, not seeming to notice Joan's hand slipped into her arm.

"Well! I'm sure I never looked ahead to this when I bore Rob and nursed him through a delicate childhood." She paused by the steps of her house and looked accusingly at Rob's father. "He always took after you."

The man looked at her palely. He had said nothing all afternoon, not even when Rob took his hand to say good-bye. "Good-bye, Father. Write and tell me how things do at the store." He had only nodded.

"You come in and get an eggnog," said Mrs. Winters.

They had both forgotten Joan. She watched them go into the house together and shut the door. Then she turned and walked down the quiet street, bright in the late sun, full of empty brightness. She who wanted everything out of life, what had she after all to tell Rose, she who was left behind in the village?

But I ought to have bought her some sort of book, she thought in the darkness, aching vaguely with heaviness of duty undone for her own. I ought to have, she blamed herself, I ought to have done more for Rose.

The old rich deep sense of family, of need to sacrifice for her own, welled up in her. "I can't ever do enough for them—not as much as Mother would have done." And now Rose was gone. She had thought only death could take away, but now life had taken as inexorably. Out of the five of them two were taken, one by death and one by life. I must do everything now for Frank and for Father, she thought, passionately, to comfort herself in the darkness before dawn. And the walls of this house were still safely about her.

Of these two, Francis surely needed her the more. Her father had God. If he were fed the food he liked—and she saw now what she had not seen before, that he loved his food and that even when his hand refused it, his eyes clung to the dish—if no one disturbed his papers, if no one came into his study when he was alone, if his garments were put in accustomed places where he could find them, there was nothing left that human heart could do for him. He missed no one or so it seemed.

. . . And indeed he missed no one. For now Mary was nearer to him than she had ever been. Her restless changeful body was not here to tempt and disturb him and make him want and deny together, and wonder, troubled, what a man chosen of God ought to do. St. Paul had said clearly in the Epistles, "It is

better to marry than to burn," but there was the scornful
overtone that to burn was ignoble. And he did not burn. It was
not in him to think of women. He desired to look on no
woman's face as woman. But Mary, alive, lying beside him,
kept him at war with himself—the old war in his members. So
now when Mary was not there he could think of her happily
and peacefully. God had seen fit to afflict him—blessed be
God's will.

And Joan, his daughter, ministered to his needs in the home,
almost as Mary had done. Sometimes he almost forgot Mary
was dead. He looked up from his plate to speak to Mary, but it
was Joan, so he remained silent. Nothing now stood between
him and the work. He could pursue secret mysteries. And he
could preach the gospel to the unsaved, now that the chapel at
South End was repaired—Dear Mary, who had done more
good than she knew with the money she had saved for him. He
had forgotten long since that there was any quarrel—Mary in
heaven understood him as Mary on earth could not. Mary's
hands in heaven were cool with blessing, Mary's voice in heaven quiet with approval. He could see her there, tranquil as she
often was not tranquil here. Now she understood. "For now we
see in a glass, darkly, but then face to face ... We shall know
as we are known." He withdrew happily more and more. He
moved about the house, a contented ghost. Only in the pulpit
did he become real to any human creature. Then the people
were his people, to whom he gave again what God had told
him. God, who in the Beginning—

He was growing daily into the likeness of what he longed to
be. It was daily easier now for him to deny the flesh. He had
almost conquered his hungry body. He could take a dish of
steaming prepared food into his hand and he could put it
steadily down and rise hungry from the table.

"Your pa looks to need red meat," Mr. Billings panted one
Saturday morning in July. He held out a slab of bloody steak to
Joan, who had answered the clatter of his wagon at the door.
"Veal's too weak for him, though it's summer. I looked at him
in church last Sunday when he was in his thirdly in the nature
of the Holy Ghost, and I says, 'It's red beef he needs.' Here
'tis!"

"I do thank you—you are the kindest man," said Joan gratefully.

"Leave it red in cooking," ordered Mr. Billings from his seat in the wagon. "Red's the thing—"

But after all it was Francis who had eaten largely of the steak. Her father had cut a brown edge from it and that was all, though Joan said, "Mr. Billings brought that steak especially for you, Father—he thought you looked pale last Sunday in church."

He smiled faintly. "I'd look better doubtless if Mr. Billings would come to prayer meetings sometimes—I never see him on a Wednesday evening."

"I'll have more of it, thank Mr. Billings," said Francis, pushing his plate. "Gee, I like it red, Jo! Hannah always makes it too dry—but this is swell!"

His father kept his eyes steadily upon his own half-empty plate. He won't eat himself, and he doesn't like to see other people eat, Francis thought, hating him ... "I'll have some more," he said loudly.

But then Hannah complained that you couldn't fill Frank up these days. He was growing beyond all his clothes. Joan could see that, when she reproached him for wearing his dark blue Sunday trousers on a weekday. "I can't sit down in those old striped pants," he complained. "Gosh, Joan, I haven't had a new suit since—since—"

He would not say "since Mother died." He never mentioned his mother, and if she were talked of in his presence, he went away.

Joan looked at him carefully. He was as tall as she, and broader. In this year he was in body a man, a great, handsome, dark, male creature. Across his lip, along his jaw, the shadow of his constantly shaven beard lay black. He was not an instant still. His body moved, full of grace. When he spoke, his face changed as his mother's had always done. He had her every look. But he was secret as she had never been secret. There was no knowing him.

For now Joan yearned to know him. For her own sake she yearned to care for him, to perceive his needs, that she might know him, and in knowing him find a sort of companionship. It was lonely to be the only woman in the house except old Hannah, who worked best if she were solitary. "Get out of my kitchen, Joan—your ma never cluttered under my feet the way you do. You're so big there's no gettin' around when you're here."

And all she had of Francis were the small things she could do for him, making his bed, mending his clothes, putting them into his drawers, for he was always away. He was away because of school and now because of vacation. At night if he stayed at home he fidgeted and took one book after another and went upstairs early. Bit by bit he had taken his freedom until now he went out of the house as carelessly as though no one were left behind him. But his father did not question him because on Sundays he still came of his own accord to church. If his mother had lived he would long since have cried out at her, "I'm sick of coming to church with you—" But because she was not there for him to cry against he went once a week and sat where she had been used to sit, and because his father saw him there he let him be, serene in the surety that his son was safe and saved. "I am glad Francis is settling down," he said to Joan.

Francis, sitting in the church, did not listen to anything his father said. He came to church not to listen to his father or to hear about God, but only blindly to find his mother. He often tried to remember what were the things she wanted him to do, and he could think of no command she had ever laid upon him except the wish that he come to church with her. It was the only rebellion against her that he now remembered, and he still rebelled against it and hated it, but because it was yet alive he could seem to see her more clearly in the church than anywhere else. In the home she had been so much his atmosphere that already her face was beginning to be blurred in his mind. But in church he could still see her very clearly as she used to sit, her little brown toque upon her head. For a long time she had worn a bunch of violets on her toque, at the edge on the side toward him where they lay against her curly hair. He loved the look of violets against her dark graying curly hair.

One night in the woods in early spring Fanny had picked a bunch of violets and put them against her black curls and he could not bear it. There could be nothing alike between Fanny and his mother. He would not even think of Fanny in church, where his mother was. They had nothing to do with each other. His mother was real, solid as life itself. Though she was dead, she was real, insofar as she had lived. His life was built on her life. Anything he might do was on that foundation, and where there was something, like this thing between Fanny and him, that could have no relation to the foundation of his mother, he knew it was not real and so it could not last.

But then he did not want it to last. He was wild to get away from it. If only he had some money—He had nothing at all except his bicycle, and if he sold that he might not be able to get away. He would go away without a word to Fanny. He had never promised Fanny anything at all. She burrowed her wild black head under his arm and whispered, "Sweet boy, you aren't going to leave me ever! If you leave me, I'll find you and drag you down—down—down. Promise me you won't leave me!" But he never promised. He never promised anybody anything, because he hated lies. He pulled Fanny's head back by her short curly hair, and he kissed her, but he never promised her. Women were always wanting promises—his mother, and now Fanny.

And Joan was wanting something from him, too, nowadays —talking to him, asking him questions—wanting to know things he did not know himself. How could he tell her where he was going after supper? When he ran out of the house he didn't know where he was going. Maybe he was only going down to Winters' store to see if any of the fellows were there. How could he tell her where he was going? Later, if he were restless, he'd go down to the woods at the south of the town and meet Fanny.

But he was wild to leave Middlehope. He must get away because he must get away from Fanny. When he had gone to South End that Sunday afternoon with Jack Weeks he had never dreamed of getting himself in a mess—not like this. He'd only thought of having a little fun and forgetting that his mother had to die. The house was so different and empty when she lay upstairs. He could not stay in it. There was nothing to do after church and after dinner, and Jack had said, "Gosh, there's a swell joint down at South End." So they had gone and Fanny was there dancing. She was dancing when he came in and he couldn't be sure she was not white, her color was so fair. Her skin was as light as the cream-colored rose his mother had by the porch, that same creamy yellow, and when he had touched her cheek it had the smooth firm feel of the smooth closed bud. Sometimes when his mother fixed flowers for the table he had sat watching her and playing with the roses. He knew the feel, the color . . . He hadn't meant anything except fun. But Fanny had meant everything right from the start. She had danced at him, danced toward him, danced for him. Jack Weeks had joshed him. She came up to the table and leaned over him.

"Sweet boy, what's your name? I gotta know your name." Her voice was black. No white woman had a voice like that, deep, soft, black. He could see her breasts as she leaned over him. He had never seen a woman's breasts. She wanted him to look at her. As soon as Jack had gone into the next room to play pool she had taken his arm and coaxed him. He wanted to go and watch Jack. He had no money and he couldn't play, but she was there . . . He knew enough not to go to her room. He shook his head when she wanted that. So she said, "Let's take a little walk, sweet boy. Don't you love the woods and the river? I know where there's a pool, so quiet and pretty—" So they had gone down to the wood . . . But you could hardly tell what she was. Her skin was as white as his, whiter than he was where the sun had burned him.

He hadn't ever really loved her. He loved his mother and so he knew what he felt for Fanny was not love. He wanted her and hated her, and he longed to be where he could not find her when he wanted her. But she was like earth in him. She was a sediment in him, a clay. If he could run away he would be like clear water, escaping from a muddied pool. Sometimes when he was with her, though he was deep in her, he wished he could rise straight up into the dark sky. At such times when he came home, even after he had bathed and was lying clean in his bed, he thought not of her but of flying in the sky, the clean, clean sky. To rise out of the dark, hot, close earth, away, away, into the emptiness where even big clouds had space enough to pass each other, not touching—Why did he want to be close to Fanny, touched by her hands, to touch her, to bury himself in her, and then come forth himself, loathing her touch, longing to be miles above her, above them all, in the sky?

He could not forget his mother. He wanted to forget her. But out of the darkness in the wood, out of the deep hot darkness, he saw her face, not angry, not even knowing he saw her, but simply as she had been when she was alive and everyday. And the moment her face came out of the darkness he wanted to get away, up, up, into the clear coolness of the sky, to leave everything he had ever known.

Joan drew the words out of him. She was always planning, now that Rose had gone away. She couldn't plan anymore about Rose's wedding and clothes, and now she was beginning to want to plan for him. She ought to have about six kids to keep her busy. The other night she was sitting on the porch when he came in—that was a night he'd met Fanny—and the old man was in bed. She didn't ask him where he had been, but she began talking suddenly out of the dark when he sat down on the step to get cool, and because he didn't want to go to bed yet. He had sworn to himself he would not meet Fanny again, and yet suddenly when he was with the fellows he had to go to her, even though his head cried prudently, "Better not go anymore, now while nobody knows! This is the time to stop, now when nobody knows."

But Fanny had her dark hands on him. He could feel the dark deep hold of her in him, and he went. Now it was over. He was back, and as he sat down he saw Joan.

"You not in bed yet?" he asked, making his voice gruff. If he were gruff enough she would not begin asking him anything. He had learned that trick with his mother.

"It's hot upstairs," Joan answered.

And then suddenly she began talking and her voice changed and sounded just like their mother's. Queer, he had never noticed it before. But now, not seeing her in the shadow behind the rose vine, it frightened him to hear what seemed his mother's voice.

"What do you plan for yourself, Frank? What are you doing with yourself?"

It was like his mother to throw a clear, direct question at him. He could almost hear the overtone of other words. "What are you doing with yourself—oh, my son!" His palms grew suddenly damp. Gosh, if it were true, what the old man was always saying, that the dead live and know! They had talked about that tonight down at the store. "Way I figure it," Mr. Pegler said, "we got no call to think that when the chemical combination we call the 'human body' is broken up that there's anything left. It's all chemistry, that's what I say." While they talked he scarcely listened. He was saying he never would go near Fanny again, but already his blood was plotting. He could feel it stirring about his heart. There was something about the still close heat of a summer night that made him think of Fanny. Outside the door of the store he could see the heat dancing above the road. A cicada called. In the back of his brain, underneath his attention to their talk, he felt the shapes that Fanny took, rising, writhing, secret in him, waiting. He had been glad—glad that the dead did not know, because only his mother could have discerned in him that dark stir. Maybe she did know? He had again that instant desire to spring from the earth, to rise, to leap into the sky, away, away.

"The only thing I really want to do," he answered Joan passionately out of the dark, "is to be an aviator. I want to fly."

"To fly?" Joan repeated, astonished. "But how could we ever get you to where you could?"

To his relief it was her own voice again. His mother would have answered strongly, "Nonsense, Frank!" And when he persisted she would have said, "Want it bad enough, and you'll get it."

But he had not really thought of being an aviator until this moment. He had only dreamed of being in the cool pure lonely upper air, freed from the earth like a bird. But now he planned instantly. What he had not thought of before came quick and complete in his mind.

"We could ask Martin Bradley. He was in the air service in the war. He dropped bombs."

Joan did not answer for a moment, and when she did her voice came differently again, another voice, small, breathless. "I shouldn't like to ask anything from him."

"Why? I thought you were running around with him. Gosh, I heard fellows laughing about it at Winters'."

"You let them laugh at me?" Joan asked, angrily.

"They didn't before me," he answered. "But I heard 'em snickerin'. Town like this everybody knows everything."

She did not answer. He rose at length, yawned loudly, and said in the aggrieved way he used to have for his mother, "Well, if you won't, you won't."

He went indoors and to his room and undressed. The longer he brooded, the more likely it seemed that there was no one to help him except Martin Bradley. And Joan would not ask—changeable, like all women. He thought for a while about women and how changeable they were. Even his mother had been changeable, and he learned to watch her when he wanted something so that he might know whether today were a day in which she was willing or unwilling. Only Fanny did not change —Fanny, steadily there in the wood at night, down by the small pool, down by the fallen tree, where the branches made a tent to cover them. "Sweet boy, don't you ever leave me. I'll hunt you everywhere. I'll drag you down—if ever you go away from me." He heard her voice always mingled with the rush of the stream, a soft, thick, singing voice. He broke into a sweat. He threw himself upon his face in his bed and felt himself sinking, sinking, into a black abyss. He was lost, he was lost. There was nobody to save him, no one to help him get away.

Joan, walking alone the next afternoon along the south road, passed the small stone house where Mrs. Mark lived, and heard her name called shrilly from the window.

She had always liked this little stone house. It stood apart from the village and it had a steady, aged look, its small-paned windows close against wind and storm. There used, Mr. Pegler said, to be several stone houses in Middlehope. All the oldest houses were stone, but in the boom times in the late nineties people got town notions and tore down the good old houses their grandfathers had made and built red brick contraptions. That was when the Bradleys built their big square brick house. The factory was going then and business was good. But Mrs. Mark had paid no attention to red brick and her house stood as it had for over a hundred years. Joan always stopped to look at it, and then to wave at Mrs. Mark's face at the window and maybe to turn in a minute. Now, hearing her name, she turned into the weedy patch and opened the door. She remembered not to greet Mrs. Mark, since everybody knew Mrs. Mark hated what she called "words withouten meanings to 'em." "Say what's to be said and be done with it," she always replied to a "good morning" or a "good-bye."

Now she began abruptly.

"I've waited to make sure and I'm sure. That great big young fellow that's your brother went down past this house last night and he met a girl same as I was pretty sure he did, but it was none of my business, or so I didn't hold it to be, until last night he came home late by the moon and it was hot and I had my curtain up and I could see the girl was colored truck. I've seen such before, but I don't hold with white and black mixing. I don't hold with your pa going down to preach to them nor with his son goin' to make up with them. Leave them alone!"

Joan, staring at Mrs. Mark, could not for the moment understand. Mrs. Mark's dry voice was harsh in her ears, but she was

THE TIME IS NOON

staring at the lashless lids, at the bony sharpness of the jaw and cheekbones. It was not Mrs. Mark's face at all, but a strange combination of lines, angles, shadows, planes, and the ears stood out transparent flanges.

"No use not seeing what's going on. Then you can handle it. I've seen plenty of them go by to South End—grandfather, father, son. They all go. South End is a vessel for this town of Middlehope. I won't name you no names. But I liked your mother. Get that boy out of this town. You look like your mother, only big as a house, aren't you? It's hard on a woman to be as big as you. Well, you're what you're born."

The angles and planes suddenly resolved themselves into Mrs. Mark's face again.

"Are you sure it was Francis?" Joan asked.

"Don't I know him since he was a baby?" Mrs. Mark retorted. "Get along now." She lay back and closed her eyes. "These legs of mine—I'm dead to the hips—inch and a quarter a year dies—I can tell to the month of the year what it's to be —Dead reckoning, I call it!" She chuckled, her eyes grim, and cut it off and said sharply, "Get along, child! You've got your job set out, haven't you?"

"Yes," said Joan.

Down the long road she walked in great steps, her big feet leaving prints like a man's in the deep dust. The late heat of the August sun beat down upon her, and her face was red. She could feel the heat shimmering about her flesh. But it did not matter. What could her mother have done for Francis? What was she to do for Francis? Her body shrank, and imagination withdrew ... She drew near home, and then turned away again. She could not see Francis—not yet—not until she had thought of something to do for him. He must go away, of course. He said he wanted to fly and she had said she could ask nothing of Martin Bradley.

She strode westward and turned at the railroad station, where the street was a dead end. The late afternoon train had come and gone, and ahead of her she saw a slight, tall figure. She recognized Martin. What was she doing here? She had turned westward, the thought of his name had carried her feet in the old way. She slackened her steps, panting softly. Francis had said Martin Bradley could help him—only Martin could help him.

"Martin!" she called loudly. "Martin! Martin Bradley!"

He stopped, turned, and waited for her, elegant and still. When she came up to him she saw he was smiling a little, and instantly she knew herself dusty and hot. She rushed on with determination. What did it matter how she looked?

"I—it's nothing about me. My brother Francis—was wondering if you could tell us how to get him into aviation?"

He stared at her, surprised. "One never knows what to expect of you, Joan." His voice was cool, tolerating, a little disdainful. But it did not matter. How did a man work in a city all day and come home without a particle of dust upon his neat dark blue shoulders? Her hands were dirty.

"It's not me," she said doggedly.

"Not you," he repeated, slowly. She felt him remembering her, and a sickness rushed upon her. But she stood sturdily, waiting.

. . . He had not, he thought, looking at Joan, remembered aviation in a long time. Even when he was in the clouds above the enemy fields, he did not think of flying. He thought only of the machine which he must move with precision, delicately, instantaneously when the moment came, to release those darts of death. Bair in his squadron was always groaning for rain. "God, I can't see them when there are clouds—I can't see where they go," Bair used to cry every day. But he himself had never allowed himself to think beyond that moment of aim, of release. Did the bomb strike the spot he had chosen? Then it was a bull's-eye. He had no more concern with it. It was like striking a note rightly upon the organ. One struck, heard the proper resonance, and passed on at once to the next note.

. . . "Aviation?" he repeated. "I don't know anything about aviation now."

"You were in the war," Joan urged. She passionately put from her the picture of herself kissing this man, kissing his hands, his lips, the white sides of his hair. If she thought of this she would be sick. And she did not matter now. It was Francis that mattered. This man looked old, smaller, shrunken. She was taller than he, though surely she had not been. She had not stooped to him. She must have grown. But perhaps she had stooped.

"But if you knew someone," she said, "you must know a pilot."

"I knew Bair, of course," he said, considering. "Roger Bair—

I flew with him—I don't know—I believe he's still flying. But we don't keep up. Of course I could—"

"Where could Frank find him?"

"I don't know—perhaps—"

"Where does he fly?"

"From a field outside New York."

"Give me a note to him—for Frank." She pressed him, ruthless with his diffidence. "He'd remember you—he couldn't forget. Have you a card? If you'd say, 'Introducing Francis Richards.' Couldn't you say 'For old times' sake, anything you do for him would be appreciated?'"

Now that she had asked a little, she could ask much. She compelled him by her asking, her eyes compelling him, her urgent voice, the rush and vigor of her big body. She opened her bag swiftly and found a pencil, short and stubby because she chewed her pencils. It offended him at once.

"I have a pen, thanks," he said coldly, and drew from an inner pocket a black fountain pen, bound properly in gold. The pen in his hand moved him to write. He took out his pocket-book, and from it drew a small neat business card. Upon it he wrote in fine script, *Introducing Francis Richards*. He hesitated. "I don't like to presume on former acquaintance," he said.

But now Joan would have dug out his vitals—let him give her something! He never gave her anything—

"You can put down 'highly recommended,' can't you? He's my brother and he's a very bright boy. Put it down."

She was breathing hard over his shoulder. He felt her there, large, implacable in her demand. He wanted to get home, to get away from her, to get home to his supper. She was distasteful to him. He shrank from remembering her. After a moment he wrote down carefully, *Recommended*. Why had he ever thought her like a lovely boy? She was only a woman and he hated women, especially when they had long hair. Besides, she was taller than he.

She snatched the card from him and ran home. It was in her hand, Frank's escape. She ran up the steps, shouting for him.

"He's in his room, I reckon!" cried Hannah from the kitchen. She ran upstairs and into his room. He was on his bed, staring up at the ceiling, his hands under his head, his face flushed and sullen, slack with despair. He turned his eyes toward her.

"Here," she cried. "I have it—introduction to Roger Bair, aviator! You can go right away—now!"

He sat up on the edge of the bed, his whole body lifted up, his face breaking into light. "I can go?"

"Yes," she whispered. She was suddenly exhausted. She sat down.

"I haven't any money," he said, frightened.

"I have—nearly eighteen dollars. I'll give it to you—"

She looked at him and instantly the tears rushed thick into her throat. If she had not found out, what would have happened to him?

"What's the matter?" he asked. "You're white as a sheet."

She stood up, shaking her head. No, she couldn't tell him she knew. She couldn't speak. They were too near to speak.

"Pack your things," she said. "I want you to go tonight. His plane maybe starts early in the morning. I hear them in the sky in the morning before I get up. I'll get the money."

She climbed the attic stairs quickly and opened the round-topped trunk and found the sandalwood box. It was half full of pennies and nickels and a few dimes, but there was a handful of quarters. The quarters were what she had not put into the missionary collection. Her father had given them to her each month on the day of the meeting. "Your mother used to give twenty-five cents each month at the ladies' foreign missionary society. I would like you to continue it."

"Yes, Father," she had replied.

But she had put the quarters in the box. Six of them had gone for Rose. The rest were now to go for Francis. She saw her mother's eyes twinkle from the grave.

What she could do for Francis was not done until he was away. For his sake she must send him as far as she could. He must not stay a night more, not if she could help it. She packed his garments feverishly into her own bag—fresh shirts, his ties, the dark red tie his mother loved, his garments. He came and went, his black hair tumbled, his eyes shining. But he was not gay. He was silent. His face was grave, tense, tightened. The loose sullenness of his red mouth, still full-lipped as a child's mouth, was gone, changed to some inner determined control. They did not speak. How could she speak, lest she cry out, "How could you do what you have done?" He did not speak because there was no one but himself in his mind. Everyone in

the world was below the horizon of his mind. He moved alone
in his life, to take his chance of freedom. If she had spoken he
would have shouted at her to leave him alone. He was sore
with sickness at the tangle he was in. He felt himself sweeping
out of it upon wide silver wings, into the sky.

"There," said Joan, rising from her knees. "Everything's in
but your toothbrush. Eat your supper and brush your teeth
before you go. You can catch the nine o'clock and be in New
York at eleven. You go straight to a Y.M.C.A. Tomorrow morning you can go out to the field and find him. You write me a
letter how things go—write soon, Frank—tomorrow night."

"Yeah, sure," he muttered. It did not seem possible he was
really leaving this room. In this room he had lived so long that
it did not seem possible he could sleep in another bed. But this
very night he must sleep in some strange unknown bed in the
city he had never seen. He'd never even once seen New York
and now suddenly tonight he was going to sleep there.

"You sell my bicycle," he said suddenly. "Jack Weeks wants
it. He'll give you fifteen dollars for it, maybe. But be sure you
have the money before you give it to him. He'll cheat you if he
can."

"I'll sell it and send you the money," she said steadily.

"If I don't get the job—" he said.

"If you don't get one job, you'll get another," she replied in
the same even tone. "You don't come back—you'll get the job,
though—I feel you will."

He looked at her deeply from under his black brows, questioning her. Did she know something? Who could know when
he told nothing? Even at the store when other fellows boasted
of the girls they knew, he was silent. No one ever saw him with
any girl. He was never with any girl. He never walked with any
girl. He and Fanny met and parted in the darkness of the wood
beyond old Mrs. Mark's house. Fanny went south and he went
north. He withdrew into deeper silence. Silence was safe—
never tell, and no one could know.

"Supper's ready, and your pa's waiting," Hannah's voice
shouted from downstairs.

"I'll go and tell him," said Joan. "He won't understand, but
he'll have to be told."

She went downstairs to the dining room. The table was set
for three. Soon it would be set for only two. She had an instant
of terror. How swift was change, how insecure was life! This

home had seemed for many years as permanent as her own body. Her mother, her father, Rose, Frank, herself, these five, had seemed as safe as setting and rising of sun. Her father came in at Hannah's call and she saw him freshly, sharply, in the power of the moment. He was a frail old man, and he was all that was left to her of what was the safety of her childhood.

He looked vaguely about. "Where's Francis? I'll sit down. I'm tired today." He took his seat at the head of the table, clinging to the sides of the chair as he sat.

"He's coming," she replied, and sat down. She would tell him quickly, now, before Frank came down. "Father," she said, "Frank's got a job. At least, probably, and he's going to New York."

He had begun to dip up the thick soup in the bowl before him in haste for its heat and warmth. When she said this he looked up at her, the spoon poised above the bowl.

"A job?" he repeated. "He isn't finished school. What's it mean? Isn't he going to college? It's strange if my son doesn't go to college. And I thought he'd begun to give weight to God. He's been so regular in his attendance at church I thought he was—"

"He has a job," said Joan, raising her voice and shaping each word plainly. "He wants to go. He's going tonight."

"Tonight!" the old man repeated, astonished. He paused and said at last, "I wasn't told."

"He didn't know until tonight," said Joan. "You have to take a job when you get it."

"What job?" he asked.

"Martin Bradley's helping him," she answered.

He went on with his soup in silence. He would talk to Francis, he thought to himself. He would not talk to Joan. Women knew very little. Francis would not tell her, but he would tell his father. He waited until Francis came in, and looking up, saw his son unwontedly. The boy's cheeks were very red and his eyes looked like Mary's eyes. He came in quickly, and sat down quickly and began to eat, and he said nothing, after all, to his father.

The old man felt cut off from these two young creatures. They told him nothing. They were full of plans of which they said nothing to him. He wiped his mouth and began, gently, "Joan tells me you are going away."

"Tonight," said Francis. "Hannah, bring me some raisin

bread." He was in sudden high excitement. "Hurry, old girl! It's your last chance—I'm going away."

"You're not!" she retorted, pausing at the door, and disappearing.

But he shouted after her, "I'm going away this very night—going to get a job in the big town!"

"No such thing—who'd have you?" she replied amiably, bringing in the raisin bread and plumping it down before him.

"He really is, Hannah," said Joan.

"Not to New York!" said Hannah. Her scraggy face puckered as though a thread had been suddenly drawn about the lips.

"Yes," said Joan.

"Your ma," said Hannah mournfully, "wouldn't have heard to it. She said Frank was to go to school till he was twenty-two. I mind, because she was counting the years until you'd be through, the three of you."

"I'm going to be an aviator," Francis boasted, his cheeks full of raisin bread.

"You'll break your neck," replied Hannah, unbelieving. "You can't walk downstairs without a tumble."

"An aviator!" said the old man suddenly. "I wasn't told." It came to him vaguely that they even told the servant more than they told him. Yet he had always done his best for them. He had prayed for them greatly. He had gone into deep agonies of prayer for their souls. "O, God, my Father, save my children's souls and bring them into the knowledge of Thee." They sat there, young and intolerably hard, not knowing of his yearning after them. They were always making jokes about things he did not understand. There was Francis now, his thumb to his nose, grimacing absurdly at the servant. He was not answered and he sighed. "I suppose," he said patiently, "you must do as you think best."

For the first time he definitely missed Mary. Mary would have spoken to Francis. But he could not think of anything to say. He sat over his tea until Francis had finished his dessert and rushed to his room for his things. When he saw him carrying his suitcase, he half rose from the table to help him, to show his son that he felt his going. But Hannah was ahead of him. She had perceived that this was no joke, and had rushed to pack some sandwiches.

"Give me that bag," she said sharply. "You'll be hungry

riding. It always makes you hungry to ride on the train. But your ma wouldn't have let this be. There's been no managing you since your ma went. There now—get away. I'll carry it myself. I've carried Joan's bag to go to college, and Rose's bag to go to heathendom—I'll carry it myself—"

"Father," said Joan, tucking on her hat, "don't hurry. Sit and finish your tea. I'll drive him to the train and be back—After all, it's only New York—it's not far."

"New York's only the place I hop off from," laughed Francis. He was free, he was free! Fanny maybe was waiting this very moment in the wood, down by the brook, in the warm dark summer night, but he was escaping her. He need not come back. He would never come back.

"Good-bye, Hannah—send me cookies once in a while." He gave her a great kiss.

She was crying a little, but she retorted in pretense of anger, "And where I'll send them to you, I'd like to know, and New York as big as all get out?"

"I'd smell 'em coming," he replied gaily. "Good-bye, Dad." He felt the cool dry old hand cling for a moment in his own hot palm and he dropped it quickly. "I'll write."

The old man rose and followed them wistfully to the door.

"You'll go to church, won't you?" he begged. "You've been so steady in attendance."

"Good-bye—good-bye," cried Francis.

The old man heard the flying gravel in the darkness and they were gone.

. . . "Good-bye, Frank," Joan said brusquely. The train stood ready to move. The steam blew back out of the darkness, white in the night. She looked at him, his eyes level with hers. He was as tall as she now, and his shoulders were broad as a man's. His face was a man's face in the shadows, angular, dark. There was knowledge in his eyes. She shrank away from the knowledge in his eyes. She did not want to kiss him. But suddenly he changed. There in a moment he changed. He threw his arm about her and put his head upon her shoulder and she could feel his cheek against her bare neck.

"Joan—" he said in a small voice. Why, he was afraid, she felt him afraid! How foolish she was to think he was grown up! He was only a little boy. Whatever he had done, he was only a little boy. She put her arm about his big young body and held him hard. But in a moment he had straightened himself and smiled, his eyes wet.

"It's very—it's funny to be leaving home."

"I know," she said, releasing him. She must always know exactly when to release him, that he might not feel he had given away anything of himself and so suffer.

"I'm glad to go, really," he said.

"I know," she said steadily.

The train whistle blew and he stepped upon the first step.

"All aboard," said the conductor.

"Remember," she whispered, longing to do everything for him, "remember—I'm here—always—like—like Mother was—"

For a second his face stared hard at her, then the train tore him away before she heard his answer.

Now she must find some sort of life in this empty house. It had seemed so small and crowded when they were all there. She had been used to going to her room that she might be alone to dream, to read, to write her music. It used to be so noisy a house. Her mother liked noise and took no pains for quiet. "I like to hear footsteps," she used to say. "I like to hear your footsteps everywhere—I like to think, that's Joan—there's Rose—here's my boy coming." She had complained against the father. "Why do you creep up the stairs, Paul? Why do you wear those slippers all the time? I like to hear a man's step ring hard and clear!" Once she said to Joan, out of a long silence as she sewed, "Your father's a good man, but I wish he would whistle or sing. I like to *hear* a man. I'm glad Frank's always making a noise in the house."

But now there was no need to go to her own room for solitude. In any room she could sit down and be alone. No one would come in, no voice call, unless it were Hannah's voice from the kitchen. "I declare, Joan, we'd better tell Mr. Billings not to send so much meat, even if he does give it. It's tedious eating at one hunk o' beef or pork the whole week long!"

"Yes, it is," she called back. Their voices echoed through the silent house.

There were fewer people from the church who came to see them. She seemed to remember that when her mother was there people were always coming, people asking her mother questions, running in and out. "Oh, Mrs. Richards, I did just want to ask you one more thing—would you have strawberry ice cream at the supper, or apple pie? I think men like pie, but—" "Mrs. Richards, Mother says could you come over a minute and look at Danny's throat and see if you think she'd ought to send for the doctor?" "Mrs. Richards, can you remember if the choir sang 'Lift up your heads, ye gates' last Easter or the time before?"

But few came in now. Sometimes if she were in the garden cutting flowers, one would stop. Mrs. Winters might say, "Did you hear from them this week, Joan? I had a letter last week. They've reached their station. I can't pronounce it. Rob says it's awful hot and lots of flies and mosquitoes. He's all worked up over the blind people. What does Rose say?" And she would answer, "I haven't heard lately from Rose, Mrs. Winters. Rose never was good at writing letters."

"Well," said Mrs. Winters, "I don't know, I'm sure." She sighed, hesitated, and then said sharply, "Those lemon lilies'd ought to been cut before they seed like that, Joan. It uses up the bulbs to let them seed."

"I'll cut them," Joan promised.

She watched Mrs. Winters down the street. Mrs. Winters had resigned from the missionary society. She did not even come to meetings. To Joan she said privately, "What I have to give'll go to Rob straight. I can't afford to drop my money for everybody anymore. We've got to do what we can for our own." Sometimes she worried. "I don't know, but I've a notion Rob isn't using what we send for himself. He keeps writing about the poor. I've said to him that the poor we have always with us, and what I send is for *him*. But nobody listens to me. What does Rose say?"

What did Rose say, indeed? There was so little in her letters. Her large even handwriting covered the pages and left them almost as empty as before. "The Lord blessed us this morning in the baptism of seven more, four women and three men. The work is prospering in spite of the opposition of many against us. But we remember 'Blessed are ye when men shall persecute you and—' "

She cried to Rose across the sea, "Rose, where is your home, and how does it look? Did you wear the satin gown? Are you and Rob in love with each other? Do you walk in your garden in the evening hand in hand, do you eat together and make little jokes together and forget sometimes the blind, the maimed, the poor?" But there was nothing in Rose's letters which could not be read aloud in the missionary meetings. They listened seriously, politely, at last indifferently. They were not real people, the converts. She could not see their faces. Still they were doubtless saved, those distant brown creatures.

"Things seem to be going so well," Mrs. Parsons said kindly. She was the president now, but they had always to prod her and correct her. They called out half-a-dozen times in the meeting. "We can't pass a motion without a second, Mrs. Parsons—Madame President, I mean—" "Oh, *yes*," murmured Mrs. Parsons, blushing, recalling her wandering thought. She had been happily dreaming while they were talking, dreaming about the story she was writing, a dear story about a young girl and a man—perhaps this time, surely this time . . . When Rose's letters were read she thought to herself that it would make a sweet story, the two brave young missionaries—her mind was full of their images, going hither and thither, two white and cloudlike shapes, blessing the dark, bound multitudes bending in devotion before them. Maybe if she could write it just as she saw it, this time somebody would want to publish it.

There was a murmur of assent over the little roomful of women, knitting, sewing, crocheting. Mrs. Billings always darned. "I've got such a lot of boys," she said with laughter. "They've got legs like centipedes, I think. I call 'em my thousand-leggers." Their minds were full of their handiwork. "Knit one—purl two—turn and knit two, purl one—" Mrs. Weeks whispered steadily to herself. "It's nice they're so ready to hear the Gospel," she called aloud. "Knit one, purl two—and turn—" Only Miss Kinney had no handiwork. She sat, smiling, her eyes large and shining, plucking at her lips with one hand.

"When I was in Africa," she would often begin, but almost immediately one of the women would interrupt vigorously, "Madame President, don't you think we ought to take up the matter of the next bazaar? Our budget—" To a neighbor she would whisper, "You've got to shut Sarah Kinney off, or we'd never get through."

And on the old, comfortable, married faces there was the same expression, "Poor thing—but you've got to shut her off— she's getting so queer!"

Yes, Rose's letters read beautifully at the missionary meetings. But they broke no silence in the house. Francis had scrawled his first letter.

> DEAR JOAN.
> I got a job, but no flying yet. I'm an errand boy and I have to do anything they tell me, but yesterday they let me help clean a plane. If I keep on right I'll maybe learn to fly some day. They tell me everybody starts like this at the bottom. Send the bicycle money to me here. I have a room across the street with a fellow I know here. I am okay.

The silence in the house grew deeper. What was there now for her to do in this house? She polished the tables and the chairs and changed the flowers every day, and learned to be troubled by the shadow of dust. It became important to her if a curtain hung awry or if a book were not straightly placed. But no hand except the wind's displaced a curtain, and no hand except her own touched anything. Her father moved from study to dining room and thence to sleep. If he went for an instant into the parlor, it was never to remain. It was to wait while she found his hat, to rest a moment when he returned, and his coming and going left nothing.

Once or twice Ned Parsons called. "Joan, want to go to the picnic Thursday?" Did she want to go? That first summer she had gone to everything. So she went once. But they were all younger than she, they seemed far, far younger. In this short time new boys and girls had grown up and she was too old for them. She felt very old. They came to her politely. "Miss Richards, will you have potato salad?" "Miss Richards, do you mind if we climb the mountain?" She might have cried back at them, "But I'll go with you—I love climbing." But there was Netta Weeks to warn her, poor ghastly Netta Weeks, trying to be one of them, trying to be noisy and gay, refusing to sit among the older folks, insisting on playing games and following the young couples about. Joan, watching, was stabbed with their contempt, their helpless toleration. Behind their cold tolerating young faces they were gnashing their teeth to cry to each other, "The silly old maid—why doesn't she leave us alone?"

"No, of course I don't mind," said Joan smoothly. "I'd rather stay and talk to your mothers anyway."

She would not walk with Ned Parsons. Ned would not do—not any longer. She wanted now to hear the authentic voice of love. His pale knobby clerk's face, his protruding eyes and weak romantic gaze—no, not Ned—not Ned, who barely reached her shoulder.

"I'm tired, Ned," she said quietly. "Why don't you ask Netta? Netta!" she called with determination. Let her deliver the children at least. "Netta, come and walk with Ned for me! I'm tired."

Netta came instantly, her round foolish spectacled face coy with smiles and seeming reluctance.

"Oh, I don't want to take your young man, I'm sure," she cried, laughing loudly.

She had been shy of Joan ever since that night in the darkness. Now they called often to each other at a distance: "Hello, Netta!" "Oh, hello, Joan—come and see me sometime." And Joan said, "You come over, too!" But they had never come to any meeting. She looked at Netta quietly and gravely as she laughed her foolish laughter.

"He's not mine," she said simply. She watched them go away, Netta already clinging to Ned's arm.

Why not? she thought. They're both searching for it.

She went home alone. Searching—everybody was searching for it. She entered the empty house in the late afternoon. It was intolerably empty, intolerably silent. There was no life anywhere—no life, except in her own body. She came upon herself suddenly in the long mirror at the end of the hall. There she was, big, strong, ruddy with maturity, ready.

I've never had even one proposal, she thought, staring at her body. She was heavier than she had been, her breasts were round, her mouth was full and red. I don't even know a man. How could he ever find her here? But here she must stay, here in this house, so long as her father lived. She must take care of his old body, feed and clothe him and keep him warm, while he took care of his soul. It was all the life she had. She was tied to him. She went to her room and took off her coat and her hat and dress and lay down upon her bed and fell into a terror of longing.

Staring up at the blank ceiling, in the blank silence of the house, she felt her body strain against her. It clamored against her, hot with lonely desire.

I'd marry, she thought desperately, I believe I'd marry almost anybody—except Ned Parsons. I want my children.

Now the silent and empty house became full with her own longing and restlessness. It was no longer important to her that a curtain was blown askew or that flowers faded in a certain bowl. Who saw these things except herself, and what activity was this for her clamoring body? She was burned by a hundred small irritations.

"I don't care what we eat, Hannah!" she cried into Hannah's astonished face.

"You needn't bite my head off?" Hannah said coldly.

"Oh, Hannah, I'm sorry!" she begged wildly. "I don't know what's the matter with me these days!"

"Well, I'm sure—" muttered Hannah, stabbing a hairpin through the knot on top of her head. "You never did have Rose's disposition," she added.

"Father, let's go somewhere—let's take a vacation!" she begged.

He was walking quietly up and down the porch. On rainy days like this, when it was not parish day, he walked up and down sixty times for exercise. He disliked the rain as intensely as a cat. He disliked to feel the soles of his feet damp. If it were his day for chapel, he went steadfastly out, carrying his large black umbrella. It was his duty. But it was pleasant if the rain did not fall on such a day. He mentioned it with gratitude in his solitary morning prayer if God sent rain on a home day.

Joan was sitting on the balustrade under the deep eaves, staring into the rain. He paused at her cry and noted mentally that he was on twenty-three. "A vacation?" he repeated. "I've never had a vacation."

"I know," she said, "so let's have one."

Twenty-three—twenty-three . . . "From what?" he asked.

"Work," she answered gaily.

"What would I do?" he asked.

"Oh, walk, talk, see something different!"

He began on twenty-four. "I'd have to pay for a supply," he said when he passed her again. "Besides, I feel no need for change. My work provides me with all I need." He began twenty-five. When he passed again she was gone.

She was gone, and when she came down she had on her mackintosh and her old blue hat. She strode off into the rain. It was raining so hard that in a moment she was sheeted with silver and the water ran into her shoes and little separate streams beat against her face. She pressed her body against the rain steadily, lifting her face against it. It tingled upon her lips, stinging like a kiss hard upon them. She fought against wind and rain gladly, wearing her body out, wild with restlessness. She was too restless to think. She could not think. She could only feel. Striding through the rain, her feet upon the wet grass of the fields, upon the moss under the trees shining in rain, her mind was full of pictures. Francis and that girl—Martin meeting her in the dell—the shapes of love. She drove herself until in fatigue her mind grew empty and then in the wet twilight she turned toward home.

When she came in, her father was waiting for her in the dining room. The night had turned cool and Hannah had built a fire and set the table. He sat by the fire, his large pale hands held to the warmth, transparent in the blaze. He looked up at her solemnly.

"You're very wet," he said.

"Yes—I'll only take a moment to change. Don't wait."

She was so tired she could be patient with him again. For of course he would wait without a word, inexorably, stubbornly gentle, until she was in her place. He held her by his uncomprehending gentleness. When she was in her place, when everything was as usual, he would be satisfied. Then he would bow his head and give his usual thanks to God.

Oh, but there was nothing now anywhere, she cried in her fresh impatience. For weariness would not last in her great strong body. Sleep came, deep, healthy, and she was hungry and ate heartily and her body was restless again and her mind hot with restlessness.

In the church on Sunday morning she held herself desperately in her seat. But she wanted to spring up, to dance, to sing, to run, to be mad and foolish, to rush down the road and find a companion, to cry to any strange man she saw, "It's a heavenly day, the trees are gold, the air is wine—come, come with me!" They'd run, they'd walk, they'd shout. She bent her head over her folded hands and smiled. Her father was praying, "Descend upon Thy people, God." She smiled, flaunting God—not God, not God this morning! She stood quickly when the hymn was announced, leaping to her feet.

"There is a fountain filled with blood," she sang carelessly, letting her big voice ring out, hurrying them all a little, hurrying Martin Bradley. She could see him glance at her in the mirror above his head. He clung with steadiness to the tempo, annoyed with her. But she was full of wild mischief. She wanted to burst from her skin, she wanted to tease, to harass, to be madly willful. She let out her voice with laughter, hurrying him, throwing them all a little askew between the organ and her rollicking voice. They sang bewildered, not knowing exactly what was wrong. She sat down and shut the book quickly and bowed her head for the benediction, her heart dancing down a sunny road. Oh, something must happen, she'd make something happen! She rose from the pew and turned about and stood waiting, smiling a little, staring at them all as they gathered their books, their coats. She'd make something happen.

Across the aisle her eyes fell upon a thick, tall young man. It was the oafish young farmer she had seen at Rose's wedding. She smiled at him suddenly, brilliantly, wickedly, straight into his small hot brown eyes. He flushed red under his red hair. His huge hands twisted his stiff straw hat around and around upon his bosom. His mouth hung a little open. He moved toward her.

"I've wanted to speak to you," he said. He had a slow thick voice and the words came quickly from his big mouth. His lips were stiff and thick and pale.

"Why don't you then?" she said willfully. Oh, she wanted to tease, to harass, to vent herself upon someone!

"I didn't know if you wanted it," he answered after a moment, staring at her.

"I don't seem to mind," she replied, still smiling. At once she hated his thickness, she immediately disliked the raw redness of his skin. But she went on smiling recklessly into his hot brown eyes. She wanted something, anything, to happen.

He took another step toward her. He muttered at her, "If I should come to your house tonight after milking, would you sit a while with me out on the porch?"

"I might," she replied, laughing.

He nodded and stalked into the aisle. She watched his broad back, his thick upper arms bursting out of the cheap blue suit. Above a stiff white collar his neck was red as beef and his head was straight and unshaped, like a block upon his square huge shoulders. His ears were close to his head. They were thick and rather small. She felt a little sick. But she thought rebelliously, Oh, well—it will be something to do tonight, at least. She was full of willfulness against everything as it was.

To this empty ordered house Bart Pounder brought himself solidly.

She had, without knowing it, come to live in the smoldering stillness, in feeling thought, in long hours alone when she sat with a book in her hands, not reading. The old man lived his angelic, attenuated life alone and she lived her life alone in aborted moods. She lived out of one mood into another, none fully understood. She was not discontented so much as stopped in herself. There was no completion in her. Nothing seemed worth doing for its own sake. Surely everything she had to do ought to lead into some larger reason. But nothing led on. Even though she swept the house and filled the vases, though she filled the old silver sugar bowl with the late red roses and set it upon the hall table before the long mirror, for whom was it done? She had her own instant of ecstasy, cut off and unfulfilled. It was not enough. It was not enough to compel Hannah.

"Hannah, see what I've done! Look at the roses!"

"They'll be dropping before the day's done—those red roses never have held together—quick to blow and soon to die, always."

It was not enough to compel her father. "Father, the roses—" His pale eyes searched patiently. "Here, Father, by the mirror—"

"Yes, yes—they are very pretty," his pale eyes drifting away again.

It was not enough.

To this newcomer she was saying eagerly, "The roses have been lovely, lovely—Only the rose beetles were so troublesome." He listened, staring at her hard.

"I'll spray them for you next spring," he said.

He was staring at her hands, at her throat, her breasts. She felt his hot simple stare and pulled her skirt lower over her knees, not knowing she did, and folded her arms across her bosom.

How did one talk to an oaf? "Have we ever met?" she asked brightly. "Where do you live?"

"Up the road a-ways, west," he answered. His voice was hard, brassy, and it seemed to come from him ungoverned. He paused between phrases, waiting for the next phrase to shape itself. His lips were stiff and hard, not used to forming words, dry and thick, except when he spoke and then moisture gathered at the corners slightly. He did not wipe it away. "We've not met—that is, not spoken. I come to church to see you, though. I've come a long time." He paused, tried to thrust his hands into the pockets of his cheap dark Sunday suit and failed. His thick thighs strained at the seams of the cloth. "Folks go to church over to Chipping Corners. I changed after I seen you once—saw you once when I was driving through town to sell a yearling bull calf."

"Did you?" She laughed, a little amused. Imagine his coming to church Sunday after Sunday to see her! A wisp of warmth curled into her amusement, a flicker of coquetry. This huge, simple creature was a man, after his sort. He caught the brief laugh and drew nearer to her upon the step where they sat. He fixed his small deep-set eyes upon her hands, clasped about her knees. He moved his own hand and let it lie, as if carelessly, upon the step between them. She could feel his thought—his simple, one thought. Soon he would lay his hand upon hers. Why would he have planned, come to see a girl, except for some simple and direct satisfaction? She warded him off. She did not move, but she threw gaiety into her voice, she let mockery fly into her eyes, bitterness in her laughter. "And I didn't know! All that faithfulness—wasted!"

He waited, immovable while she laughed, and when she was silent, he said, "I figure it wasn't wasted. It was only the beginning of something I'd set myself to do. I figured someday I'd sit on the porch like this with you. And here I am."

He sat in vast waiting. She looked at him now, afraid. "I figured," he went on in his slow stiff-lipped way, "the day would be when I'd lay my hand on your hands—like this." She watched his enormous hand move and motionless she watched it descend and cover her two clasped hands. "Like this," he said again.

She felt his hand hard and stiff against her tender flesh. She looked at his hand. It was broad and thick, the fingers thick to their tips, the palm meaty. The little finger was sharply bent as though it had been broken.

"Did you break your little finger?" she asked aloud. Why did she ask when she did not care? The hand filled her with repulsion.

"No," he said. He did not remove his hand. He held it there, thickly covering her hands, heavy as a stone upon her two hands. "It's work that's done it—nothing but work. This other one's the same." He held up his other hand to show her and she saw it in its hugeness. She could see even in the dim light the large freckles upon the forearm, where his sleeve was too short, the rough red hair upon the flesh. Upon the back of his hand there was this wild red hair. She shrank under the cover of his hand and tried to shake it off. But there it clung, pressing down.

"Take your hand away," she said violently. "I don't like to be touched." He waited an instant, and then he took it away without reply. She felt him waiting. He took it away, but he was waiting. He would surely put it there again. She stood up abruptly. "I must go in now," she said quickly. "I have some things to do."

He rose clumsily, his body huge and thick, taller even than she was. He stared at her stubbornly, and for a moment again she was afraid of him. But he said calmly enough, "Good night, then. I'll come again—if you say so."

"Good night," she said, already at the door. "Good night—"

She ran to her room without looking back. She would never say he was to come back, never! It was good to be back in the house, in this lonely house. Where was her father? She ran downstairs again and knocked at his door.

"Yes?" he called. "Come in."

She went in quickly. "Father?"

"Yes," he replied. He was sitting in his old Morris chair by a small dying wood fire, his hands folded in his lap. He had on his old patched plum-colored study gown, and above his thin face his white hair stood a little disordered, so that she knew he had just finished his evening prayer. He turned his mystic eyes toward her.

"Father," she said, "I just—I suddenly felt a little lonely."

She had never said such a thing before and he looked at her uncomfortably. . . . She looked like her mother, he thought in alarm. Mary had been used, when she was younger, to come running into his study like this at night after he supposed she was in bed and asleep. "Paul, Paul—I'm so lonely." "Lonely? But I am here, Mary." "I can't feel you near me, Paul. You seem somewhere else. You live away from me so." "I must be about my Father's business, Mary." . . . He felt his daughter's hand on his arm and he was very uncomfortable. It was a light touch, but it had the hot shaking quality that Mary's had sometimes—especially when she was young.

"Are you ill, Joan?"

To his horror she fell upon her knees and placed her face upon his arm. He did not move. He felt her shake her head. "Lonely, lonely," he heard her whisper. He must, he felt, do something. Diffidently he put up his other hand and touched her hair once. It sprang warm and curled about his fingers and he took his hand away quickly. He must think of something to say.

"Would you—do you think you'd like to help me at the mission? It would give you something to do."

But who could ever understand women? She lifted her head sharply and gave him a long look, and then she began to laugh, so long, so loud, until tears were in her eyes. He waited, pained. He had wanted to help her. At last she stopped laughing and wiped her eyes.

"I'll help you," she said. "Yes, perhaps it will give me something to do. . . . Good night, poor dear."

She bent and kissed him, a touch upon his pale high forehead, and went away. She was better, he felt happily. The laughter had done her good, though he could not understand it. But if it had done her good—he believed he had once heard a doctor say that laughter was medicinal. But why "poor dear"?

What was it Martin had promised and never given, what had he touched in her and not taken from her, what stirred in her and was not completed? Something now bloomed in her, lonely as a vivid flower in a field, solitary of its kind. She came to a sort of maturity, and this man who beset her doggedly had no more to do with it than a bee, stumbling upon a vivid flower, forcing its petals into a troubled readiness, because the hour was come. For he made no secret of why he came. He came each Sunday, doggedly, now without asking. Each Sunday, she perceived, he came with his plan of one more step he would take toward her. Having touched her hands at first, he took her hand the next time and held it. This, his way said, he had a right to do. Having held her hand, the next time he put his hand upon her waist. She drew away, sick, yet stirred by each fresh movement.

If she grew angry at him, and she was always angry at him for each fresh outrage of her, he waited or he made his answer through stiff, unmoving lips. "Don't touch me like that, Bart Pounder!" she cried at him, her voice low. Of course her father would not hear in the study, who never heard anything.

"No?" Bart answered, and did not move. Then she would seize his great hand and throw his arm from her as though it were a snake. He let her throw it, but before he went away it would be about her again. And then, feeling the heavy dogged clasp, she might be silent, she might sit shuddering and stirred within the clasp. So one night he would touch her breast. So one night he would kiss her lips. She knew the way, but not the end. When he had kissed her, then what was the end?

In the night when he was gone she awoke, cold and hot, to ask herself the end. She was afraid in the night, in the empty house, with only the old man lying lightly asleep, to be near. Rose and Francis and her mother—they were all as though they had never been. She was alone and there was no one near —no one to whom heart could cling. She wanted her own. Oh, where were her own? Around her life was deep, tremendous, remote, silent. She moved alone in all the silence, she who loved warmth and nearness and the safety of human closeness. She would grow older and older, like Miss Kinney, waiting . . . waiting. Old people lived forever while the young waited. She was wicked. She was not waiting for her father to die. She loved this house, the village, the people she had always known. Oh, but they had never known her. They had seen her growing up, a tall child. "How you grow, Joan! My, you're going to be a big girl!" Yes, she had grown and grown beyond them all. They knew her no more. They lived on in their little houses contentedly but she wanted everything. What could be the end?

Then came November. She could not stay within the confines of the house. The house was full of herself. In whatever room she sat, it became full and bursting with herself, and she could not stay for her restlessness. The dreaming of the autumn was over. The dying heat of Indian summer was finished in the still evenings.

And she could not stay in the confines of the garden. The garden she had cultivated was dead and finished and in the November sunshine the shadow of the church steeple fell sharp across the frost-gray grass. But abroad in the woods along the road, there was wild beauty. There was madness in the woods, there was fullness in the red apples and in the dark wild grapes upon the stone walls, and in falling nuts and late yellow pears. In the energy of every color edged in the sharp clear cold she was whipped into intensest restlessness.

She went to her father. "Give me the work you wanted me to have. I'm ready. I want something to do." She seized the excuse to get away into the fields, to walk miles along the dusty gorgeous roadsides to South End. "I need help with the young people," her father said. He spoke with gentle excitement. . . .

He would not of course tell Joan, but this was an answer to prayer. He would not tell her because once when his son Francis was little more than a child, and he had said when he did something—he had forgotten now what it was—"It is an answer to prayer," the child had answered violently, "Then I won't do it." The young were so difficult to understand. And they had been such a problem to him at the mission—those large dark young men and the dark painted girls. He was helpless before their singing. They could take a hymn straight away from him, as they did "Oh, Beulah Land" the other day, and so with the singing of it that it ceased to be a hymn. They became stamping feet and clapping hands. There was one girl especially who snapped her fingers like a horsewhip at every intensified beat. Once she had leaped to her feet and had begun to sing alone a song he had not announced or had not even heard of. "Singin' with a sword in mah hand, Oh, Lawd." She sang it with her hands on her hips, swaying as though she were dancing. He had pronounced the benediction hastily and come away. "The Lord is not pleased." But perhaps if Joan came, God would use her. He looked toward her with sudden dependence. She was so large, so strong. The young were so strong. He felt he would like to put out his hand and touch her arm. But he had never done that sort of thing and so he did not. He merely smiled delicately, without quite meeting her eyes.

"You will see what is needed," he murmured. "When you get there you will see what is to be done—I feel sure you will be guided." He gazed wistfully into space.

Upon a glowing afternoon she walked to South End. She wanted to walk, to walk along the rough road, searching passionately for every beauty. There was an immense dead oak once struck by lightning wrapped like a blazing tower in crimson woodbine. Here upon a rock a tiny flat vine crawled like a small scarlet serpent. The sunshine poured down from a golden heaven. The far hills were blue. In the streets of South End the sunshine glittered on every tin can and bit of broken glass and red ray of dress. They loved red here. The babies wore red slips and the young girls wore red blouses and red ribbons in their tightly braided hair. Red geraniums bloomed in rusty cans, and late zinnias shone cerise and scarlet from careless seeds.

Into the chapel they crowded, dark skins, red ribbons, rolling restless black eyes. They gathered, black skin, brown skin, skin of amber. They called zestfully to one another. They did not quiet until her father began to speak. Then they listened in a stillness that was not quiet. It was silent as a storm is silent before wind breaks. When her father announced the hymn, a small brassy organ began to throb and instantly the singing burst forth, loud, syncopated, full of wild music. "Like a river glorious is God's perfect peace," they sang, swaying, moving, surging.

... But there was no peace—they wanted no peace. Oh, who wanted peace? She caught the excitement in her own blood—no peace, no peace—how could there be peace if one were alive? Only let life flow in upon her—let all life come, O God! She flung out her heart in the cry. Suddenly she thought of Francis. Was that life, too? He had found a sort of life here. She looked over the crowd quickly. No, she was glad she knew no one among them all. Suddenly she felt she could do nothing for them—nothing for any of them. Let them live—let them live—let all life go on. She did not listen to anything her father said.

When he sat down she rose and went out quickly. Behind her the people crowded out of the chapel, hurrying to laugh and to talk. They overtook her and she saw that they had taken off their shoes and were walking barefoot down the dusty road, carrying their tied shoes in their hands. They were laughing, and bursting into fragments of singing, and by twos and threes they stopped at cheap ruined houses. She went on out of the town and into the country road. On her way home Mrs. Mark tapped on the windowpane and she went in.

"Where've you been?" said Mrs. Mark from the bed.

"I told Father I'd help him at the mission—but I think I just can't," she said. She couldn't keep from answering Mrs. Mark straightly.

"What you want to help for?" said Mrs. Mark. "They don't need help—they have a grand time. Go on home and find something to make you half as happy as they are."

She looked at Joan crossly. She could no longer move her right leg. Now, before she could get onto her crutches, she must shift her leg like a log with both hands.

"Get along and do as I say," she said.

"Yes, Mrs. Mark," said Joan.

She hesitated, hating as she always did to leave a creature so helpless. "Go along," said Mrs. Mark. "I've got to get up and stir up my supper," No one ever saw Mrs. Mark get up. And so Joan went away. She went away down the road, the sun smoldering crimson among the vivid trees.

The air was completely still, cold without chill. Next Sunday, she thought suddenly, it would surely be too cold to sit upon the porch. She would have to light the fire in the square sitting room and let him come in. She had not wanted him to come in. One excuse after another she had made to keep him waiting.

She did not want to open the door of the house to him. But since it was so cold now, if he came into the front sitting room, and if she said to her father, "Come in to the fire, where we are," if her father sat there, then the man could not touch her lips. He would have planned to touch her lips. She withdrew from the imagination of his thick pale mouth, wind-cracked, dry. She felt again the hard coarse pressure of his great arms about her. That was last time. . . . But if her father were there, she would be safe. But perhaps she did not really want to be safe. She pushed away decision recklessly. Whatever came, let it come.

Yes, Mrs. Mark was right. She must tell her father that she could not help him—not at the mission. The people were stronger than she. They would sweep her into themselves, as they absorbed into their own richer rhythm and tunes of the hymns. If she stayed among them, if she were often near them, hearing them sing, soon she would be singing with them and not against them. She laughed softly, remembering, walking down the road alone, with what determination her father had held to time and tune, his look absorbed, his thin, high voice steadfast against the rush of throbbing other voices. Through the deep November dusk she heard again the beat and rhythm, the beat and crying, of the dark crowd. Her body fell into the measure of the beat and movement as she walked, and in her ears her blood pulsed—no use, no use for her to try to save someone when she could not save herself. She wanted earth, not heaven; life, not salvation from it. Her feet stepped the dusty country road to the tune of old desire. She was as light as air, striding through the potent windless night.

... She became aware of a horse's cantering step, and she paused and stood aside among the weeds and the rhythm paused a moment in her, waiting. She looked through the dusk and saw an awkward sturdy man astride a thick-boned farm beast. She knew at once who it was.

"Well, look who's here!"

It was the phrase he used every time he saw her. She drew back a little farther from his path.

"Good evening, Bart!" she answered. She was the more fastidious in her own speech because his speech repelled her. But he did not notice her withdrawal. He leaped down from his horse and came near. In the twilight she noticed suddenly, unwillingly, upon the open roadway, the fields about them, that he looked better than she had ever seen him. He wore his work clothes, blue jeans and a coarse blue shirt open at the collar, the sleeves rolled above his elbows. The twilight hid his stiff dry lips, his thick nose, squat along the bridge. There was only his outline—his square shoulders, his thighs, his limbs. He looked huge, magnificent as a bull. The turn of his head was set well upon his strong thick neck. Here, where he belonged, he was a handsome man, a fine animal. When he came near her she could smell an odor of hay and earth—a clean, hearty smell. She leaned away from him, breathless.

"Where you been?" he cried at her. "It's luck, meeting up with you like this!"

She felt his instinctive movement to touch her, to put his arms around her waist. She felt his arms about her waist. Now his hand was creeping toward her breast. He had not touched her breast before. She stood still, despising herself, and unwillingly longing for his hand to touch her breast. Yet when the touch came, she sprang away from it.

"I must go home," she said, her voice stifled, her blood roaring in her ears. "I must go home. Let me go!"

"Well, well, well!" he exclaimed in mock surprise. "Who's holding you?"

"You are," she answered desperately. But she had not moved.

"Who—me?" He pressed her breast slowly.

"Yes," she whispered, sick, and longing.

He dropped his hand suddenly.

"Who—me?" he said again and laughed.

She turned her look on him and unwillingly she saw him, a big handsome man, handsome in his own place. Without a word she started to run into the dusk, desperately, home.

Inside the front door she stood motionless, her hand upon the door she had just closed. The house was utterly silent about her. The familiar rooms, the furniture, the clock in the hall, everything was as she had always known it. It was intolerably still, intolerably shabby, empty, hopeless. Under her stare the familiar rooms grew strange and aloof from her.

"How could I let him touch me?" she asked herself wildly. The house remained silent about her. She was shut off from all of life in this house.

"Hannah!" she screamed suddenly. "Hannah—Hannah!"

From the attic Hannah's voice dropped down thin and distant. "What you want?"

"Where's Father? Isn't he home yet?" She had no one else left.

"No, not yet."

"I'm going to find him," she cried.

She darted from the house again, and at the instant his old car drew up at the door and he stepped backward out of it his absurd careful way. He was never quite used to the car.

"Father—Father," she cried at him.

He turned his head. "Yes, what is it, Joan?" He began collecting his books.

She wanted to go to him and lean against him. She wanted to feel someone near her. She had never so leaned against him, but being now impelled by need she took his hand. "I'm glad you're home. I was worrying a little."

"But I am not beyond my usual hour," he said mildly, in surprise. "I am not usually home before six. I remained to speak to the people."

His hand hung in hers, delicate, bloodless, cool.

"Anyway, you're home now," she said breathlessly. "Come in

to supper. I'll open a jar of the red cherries. Let's light the fire. Maybe there's a letter from Rose or maybe even Frank."

He did not reply. He wanted to take his hand away, but he did not wish to be unkind. He let it lie one instant uncomfortably and then withdrew it. She did not prevent him. It was impossible to cling to that hand.

In the night she woke. It was raining. The night had turned warm and wet and still. There was only the soft downward rush of rain. Suddenly she felt safe again, safe and secure, after all, in this house where she had been born. The rain shut her in, the rain held her safe against intrusion. She slept deeply, and in the morning she woke, quieted. The day was slumberous with rain and quiet, and day after day the week passed. She sat by her window, sewing. She looked over all her dresses one by one. She still needed nothing new—there was no reason yet for buying anything new.

She woke on Saturday morning to sunshine, to scold herself and to laugh with relief. Tomorrow she would tell Bart never to come again. She did not want anything from him. She had so much. She was very silly. For they all needed her as much as ever. Rose had said in her very last letter:

> Please buy me two pairs of black stockings and a paper of pins and three spools of white cotton thread and some needles. Such little things we cannot buy here. We are now wearing native garments, but the needles are blunt and short and hard to hold. You will rejoice with us that on Sunday four more, three women and one man, were received—

She would buy the things today. She would find Rob's father in the store and say, "They go all the way to China, Mr. Winters, to Rob and to Rose." He would want to put in something—he was so kind and gentle and always wanting to do nice things, even if they were rather silly things. He kept giving Mrs. Winters bottles of perfume, or when he went to New York to get his stock he would bring her home a flashy ring or a glass necklace. Mrs. Winters grew so provoked with him. If the jewelry cost too much she would say plainly, "I'm going to send it right back, Henry Winters. Me with earrings!" Sometimes she could only get credit, and then she had to buy whatever she could, so she bought flat silver. She had a great deal of flat silver.

But certainly Mr. Winters would want to put in a gift for Rose. Joan's mind ran over the big one-room store. What would be nice? Rose had never mentioned the peach nightgown. Joan, remembering, had a pang of missing it still. It was so pretty. She would probably never have another so pretty.

She leaped from her bed and was suddenly gay. The house was itself again. Rose and Francis were alive, needing her—her dear old father. She was gay with him at breakfast and laughed when he looked at her in bewilderment.

"I'm only making fun," she cried, and dropped a light kiss upon the ends of his white hair. "The rain's over!"

"Your mother used to have days," he remarked with mild patience.

Her heart shadowed. "There—I'll stop teasing you," she said remorsefully.

Well, it didn't matter. She must get the things for Rose. She would buy a little gift, too, to put in. She had several dollars saved. She could get some ribbon—but there they wore native dress. Why didn't Rose tell her how they looked? Or perhaps a pair of silk stockings. It was impossible to believe that Rose did not secretly adore silk stockings. She put on her hat and her old brown coat and went down the street, singing under her breath.

In the store at the far end, among the cotton stuffs, she saw Ned Parsons and turned her head. She did not want to bother with him today, but probably she would have to—he'd call or come bustling up. But he did not. When she glanced toward him he seemed to be absorbed in a list he was checking. He did not seem to see her. She searched for Mr. Winters, and found him at last in the stock room, surrounded by half-opened packages and boxes. He stood tall and narrow, his too narrow shoulders drooping about his narrow chest. It was known that he was "consumptive" and only Mrs. Winters' constancy and determination had kept him alive. Left to himself he would not have touched milk or butter or eggs. But twice a day she came to the store with a tumbler of eggnog and stood watching him while he drank it. Everybody knew that once, when he was young, in desperation he had poured it into a bale of new white cotton sheeting while she was looking about, but she had caught him because he had poured it too quickly. The stuff had slipped down the sized cloth in trickles of yellow. She had never forgotten it. "The wicked waste!" she had cried hundreds of times in remembering it. Hundreds upon hundreds of times she had stood watching him drink the eggnog down, never trusting him. Once goaded by the smiles of clerks he had muttered, "You don't need to stand there—seems as if all the times I've drunk it would count."

But she had retorted, "I've never felt I knew exactly what you'd do next, Henry Winters! If it wasn't for me, you'd be in your grave." His life, saved thus daily, belonged to her.

"Mr. Winters!" Joan called across an aisle, beaming at him. "I've come to get some things for Rose. I thought you'd be interested."

His face cracked into wrinkles, and she warmed to see him. He was so kind!

"Well now, come along and let's see." He was all excitement at once, his bony body moving in little convulsive darts of overflow. "I'm just unpacking some perfume. It so becomes a lady—like a flower scented, I always think."

"But to send so far? A bottle might break."

"Yes—yes—stupid of me. Well now, let me think. A brooch? I have some nice costume jewelry." Why did Mr. Winters seem so excited today? He fumbled in a package and brought out a pasteboard box and opened it. His hands were trembling, and he did not quite meet her eyes. "Look, it's pretty stuff, isn't it? See, here's a garnet set. I'm partial to garnet. This is amethyst —glass, but it looks real, doesn't it? This is pretty, isn't it—and these blue beads." He touched the glass beads with a long, delicate forefinger, the nail blunt and broken.

"Well," said Joan, hesitating. It was so hard to tell him Rose never wore jewelry. "I think," she said warmly, not to hurt his feelings, "if we chose some silk stockings—They're easy to send."

He closed the box at once. "You're right," he said quickly, and hurried ahead of her.

In the store, people were beginning to come for their day's shopping. Since it was Saturday, wives were in from the country, the older ones in calico waists and dark skirts and little stiff hats, and the young women in wash dresses, the sort Mr. Winters hung on a rack and sold for a dollar. Three or four of them stood by the rack, turning the dresses eagerly. She could hear them. "There—that's real pretty." "I don't care for checks, though—looks like apron stuff." One of them, a plump squat woman who had a coarse pretty face, said, "Yes, when I'm dressed up I like to feel dressed up. Joe likes something fancy on Sunday, too—he's partial to lace." She listened, watching them, smiling yet feeling them strange to her. They would be shy of her because she was educated, because she was the minister's daughter. She said impulsively to Mr. Winters, "Wait on them first—I'm in no hurry."

"No indeed," he said heartily, although any other day he would have obeyed her. What was the matter with him today? She smiled at them when he went back unwillingly toward them. But they did not smile back. Their eyes met hers blankly and they took her courtesy, not recognizing it. She waited, foolishly hurt.

. . . Perhaps, she told herself afterward, it was because she was already hurt that it seemed to her that when Mrs. Bradley came in a moment later she thought her cool. What did it matter whether Mrs. Bradley was cool or not? What if Mrs. Bradley only gave her a little nod and held her tight lips without a smile? Had someone told her perhaps after all this long time that Martin had once—Mrs. Bradley always hated any girl whom Martin liked—people laughed at her about it. But then Netta came in and Netta was not cool. She was too warm, too pitying. Netta waved to her and then came near and whispered to her, "I want you to know that I shall always stand by you!"

"What do you mean, Netta?" she said aloud. She had always the instinct to answer Netta's whispers very loudly.

But Netta turned now with fresh warmth to Mrs. Bradley, who was listening. "Oh, Mrs. Bradley, I want to tell you I think the way Martin played last Sunday was just wonderful! It's so sweet of him to want to keep on playing in this little old village when we all know he could—I said to Ned last night—" She drifted away with Mrs. Bradley, laughing coquettishly. "And Ned said—" She glanced at Ned at the far corner and waved. "There he is—he's calling me."

. . . "Now let's see," said Mr. Winters. He had been arguing mildly over the dresses. "Wouldn't you care for the blue instead, ma'am? It seems to me blue favors you more than pink—and the blue is a little bigger." He shook his head at Joan and ruffled his gray spiky hair that stood high and stiff above his narrow, veined forehead. "She took the pink," he whispered to her with pain a moment later. "A fat woman will always choose pink. I've seen them do it for twenty years. Now then—" He was so kind, so very kind.

When she had the little heap ready he ran into the stock room in the funny jogging trot he had when he saw customers filling the store, and came back holding the blue beads out to her. "I want you to have them," he said. "They favor you."

"Oh, no," she said, amused. "I couldn't."

Then to her surprise he became suddenly incoherent. He was staring across the store and she followed his eyes. There was Mrs. Winters, her back to them.

"You take them," he said, and stumbled on. "What I say is it's not the old man's fault. Whatever they say, you remember that. We all grow old, I guess."

He plunged away from her and she was left, holding the blue beads. She picked up her package and quietly went home ... So something was wrong about her father.

She entered the house softly, every sense sharpened. While she had sat brooding over her own restlessness, dwelling upon her loneliness, her father had been needing her and she had not known. When would she learn not to think of herself? While she was playing through a summer her mother had sickened, saying nothing. In the silence of this house her father was suffering without speaking.

She took off her hat and went straight into his study without knocking. On Saturday morning he would be writing his sermon. He wrote out all his sermons in an even large hand, whose lines were now becoming a little trembling. Upon his shelves lay piles of manuscript, dated neatly. He never repeated a sermon. It would have seemed dishonest to him.

But he was not writing. He was sitting as he always did in his old Morris chair, drawn close to a small, neatly piled fire in the grate. He was as close to the flickering blaze as he could be, his pale hands outspread above it. He turned his head slowly when she came in and stared at her as though he did not recognize her. She realized suddenly that now he often looked at her like this. Seeing him sharply in the sunny room she saw how pale he was. He had always been pale, his skin white, his pale reddish hair changing imperceptibly to whiteness, but now he was as white as a figure of snow, his eyes scarcely deepening into silvery blue. She longed to run to him, to enfold him, to tell him he was not alone because she was there, young and alive. But she knew that it would frighten him. She made her voice casual.

"See, Father, what I am sending to Rose. And I oughtn't to interrupt you, but I thought perhaps if you had something you would like to put in it, too? It would be so nice for them."

He stirred himself slightly, moistening his white lips. "Yes," he murmured. "Of course. I gave them a copy of the Old and New Testaments, revised."

He rose, lifting himself out of his chair by his hands pressing upon the arms. "Yes," he said helplessly. He stood a moment and put his hand to his head. "What was it? Yes—yes—" He opened a drawer in the table where he kept his small supply of writing paper and took out a fresh pad and a new pencil. After a moment's thought he drew out another pencil. "They would find these useful." He held them a moment jealously. There was something precious to him about fresh paper and pencils. "When I was a boy," he said suddenly, "we were very poor and I had difficulty in procuring writing supplies. I used to write upon the brown paper wrapped about the food. But raw meat always ruined the paper."

"They'll be easy to send," Joan said. She could see the little serious boy, wanting paper and pencils. He gave them to her reluctantly and that she might watch him, she wrapped the package there and addressed it. "Think how far this has to go over land and sea!" she said, forcing her voice to brightness. He had sat down again and was putting the half-burned bits of wood together, and he did not answer.

"There," she said, "it's ready. And you'll want to go on with your sermon." When still he did not answer, she touched his shoulder. "Won't you, Father?"

He looked up at her with a sudden nervous gesture.

"Yes, of course," he said quickly. "Of course—of course—"

Yes, surely there was something wrong. She could feel it in the church. In the church there was restlessness. The choir loft was half empty. There had been two new people in the choir lately, a youngish man and a woman, newly come to the village. Today they were not in their places. There was whispering and rustling, and at last Mrs. Parsons, looking frightened, sang the same solo she had sung last Sunday.

Joan glanced sharply about the church. She knew them all so well that now when Mr. Parker was not there, when Mr. and

Mrs. Weeks were not there, when the Jameses and the Newtons were not there, it was as though holes gaped suddenly in sound familiar fabric. Why, a lot of people were not there. But Netta was there, and Mr. and Mrs. Billings, stout, red, and all their three sons. Mr. Billings looked belligerently ahead and Mrs. Billings nodded a little beside him, struggling against sleep, as she usually did. It was comforting to see her, so usual, as though nothing could be wrong. Her fat red hands lay clasped in her lap. She always said with a laugh, "As soon as my hands lay, I go to sleep. Mr. Billings teases me dreadfully about it—but then!"

In the back, Bart Pounder sat solidly. She caught his eye and looked away. But there was Dr. Crabbe! Why had Dr. Crabbe come to church today, when he never came?

Then her father stood up, tall and white. He seemed not to see the empty pews. He closed his eyes and over his face there came the old unconscious reverent ecstasy. "Let us pray. O God, our rock in time of storm—" His grave voice floated about the high and shadowy chancel.

He opened his eyes and began to preach, and she was somewhat reassured. Then he had written his sermon yesterday after she left him . . . There was a slight rustling in the church. Martin Bradley turned his music at the organ. Across the aisle, Netta took a hymnbook from the rack and read it ostentatiously. Joan felt the angry blood rush to her cheeks. She wanted to shout at Martin, to snatch the book from Netta's hand. But she did not. She sat very straight, her eyes fixed upon her father's face, listening intently. He read his sermon carefully from beginning to end without once looking up, without lifting or lowering his voice. She did not hear a word of it.

Once she saw, how blind not to have seen before! But they had all been so known to her, the familiar people, the well known, the people who had been like a fringe of family, an outer wall of safety. She had grown up secure in their friendliness. They had their little ways. Had they not all laughed at the breakfast table when their mother begged their father, "Don't preach about foreign missions too often—remember the Kinney's!" Or she had said, "Mrs. Winters didn't like your quoting St. Paul about women last Sunday—that is an irritating verse, Paul!"

But these were dear faults, the whims of people loved and

known. Then how, suddenly, could people become hostile? How could walls fall and safety fail when one had nothing?

She listened day after day at the study door and heard her father's footsteps, walking to and fro, soft, and all but soundless. Sometimes they stopped and she heard a deep murmuring, a sighing that was almost a moan.

But when he came out he was himself, very still, very composed. He came and went to his tasks. And she would not ask Hannah anything, although Hannah always knew the village gossip. Hannah was cross in the kitchen because she was making desserts which were usually too much trouble, and because he was still steadfast against temptation. He put aside even her chocolate pudding which he loved.

She would, she decided, walking about the garden, thinking swfitly, go and ask Ned Parsons. Ned, who had loved her— surely he had almost loved her?—would tell her. She would not give him the time to put her off. She would say straightly, "What is the matter with my father?"

She put on her hat and went to the store. It was nearly noon and women would be at home cooking their dinners. He was there, checking piles of gingham at the back counter, his pencil behind his large ear, his coat off and his dark vest unbuttoned.

"Oh, hello, Joan!" He scarcely paused. Once he would have rushed to greet her! The store was empty. Even Mr. Winters had gone to lunch. "What can I do for you?"—Ned, the clerk. She remembered his face, mooning at her above his guitar.

"Do you still play the guitar?" she asked suddenly.

He looked at her above a pile of flowered stuff, his eyes round. He laughed, embarrassed.

"Yes—I do." He coughed and swallowed and fumbled at his ear for his pencil. "Say, I have to thank you a lot for something, Joan. I guess you didn't know what you did when you told Netta and me to go off that time. We—I guess I saw she was a kid, too. But she was a little older—not enough to amount to anything now, but when you're kids—" He laughed his high silly laugh.

"I'm very glad," she said. She looked at him clearly and fully, but he was fumbling over the folds of the garish gingham.

"Yes—well—" He glanced at her furtively and grew very red and went on fumbling busily. "We've always expected great things of you, Joan. I always thought you were too good for us—your education and all—and your music writing."

"Ned Parsons," she said suddenly, "tell me what's the matter with my father."

He looked up at her then, startled by her suddenness. "Well, now—"

"Straight!" she commanded him.

"Oh, nothing, but some folks think he's too old," he blurted. She gazed at him intently, taking each word. "Then there's some says he pays more attention to the niggers down at South End—they say that you have to be a nigger or a heathen or he has no interest in anybody." He began shifting piles of cloth.

"Then what?" she demanded, despising him.

"Oh, well—you know how people are in a little town. They want a young fellow—up-to-date and all that. There's a fellow over to Lawtonville they're talking about."

"I see," she said clearly. "Thank you, Ned."

She turned, and he called after her, "Not that there isn't a good strong handful that don't want him turned out. I'm one of them—Netta and I both are, Joan!"

"Thank you, Ned," she called back.

So now she knew what it was. She was like a child, bereft. Grown people, those whom she had trusted, had turned and left her. They stood alone, she and this old man.

People were tired of them. They had grown tired of the same face in the pulpit, saying the same things, the same eternal things. They wanted something brighter and more amusing. She began thinking of them one by one. Which of them would stand by her father, which of them would not? But when she began thinking and remembering how they had last looked, how they had last spoken, she could not be sure of any of them, not even of Miss Kinney, who would be swayed by the last person she heard. There was Dr. Crabbe, Mr. Pegler, Mrs. Mark. But they were not the church, and Mrs. Mark had her legs. There was no one of whom she could be sure.

She entered the house and went quietly to her room. Then it came to her that there was no more shelter in this room, no more safety in this house. All that she had thought was safety forever about her was gone, unreasonably gone and not to be regained. This house in which they had all made a home belonged to their enemies. It belonged to the church. It could not be a home, this house given and taken away at the whim of a crowd. They had built a home under foreign shelter.

She stood by the window, staring across the wintry garden. All these flowers her mother had planted in foreign soil, the lemon lilies, the ferns they had dug from woods and streams. Her mother had wandered through woods in spring with a trowel and a basket, crying aloud over bloodroot and trillium and feathery mosses. Before she went, Joan thought savagely, she would dig them all up and throw them away. She would chop the roses at the roots and hack the lily bulbs. Who could help growing old? They were all growing old. They were old— old—the church was nothing but old people. Yet who turned Mr. Parker out of his house because he was old, and who took bread away from Mrs. Kinney because she was over eighty years old? Then she was suddenly afraid. What did people do when the roof was taken from over them and wage was stopped and there was no more bread? What would she do with this old man? She had no one.

But they helped her to be proud. On Sundays before their strangeness she could pretend she knew nothing. She could receive coldly their meaningless friendliness. She sat in the pew where once they had all sat to hear a proud priest, listening fiercely now to an old mumbling man.

For it was impossible not to see that he was now nothing but an old man. He mounted the pulpit steps wearily and he clutched the handrail when he descended. Only for a moment, that first moment when he faced his failing congregation, did he throw up his head and straighten his shoulders. Soon he forgot. Soon he was poring aloud over his manuscript, reading strange dreamy stuff to which the few listened, bewildered or scornful.

"And I dreamed I saw as though the heavens were rolled away, a fair land, through which flowed serene a river. The name of the river was Peace, and there was room for everyone there on its banks, the young and the old, and they lived together safely. Dreams are not meaningless, not vagrant. Dreams—"

"I must take him away," she planned passionately. She wanted to run up now and lead him away and shelter him.

Yet he would not be sheltered. In the house when they were alone it was necessary to pretend with him that everything was well. He came home from a meeting of his vestry, stricken and bewildered, muttering replies to himself. Waiting for him, standing at the dining room window watching for him, she wept when she saw him dragging himself across the gray frost-bitten lawn. His lips were moving and he made angry, futile gestures that were like weak blows.

But when, anguished with tenderness, she ran to the door, he pushed her feebly away, panting a little. "Is—is supper ready?" he asked. "I feel—a little faint."

"Oh, what has happened?"

"Nothing—nothing," he replied with unusual irritation. "I'm just a little tired. I'd like to have supper right away—as soon as I wash—"

He went slowly upstairs. Standing at the foot, she heard him moan softly at the top step. "O, God—" But after a moment he went on and he did not call her. She must, she perceived, allow him to remain what he had always been. He must remain a priest or he would die. But a little later, out of the absolute silence in which they sat at the table, she asked again, "Father —can't you tell me? Couldn't you talk it over with me?" He answered, "Women do not understand these things. There is nothing in which you could help me. I trust in God." She smiled at him, pitifully, and let him be. At night, lying awake, she could hear him praying, in long stretches of monotone. He was still putting his trust in God . . .

And if he gave up his trust in God he would have nothing left. People had drawn away and left him. One by one they had all gone. Mary was gone. She used to lie here in this bed and in the night when he awoke to a strange aching loneliness he could look over and see her dark head or put out his hand and touch her warm breathing body. Now his own feeble warmth could scarcely change in a whole night the chill of the sheets. And in the night they all seemed to mock him. The members of his spiritual family! In the night he even wondered if what they said was true. Perhaps he was getting old. But if he was too old to preach, what could he do? There was the little insurance he had all these years in the Ministers' Relief Fund. Mary had made him take it when Joan was born. It had seemed not trusting in God, but she kept at him. And he could draw it out in another two years. It would all be his, then. He planned in the darkness that he might rent a little room in South End and go and preach to the unsaved. "And the common people heard him gladly." "For so persecuted they the saints before you." He began murmuring the strong resolute words and after a while they helped him. He began to feel the old arrogant determination to make his people do God's will. No, he would not retreat before his people. The Lord had appointed him—the Lord alone could dismiss him. He would not speak to anyone. He put his trust in God. He slept fitfully before dawn . . .

But if he would not tell her, she must know otherwise how to take care of him. She went to Mr. Weeks, who was the church treasurer. She remembered Netta's father as a poor man, a mechanic who had moved to the village from elsewhere and opened a small grocery store. Soon he was unaccountably prosperous, enough so to buy the shirt factory at South End, though he had not opened it yet. But they had never bought of him because her mother said they were used to Mr. Winters' general store. She did not like Peter Weeks because he asked outright what Winters was selling for, and twisted his tight small mouth to say, "I'll let you have it two cents under his price—anything you want."

"No, thank you," she replied coldly. When Mr. Weeks had joined the church and Hannah said, "Reckon we'd oughta buy a little of him now and then," her mother had replied proudly, "We don't do that sort of thing."

She entered the grocery shop, her head high and her heart water within her.

Netta's father hastened toward her. "Well, well," he cried, but she would not answer his meager joviality. "Mr. Weeks," she said directly over the counter, "I've come to ask one thing—when does my father have to go?"

"Well, now," he considered, taken aback. His angular wizened colorless face fell into his conventional shopman's smile. "You and Netta are old friends—I want to do all I can."

"It's not necessary," she said steadily. "I'll take care of my father."

"The fact is," Mr. Weeks said, moving a cud of tobacco in his cheek, "the old man's kind of stubborn. Won't give his resignation."

"I see," said Joan.

"We're waiting for that. Can't technically close him out before then. The fact is, we'd want to get a new man started as soon as we can, but I'm treasurer and I know we can't afford any overlapping. Finances in bad shape, but I'm getting things in order—"

"I see," said Joan. "Then the sooner we go the better."

"He'd better hand in his resignation, you see, Joan." He moved his quid. "I don't want to be hard on him—you and Netta—Say, hear Netta's going to splice up with Ned Parsons? She was a long time going off, Netta was, but she did well in the end. Ned takes after his pa, I'm glad to say, instead of his ma. He works steady. I'm thinking some of starting up the factory, and if I do I'm going to put Ned in charge—that is, if he goes ahead with Netta."

"I'm very glad for Netta. Will you tell her? Good-bye." She forgot Ned and Netta at once.

Across the table at supper when Hannah was gone she said, "Father, let's do proudly what has to be done. We'll go to the city—I'll find a job. And Francis can help. We'll start again."

He had been eating rapidly and hungrily. Of late, with all the worry, he had let himself eat more. He often felt faint and he needed strength. Tonight the stew had been unusually good, and the steamed pudding. But Joan was so quick. He stared at her and put his hand to his mouth, and she saw he was sick. She ran to him, but he fended her off with his arm and rose and went out. When after a long time he did not call her, she went to find him. He was in his room and when she called he cried feebly that he was undressing and she could not come. She sat down on a little stool by the door and waited. But the door did not open, and at last she opened it softly. He lay on his back, his folded hands on his breast. His eyes were closed and he was drawing deep breaths, snoring now and then. He had crept into bed without calling her and gone to sleep. She closed the door and went to her own room. He did not want her.

For her there was no sleep. She could not sleep in such uncertainty, in such loneliness. Rose was far away and Francis had written only once. But she remembered Francis, how he had leaped from his bed and dashed for Dr. Crabbe that day. She went to her desk and began to write to Francis. "We must go. You see how it is," she ended. "We had better come to New York and I could get a job. At any rate, we must get out of this house."

She sat a while and added, "I have no one to count on but you. And he is your father, too."

She sealed and stamped the letter and lay down in her bed, listening, to fall at last into sleep.

She woke with the feeling of a strange sound just heard. She had heard it in deep sleep and waked instantly from old habit with her mother. She lay awake, taut, listening. What was it? The house was very silent. The night was still. Then it came again, a loud choke, a snore, a voice struggling and stifled. She leaped out of bed and ran to the door between his room and hers. But he had locked it. Sometime, without her knowing it, he had locked it so that he might be quite alone. She cried through the panel, "Father—I'm coming—" But he did not answer. There was the door from the hall. She ran down the hall, calling upward to the attic for Hannah as she ran. This door was not locked, thank God! She pushed it open. The room was dark. There was no moon and even through the open window only darkness streamed. But out of that darkness she heard his strange breathing. She fumbled for the light and heard on the stair Hannah's stumbling and muttering against the darkness.

"Hannah!" she cried. "Go and get Dr. Crabbe. Something's wrong with Father!"

Hannah's voice grated through the darkness. "He's overeaten. He's always held back, but last night he kind of let go and ate. I noticed him on the pudding." She reached the door as Joan found the switch. The light flashed down upon the bed, upon him. They stared at him in the instant together. He lay stiffly, his arms flung into a shape of agony. His mouth was twisted across his jaws and pinned there, held by invisibly crooked muscles. His eyes were dim, half-open. His usually snow-pale face was stained with purple—

"My soul and body!" whispered Hannah. "It's a stroke!" She turned and padded away . . .

This figure on the bed did not stir. She was afraid of him—so strange, so twisted. She lifted his hand to place it nearer his body in a more easy pose and the arm was stiff. She could not move it. A dribble of saliva ran from the loose corner of his mouth and she lifted the sheet and wiped it away, sickened. "Father, Father!" she cried. But he neither saw nor heard. He was absorbed in the heavy breath he drew.

And then, as she stood there alone with him, the breathing stopped. At one instant the breath came, deep and thick, roughened, grating, like something dragging harshly over a rocky road. Then it stopped. Even as she stood, crying to him, it stopped. She waited, in terror, for it to begin again. But the strange purple faded out of his face, gravity fell upon his crooked mouth, and the twisting left his flung limbs. The body seemed to relax, to curl, to shrink. The breath was finished. She turned away and ran—ran down the stairs, calling, "Hannah, Hannah!"

The front door opened and Dr. Crabbe was there, his overcoat over his striped pajamas, his hair a fringe of tangle about his baldness. "Father's gone—he's gone!" She shrieked at him as though she were a little girl. "Oh, Dr. Crabbe—oh, what shall I do!" She began suddenly to cry aloud.

He lumbered up the stairs, and she followed behind him, and Hannah behind her, a frenzied procession. She could not keep from sobbing, every breath arose a sob. She felt weak with sobbing. They were by him but he had not moved. There he lay, just as she had left him, Dr. Crabbe lifted his arm. It lay limp in his grasp and he put it down gently. Hannah began to sniffle. "It was a stroke, wasn't it, Doctor? He always kept himself starved and last night he took three helpings of my dried fig pudding and the hard sauce. I was that surprised, beside all else he'd eaten—"

Dr. Crabbe did not answer her. He did not say to Joan, "Stop sobbing, child." He looked down into the proud dead face, seeming not to hear her. It was a proud high face, even though dead. "The old son of God," he murmured, smiling. "He stood up in the vestry last Sunday and told them God called him, not man, and that he would die before he resigned. He was lucky—not everybody can die when life is ended." He bent and with gentleness he touched the eyelids and closed them and laid the hands upon the breast.

But she kept on sobbing. She could not stop her sobbing.

They were all very kind, of course. They sent a great many flowers. The house was full of flowers, and on the floral pieces were little notes speaking of his "wonderful service." "So many years," they all chorused. Now that he had, in a manner, resigned, they were eager to praise, to appreciate. Mr. Weeks came to see her and to say uncomfortably, "I didn't mean any harm, you know. It was just business—things getting sorta rundown—if I'd had any idea—"

She heard him listlessly, hating him. She had to watch herself all the time or she began that foolish sobbing. She wept the instant she was alone—not for him—not for him—"It doesn't matter, Mr. Weeks—"

Dr. Crabbe telegraphed for her to Francis. He said, looking at her sharply, "You need to have someone here with you—there's no one else." She said, "Maybe he can't come—he's just new at a job—I don't know—" She desperately wanted him to come. She needed the sense of her own beside her. But he did not come. There was no answer even to the telegram. They wouldn't let him off, she thought dully when it was the hour for the funeral and he had not come.

She went with Hannah to the church quietly. Mrs. Winters was there first, just to see that everything was right. "Wait a little, dearie," she said. "Wait till they're all seated." She was so kind. But even she had said when they stood looking at him in his coffin, "If he hadn't been so set on that South End—"

Yes, they were all kind now, when it was too late. She sat in the pew quite alone, and the preacher from Lawtonville mounted the pulpit, and before him lay the casket. He mounted eagerly and then remembered and slowed himself. But it was difficult to walk slowly today. The eagerness crept out of him, his eyes, his voice, the nervous quickness of his hands. Would he please the people, his eagerness was asking? And across the dead the people were looking at him closely, intensely. Would he please them? He began praising the dead man eagerly, fully, remembering to round his sentences, to use the metaphors he had planned. When he prayed he had a small sheet of notes before him upon the pulpit and he opened his eyes now and then to glance at them. He must make a good prayer. It was so necessary for Minnie to—

"And may we so live, O God," he prayed fluently, glancing secretly at the bit of paper, "that at the end—"

After it was over, Netta wanted to come home with her, and Mrs. Winters said, "Now don't stay there alone—come over to us." They all said, "Let us know if we can do anything." She smiled and thanked them, knowing there was nothing.

She was alone, wherever she was. It did not matter. She wanted to go away from them because underneath all their kindness she could feel their relief. Before her they were decent and grave. But they would go to their homes and look at each other and murmur, "After all, it was best—for everybody concerned." So she went back to the house quite alone. She must not begin that sobbing again. She had begun to be sick with sobbing.

They were all very kind. Dr. Crabbe came to see her and worried her with his insistent kindness. "What are you going to do, Joan? You've got to do something, child!"

She had answered at first quite eagerly. "Yes, of course, Dr. Crabbe. I thought I'd go to New York and be with Frank. He has a job, and I could find something, I know."

"Hm," said Dr. Crabbe, staring at her with dissatisfaction. "Looks to me like you better take a good dose of castor oil. Stomach's probably stopped working with all this—only natural. You look yellow. Have you any money?"

"Oh, yes, Dr. Crabbe," she said hastily. She wouldn't take money. She was proud with all her mother's pride ... "Just because my husband's a minister is no reason why my children should wear other people's old clothes. Never take gifts, Joan!" ... Besides, she had a few dollars again in the sandalwood box, and in her father's old purse she had found a dollar. His salary had been due next week, but of course now— "Plenty, Dr. Crabbe," she said brightly. "Honest!" He glanced at her. "How much?" "Oh, lots! Besides, Francis is earning." "Hm," he said grudgingly and went away.

They had not ceased to be kind. They said, "Take your time, Joan." But the third day the new minister and his wife came to see the parsonage. "Not to hurry you at all, Miss Richards," he said. He was very happy in this new call. His salary would be nearly two hundred a year more. With two hundred—then his red-haired young wife called to him sharply, "George! We'll have to ask them to repaper the dining room anyway—and do over the floors." Joan followed them about. "Yes, there is the pantry—that door is the cellar steps—it opens the other way." All the familiar corners of the house she had always known as instinctively as her own body she was revealing to strangers.

"Don't know if I'll like her," said Hannah, grumbling when they were gone. "She looks the kind that would skimp on butter and count the eggs." She clattered the pans in the kitchen. "Said she didn't know if she wanted help at all except this place is bigger'n she's used to—I'll lay it is—she don't look used to much in my opinion."

"Don't hurry," they all said, but she was in a fever of hurry.

Pack up his few things—send the clothes to the mission. She had said to the new minister when they were looking at the bedroom, "Would you take a few clothes of his to the mission? He'd want the—"

The young man pursed his full lips. "I'm not sure just when I'll be going—I've not decided about going on with that work—the people in the church—"

"Never mind," she said quickly. "I'll take them myself."

She was going away, just as soon as she could get things packed. She was glad there was so little—glad nearly everything had to be left because it belonged to the people. Even the dishes from which she had eaten bread and milk and the cakes her mother had made and meat and vegetables and deep pies —old familiar precious dishes—"Run and get me the tall cake dish, darling!" "Where's the bowl we put fruit in, Hannah!"— even the dishes were not theirs. Nothing had been really theirs. She would take the round-topped trunk—her clothes, the books of course, her mother's own linen and silver. Perhaps she'd better not take anything at first, just pack and store them somewhere and find Francis. Strange of Frank not even to write!

Then nearly a week after the death, there was Francis' letter. She came from the study where she had been sorting her father's books and there was the letter in the hall. "Looks like Frank's writing, but the postmark isn't New York. I can't make it out," Hannah had called.

She went at once and opened the letter quickly. No, it was not from New York. It was from a place in Michigan, but it was Frank's letter.

DEAR JOAN—

I lost my job and here I am with a couple of fellows. I'm looking for work here. They say there is a lot of work at General Motors. I expect I'll get a job. As I am a little short, please send me anything you can.

He did not even know. He had not heard. She tore the letter into small pieces and left the heap upon the table.

. . . So what could she do? The house stretched about her, empty, inexorable, waiting for her to go, waiting to begin another life. It was through with her. She was terrified of this house. She ran out into the garden. It was nearly Thanksgiving.

She had not thought how nearly Thanksgiving it was. But now a load of cornstalks was being drawn to the church door, the cornstalks they always used as a background for pumpkins and fruits. There was a loud shout from the wagon as it drew near, and the horses stopped in front of her, breathing out steam. A strong bulky figure leaped down from the wagon and came near her. It was Bart. She smelled the odor of the dry stalks upon him, clean and earthy. Suddenly she began sobbing again, the sobs that jerked at her very entrails. "Oh, Bart," she sobbed. "Oh, Bart, Bart!"

He came toward her, smiling, steady, sure, safe. He had his arm about her and she clung to him and he led her into the empty house. There in the empty sitting room she felt his lips upon hers at last. She was still for a moment, feeling. His lips were stiff and hard upon her mouth. Deep within her body her heart drew back in strange dismay. But she clung to him, sobbing. He was strong as a rock, his arms about her were like the walls of a house.

III

THIS RING UPON HER FINGER WAS
new and stiff. She had never worn a ring before, because it
soon irked her. Someone had given her a ring once when she
was a a little girl and she had wanted to wear it because it was
so pretty, a red bit of glass set in a loop of silver-washed metal,
but she could not. In a little while it made her restless and she
took it off. But this ring she must not take off. She must learn to
wear it. She had set it herself upon her hand, a wide bank of
gold, old-fashioned and heavy. Bart had searched among the
rings upon the counter in the little jeweler's shop in Clarktown
while she stood waiting until he had found a ring like his
mother's. "It's got to last a long time," he said. When the clerk
had fitted it to her finger and given it to them, Bart had tried it
on his own hand. But it would go over no finger except the little
one, and there it stuck upon the crooked joint.

There was no need to wait. There was no one to consider.
Why should she consider those who had not considered her?
She would slip out of that old life. It could be nothing to any of
them what she did. She did not want to tell anybody she was
going to marry Bart Pounder. She did not want to see that
surprised look—"Bart Pounder?" She silenced her own heart
savagely. "Yes—Bart Pounder—who else is there?"

She went to Mr. Winters, who was an elder, in the evening
after store hours. He was there alone, searching over his

shelves for something someone had wanted in the day and he could not find. It was his usual evening occupation. "If you can just wait till tomorrow, I can find it," he said a dozen times a day. Upon bits of paper he scrawled, "Mrs. Parsons—ink eraser"—"a spool of sixty white for Mrs. Bradley"—"Billings a chipping knife." When she came in tonight she could hear him muttering mildly, "Now where in tuck did I put that?"

"Mr. Winters, will you please tell them I shall be leaving the manse right away?"

He left off muttering and turned to her, kind, protesting. "Now don't you let them hurry you."

"No, but I have made my plans."

"Going away?"

"Yes, I'm going away."

Next morning Mrs. Winters came bustling up the steps. "Joan, I came right over. Mr. Winters told me. What are you going to do?"

"I'm going away, Mrs. Winters."

"Yes, but—"

"I'm not a child, you know. I'm grown up. I have my plans. I'll write you."

Mrs. Winters could not help. No one could really help. It was better to be silent, to make her own life. She would not forget that only by death was her father saved from these people.

But when she said good-bye to Hannah, she clung to her a moment. Hannah said, patting her back briskly, "Did you write me that little letter, Joan, so's if I don't make it with this new minister's wife, I could go and try some of the summer folks over at Piney Cove?" Joan released her instantly. "Yes, Hannah." She opened her bag and took out the letter. *This is to introduce Hannah Jackson, our general servant for more than twenty years. We have always found her clean, honest—*

"It's hard on a body," said Hannah fretfully, "at this age to be having to find a new place and I haven't chick nor child."

"Yes, it's hard," said Joan quietly. "It's hard at any age."

There could not be, of course, any white satin nor any of that dreaming. White satin would have sat strangely upon her with Bart standing by her in his bursting blue suit. So she put on her old orange wool dress and her brown coat and the small brown felt hat and she and Bart stood before the county clerk, repeating his words. He was a small, wry-faced man with big loose lips in a wizened face. The day was cold with November and his thin-curved nose was damp and red, and he wiped his hand across it often. "You can sign there," he said, pointing with his nail-bitten forefinger.

She signed her name steadily, "Joan Pounder." Steadily she forced her hand to the name she had taken for her own, shaping its unfamiliar letters for the first time. She stood and watched Bart hold the pen clumsily like a farm tool in his great hand. He wrote his name in a childish angular scrawl beside her neat small script. She stood for an instant looking at the two names. Then she said, "Take me home, Bart."

"Giddap there!" he shouted at his two horses. He clacked the reins across their backs and they began to trot briskly, their rustbrown coats shining in the wintry sun.

"I'll get a car one of these days," he said. "But I've got to get ahead a little. And a car's no good for plowing. Got to have horses on a farm, car or no car." He turned to grin at her. A look she was beginning to know came over his face. His nostrils thickened a little, his lips parted and loosened. "I don't know if we could sit so close in a car though, my girl," he whispered heavily. He had small yellowish soft-looking teeth set in gums too wide and pale. She looked away quickly.

They were moving out of the country she knew into a rugged hilly land, whose valleys were dark with woods. Between the rough fields were stone walls piled of the stones from the land. Everywhere the last colors of autumn were subsiding into dun and gray. Only the oak trees still burned dully red, but a few more nights of frost would strip them, too. Then it would be winter. She was glad for Bart, she told herself, gazing straightly into the dying landscape. If it had not been for Bart she would have been quite alone and winter was coming. In so short a time had she been left quite alone.

Then at a bend of the narrow earth road rose a big frame house with green blinds, an oblong of white against the land. A few great maple trees stood about it, their skeleton limbs not hiding it.

"There's the house," said Bart, pointing with his whip. "The folks will be expecting us. Don't you mind my mother."

He had never mentioned his home before except to say shortly, "I live with my folks. I'm to have the place if I stay with them—so I'm staying."

They drew up and the door opened and now she was near

enough to see them, his father, his mother, his brother. They came out, one by one, his mother last, and stood waiting for her. Her heart rushed eagerly toward them; she peered through the dusk to see them—father, mother, brother. But she liked the house, so cleanly white and green, she liked the maples. Under their bare limbs the unraked leaves lay in a carpet of ashy gold.

She wanted to like everything. Here was to be her home. She was glad they were all to live together. She did not want to live alone with Bart. A tag end of Scripture flew into her mind: "And the lonely he hath set into families."

She jumped out of the buggy and ran across the dry frostbitten grass and through the rustling fallen leaves toward the three waiting figures. She ran toward the woman, holding out her hands. She put her arms about the stiff body, and smelled a faint soapy cleanness upon the cheek beneath her lips. "I'm Joan," she said. She wanted very much to have them love her. She would make them love her.

"Well!" said Bart's mother. "Well, I'm sure—" Under her lips Joan felt the passive plump cold cheek.

"Here's the old man," said Bart. "And this here's Sam—my kid brother."

She put out her hand quickly and felt it taken twice by huge stiff hands, the same except that the old man's hand was cold and the young man's hot and damp in the palm, and did not quickly let hers drop. The old man did not speak. "Pleased," Sam muttered. He had small hot brown eyes like Bart's, under rough hedgy red brows. They stood staring at her, unblinking, out of the twilight, and she stared back at them until the silence was heavy to crush her. She must speak and break this deep silence.

"It's a lovely house," she said at last.

"Won't you come in?" said Bart's mother.

"We'd better go in," said Bart.

They turned and tramped in silence into the house, and she followed them into a small square hall from which a staircase rose steeply. There was a hesitation she did not understand. Then the mother said, "Well, use the front stairs for once." But the two men went through the hall to the kitchen, and Bart said, "Reckon I'll wash up in the kitchen, too."

"Come on up and I'll show you the room," said the mother. She mounted the stairs, not touching the rail, stepping carefully, and Joan followed, her bag in her hand. The stairs turned sharply into a narrow hall encircled by closed doors.

"Here," said the mother. She opened a door and went in first and Joan followed her. "You'll find everything handy, I hope."

"Oh, yes," said Joan eagerly, staring about her. There was a maple bureau, a washstand with a pitcher and basin, a rocking chair, a double bed. Upon the bare clean painted floor were bits of old flowered carpet, neatly hemmed.

"We have a bathroom," she heard Bart's mother say. "It's down the hall. But the men don't use it. They take the tub to the woodshed when they need to wash. I can't have the smell of stable in the house. But you can use the bathroom with me, I reckon."

Joan did not hear her. There was only this double bed. There she must sleep this night with Bart, this night that was already come down upon her. She had not wanted to think of it. But now the night was here.

"Well, we'll be ready to eat as soon as you come down," continued Bart's mother. "I'll just go and stir up the potatoes." She went out, closing the door, but Joan did not hear her footsteps on the stairs.

In the dusky room she sat down. She felt as though she had been running too quickly for a long time and now motion was stopped forever. Silence was deep about her. Through the window she saw the endless rolling twilight hills, the dark trees, the faint pale lines of dividing stone walls, the empty shorn fields. There was no other house to be seen. She ran, half afraid, close to the window, but there were no other houses. A great gray barn loomed directly in front of the house. She could see the shadowy figure of Bart's father moving in the light of the oil lantern he carried. His head was lost in the early darkness but she saw clearly his shapeless legs in overalls, the clump of his hand grasping the handle of the lantern. He slid the barn doors shut and came toward the house, his shadow warped and monstrous upon the dry ground. She stood in the chill darkness, afraid to live. For the moment she passionately envied her mother, safe in her grave, having no more to face the fall of night, the dawn of day. She was afraid of night, afraid of day.

Then she felt the ring upon her finger. She had forgotten it for a while in her excitement, but now she felt it, strange and stiff upon her flesh. She turned resolutely and found matches beside the oil lamp on the mantelpiece and struck a light and lit the lamp. It was very clean and the chimney shone. The flame licked about the cleanly wiped wick and there was a streak of smoke. She turned it down quickly—but there the black was.

It didn't matter—she was relieved with light. She took off her hat and then lifted the pitcher and poured out water to wash her hands. The faint clink of the pitcher was like a crack in the silence. The house was full of silence, the same silence that hung over the hills and the woods. She found herself moving carefully that she might not break the silence again. She opened the door and tiptoed down the carpeted stairs, down the dark narrow hall. There was no voice to guide her, nothing except a vein of light under a door at the end. She opened it and there they all sat at the table, waiting for her. They did not speak when she came in. She took the empty chair by Bart, trying to smile. No one spoke, but Sam was watching her from under his bushy brows. Bart's mother rose and went into the kitchen and came back with a dish of smoking boiled potatoes.

"We'll eat now," she said.

She had known silence before. After her mother's death there had been silence of a voice no longer heard. There was the increasing silence in the house after Rose had gone and then Francis. There was the silence in which she had lived with her father and in which he had died. There was the silence into which Bart had come, from which he had taken her, the silence of herself, bereft.

But none of it had been like this silence. They sat down and suddenly in the stillness, in the stillness of field and wood and tree and night sky about the solitary house, Bart's father said shortly, "We'll have the blessing—God, for what we are about to receive, make us truly thankful. Amen."

But the prayer did not break the silence. They were crowded about the table in the small crowded room. Beside her sat Bart's father, his elbows squared. In the silence she could hear him breathing as he ate, helping himself to potatoes, to bread, to cold meat, pouring out skim milk to swallow it down in gulps. Across the table Sam sat, eating, watching her incessantly. Beside her was Bart, beyond, his mother. She did not look at their faces. She kept her eyes on her plate, but around the plate was a circle of hands, their hands, great, warped, clumsy

hands, thick and brutal with animal work. She thought suddenly that she never wanted to touch them and pressed the
thought down instantly. She must not think such things. They
were good people, honest, hard-working. Their faces were decent, honest faces. She belonged to them now. This was the
home which was to give her food and shelter the rest of her life
—the home she had chosen. She gathered her reasoning
thoughts. Her mother would have talked cheerfully, quietly,
making friends, and she herself must try. Perhaps they were
shy of her, too. She looked up brightly. "I've never lived on a
farm before," she said. "I know I'll like it—I love the country."

No one answered. Bart's father reached for the bread.

"Got anything else to eat coming?" he asked his wife.

"There's some apples stewed up," she answered. "Or I could
open a can of raspberries."

He thought a moment. "Apples," he said.

She rose and brought back a bowl and set it on the table. It
passed from hand to hand in silence.

After the meal was over they sat in the small crowded room.
She had tried to help clear away, taking out the dishes, searching for the dishpan. "I'll wash the dishes," she said. But Bart's
mother poured the water into the pan and tied on an apron.
"You can wipe," she replied. So Joan wiped, and Bart sat in the
other room with the men. Now that the men were alone a little
talk went on. She could hear the flat toneless voices.

"You finish that cornfield today, Sam?"

"Pretty near—tomorrow anyway."

"You aiming to take tomorrow off, Bart?"

"No, I guess not."

"Apples ought to be sorted. Shaler's comin' for them the day
after."

"All right."

In the kitchen she searched herself desperately for something to say. What would Bart's mother like her to say? "This is
a nice kitchen—I like a big kitchen."

There was no answer for a moment. Bart's mother swept the
cloth about the greasy edge of the pan. "It makes work when
you have everything to do yourself," she answered. Her face
did not change its dull worried look.

"I'll help you now," said Joan eagerly. "I want to help all I
can."

She opened the dish closet and began to put away the dishes

she had just finished wiping. "Let me see—the plates here—and these spoons—"

"They don't go there—the good spoons I put in the drawer. Those are kitchen things—you'd better let me put them right."

She pushed Joan aside and began to sort the dishes and silver.

"There—"

"I'll know tomorrow," said Joan humbly. She went into the other room. The three men fell silent at once. They sat about the table, set for the next meal and shrouded with a gray-white cloth. She sat down on one of the straight chairs, wondering what was beyond the closed doors. There must be many rooms in this big house. But it was as though there was only this room where they ate, the kitchen, the rooms for sleep upstairs. She sat, afraid to go upstairs, although she was very tired, too tired to try again to talk. Tomorrow in the morning, when the night was over—There was yet the night.

The father yawned suddenly and enormously. "Got to get to sleep," he muttered.

He rose, and opening the cupboard beside the scaled fireplace, he brought out a squarely bound Bible and his spectacles. "Mother!" he called, and Bart's mother came in, untying her apron as she came. She sat with it across her knees, her hands limply clasped upon it. He opened the Bible and searched slowly for a mark, moving his callused finger from page to page.

"The thirtieth chapter of Isaiah," he announced, and began to read slowly, hesitating over the long words, "Woe to the rebellious children, saith the Lord." It was a long chapter, but he read it to the end. They sat, motionless as stone. Were they listening? She looked from face to face, but she did not know. The mother sat with utter emptiness upon her face, lax with the habit of weariness. It was not possible she heard. Bart sat staring at his great hands. She saw his eyelids droop—he was almost asleep. Sam's eyes were upon her ankles. She drew them quickly under her chair.

"Let us pray," Bart's father said, closing the book, and they knelt. Now forced to speak sentence upon sentence, the old man's voice dropped into a mumble. He repeated bits of Scripture, made half-formed petitions, accepted ill fortune with a strange heavy patience. "We know that whatever comes it is from God. We plant but we may not reap. Man soweth but the harvest is with God. Help us to take what comes to us and work at whatever our hand finds to do. Amen."

They rose into silence again. Bart's mother tied her apron about her waist and went back to the kitchen. The father put the book and his spectacles back into the closet and sighed deeply. He turned with heavy abruptness and went to the kitchen. She heard a basin clatter in the zinc-lined sink and heard him dip and pour water. There was the hiss of lather, the dry stroke of a razor against the stubble of his beard. There was the clash of water flowing and of water emptied. Then he walked heavily through the room and up a small back staircase she had not seen.

"Well," said Sam, rising, "I guess I'll go to bed." He rubbed his great hand through his red hair. She saw him staring at her, at Bart, avid. Secrecy, hot and fierce, was in his eyes. She looked away quickly and he went into the kitchen. His mother was still in the kitchen, moving about, wiping off the top of the stove, putting away pots, filling the kettle.

"Sam, you get me some wood first thing in the morning," she said.

"All right. Where are the apples?"

"Don't leave the cores under your bed for me to pick up the way you did this morning."

He did not answer. He came into the room where she and Bart sat, and grinned at them. "Well, sweet dreams, you two!" he said, and went up the small back stairs.

She did not answer. One by one they were forcing the night upon her. The mother was waiting for them to go. In the kitchen she was sitting now on the reed-bottomed chair by the stove, waiting.

Bart got up suddenly. "Ma always comes up last. We'd better go."

"All right, Bart," she said faintly. She turned to go into the hall to the stairs down which she had come. But he called her abruptly. "Come this way— we use the back stairs every day."

"All right, Bart," she said, and followed him up the steep dark stairway.

It was dawn. When she opened her eyes the low ceiling seemed close, like a dim sky. The small room was full of pale quiet light. She raised her head and leaned upon her arm and looked out of the window.

Bart had said, brusque with embarrassment, "What side you want to sleep on?" and she answered quickly, "Outside—next the window, please." He was ready before she was and he had rolled heavily to the wall. She had looked at the window all the time she was getting ready. It was a window away from this room, a window toward the hills.

There the hills were now, dark and still under the faintly coloring sky. She looked at them with a quiet wintry sadness. This was the way old people must feel, as she felt this morning, very old people, from whom everything had been taken away, or who knew that now nothing more was to be theirs. Nothing more now was to be hers except the things old people may have, a roof for shelter from rain, a fire for warmth, food, sleep, and within their hearts the emptiness of no more to come. All the emptiness in life was inside her, nothing but emptiness. She was a hollow figure, standing alone in a great silent empty plain. No one was near—no ear to hear her, no voice which she could hear. Behind her she heard the rasping steady breathing of Bart. Now that he was at last asleep he slept thickly, lumpishly. She must not look at him, must not imagine how he looked. Here was the window through which she could see the hills.

She crept carefully out of the bed and into her clothes. When she was dressed she knelt beside the window and watched the changing light. Let her not think, let her not remember anything. But she remembered suddenly one thing. Once when she was a little girl and she heard that quarreling in the room next to hers—were they quarreling?—she had got up out of bed, troubled, quivering, to listen at the door, to know what was wrong. She heard her mother say in a small, death-like voice, almost a whisper, "Is this all? Paul, is there nothing more than this?" And her father had answered more sharply than she had ever heard him speak, "I don't know what you mean, Mary."

But she knew what her mother had meant. This morning she knew.

"You up already?" Bart's sleepy voice came suddenly from the wall.

"Yes, I'm up, Bart."

He yawned loudly. "I'm awful sleepy this morning. Guess I'll take another nap."

"All right, Bart."

. . . What could she pour into such emptiness to fill it? There was nothing deep enough to fill it to the bottom. Everything she did was so small it only floated on the surface of the fathomless emptiness. She watched the dawn brighten, and slowly the hills turned blue and over their rim the edge of the red sun rose and swelled into roundness and light poured over the land. Day was here again. Her frantic body was nothing in the hugeness of the day and night. This shell of walls and roof were all she had for shelter from the moons and suns and roaring winds or racing million stars, and from all the carelessness of people passing by. She turned from the window and began to unpack her bag and put her clothes away into the drawers.

In the days, she learned to work as she never had. She wasted no time on talk. Words echoed too hollowly in that void. She learned to be as silent as the others were, as chary of unnecessary speech.

"Bart, what time are you getting up to plow the wheatfield?"

"Half past four."

No use to say more than that. Half past four meant breakfast at five. And before breakfast there must be the praying and Bible reading. She sat in stillness, dawn after dawn, staring out of the dusky windowpane while Bart's father read the Bible, one verse after the other, following the lines with his thick cracked fingertip. She dreaded the deepest winter when the window would be black and she could not see the hills lightening with morning. But deepest winter came and then all she could see in the window was only a mirror. In it she saw five people sitting about a shrouded table, their heads patiently inclined. She saw herself one of them and she turned her head away.

Setting the cold skim milk on the table, the cold bread, the pat of pale milky butter, she watched the window, watched for the dawn. It seemed sometimes it would never come. Sometimes they had eaten what there was to eat—eggs were not to be eaten because they could be sold, and coffee was an indulgence, a strong drink with which to indulge the flesh—and she was washing the dishes, before that light began to break, streaming over the hills like music.

. . . Music! She had forgotten there was music. Behind one of the closed doors there was an old upright piano. She touched it once, softly. But its faint notes jangled and twanged out of tune and she closed it. Sometimes Bart's father came into the kitchen on a Saturday night where she and Bart's mother sat in silence mending the clothes the men wanted to put on after their weekly baths.

"Here," he said gruffly, "see if you can pick out that tune." He had a shining red hymnbook open to his hand. He had to choose hymns because he was superintendent of the Sunday school, as he had been for thirty years. The mother rose, sighing, and took the book and went to the piano. Behind her he stomped, stocking-footed, grumbling. "Since they went and got these new hymnbooks I can't go by the old words anymore."

She heard the warped tune wavering in the cold other room, a treble picked out with one finger. She waited for silence or for a shout: "Never heard such a heathenish dancy tune!" But if it was what he wanted, there was only silence. Silence was his thanks for anything, and his only praise.

... Once she had tried to be gay, for she was so made that she could not keep from growing a little fond of what she must care for, and once she said to the mother on a Sunday morning, "You look nice in that brown coat."

The mother looked half-frightened and shy to sickness, and Joan smiled, still trying to be gay. "Didn't anyone ever say you looked nice before—not even *him*?" She nodded toward the father.

But he stared at her, his mouth a grim, wide line across his jaw, bewildered by her gaiety.

"I hate polite talk," he said. "It's not honest. I expect my wife to look right. If she doesn't, I tell her so."

On that day they had gone to the church as they did every Sunday. Through snow and rain and wind they went as steadily as through sunshine, and Bart's father whipped up the horses, worried that he must, because it was the Sabbath and these were his beasts. Once, reading in a chill dawn, he came to the Commandments. "Thou and thy beast," he read, and suddenly he paused and whipped off his spectacles and looked about at them. "I wish it had gone on and said *how* to rest the beast on Sunday when you have to go to church." He stared at them, one after the other, and the light from the oil lamp fell on his lined anxious face. Joan saw in that moment's light the troubled puzzling of many years spring into his deep-set grayish eyes. Every Sunday morning he had waked to it.

Sam mumbled, his small red eyes lighting under the clownish thatch of his hair, "Pity it doesn't mention a car!"

But his father glared at him. "You and your making jokes of everything," he shouted suddenly.

Sam bristled feebly. "Well, a joke's no harm that I can see. Anybody'd think a joke in this house was a sin!"

"Shut up," his father bellowed.

"Abram, Abram," the mother broke in, "and you with God's word open on your knee!"

In the silence he began to read again, his burden still upon him. He fretted constantly because he could not find ways of literally obeying what he read.

And none of these things filled the emptiness within her. Now she knew where every dish and spoon belonged and where the rooms must be brushed and wiped and she knew the secret of every room, the parlor where they never sat, unless some relative came to see them. . . .

"This is my son's wife Joan, this is Bart's Aunt Emma."

"Uh-huh, well, I heard Bart was married, but I didn't get invited to the wedding."

Aunt Emma's black eyes stared at her out of an enormous fat face, as expressionless as the underside of a pie. "You're a right hefty somebody, aren't you? Almost as tall as Bart! Is she a good cook, Minna?"

"I do the cooking." Bart's mother said stiffly, and added unwillingly, "She's handy, though, about the house."

"Who were her folks?"

Her folks! Had she once had people of her own, who had been hers and whose she was?

Bart, called in from the stable to see his Aunt Emma, said shortly. "Her father was the old preacher over at Middlehope."

"I heard tell of him," said Aunt Emma. "Folks said he was a little off."

"My father?" Joan gasped.

"Nothing but his age and all, I reckon," said Aunt Emma placatingly, and Joan saw this woman did not mean to be unkind. But still she was stabbed. So people had spoken of her father!

There was the dark parlor, where they never went, not even on Christmas Day. . . . But then, what was Christmas in this house of silence? There was a tree at the Sunday school in Chipping Corners on Christmas Eve. Christmas fell that year on a Sunday and the horses must take them, Bart's father said, to what was no better than a merrymaking on the Sabbath. But it was not so very merry. The tree was a slightly crooked pine, sparsely scattered with tinsel from a ten-cent store. But there was a star, a white paper star, stitched around the edges with tinsel, and Bart's father read the story of the star, and the children came forward, the pinched frightened-looking farm children who worked early and late at chores, and the smug little children of small village storekeepers, with here and there among them the angelic face of a child who would never belong anywhere. Looking at one of these, a little brown-haired girl, staring at the few candles upon the tree, dreaming them into hundreds, Joan saw herself. She watched the little girl, smiling, catching from the child's eyes a solitary gleam of Christmas. She made her way to the little girl's side and said, "Merry Christmas!" But the words were strange to the child. She did not know the greeting. She pointed a thin little finger at the tree and cried out, "That there one is a-fallin'!" She drew close while Joan straightened the candle, and stared on, lonely and entranced.

So they came back to the farmhouse. They sat down to a better dinner than usual—roast pork and baked apples, and for dessert a bread pudding with raisins. She had made little gifts. She took some of her money and spent it, not for them, but for Christmas—wool for a pair of slippers she crocheted for the father, silk for a knitted green tie for Sam, and a brown one for Bart, and for the mother a handkerchief with a bit of lace at the edge.

She had wrapped the gifts in bright paper and put them on the table. They shone gaily red on the white cotton cloth, but no one spoke or seemed to see them, and at last she could not keep from saying, "Aren't you going to look at your presents?" Then, one by one, clumsily, shyly, almost unwillingly, they took the packages and opened them, all except the father, who left his unopened. The mother said, "I don't know how to thank you, I'm sure."

Sam said, grinning at her intimately, "Green's my girl's favorite color. If it had been blue now, I'd have given it back to you."

Bart said, "Is that what you've been doing every night on the sly, sitting up when you ought to have been in bed!"

The father, because the unopened package was so large

upon the table, put it on the floor under his chair. After he had eaten he took it with him and went upstairs and when he came down he wore the slippers.

"Do they fit you?" she asked, wistfully.

"A mite short, but I can wear them," he answered.

Without speaking she went upstairs to the cold bedroom and shut the door and sat by the window and looked over the gray hills. A year ago today they had gathered in the pine-scented church where her mother lay dead under the Christmas star. It was very long ago. Her mother was locked away into the earth, into all that was gone forever.

That little girl, dreaming the few candles into hundreds upon the scanty Christmas tree this morning in the bare little church!

She could not keep down her heart, after all. It would come up like a bubble in a breeze whenever she forgot. And she forgot very often. She forgot in the joy of snow. There was the old childish rush of pleasure over snow, the soft wide whiteness of the new earth. She put on her boots and her old red leather coat and plowed through the woods in an ecstasy. Then the universe shrank small and warm about her and she was not lonely, not for this moment. And the snow melted and underneath were small green plants, leafing and sprouting and ready. In the afternoons, when the work was over, there were waiting for her the hidden rosy buds of arbutus and the pearly whiteness of bloodroot. She could bear the loneliness in the house, thinking of all that was waiting for her in the intimacy of the earth over which she wandered alone and was not lonely. She took pleasure in small things, small flowers and small curious stones and in little dells. She discovered valleys, named them to herself: "My dell where I found the dogtooth violets"; "My pool—" But she avoided the pale tremendous largeness of earth and sky at dawn, and twilight, and at night she drew the shades because the sky was so wide and glittering with the cold far stars.

So the year passed, and another Christmas, and she gathered to herself all she could possess to fill her emptiness.

And she still had something of her own to put into her emptiness. Rose and Francis were alive. They were somewhere in the world and so they belonged to her. Early in the new year Rose wrote from across the seas that she was soon to have a baby. When the letter came, Joan put her hand to her lips to press them shut. She must have her part in this. She wanted Rose's baby, too. And Rose must come home now. She could come here—this was her home and Rose could come to it and have her baby.

She planned quickly. It was a good place to have a baby, quiet and clean, and there were the hills. It would be spring when the baby was born and she could set a basket out under the trees. She curved her arms, feeling Rose's baby in them. Rose wouldn't know how to take care of a baby. She laughed aloud—Rose with a baby! Someone must be told. She ran to find Bart. He was in the field, building a stone wall.

"Rose is going to have a baby," she cried, waving the thin foreign sheets at him. "I must write to her to come home—"

He went on lifting the stones. There was this stretch of wall and another before sundown. "You know how Ma is," he said.

"You mean—she wouldn't want Rose?"

He laid a stone in silence before he spoke. "She always took kids hard," he said heavily. There were some women who came out into the fields and helped, but Joan didn't seem to think of it. Well, no one should say he wasn't good to her. "We never could have the other kids home after school much," he went on. "She always took them as work. She was always afraid of the muss they might make in the house."

Something in his voice made her suddenly see Bart, a small overworked boy with no chance to play. She looked at him for the first time, instantly moved by the little child she saw.

"Didn't she ever invite any children over—to a party or something?"

"We never had a party," he said slowly, striking a rough stone into pieces. "She was afraid of the trouble, and he was afraid of our learning something sinful."

"Didn't anyone ever invite you?" she asked, troubled. When she had been a child a party was nothing—her mother would cry in gaiety. "Let's have a party!" And almost at once there was a party, the house full of noisy children, prancing about, dressed up, an orchestra blowing on combs and drumming on tin pans.

"You don't keep getting asked if you never ask," said Bart.

. . . In the kitchen she said to the stout pale woman sitting eternally by the kitchen stove, "My sister Rose is going to have a baby—I'm so happy!"

Bart's mother sighed. "Children are a lot of trouble. They mess the house up."

"Weren't you glad when your children were born?" Joan asked, angry for that little boy.

"They're good," she answered. "They've always been good boys. But they've made work. I got so I just couldn't make pie for them. It seemed too much to work for a long time and roll out the pie and see them eat it in a few minutes as quick as though they was drinking milk. I gave up making pie in their teens. Three men can eat up a whole pie at once and your work's gone for nothing, seems like. It didn't seem necessary."

She sighed again, in the midst of the clean kitchen.

"But my sister is coming home . . ." Joan began again. She would not give up quite so easily as this.

Then she thought of a key to open the door of this house to Rose. Once a month in the middle of the week Bart's mother put on her second-best black dress and one of the boys or Bart's father hitched up and drove her to the church to a missionary meeting. Joan never wanted to go. She always said, "I'll have supper ready for you when you come back." But once or twice she had gone and sat quietly through the meeting. It was like all the others she had known, the good mothers sewing, listening to tales of famine and flood and falling down before idols, their eyes absorbed, turned inwardly upon their houses, upon the house where each must be back for supper. There was the tinkling dribble of small silver and copper coins and it was all over. Still they went, since it was a duty.

"You know—did I tell you?—that Rose and her husband are missionaries?"

"Yes, you did tell me," Bart's mother said. "I always thought it kind of queer that you never cared more about the meetings, they being missionaries themselves. Well, I guess I'll stir the potatoes. Does seem as if mealtimes come round quicker than anything could."

She rose from her seat by the stove, sighing.

No, there was no room here for Rose's baby to be born. She wrote to Rose, "If I ever have a place of my own—" For she had no place of her own, after all. She must let Rose have her baby in a foreign country.

Into the emptiness she began to put an image of Bart. She needed an image in her emptiness and so she took a little here and there of what she had. "He's my husband," she said to herself. So she took fragments of Bart and shaped them with the welding of her imagination into an image. She took his size, the breadth of his shoulders and his strong neck and his length of limb. But she did not take his hands, clenched, hard, swollen, so that he could never really straighten them or never seem, when he took her hand in his, really to hold it. She took his square jaw, his close curly dark red hair. But she did not take his stiff pale lips, nor his deep-set reddish eyes. She even took his silence and made it strength. And the breath with which she breathed life into this image she made was the moment in the field when she saw him as a small awkward country boy, wanting the merriment of parties, of play, and doomed to work, to get up and milk the cows before he went to school, to milk cows and chop wood and carry feed and water to the beasts when other boys were playing ball and sledding and skating and giving and going to parties.

For of course there had never been any fun in this house. There was no room in which fun could be made. The parlor was full of the old-fashioned horsehair set, the polished table, the bright rose-flowered carpet, still clean after fifty years. The sitting room was full of the jangling piano, the cabinet of shells and hair flowers and little boxes and bits of glass. Poor Bart—poor little working boy!

She began to be kind to Bart, to talk more to him. In that silence of his, what might there not be sleeping but alive? She might find thought and imagination—if not love, perhaps thought and imagination. It would be good to find these buried under the vast silence, the silence he did not break in the day—for it was not broken by his saying, "Where'd you put my old pants?" or by her saying. "They are mended and hanging on the second hook behind the door"—which he did not break in the night, which he would not have broken if she had cried aloud what she so often cried with inward desperate tearless weeping, "Is this all, Bart? Is this all it is?" For he took her night after night, swiftly, and in the same silence in which he ate and drank or in which he fell into instant sleep.

But sometimes in the day when she was away from him she remembered the little longing boy she saw in the field. From that little boy Bart might be born again, a man such as his father and mother had not made him.

"Bart, would you like me to read to you sometimes?"

"What?"

"My books. They were in the round-topped trunk I brought with me, remember? I've set them on a shelf in the attic. Your mother said they wouldn't be in her way so much there."

"Sure."

He was so amiable that the image in the emptiness stirred with life. In their own room that night she opened the book she had chosen. In the afternoon, after the work was done, she had gone to the attic and had sat down and one by one she had taken down her books. Here were the books she had had in college. On a page she found Mary Robey's name scrawled: *When this you see, remember me.* Yes, she remembered. It was another life—a life finished with its end. Strange how life could end abruptly and begin again, wholly different, so that one was another person! But these books, some of them her mother's, were like a frail mesh, binding that past to this hour. Perhaps they would bind Bart and her into some sort of life together. *Story of an African Farm.* It had been when she first read it a troubling book, with the trouble of reality and of herself in the child on the farm. And then Miss Kinney had made Africa vivid in darkness, and she could see it all.

She began to read to him. He sprawled upon the sheepskin rug before the empty fireplace. She began to read in a quiet even voice, eagerly. Perhaps this was the beginning of a sort of companionship. Perhaps she had not tried enough. She read on a while, and then the old sense of troubled reality came over her again out of this book. It became at last too much for her. She looked up, trembling, pleading. She laughed shyly, her eyes wet.

"Bart, this child is so much like me that I—"

He was asleep, deeply asleep, his mouth open. He must have been asleep a long time.

Though she put her books away to read alone sometimes, going up the steep attic stairs to them alone, she was still kind to Bart, who was only a boy. She saw now that there was nothing more in him than what was to be seen by anyone. He would never be anything but a boy. Once reading of a man and a woman in one of her books, she found herself weeping. It was like waking from sleep to find herself weeping. It was not a surface weeping, not tears only, but some hurt in the roots of her. She was a woman now. There was no more of the girl Joan left. She knew why she wept and she said steadily to her weeping heart, "Be just. I married him for a home and for safety, and I have these two things."

But the book made her think of the way she used to kiss Martin Bradley. She did not love Martin Bradley. She did not want him anymore. But there had been those kisses, the only ones she had ever given any man. She did not kiss Bart. She could not kiss Bart. When he pressed her she touched his lips quickly, she kept her lips still and patient beneath his. She said to herself day after day, "I must always be just to Bart."

Sometimes passive in the night she thought, reproaching herself, "I have injured him. On one of the farms in these hills there would have been a woman to love him in his own way." She remembered the farmer and the girl who had come to be married in the manse. The man was like Bart, she thought, filled with remorse. "I have deprived them both so that I might have a place for myself. I must make it up to him."

So she was very kind to Bart. She denied him nothing, by day or by night. She went when he called from the barn or the yard. "Bring me a pail of fresh water this morning. Jo—I'll be in the west field."

"Yes, Bart."

"Come and see the two old hogs fight, Jo. It's a sight to make your sides split!" She stood by the pigpen with him, watching, revolted by the angry grunting beasts.

At night he said roughly, "Don't you go to sleep yet, my girl."

"All right, Bart."

She had at first hated the silence of the house. It had pressed upon her, intolerable to bear. But now it was a cloak under which she could hide. She was glad for their habit of silence. Since none spoke and none revealed himself, she also need not speak nor reveal herself to any. Silence was shelter. And day and night she was kind to Bart. . . .

Out of her steady determined kindness to Bart she conceived her child. She waited, breathless with joy, in a shining mist of joy, until she was sure. And then she was sure and then she was no longer alone. She was never to be alone again. She was in the full company of her child.

So she did not need any longer the image of Bart. She could accept Bart as he was. For instead of the image there was now the reality of her child. She carried that reality with her everywhere. There was this steadily growing secret life within her.

Soon, like a bud pushing daily more steadily to the light, this life would also come into the light, and she would see her child. But she held him as securely her own already as though she had him, flesh and blood, in her hands. She was not impatient, for she had him. It was enough that he was alive, growing, moving. She carried him with her into every realm of her being. He was not only in her body, he was in her heart and her mind. For him she made her life. Even when she read she put what she read consciously into his making. "That's a lovely thought," she would say to herself. "That I put into him." But she needed a place for him in this house. She found an old broken armchair in the attic and mended it and made it soft with a ragged quilt and there she sat, by the small gabled window toward the west, dreaming, sending her dreams through her beating blood, her blood that was feeding and fashioning her child.

Now she took stock of all that made her life to see what she wanted for her son. This house was to be his home, this land, these hills must for years be his home and his world. She pondered it all, everything, examined each separate part, to see what she wanted for him. Here he and she would live together, taking what they wanted, making what they had not. She would take the great shadowing sheltering trees, she would take the undulating hills, the valleys full of woods, the curious aged rocks, the stream at the edge of the cornfield, the marsh where lady's slipper and wild iris grew, all her small private possessions. She would take the barn with its great hayloft, the cattle lowing and giving their milk.

She would go to the barn herself and even now take the milk for him whole. When Bart's father said, "We sell the cream," she would say, "My baby shall have cream. It is more important for him to have cream than for it to be sold to city people." She would take the eggs they guarded as jealously as jewels. He must have eggs every day. She began even now for him, now when her body was his source of growing. So she had had to tell them about him. She kept it as long as she could to herself, so that in the silence she and the child could live together. But for his sake it was told.

"Bart," she had said one night in the bedroom when he stepped out of his blue jeans. She stooped to pick them up and hang them on the nail behind the door. "I'm going to have a baby."

"Are we?" he cried. She paused, astonished at his "we." It had not come into her mind that the child was anyone's except her own. His square unshaved face broke into a great grin. "I been wondering when that was going to happen."

She had gone on distinctly. "I want you to get me a quart of milk every day with all the cream in. And I want two eggs for my breakfast. The baby ought to have them."

He scratched his head and looked at her. "Don't know about that—Pop's kind of low since the fruit trees got frosted."

"It's got to be, Bart," she replied.

"Sure," he said amiably. "If you say so, I'll put it up to Pop."

"I never coddled myself." Bart's mother said next day in the kitchen. "I raised the boys on skim milk all right. Folks don't need cream. It sells good and we're short."

Joan did not answer. She could use stubborn silence now, too. She went on steadily kneading bread. She had learned how to make good bread, great snowy loaves, brown crusted. Some day her little boy would run into this very kitchen, "Mother, I'm hungry." She would answer, "Yes, my son." She would go and cut him a full slice of the bread she had made and butter it thickly before their very eyes, and give it to him. "There's plenty more if you want it, my son," she would say clearly before them all. She would take ruthlessly for him.

So now she went openly into the cellar and poured out cream and put it back into her skim milk, cream that was bottled, ready to be sold. She went to the nests in the chicken house and took what eggs she wanted. They watched her, their silence loud with astonishment and anger, so that Bart was afraid before his father and tried to placate him with extra work. Let him, she thought triumphantly, let him do that for my child.

Only Sam said aloud, with envy and hostility, "Say, it's luck for you, ain't it!" His mother hushed him, outraged. "Sam, be quiet!" But it was outrage because it was not decent to know that Joan was to have a baby. It was another thing about which to be silent. Joan spoke quickly, tranquilly. "Why luck? I want my child to have a strong body, Sam."

But to such frankness he had no answer. He grew red and retreated into their common silence and said no more. They were shocked at her indecency. But she was not afraid of their silence anymore. She had learned how to live in it now. She took what she wanted and was not afraid.

And then one day there was a letter for her. She had no letters these days except from Rose, for Francis did not write. He had lost himself in the world and she did not know where he was. She could only wait for him to come back. She tore at this letter quickly, for the stamp was not foreign. But it was not from Francis. The paper was stamped with the words, MINISTER'S INSURANCE DEPARTMENT. She read it quickly. There was a check pinned to the corner. Her father, the letter said, had for years carried a small insurance. Since they had not known of his death until recently there had been a delay in sending her the money. More than two years ago he had written saying his wife had died and he wished his elder daughter to have his insurance in case of his death. The check was for five hundred dollars.

She sat down on the old stump by the mailbox. If she had had this letter before her child began to live in her—but she had not.

She was held now to this house. She must keep this house to be a home for her child, a family into which he could be born. Money could not buy her freedom. She had taken their blood into her and mingled it with her own blood. She could never be free. She sat, gazing over the morning fields. On the hill across the valley she saw Bart plowing, small against the earth. She heard his voice crying at the horses, faint and very thin in the distance. Money could not free her. She had taken him into herself. But she would not tell him of this money. At least that would be hers. She would put it into the bank in some town where they did not go and keep it in her own name. She would know it was there if she needed it, a secret power.

But she was jealous of Bart. As the days passed, as the child moved in her and grew, she wanted it to be all her own. Bart's part in its creation was so little, so unconscious, so accidental.

And Bart could not be a father when he was only a boy. He was longing for a car now, exactly as a boy longs. She listened to him. "Jo, I just got to get me a car. I got seventy dollars in cash now and my share of the pigs and pullets. I got a good notion to go on and get me a car." He was excited by the thought, pleading for her agreement. "Don't you think we ought to have a car? It's so slow these days not to have one. Every fellow my age drives his own car, and it looks foolish to go to church or town in that old surrey, hitched to the plow horses. If Pop wasn't so old-fashioned—he's got money in the bank—I know he has."

She smiled in secret triumph. This great boy the father of her son! She smiled tolerantly. "Why, yes, Bart. Why not?"

"I could get me a used car," he said in excitement. "I could paint it up all new. Say, do you like red or blue? Maybe a nice green. I'm partial to green."

He went off, planning. She said to herself, "Let him have his car. It will mean more to him than the child. I can have the child to myself."

The next Saturday, when he came home in an old car, she went out and admired it. The owner said loudly, "He's the quickest fellow to learn to drive I've ever seen. I told him a few things and he's got the hang already." Bart said, "Move over and let me see." He shoved himself into the driver's seat and studied the gears. "Let's see—" The car moved slowly. His face grew solemnly ecstatic.

She smiled, content. Her child was her own. It was more easy now to be pleasant, to be kind. She was very kind to them all, these days.

But she wanted someone to whom to talk. If her mother had been alive she would have run to her. "Mother, I am going to have my child!" She could see her mother's dark eyes go joyous in that brightness, as though an inner light had been turned on, like windows shining in the night. "Oh, my *darling*!" She could feel the quick warm arms about her. And she yearned for Rose and Francis. It had been so long—how had they grown so separate? She wanted to see him again. As if an answer to her longing, a letter came from Rose. Rose's child was born, a little delicate boy, so delicate they had not dared to hope to keep him alive, but he lived. He had been born on a warm April day in a Chinese city, a fair little boy who looked like Rob. Rose had no milk for him. Her round breasts were useless, for the nipples were too small. They would not rise and the little boy could not grasp them in his lips, or he was too feeble to try. So they had hired a Chinese wet nurse, a peasant woman whose baby was a girl. She was willing for money to take the girl's milk for Rose's little boy. "We feel only our prayers have kept him alive," Rose wrote. Joan, reading the letter closely, longed for the frail child. She looked at her own swelling breasts proudly. If the children had been together, I believe I could have fed them both, she thought in triumph. I shall have so much—far more than enough.

Bart's mother said, "Reckon I can help you when your time comes. And Mrs. Potter over at Clarktown is a midwife, if anything seems out of the way."

But Joan said, "I've made my plans. I shall have Dr. Crabbe."

"It doesn't seem as if you had to have a real doctor," Bart's mother objected. She was peeling potatoes and she looked at Joan reproachfully. "It ain't like a sickness."

"He knows me," Joan answered tranquilly.

She was ironing a small, plain white dress she had just finished—six little dresses. Bart's mother had said, "There's some of Sam's old baby clothes in the attic."

"No," said Joan quickly. "No, I don't need them." She could not have Sam's old garments on her little tender-fleshed son. The thought revolted her. She could not bear to touch Sam even in accidental passing. But she opened the round-topped trunk and searched over the baby dresses, the little petticoats and shoes, and the red jackets Francis had worn. They were old and much washed but still dainty, because her mother had made them so fine of good lasting stuff and with small embroidery and tiny worked buttonholes and narrow laces.

One day in late October she hitched an idle horse to the buggy and drove to Middlehope to see Dr. Crabbe. She chose a Monday, when people would be busy and she might meet no one. Bart said proudly, "I'll drive you in the car if you'll wait till the work's done." But she could not trust her son to his slow-witted driving. She said quietly, "I'd better go earlier, thank you, Bart."

So she had driven gladly alone through the still October sunshine. She had made it habit now to choose things for her son's life. I choose these colors, she thought happily, that red vine in that oak, that yellow white-barked birch that little gay chipmunk. Together they would see all these things, and soon, in only a year or two, they could talk about them. Then there would always be someone with whom to talk. She must watch and find out all she could, see all she could, with which to enrich his life. These hills should not imprison him, nor should the woods seem dark or frightening. He must never feel lonely in this silence. She must be always there.

She drove into the quiet sunlit street, and past the church-yard, the church, the manse. Upon the manse steps sat two small children, a boy and a girl, eating slices of bread, staring at her as she passed. She heard a woman's brisk voice calling, "Mollie, where's Donny?"

"We're here," the little girl piped back.

"Take good care of him," the voice answered. In the garden she saw a youngish man raking leaves, bareheaded and a little bald. It was the new minister. Monday was his holiday as it had been her father's. But her father never raked leaves—he spent the whole day in his study, reading books he had not time for on other days or making parish calls. The new minister? He was no longer new. He was the minister now, his the house and children. It was impossible to believe that the two small children were not the ghosts of herself and Francis, so short the time was since they had sat on the steps eating bread and sugar. She could hear her mother's voice: "Joan, where's Francis?"

"We're here, Mother!"

"All right, darling."

She must find Francis, she thought ardently. She took her mind from her errand to think of him, troubled, her conscience stirring. She ought not have let him go so long. But he did not write and she had no way to find him. She must send letters, many letters, send them out like arrows, until one found him and brought him home to her again. . . .

In Dr. Crabbe's office she waited, and then in a moment he was there, his hair a curly white rim about his bald crown, his blue eyes dim and rheumy, his hands shaking.

"My goodness, it's you, Joan Richards! Why on earth haven't you—Where's that Godforsaken hole you hide in, anyway? I've been driving all round that country seeing sick folks and never see hide nor hair of you!"

She found her lips trembling. She wanted to cry. She wanted to cry and cry and tell Dr. Crabbe everything, to be the little girl again, to catch for a moment the warm old circle about her. But she steadied herself. No use trying to go back.

She laughed and took his hands, feeling their shaking.

"Dr. Crabbe, I'm going to have my baby—and I want you to help me."

"Well, well, well—I keep on living and living. Your mother came to me with those very words. Let's see—sit down, child

—I want to ask you a few things. Let me look at you." She gave her body over to his hands gratefully, confidently. He peered and puffed as she remembered he always did, breathing hard as he grew absorbed.

"There—you've got a glorious body, Joan—sound as an apple—no trouble at all—everything's just beautiful. God, I like to see a good body!"

He washed contentedly, talking cheerfully. "Old Mrs. Kinney's not dead yet, Joan—had pneumonia last winter and I had to pull her through it, damn her! She thought sure she'd go. You know how scary she is of everything—won't even ride in an automobile But she got well. I swear I'm going to live to bury her You heard Netta and Ned married, didn't you? They're going to have a baby next month, but she's a different story—slack built sort of female—I don't know what's going to happen there I'm dubious, that's all, I'm dubious!"

He asked no more questions of her until she went outside. Then he shot his white eyebrows over his eyes at her and said sharply, "You happy, Joan?"

She smiled at him. "Why not? I'm going to have my baby."

And jogging home alone she began to sing. She hadn't sung in months. Now she thought she could, if she had a little time, make a song of her own again. The tight dark isolation of her heart was over. Yes, actually, there was a song in her mouth. She held it lightly on her lips, waiting for it to shape. Here was a phrase, and here. When she reached home she went straight to the attic and found a bit of paper and put down the two lines and then a third.

But although she waited, the end would not come. The song hung there, unfinished, and she let it be. It was a song written to a child not yet born. The end would come in its own time.

Waiting for her baby in overflowing tenderness, she wrote to Rose more warmly than she ever had. "Tell me all about little David, I feel he is mine, too." She tried to see the little fragile fair baby, nursed by a brown woman. She wondered about his home and the Chinese landscape. If only Rose would tell her more—she couldn't see anything of Rose's life. When she tried, she saw a static picture of a church, shining among dark vague temple shapes, and a stream of brown people leaving the temples, pouring into the church. But that could not be life. The work was going well, Rose said. Little David had had a fever—

malaria, they thought, but he was better again. The Lord blessed them and they were receiving nearly fifty new members this year. Rob was opening new territory. The people were hostile and he went in danger of his life among them, but they were not afraid. They persisted steadily in God's work, preaching the Gospel to unwilling ears, trusting to God for the harvest. She hoped Joan would bear her child more easily than she did. David interfered a good deal with her classes, but he would soon be older.

I wish I had him, Joan thought, folding the pages. I could take care of him easily. I believe he bothers Rose. I can't think of her holding a baby and bathing him and dressing him.

But Francis never answered her letters. She thought about him while she was waiting, worrying about him because he never wrote. She seemed to see him now always as he had been when he was a small boy in a little red sweater, his eyes very black above round scarlet cheeks and his black hair curling a little at the ends.... "Joan, take Frankie with you if you are going to the Winters' to play." ... "All right, Mother—come on, Frankie!"

If sometimes she was impatient with his short steps and his constant tagging, one look at his face and chubby body softened her. None of the girls had a little brother so pretty. What if she'd had a pale-eyed weazened little runt like Netta's Jackie? She was always proud to walk along the street with Frank. They might meet a stranger who would surely say, "What a beautiful little boy!" Then she could always reply proudly. "He's my little brother!"

But he never wrote to her.

Then one clear frosty morning when she was doing the Monday's wash under the elm tree in the yard she looked up and saw him walking down the road to the house, a small suitcase in his hand. She could not believe it was he, but she knew the way he walked. And it was like him to come suddenly, without a word. She straightened herself above suds and ran, clumsy with her child, to meet him and take him in her arms.

"Oh Frank!" she cried, laughing and wanting to cry. "I've been thinking about you so much. Why haven't you answered my letters? I've written and written!"

Ah, it was good to have her arms warmly about someone!

He had grown. He was taller than she now, he was handsomer than ever. But so thin! Her eyes took him all in at once—that was the same blue suit he had when he went away. Now it was worn and gray at the wrists and elbows, and he had turned the cuffs of the trousers inward. But it was his face at which she looked. His rosy boyish color was gone. His face was sharp-boned, sunken at the jaws and the temples. He looked tired enough to die.

"I only got two letters," he said. "It's taken me a while to come—to get here."

"It's home," she said quickly. "Where I am is always home for you."

He did not answer. He walked beside her to the house, and followed her in. She took him into the dining room, the only room that was warm, and the day was chilly with autumn. Then she did not know where to take him. "Wait," she said. "I'll ask Bart's mother."

In the kitchen she said, "My brother has come." She paused, "May he—What room shall I put him in?"

Bart's mother looked up from the stove, astonished. "How long'll he be here?" she asked after a while. No one had ever come here to stay.

"I don't know," she answered. "I haven't had a chance to talk."

Bart's mother lifted the lid of the stove and pushed in a knotty stick of wood. The lid would not fit down and she clattered at it.

"He can sleep with Sam, or in that old bed in the attic. We used to have a hired man up there when times was good, but nobody's slept there for a long time. It's all right as long as it's not summer. There's some quilts in that old chest under the eaves."

She went back to the dining room and took his hand. It was callused and hard, so hard that she looked at it quickly. It was grimed with so deep a grime that it looked as though it could never be clean. "What have you been doing?" she cried. His hands had been slender, the joints supple. It was still a slender hand, it would always be slender, but the skin was scarred and the nails black and broken.

"Been in machine shops," he said, "and this last six months I've been in West Virginia in a coal mine."

"In a mine!" she said, astonished. "I though you wanted to fly."

"I do," he said. "I lost my job—nobody can hold a job these rotten days—and I went south with my pal. We heard there were jobs in the mines." He made a grunt of laughter. "Do you see me in a mine, Joan, wanting to fly?" He sat down and put his grimy slender hands through his too long heavy black hair and leaned upon them.

"Come upstairs," she said. "Come up to my room. I must know everything."

He followed her up the front stairs, not knowing why she hesitated a moment and then said firmly, "Yes, come this way." She led him into the bedroom.

"Gee," he said, "I'd like a bath, Joan. I've hiked and hitch-hiked for days."

She hesitated again. There was the bathroom, but—the child made her strong today for Francis. Someday the child would be a man like Francis, and he would not wash himself in a wooden tub in the woodshed. "I'll show you where the bath-room is," she said.

While he bathed she went downstairs. She was foolish enough to be afraid for a moment of this fat silent woman moving about the kitchen. She listened to know if Francis was quiet. He used to be so noisy, rushing the water out of the faucets, dropping the soap dish, his strong bare footsteps thudding about. But he was very quiet now. For a moment she was so foolish as to think she would not tell Bart's mother. She could put everything in order— Then she straightened herself. She would not be afraid, she was going to make a life for her own boy here in this house.

She went to the door of the kitchen. "Francis is using the bathroom," she said quietly. "He has come a long way—he's very tired."

Looking down, she met Bart's mother's eyes fully—pale eyes whose brown had no depth. They were the color of shallow leaf-stained water flowing over stones. She gazed into them steadfastly, defying them. Sometimes it was good to be tall and towering. The pale eyes wavered and fell.

"There ain't too much hot water," she said. "If he uses too much there won't be enough for the dishes. How long did you say he was staying?"

"I don't know," said Joan.

She set his place beside hers for the noon meal, and went

back upstairs. He was dressed again and sitting in the bedroom. Now that he was clean, he looked very pale.

"You are much too thin, Frank," she said, instantly troubled.

He gave the grin above which his eyes used to sparkle. But now they remained somber. "I haven't eaten my fill steadily," he said. "Seems to take a lot to feed me, Joan. I didn't realize it before when I wasn't doing it myself."

He looked about the room restlessly. "What sort of a place is this you're in? I haven't seen your—I haven't seen Bart yet. I can't seem to think of you as married." His eyes swept her figure delicately and moved away.

She said at once, "You see I'm going to have a baby soon, Frank."

"Yes . . . I hope you're happy."

She did not answer. Now that Frank was here something of her own was near her again. She wanted to talk to him, to confide in him as she had never confided. But he kept his eyes steadily turned from her and his reserve held her away. "I'm happy about the baby," she said.

She waited but he did not answer, so she knew they could not speak of herself. She said, "Now tell me about yourself—everything. I've thought about you so. Why didn't you keep that job?"

"I never could work up in it. They kept me greasing parts and cleaning—all the young fellows who'd been to schools kept coming in and getting ahead. There isn't any fairness in this rotten system, Joan. I've learned a lot since I've been away. I used to think if I worked hard and good, I'd get ahead anyway. I soon gave that up, like I gave up all that stuff Dad used to preach. He didn't know anything real—all that talk." His face was set in a bitter half-grin.

"He believed it," she said quickly.

"Oh, sure," he replied. "That's why it was so poisonous. He was good enough, but that's no use—not on this earth, not with things the way they are. There's no chance for a fellow who hasn't influence or money or something. Remember that letter you got me? That letter didn't help me. Bair hadn't any use for Bradley. He hardly looked at it. I got the job because they happened to need a hand just then. It was summer and things were busy." He examined hs hands carefully as if he had never seen them before. "Well, then things weren't so busy and they dropped me, and there was nothing to do about that. I was hoping to get to be one of the regular ground crew. And about that time you wrote about Father—but I didn't want to come to Middlehope."

"No, it was better that you didn't."

He looked at her sharply and she added, "I mean you couldn't have helped—it was all over."

"That's what I thought. So I went to Michigan with a fellow and got a job in the factory there. It was furnace work. I couldn't stand it. I had to stoke the furnaces all day—my skin cracked on me—I was half-roasted. I used to look at my hands and expect the meat to drop off of them. Then I got into some trouble there. I got taken up by some fellows who were arrested for trying to start a strike. Joan, there wasn't a job in that factory fit for a man to live by except the gatekeeper's job. He could stand out in the sunshine and air. The rest of us just stood ten hours a day doing one thing, stoking, riveting, hitting the same place in each car as it came along. If you were on that assembly line you couldn't stop a minute even to breathe or straighten your back—the next car was there and you had to do your share. Another man at the furnaces with me was named Jim Duble—he was a West Virginia fellow, and his dad had been in the coal mines. He swore he'd never go back. But he did go back and I went with him. He said at least it was cool in the mines—cool and dark. I'd stared into that fire until I thought my eyeballs would burst. I thought if I could just get into some cool dark place . . . but I couldn't stand the mine. Every day I had to go down and down—into blackness." He was twisting his grimed hands and she saw him tremble a little. A light sweat broke out about his lips and he wiped it off and went on twisting his hands. "I'd look up at the sky before I went down. Then I'd have to go down. I had to stand being in a hole in the darkness, the earth and the rocks clamping me in. I never could stand being shut in anywhere, even when I was a kid. One morning—soon after I got your last letter—I looked up like that. It was the brightest morning I'd ever seen, sunshine everywhere and the leaves all glittering yellow—everything was sunshine. And I looked up and there was a plane flying high in all that light. I just laid down my stuff and quit. I guess you won't understand. But I quit. I said, I'll never go down again, not if I starve, not if I never fly. At least I won't go down again."

"I do understand," she said. "I understand better than I can tell you."

"I don't see—" he began, and the door opened and Bart came in.

Bart stretched his hand out toward Francis heartily. "I heard downstairs you were here," he said. Upon his square unshaved face was his aimless good-natured grin. She saw him sharply, in Francis' astonished eyes. She saw Bart's rough looks and heard his crude laughter, she saw his simple mind. She saw his thick nostrils and little deep-set meaningless eyes, his huge useless strength, as useless as a beast's unless it were harnessed to some primitive tool.

Her eyes met Francis' eyes with brave pleading.

"You see I do understand," she said.

She had been living here on this hillside, and beyond the rim of the stable hills the world had been roaring and whirling around her, as huge and unknown as the night sky against which she had drawn the shades, lest she be lost. Francis had been caught and held in that whirling, tossed and caught and thrown up again into this one still spot. She listened to him, hour upon hour. He did not pour out talk upon her. He was too wounded for that. In fragments, in torn bits of himself, in scattered words, he let her see. They wandered into the orchard, and into the woods. They sat by the stream in the valley under the falling leaves. In the house he was completely silent, with a guarded stopped silence. But alone with her outdoors he talked, pausing often to breathe deeply, to wipe his forehead when the sweat burst out, to break off suddenly, "Well, there's no use in going into all that." There was nothing left in him of that willful boy, tumbling down the stairs in the sunny old manse, crashing into the dining room shouting for food, whistling noisily everywhere, planning loudly for pleasure, arguing eternally for his own way. He moved, guarded and controlled, his head bent downward a little, as though he had been walking for a long time under a roof too low for him. But from the scraps she pieced out what was whirling about this still spot of earth. In the silence of the woods where the stream slipped so softly over smooth stones that it was scarcely to be heard, she listened.

"Things are shutting down on us everywhere now. You can't get jobs. They don't want you. Nobody cares if you starve."

He said, "I came near starving right there in New York City —food everywhere, restaurants full of food, shops full of food, groceries, delicatessens, wagons full of food, people sitting eating everywhere. And I was so hungry I went crazy and went up to a taxi stopped at a traffic light. There was a woman inside —an old woman. I wouldn't have spoken to a girl. I said, 'Would you let me go with you to any restaurant to get a meal? I'm faint with hunger.'"

"Frank!" she cried. "Why didn't you come home?"

"What for?" he answered. "That wouldn't help. I can't keep coming home all my life. She wanted to give me money. She said, 'Here's a dollar.'"

"Oh, Frank," Joan said.

"I wouldn't take it. That wasn't what I wanted. She said, 'I'll lend it.' And I said, 'I can't pay it back.'"

"Then what?" she whispered.

"Then the light changed and the taxi went on," he replied.

A leaf floated slowly down, upheld by the breeze, and settled upon the small placid pool. Its shadow lay, magnified through the clear water, upon a rock at the bottom.

"And?"

"I fell in with another fellow who hadn't any job, and he took me to a joint he knew and the fellow that ran it gave us some stuff left over from what he didn't sell—lemon pie and stuff that spoiled if he kept it."

She was silent, staring at the shadow of the leaf, so clear, so dancing. A squirrel capered up a tree. She could see its inverted reflection in the pool.

"If you had come home—"

But he straightened himself impatiently and threw a stone into the smooth pool. It broke into a shimmer of ripples and the leaf tossed like a little ship upon the little waves.

"Don't you see it wouldn't matter? There's hundreds of fellows like me, trying to catch on somewhere, hungry as hell— running home doesn't help them. There's got to be a place for them. Gosh, when I think of that stuff Dad used to talk—all that holy salvation stuff! Listen here—not one thing he said was ever any use to me."

"He honestly believed—" she began, troubled.

"Yeah, and what of it?" He was snarling. She saw a hungry boy wandering along the city streets, his hat over his eyes, his body aching with hunger. "You've got to do something more than talk these days. Something's got to be done, and be done damned quick! There's a lot of us feeling like that. And I stick by them! I stick by the hungry and the fellows that can't get jobs!"

He was shouting, his voice ringing through the quiet woods. He had sprung to his feet and she looked up at him.

"Why, Frank, you look just like Father!" she said.

He stared back at her.

"Oh, my God!" he whispered.

He dropped to the log beside her and began scuffling at the small stones.

"I mean—"

"I know what you mean," he said bitterly. "It's the damnedest thing, the way you can't get rid of your ancestors!"

He fell into moody silence and she was bewildered. "Come on home to supper, anyway," she said at last. At least today she had that to give him, food upon a table and a roof under which to sleep. She would take him home. He rose to follow her, and they stood a moment looking at the pool. It was smooth again and the little leaf was quietly sailing on a wave, sailing nowhere, and the stone he had flung lay lost among the other stones at the bottom.

But here was no home for Francis, though with all her strength she sought to make it a home. She took the walls of this house and encompassed him about for his shelter. She made his bed in the attic soft with quilts and put sheets upon it for comfort, although Sam slept without sheets, and not until she came had Bart used them. But Francis should use their mother's sheets which she had brought with her. She dragged the boxes and trunks to make a sort of room for him near the bookshelves. And at the table she plied him with food, passing him the butter, the bread, the meat, relentlessly under their eyes.

"I'll make a pie," she said to Bart's mother. She had not cared before, but now she wanted to make it.

"It takes lard," the older woman said, grudgingly.

Then Joan shamelessly made use of Bart. "Bart says he likes pie," and when she saw Bart's mother give way she used this means again and again. "I made a raisin pudding, Bart." "Bart, I made cookies today—Francis, they're the old ginger cookies, like Mother's." Bart ate, enchanted. "Gosh, Jo, you're a famous cook. What's the matter you been keeping it all to yourself?"

She smiled, her eyes on Francis. His thinness was daily growing into a slender resilient strength. When they were alone she urged him, "Eat, Frank. I want you to get your strength back."

"Yes, I'll take food," he said sturdily. "I've got to begin again, I'll stay until I am able to begin over."

He was so beautiful she could not stop looking at him. His hands were free of the black of the mines now, but they were hard, clean and hard. He helped silently about the place, chopping wood and filling the box in the kitchen and in the dining room, helping her wring the clothes and hang them, carrying water to the barn. She would give him something when he went back to work, buy a new suit for him. She would coax him to take it. But now she gave him a pair of the blue jeans that Bart wore. "I'll take your suit and clean it and press it." She brushed and pressed the stuff with careful pleasure. It was not work to touch and clean and mend that which clothed one's beloved. Strange how garments partook of the bodies which they clothed!

But none of this made his home. In the attic they met sometimes alone, and they knew that their only home was all that which they had shared and which was gone now. They talked long hours here together, he talking again and she still listening. She led him on to talk and now he talked more easily. His speech did not come in such wrenched, broken sentences. He was growing a little healed. But as he was healed he was restless. He was like an animal held by a wound, and one day he would be well of it and ready again to go away. But they talked always and only of him—and she wanted it so. She fended off day by day the question which she saw hanging upon his lips, daily nearer to utterance: "Joan, how did you come to do this?" She talked feverishly of himself. "What do you want to do now, Frank darling? When you get rested and ready to start again—" In the attic she poured out the names their mother used so lavishly upon them all: "darling Frank," "dear heart," "dearest Frank"—all the names for which she had as yet no other use—no use until her baby was born. So that she might fend off that question she talked constantly with him about himself, because in such talk he forgot her. "I want to fly," he said, over and over. "I've got to fly—I can do it. If

I had a chance I could do it. I feel it in myself—the power to do it. I'd know how to do it if I could just get at the controls. They wouldn't need to tell me but just the once—"

He liked the attic. He came to it now whenever there was nothing he could do, when she was busy about the house, when they were not at meals. She found him here when she was free by the gable window, staring out into the sky, over the hills and fields. "I can almost imagine sometimes here that I'm flying," he said. "That elm tree top just outside hides the ground. You see Joan? You look straight over it to the hills and it seems far up."

Yes, she knew Francis must go. They were pushing him out by their silence, by their steady disapproving silence. She said, placating Bart's father, "Let Francis shell the corn for you today."

"I've shelled it myself for thirty-five years," he said grimly.

"Francis can bring up the milk for you," she said to Bart's mother. "Francis and I will gather the eggs."

"The hens don't take to strangers," she said, and Francis stumbled upon the dark cellar stairs and spilled the milk. "You better go and set somewhere," she said bitterly, and cried at Joan, hastening with a cloth and a pail, "Don't bend over—you'll hurt yourself and I'll have the care of you."

No, here was no home. And he never really gave himself up to her here. For with all their talk, they never spoke of why he had gone away that day, of why she had urged him to go away and why he had eagerly gone. Part of him still hid from her.

One morning after breakfast, when he had been there less than three weeks, Sam beckoned to her with his great thumb. She followed him into the hall and he shut the door.

"You kinda follow me after a half hour or so," he whispered to her. "I'll be in the barn cleaning out the manure. Got something to tell you."

"Why don't you tell me now, Sam?" she asked, surprised. His full red face was strangely unyouthful, close to hers like this. He had already lost his front side teeth. He was not yet twenty-five.

"You'll thank me for not telling you here," he replied. "It's about your brother."

She stopped, frightened. "All right, Sam," she said quietly.

In the kitchen, over the dishes, she searched for excuses. "I believe I'll stir up some applesauce," she said to Bart's mother.

"I'll go out and pick up some corncobs to start the fire up a little."

"I told Sam to get them last night," the mother answered.

"He forgot," said Joan. "I'll tell him."

In the barn, above the smoking manure, she heard Sam's coarse whispering. He leaned upon the spade, his little hot eyes boldly upon her, glancing now and then at her fullness.

"I heard something last night Jo. Never mind where I heard it, but I heard it, straight from a colored girl. She's looking for your brother. Says he owes her something and she's going to get it She's not all colored—she's pretty near three-fourths white. Name's Fanny. She heard he'd come back."

"How did she hear?" Joan asked. She knew he was staring at her, but she would not seem to know. She could penetrate that shallow skull. He turned away and spaded with elaborate ease about the edge of a stall. "Oh, women like her—they got ways of knowing they find out anything they want to find out."

She did not speak. She stood watching his spade searching out the filth and lifting it. The stench overwhelmed her—rank, penetrating hot. He stood in it, breathing it in and out. She turned quickly and went outside the barn, panting for the clean air.

But she was grateful for the warning, else how would she had known so swiftly what to do that next afternoon? It was a still, fair afternoon, and she had just come down from the attic. She had gone to find Francis but when she lifted the latch he lay on the bed, his hands folded under his head, asleep. He lay very still, breathing so gently she could not hear him. Upon his face was a look of deep repose She closed the door again, softly Let him rest. He seemed so seldom to rest. In the close tense stillness in which he now held himself there was no rest. He had in so short a time changed all the loose gamboling ways of his youth to this controlled stillness of the body. It was as though under his clothes his body were bound in secret chains. So let him rest.

She went out into the sunshine of the afternoon. It was not late, but the sun would soon be gone. She turned westward down the road, to walk a little while, her face toward the sun. In the barn the men were milking. She could hear Bart's voice roaring at a cow: "Stand over there, Bessy! Careful now, you—"

She set her face steadily westward.

It was then that she saw the girl coming toward her. She came up the road, walking with a sort of springy dancing step, and she had a child with her, a little boy. She had been carrying him, but when she saw Joan she set the child down in the dusty road and led him toward her.

Joan stopped, waiting, looking at the two. Of course this was Fanny. She remembered now she had seen this face, this gay careless passionate pretty face, the last time she had been at the mission with her father. This girl had been there. She remembered her wearing a thin red flowered dress through which her skin had shone, golden. The girl's face looked up to hers, a face like a dark petunia, the full red lips, the great dark swimming eyes, black iris, clear white, passionate eyes and mouth, smooth round dark cheeks, strong short curly black hair under a small bright red felt hat.

"Are you Frank Richards' sister? You favor him mightily." The girl's voice was like honey, thick-deep, sweet.

"Yes," Joan said—no use trying to say anything else. "I'm his sister—what do you want of him?"

"I heard he was here."

She looked down into the black eyes. . . . And why should she now remember Miss Kinney, standing before the missionary meeting, talking about great eyes peering through the jungle, jungle eyes?

"He's gone," she lied. "He's gone back to his job."

"Could you kindly tell me where he is?"

"Far away—away out west."

"Is he coming back soon?"

"No—not soon—perhaps never. He didn't say."

In the twilight the child suddenly began to cry softly, and the girl slapped him sharply on the cheek. "Shut up, you!" The child turned and buried his face in her skirt, and sobbed noiselessly. He was too thinly dressed and Joan saw he was shivering.

"He's cold," she exclaimed.

"He wouldn't be so cold if he'd walked more instead of fretting me to carry him," the girl said petulantly. But Joan dropped to her knees, not able to bear the child's noiseless weeping. A little child ought not to know how to weep silently, she thought. He must have been many times afraid before he could have taught himself to weep like that.

She began to unbutton her jacket.

"I have a sweater underneath," she said. "Let me wrap it about him." She took off the garment and knelt upon the ground and slipped the child's arm through the sleeves and turned them back over his hands. Without knowing it she was coaxing him, talking to him tenderly, persuading his little chilled body into the wrap. "There now, little boy! Now, this hand, now we'll button it up warm and tight. See, I'll put your own belt around to hold it close. There . . . there . . ."

The child, won by her voice, looked at her, and she saw his face fully, near to her own. Her heart turned in her breast. Francis had been beautiful, but this child was the most beautiful she had ever seen. This little face was the face of a dream child. She stared into it, trembling, drawn, repelled. Francis, her mother, her father, her own self—all of them were there in this jungle child's lovely face, but to them all were added the darkness, the passion, the power of the jungle.

"He's your own brother's child." She heard the girl's deep wild voice. "He put this child in me. He come and met me in the woods down by the stream and put this child in me and then he went away and left it on me. I got no way to keep him. If a man fathers a child in me, he's got to take it or pay for it, one or other. Else I can't make my living. And I'm wanting to settle down. I got a colored fellow will marry me if I can do something about this child. It's your own brother's—I can prove it."

"Don't tell me anything!" Joan whispered. "I believe what you say. I don't want to know. Let me think."

She rose to her feet and stood looking at the child. He looked back at her silently, comforted by the jacket, trying to hold his lips against quivering. From under his fabulous lashes he looked up, his eyes unearthly large. He could not possibly understand. He was too small. And yet he seemed to know his circumstances. She loved him suddenly, and she knew she could not let him go—she must keep hold of him—her mother, her father, Francis, all of them were here in this tiny body. His blood was theirs.

"If you will wait a few days," she began, breathless, still looking down at him, "not more than a week—say a week from today—I'll bring you a little money. I have to get it from the bank. I haven't much, but I'll surely help you. And I'll think what to do—if you'll just go home now. I'll be here a week from today at this same time with the money. You can trust me, can't you? My father used to preach in South End."

"Yes, I used to hear him." The girl laughed, a full deep laugh. "Lordy, I used to think what a conniption he'd have if he knew he was a granddad!"

Joan said, "Our parents are dead."

"Yes, I know. The chapel's shut up. They say it's going to be a dance hall next summer— fellow name of Jack Weeks is going to open a beer hall there as soon as the main road's finished—a little peakedy white fellow but his dad's putting up the cash. Going to open the factory again, too. The state's working on a big new road now right through South End, and everybody says business is going to be good—we're all going to make money." The girl spoke eagerly, her mouth a poppy for redness in her glowing face. She was restored to good humor. "I've got to be gone, I guess. My fellow's waiting down the road. He's got a car. Well, thank you ma'am, if you will help me. I call this child Frankie, after his pa. I call them after all their pas— the two girls, I twisted their names. Willa, I call one, and the other—Here, you take off the lady's jacket, Frankie."

"No—let him keep it," said Joan. "And take care of him." She turned and began to walk away.

"Oh, sure I will! I'm always good to them—nobody can say I'm not good to them."

She looked after them once, quickly. That small creature was trudging along over the rough earth road. She could see her jacket warm around him, glowing through the twilight a spot of scarlet.

Oh, what had Francis done?

In the house there was the smell of wood burning in the kitchen stove. The cover had been taken from the table and in the kitchen, the men were washing. She heard Bart say, "Where's Jo?"

"Upstairs, I guess," his mother answered. "I've had no help from her tonight, I know."

But she tiptoed through the room and went straight upstairs to the attic. Francis was still asleep. No, he was not asleep. He was lying awake, and he had lighted the candle on the box.

"That you?" he asked.

"Yes," she said. She came over and sat on his bed. She had

no time to waste. In a few minutes Bart would be shouting for her.

"Francis," she began and stopped. "Francis—there was a girl here this afternoon—from South End—looking for you. I met her on the road."

She felt his body gather and grow tense. "She was here, looking for me?"

"Yes—but I knew before."

"You knew?"

"Yes."

They were both whispering. He sat up. "If you knew, why didn't you tell me?"

"I couldn't—you didn't tell me."

"I wanted to get away. . . . Damn her, she used to say she'd find me wherever I went. That's why I couldn't come back home. Thought I was safe here. How'd she know? I haven't stirred out. I haven't seen anybody."

"She heard somehow." He did not ask of the child.

"I've got to go away now."

"But why are you afraid of her, Frank?"

"I'm not afraid of her—she's only a whore. You can't understand."

"Then what are you afraid of, Frank? I could help, you know. I'll think of some way to help."

"You can't help—you don't know." He began picking at the old tufted quilt he had put over his knees. "You—I'm not afraid of *her*—it's *myself*—you can't understand. I'm spoiled, see? I'm afraid of—wanting to go back to her. I—I'm not decent. I—I want her—a woman like her. You don't know. I don't know what's the matter with me. I make myself sick. I want her and then I'm sick. I'm sick when I remember her—other women like her—but I want her. It's the only kind I can —can want. You'll never know what I mean—nobody can know. I can't get away from it—I want to get away, but I can't."

But he did not speak of the child. He did not know of the child. He must never know about the child. . . . "Me in a coal mine, Joan, wanting to fly!"

"Jo!" Bart's voice shouted up the stairs. "Time to eat!"

"You shall get away—poor Frank, you shall get away!" she promised. Somehow, she could do it, she said to herself fiercely. She could do what ought to be done.

She rode over them all. Bart, astonished, cried, "But you don't know how to even get around in the city! You'll get lost— and I can't go with you right now. We're butchering this week —don't know if Sam could go, even."

"I don't want anybody. Frank knows the way there and I can get back."

She forced her own will ruthlessly.

"You're near your time. You might be took," Bart's mother said. New York! It was a hundred miles away. She knew all about it and she wouldn't go there for anything, and never had. Things happened there. You could read about it in the newspaper. Everybody said—

"I'll be all right," said Joan. "I have more than three weeks to go."

"You can't tell so near," the woman fretted.

"Dr. Crabbe says so," she answered with composure.

"How can *he* tell? Can't anybody tell exactly when a woman takes."

She did not answer. She went on wiping the table, putting away dishes, sweeping the crumbs, planning. She was going with Frank herself. She was going to find Roger Bair herself this time and tell him about Frank. She could do it.

"It's not decent for a woman in your fix to go among a lot of men strangers." Bart's mother was watching her from the stove.

She turned on her. "You mean it's a shame for a woman to have a child?"

"No," the other woman said, embarrassed. She was wiping out the zinc-lined sink and she did not look up. "It's not shame —not after the birth. But before, a decent woman doesn't show herself."

"I do," said Joan. "I don't care—I'm proud." She was triumphant over this house now, triumphant over their silence, over their stubbornness.

"You going to New York?" said Bart's father at the dinner table. He shot his eyebrows over his eyes at her.

"Yes, I'm going," Joan cried.

He grunted and filled his mouth with bread.

"Bring me back something, Sis," said Sam, grinning. He had finished his food and was picking at his black nails with the tines of his fork.

She saw Francis look at him and then stare down into his

plate. He ate doggedly, saying nothing. But after the meal he hung about her as she worked. "Don't come," he muttered. "It doesn't matter about me. I'll find something. There are lots of fellows like me—I'll go on away again."

"We're going tomorrow," she said cheerfully. "I've always wanted to see New York."

But of New York she never remembered anything. She stayed by Francis closely, getting off the train, going down into subways, going up into elevated trains, walking along the streets that were swaying with crowds. He seemed to know his way, going on with certainty from one place to another. She looked at the faces flying past her, a glimpse at this face, a glimpse at another, before they passed. It was as though they were all whirling about her and Francis, and only they two seemed to have direction.

Or were they lost, too? Once in a subway, deep underground, he took her hand. "Don't you get lost," he said.

"I shan't lose you," she promised him, holding fast.

They climbed at last into a bus. "Now," said Francis, "we are nearly there." He sat down beside her. "There isn't any hope, you know, Joan. It's nonsense. He won't remember me—he doesn't know you." His face was bleak in the early morning.

"Are you sure this is the time he will be there?" she asked. She did not answer his despair. She would do anything. All these houses and people—she was not afraid of any of them.

"Yeah," he said listlessly. "I looked up the plane schedule. He comes the same time he used to. I was always there to see him come in and take off. He'll be there unless he's dead. He's nuts about his plane."

"Then I'll see him," she said tranquilly. "I brought enough money along. Even if I have to buy a ticket and ride somewhere in his plane, I'll see him."

The flying field was as big as the whole farm laid smooth. She had never seen so wide and smooth a place. She had never seen a plane before, except as it flew, a bird among birds, in the sky. But then it was impossible, gazing at that far shape as she stood alone upon a hillside, impossible to believe that it contained in its body human beings. Only its purposefulness seemed guided and human. Birds fluttered and swerved, dipped and soared and drifted in dreaming circles. But a plane went straight to its desire.

They were walking across the level field.

"Here's his plane," said Francis.

She forgot to look at Francis—she did not hear the eagerness of his voice. She was staring at the great plane. It was enormous, more huge than her imagination of it. She gazed at it, forgetting everything else, herself, her life. All her wonder was held in this shining shape of silvery metal, seeming to touch the earth so delicately, seeming to spurn it, its wings forever outspread ready for instant flight, its never-folding wings.

But out of the wonder someone was speaking to her. "What do you see?" She looked up at a man taller even than she was—it was strange to look higher than herself—she was always taller than everybody. He looked down at her, a man in a khaki shirt and breeches, a visored cap on his head. Under the cap his face was lean and hewn, the cheeks flat, the eyes bold and blue.

"It's the plane," she said. "I've never seen anything so beautiful before. It's—it's concentration—the clean shape—it's the very shape of flight—it's motion put into shape."

She turned her head. She stared at the plane dreamily in ecstasy. She was thinking. I'm glad I saw this before my baby is born. I'm glad I have this to go into his last making.

She was recalled again by the man's voice. "Are you a passenger? Are you going?"

"Oh, no," she said quickly. "I couldn't—I have to go home—I came here with my brother. He wants to fly." She looked around for Francis and saw him standing a little way off, twisting his hat in his hands. "There he is! Wait—perhaps you could tell us where to find Roger Bair. He's the pilot."

Francis came up to her and caught her words.

"But, Joan," he whispered.

The man smiled. "I'm Roger Bair!"

"Are you?" she cried, and laughed aloud. When she looked at his face now she saw very clearly the straight brow and nose, the deep lines from mouth to chin, the brown weathered skin. It was impossible to tell how old he was from his face, and the cap hid his hair. But his eyes were blue, a clear imperial blue. Looking up in the morning light she seemed to be looking through his face to the sky, his eyes were so blue.

A young man in overalls came up panting. "All right, sir—she's ready."

"All right—I'm ready. Look here"—his eyes came back to Joan's face—"what's this about your brother?"

"I've always wanted to fly, sir!" Francis said quickly.

"I seem to remember your face," the man said, looking at him.

"I worked here a little while."

"Ground crew?"

"No, sir. I never got that far. I was just a sort of extra. Then they cut down their men. It was after an accident, I guess, and they took off some planes."

Roger Bair looked from one to the other of them. They were both beseeching him. "Look here," he said hurriedly to Francis, "I'm not a potentate. I don't know what I can do about jobs. But—you feel about this plane like she does?" He looked at Francis and nodded toward Joan.

"Yes, sir," said Francis. He wet his dry lips and looked steadfastly back at this god who could deliver him.

"All right. Show up here two days from now at this same time and I'll see what I can do. Now I must go—" He turned to Joan and his face wrinkled deeply into the warmest smile she had ever seen. "Some day you'll fly with me."

"Shall I?" She smiled back at him. It was impossible, seeing him, not to let her smile respond to his, and not to believe him.

"Yes!" he shouted confidently. He was already running. Now he was in the plane, and she could not see him.

The steps were drawn away, the door closed, and the great roaring creature moved to mount into the air with the heavy lightness of an eagle. She stood, not knowing that any soul was near, watching him fly higher and higher to disappear into the far mists of the morning. He was gone. Without a word she followed Francis and he put her on the train.

"You'll be all right now," she said.

"Yes," he said. "I'll be all right."

She was going back, alone again. But she had those words, like a token, like a flower left in her hands. "Some day you'll fly with me." Anything was possible, as long as life lasted. Her heart flew dancing out of her breast and gamboled among the shining clouds, following him merrily. I believe I shall, she thought. She held the corners of her mouth into a smile, because she could have laughed in sheer exaltation and delight. Beauty! The world was full of it. Her face lit and sparkled, but she said nothing at all. She let her pure pleasure flow through fields and villages. She thought of him in purest pleasure, remembering him, shaping the memory, holding fast in her mind the movement of his body, the lines of his face, the color of his eyes. And there was, for life in the image, the memory of his smile.

The house was dark and close. To come back to this house, its closed windows, its empty rooms, the small huddled dining room, the kitchen where the men washed, where the food was prepared, where they sat more and more about the iron range now that winter was closing in, was to burrow into the earth. She could never forget, so long as she lived, that wide smooth field, the light of the rising sun, the shining silvery lifted plane. And Roger Bair was a part of it, the embodiment of that morning, just as Bart was the embodiment of these backbreaking fields, this earthy life filled with nothing but the work for food to eat, food forced from the earth, washed, cooked, eaten.

For here they spent their days in getting and eating the food. They went to bed early, exhausted, and slept like beasts, suddenly, heavily. They rose at dawn to get their food again. And they thanked God for this. It was the life of moles, burrowing through the sullen earth. They never lifted their eyes from earth to sky. The seasons were for the fruition of their crops for food. Snow might fall but there was no beauty in it. It was a cause for anger if it fell too long; if it fell too lightly, the wheat suffered. Spring was measured not by bloodroot in the woods and arbutus under the brown leaves around the roots of an old oak, but by the frost upon the fruit trees, and summer was cursed by insects on the potatoes and the beans, by storms too harsh for corn and ripening grain, and autumn was gloomy with a harvest too scanty. They were bound into the earth, mind and body, and their souls were never lifted. When the old man prayed, he pulled God down to earth.

But sometimes she heard a far rushing sound and then she ran out, though the wind were bitter from the north, and looked up into the clouds to search in that distance for the diving shining shape. Sometimes she found it, glittering like a daytime shooting star. Sometimes it was lost in cloud and she would only hear its passing. But she could always imagine it was the plane beside which she had stood, into which he had climbed. She could imagine it, and so make it a light in her darkness, and he was there, a companion in her loneliness.

And, she argued to excuse her dreaming, if she thought about him the baby might grow a little like him perhaps. Surely dreams were not wrong, not if there was nothing else, especially not if her hands went on doing their duty day after day.

She came, as winter drew near, to spend more and more time in the attic, high among the treetops. She sat there often while the swift evening fell, gazing out of the gabled window, hearing the icy branches crack as they swayed about her. Was the plane flying, she wondered, through these frosty clouds? . . . Francis had his job, he wrote her. Roger Bair had been very kind. He was going to be taught to fly some day. He was learning everything about the plane. If he got there early in the morning, Roger Bair taught him things. He always was there early and he always was there when Roger Bair came in . . . She sat in the stillness of the attic. Francis was safe now. She could take her mind from Francis. Down in the earth, in this house, buried among these hills, she could remember the sky and that clean springing soaring shaft of flight into the sky.

When the attic grew dark, as it did early these days, she curled for warmth into the quilts where Francis had slept. She had left his bed as it was, and now it was a place for her. For she could not sleep with Bart now. She was restless with him, and it was no slight restlessness of the body. This was a restlessness which fell upon her like a sickness that first night of her return. She was afraid of this increasing restlessness. In the night she drew far from him, lest she touch him, even inadvertently. At first she lay far from him, grateful for the width of the old bed, so that in his sleep he might not fling his heavy arm unknowingly upon her. Then one night she crept in the darkness to the attic bed, and there alone fell instantly into deep sleep. He found her there, astonished, angry. She woke the second time to see him in the doorway in the woolen underwear he wore at night as well as in the day.

"What'd you come up here for?" he cried resentfully, staring at her over the lighted candle he held. "What's the matter with you anyway these days?"

"I'm restless," she answered. "The baby's so near." Her conscience stirred. She would have been restless without the baby. This was another restlessness. Then her courage welled up strongly. She would make a life. She was not afraid of Bart. She went on calmly, her heart thudding, "I shall sleep here as often as I like, Bart. I'm going to do whatever is best for the baby now. I've got to think of him."

He stared at her over the candle. The upward light threw into relief his thick stubborn jaw, his wide coarse dry lips, the broad base of his nose. The forehead and the small grayish eyes receded into shadow.

"I have my rights," he muttered. "You got to give me my rights."

"I'm staying here," she said. She must speak very plainly to him. He understood nothing else but the straightest, plainest speech. "I'm staying here as long as it's best for the baby." She turned over and closed her eyes. Her heart was beating very hard and she must still it. This sickness, this fearful repulsion, must not go into the making of her baby. She must think of other things, lovely things. She would think of the sky and of the driving silver stars. She lay waiting until she heard him stumble down the stairs and until she heard the door slam. Then she leaped from her bed and searched the sky. But there were no stars. Outside was the deep darkness.

She went on the day she had promised toward the bend of the road where she was to meet Fanny. It was a sullen day, the snow drifting from smooth, frigid gray clouds. She had brought some money. For the present she would bring a little money each week, but soon she must think of some way to earn more. She held it in her hand, the precious stuff. It could not be more precious to Fanny than it was to her. She would tell Fanny she had only a very little and her own child coming. But Fanny was not there. She waited a while, gazing over the bleak hills, not daring to leave too soon. She walked up and down until she was cold, so cold that the child within her felt still and cold, and she grew afraid for him. Troubled, she resolved she would come again the next week, on the same day. She searched the whitening landscape, the bitter wind tearing at her coat, at her hair. But there was no living creature in sight. The road wound emptily into the distance. She turned and went back to the house.

Before the week was gone, on Christmas Eve, her child was born. She had made this year no mockery of preparation for Christmas. Her mother was three years dead. She remembered and put away the memory. Another year there would be a reason for Christmas, a little child for whom to make gifts and cut a tree and trim it. And then in the twilight, the birth began.

But she had the child so easily that it was like a gift. She had been ready for any pain. She remembered scraps of whispers here and there through her years of girlhood—her mother, hurrying in sometimes in the early morning, pale but cheerful, to be at the breakfast table, "Yes, dear, I *am* a little tired. I was at the Watsons' most of the night. They have a dear little baby girl." Later, neighbors running in, she could hear, when she was dusting in the hall, her mother's lowered voice. "Dr. Crabbe sent for me. No, things didn't go just right, but she pulled through. It's a miracle the child was saved. What? Yes, she suffered *agonies!* If only the child is all right—you know what I mean. You never can tell—"

Once Hannah said primly, "I've never married, but there are rewards. I've been spared some agonies, anyway."

She had been ready for agonies, though Dr. Crabbe had said, "You're made for this job, Joan—measurements perfect! Don't often see a woman like that these days—spindly lot, living off pineapple and spinach and looking like yellow wax beans!"

Yes, the child had come like a gift. In the afternoon of Christmas Eve she was in the attic, looking out of the gable window at a deep orange sunset sky. She had had the premonition of pain, and recognized it instantly. She laid herself upon the bed and waited and almost at once the rhythm of pain began. She went downstairs and called Bart.

"Go for Dr. Crabbe," she said. To Bart's mother she said quietly, "My time's come. I'm going to be in the attic in my own bed."

"You're not going to give birth in the attic!" Bart's mother cried. "Folks will talk! My son's wife lying in the attic like hired help!"

"Who will know?" she answered quietly from the stairs. She wanted her baby born there among the treetops, high above the earth. She had been preparing for him there. His little clothes were there in the tray of the round-topped trunk, and the few things Dr. Crabbe had told her to have ready.

"The doctor will tell," Bart's mother cried up the stairs after her. "It will be a shame to us! And if I have to fetch and carry for you, it will be extra steps. There's enough work as it is."

"Bart will sleep better," Joan answered, and heard no answer.

In the attic she made ready. She made everything ready to the measure of the rhythm of pain now quickening its swifter and swifter paces. When its beat brought the sweat upon her forehead and her upper lip, and the palms of her hands were wet, she laid herself upon her bed and stared straight into the rafters, gathering herself for each crisis of the pain. Soon Dr. Crabbe would be here. He had said, "Five hours, perhaps, since it is the first time." Three hours were gone. He would be here at any moment. She could almost catch the rumble and racket of Bart's old car. God send he would drive carefully! He was so absurdly proud of driving that he scorned to be careful. Like a child he boasted, "Look at me pass that fellow!"

Don't think about Bart! This was something she was doing alone. She was having her own child, her first child, the first of many children. Children were to fill her life, all her little children. Now her life was really beginning. She had waited so long for her life to begin. The pain gathered in her, deep, immense, pulling every fiber of her body into a focus of bright pain. Why did people say pain was dark and dull? If one let pain come free—like this—like this—letting it possess the body, letting it gather and mount and soar, it was bright, a shape of edged beauty, acute and clear, rising, tingling, flying upward into purest feeling—a winged body, mounting, soaring into the sky. Above her was the sky, black, deep, soft, a blackness for pain to shine against, to pierce—to pierce and rend and tear.

Something broke in her, her very being gushed forth. She might have been terrified at this melting and flowing. But she was not afraid. By body's sense she knew this was right. Then, almost immediately, the child was born. She gave one great involuntary cry, a cry mingled with the child's first cry. There were footsteps and Dr. Crabbe's voice roared up the steep stairs. She saw his curly grayish head rising at the door. "My God, Joan!" he rumbled, hurrying, stumbling. She was smiling, panting, saying over and over, "Dr. Crabbe—Dr. Crabbe—"

He was bustling, hurrying, cursing. But she had everything ready. He was there instantly at work, grumbling at her, grinning. "Had to be forehanded, didn't you? Damn these capable women anyway! It'll be a pretty kind of world for the profession if women go having their babies by themselves—and it's about all that's left for me to do nowadays—nobody getting sick much and old Mrs. Kinney still hanging on. It's a biggish baby, Joan—a boy!"

All Christmas day she lay upon her bed under the rafters in the deep quietness. Beside her lay the child. She would never be lonely again, never. Her body had divided and made this second self. She was contented as she had never known content. It was body content, content of instinct. Mind did not stir, heart slumbered. But the womb had fulfilled itself richly and she slept and the child slept. Twice she woke, once at Bart's heavy tread, catching upon the stairs. "Dang these stairs—here's your food, Jo."

"Thank you, Bart." She was hungry and she ate while he sat waiting, tipping back on his chair. He had stared curiously at the baby once. "Most as big as a calf," he had said, grinning. She did not answer. He had nothing to do with her child.

"Looks like snow," he remarked.

"Does it?" she said. She looked at the window. Yes, the sky was softly, deeply, evenly gray. He took her bowl and spoon and clattered heavily down the stairs. The clatter was scarcely gone before she slept again. She woke once to find Dr. Crabbe gazing down at her. "Sleep, girl," he had murmured. "That's right. Sleep deeply. Everything's fine—nothing for me to do. I'll be getting back before the snow gets any heavier. It's six inches already."

Snow—it was snowing, then. She was glad. Fanny wouldn't come through the snow. She was safe. She and the baby were safe under this roof. The snow was covering them, warming them, giving them its shelter. She slipped deeper into her covers and felt the body of the child, warm, robust, sleeping. The child was here. She returned into her sleep.

Surely this child was the best child that was ever born. He lay for hours in the rough little cradle she had found under the eaves. She had taken an old pillow and cleaned it and made it into a mattress and cut up two of her mother's linen sheets into small sheets, and she made a tiny pillow and edged it with the fine crocheted lace upon her mother's wedding petticoat. The petticoat was in the round-topped trunk and there she found it, yellowed and scarcely worn, and very fine. Her mother had been an only child and her wedding clothes had been fine, and she had had good linen, though her father had been poor—a professor of Latin in a little Southern university. She scarcely ever talked about her father and mother, because they had died close together the last year before Joan was born. There was no home to go to anymore—no home to take her baby and show her off. She used to say, "I did so want to show you to my mother, Joan. You were the loveliest baby, and she loved babies. It was so hard not to have her see you."

Yes, it was hard. Looking at her own baby, Joan cried out in her heart, "I wish I could show him to her. I wish she could see him, somehow. Maybe she does see him."

But even if she saw him from some far heaven of the dead it was not enough. She wanted to cry out to her mother, "Look at his little hands and feet! See how quietly he lies. I believe he will have curly hair. Isn't his hair the goldenest gold?"

She wanted to hear her mother's voice, eager, excited, agreeing, praising, "The loveliest baby, darling! I always knew you would have lovely babies."

But there was only silence, and she sitting alone by the crib, holding his plump, passive little hand. He was so good. He would lie letting her hold his hand or cuddle him to her. It did not matter how firmly she strained him to her, he never cried. He ate and slept and never cried when she put him down. He lay in his crib, staring at the rafters, breathing gently, slowly. He was so quiet, so silent. Even Bart's mother said grudgingly, "He's pretty good. But I declare I don't see the use of washing out his diapers every time they're a mite wet. The soap jar's nearly empty again. It's a chore to make soap, too."

She grew strong quickly and went downstairs. Everything was exactly the same and yet it was all different now that her baby was born. This was her home. She was rooted here now.

"Seems to me it's about time you was moving into your right bed again," said Bart to her one night. She was putting away his blue shirts she had just ironed. He was in bed, ready to sleep.

She was suddenly breathless. "The baby would disturb you, Bart."

"He doesn't make any noise," said Bart grumpily from the bed. He was watching her, the thickened look creeping about his lips and nostrils. She hastened a little and then remembered. She was not afraid. She did not answer. She put away

Bart's heavy shoes and hung up his work garments. "Shall I open the window, just a little?" she said quietly.

"No," he grunted from the bed. "It's as cold as sin outside."

"Then good night," she said. She blew out the lamp quietly and escaped him in the darkness.

She climbed the attic stairs and made ready for bed. In the cradle the baby lay sleeping. She threw open the window wide and felt the clean icy air rush in upon them. I'll keep him where I can open the windows, she thought. He's going to live up here with me.

She lay there in the keen darkness, awake, the cold air coming and going, an energy in her blood against sleep. She was perfectly strong again. The baby was three weeks old. Dr. Crabbe said he wouldn't come anymore—she didn't need him.

"You never needed me anyway, darn you," he said affectionately, accusing her. "You've got health enough in you to heal any sickness." Yes, she was strong—strong enough for anything, strong against anybody.

Echoing at the edges of her thought was Fanny's voice. Fanny might come any day. The heavy snows were melting. She must get word to Fanny. That little dark child belonged to her, too. She must do something, she must think what to do. But now she would know, she was so strong. Things came to her when she was strong like this.

And next day she thought of how to get word to Fanny. She met Sam on the small back stairs and waited for him. The stair was too narrow for passing. As she waited for his clumping step, waited for his rough grinning face to pass her, she thought of it. There was a look on his face, a look she hated and would not see. He could not see any woman without that look. But she could use even that. "Sam," she whispered, "will you do something for me?"

"Sure," he said. He clamped his hand heavily upon her shoulder and patted it. She did not flinch. "Do you see Fanny sometimes?"

He dropped his hand and his grin widened. "Now you're trying to find out something."

"No, no," she said quickly. "I only want you to tell her something for me—tell her that I'm ready to do what I said."

"What did you say?"

She fenced him off. "Now *you* are trying to find out something."

"Yes," he parried. His hand was heavy on her shoulder again. "I got you."

"No more than I have you," she said smoothly. "I would tell your father, you know."

His hand was dead on her shoulder. The grin was stricken from his face. "You *wouldn't!*" he whispered.

"No, of course not!" She laughed, sick within herself. "Of course I won't say a word. You *will* tell her, won't you, Sam?"

"Sure, I'll tell her," he said. "I'll tell her—I'll tell her tonight maybe—"

She went upstairs and took the baby from the cradle and rocked him against her, sick, sick. She must remember that little dark angelic face. What she did was for him—for them all.

She looked at the baby. He was so fair, his eyes blue like her father's. I'll call him Paul, after Father, she thought. She had not known what to call him. Once she had asked Bart suddenly, "Do you like the name Roger, Bart?"

"What for?" he had asked stupidly.

"For the baby"

"I don't know," he had answered, pondering. "We had a sorrel horse named Roger. Pop sold him because he wouldn't go in a team. He'd rear and pitch if he was put with another horse."

No, she thought, looking at the child's broad pale forehead and wide blue eyes, Roger didn't suit him. Roger meant someone else. Paul—she named him Paul.

"Shall we call the baby Paul?" she said brightly at the supper table.

They looked up at her out of the silence. Whenever she spoke they looked at her astonished, unable to comprehend at once what she said, since she did not speak of the things of which they were thinking—the field just sown, a horse to be shod, the pig's litter. Then Sam spoke. "Paul—it's all right, isn't it? Pop will like it."

"It's short and handy," said Bart.

"They can't nickname it when he goes to school," said Bart's mother.

The old man waited, his jaws full of dry bread. He swallowed hard and gulped the skim milk. "It's a good Gospel name," he said.

"Then it will be Paul," said Joan. She smiled. It would have been Paul anyway.

She had often dreamed in the silence of this house of children's voices, of the chatter and singing, of the shouting and laughter. The house would be full of lovely sound when a child was born. Even a child's lusty crying would be good to hear.

But Paul was so still. He never cried. Not unless he were hurt and in physical pain would he cry. She waited for the sounds of bubbling laughter, of cries and little angers. Frank, she remembered, searching her memory, had been always bubbling and cooing and roaring with laugher or crying. But Paul was still. She coaxed him with singing and prattle and smiles. But he stared back at her quietly, his face grave, his blue eyes wandering from her face. She held him in her arms and shook him in play and he bore it patiently. The most he ever gave her was one day when she touched his cheek with her finger and moved it about his chubby jaw, his lips. Then for an instant he smiled, as though she had touched some nerve or muscle. But when she cried out in delight, it was over. When she took her finger away, the smile was gone. It was like a ripple when a finger is trailed in water. She could not be sure it was a smile.

She wrote to Rose. "Does David laugh and smile? Does he make sounds?" Rose replied, surprised, "You forget David is nearly a year old. He is trying to talk. He is very delicate and he has been ill so much, too." She sent a small photograph of a grave little boy, held by a cheerful dark-faced Chinese woman. She studied the small shape. It was a delicate face, a thin body held very straight. The eyes looked out, intense, tragic, and the mouth was pursed into some rebellion. Her heart rushed to him. If I had him I'd build him up, she thought. He needs good food—he ought to get out of that climate. She went and picked Paul up from his crib. He was beautiful. She took pride in his size and health. His body was fat and solid, the dimpled hands chubby, his thighs broad and well-fleshed, his cheeks scarlet and his lips apple-red. But he was so lazy.

"Lazy, lazy!" She laughed at him and nuzzled her face into the fragrant creases of his neck. "Sit up, lazybones! It's time you were sitting up!"

But when she took her hand away from his back he fell against her, softly, effortlessly, and leaned upon her. "You don't try," she scolded him. Then, sick with her love for him, she held him against her. Children were not all the same, she thought, cuddling him. Not all children could be the same. And he was so dear to hold, a lovely baby to hold, leaning in her arms, willing to be held.

"David is so independent," Rose wrote, "He is so difficult to keep in bed when he is ill. He is a very difficult child to control."

She kissed Paul's soft whitish hair under her chin. Against her bosom he lay, his full pink cheek pressed against her breast. He did not cry even to be fed. It was as though he did not know her bosom lay there beneath his cheek. His lips never went seeking. He was like a pretty, plump doll. She held him to her firmly.

"Not all children can be the same," she said.

And after a while after the winter was passed and spring came again, he began to hold his head up a little and to reach sometimes for the toys she made him—a red dog she sewed, a green rabbit. Perhaps if his toys were bright he would see them better. He would reach for them and hold them and soon they would drop from his hands and he would not miss them. She ran to pick them up for him, to play with them for him, to coax his hands to hold them.

One windy April day she took him outdoors, and above the gusty wind she heard a steady roar. She looked up quickly to see the plane driving through the huge white clouds, flashing across the blue between. "Look, look," she cried to Paul. She held him up, and with her hand under his chin she forced his gaze upward. And if by any chance Roger Bair was there, so high above her, would he look down and see a woman holding a child up to him? But Paul's eyes could not catch the swiftly moving shape.

"Look, Mother's boy! See, darling!" she cried. But his eyes slipped away quickly. She followed them. At what was Paul looking? He seemed not to look seeingly at anything, his gaze as silent as his voice.

But the silence was not as it was before his coming. It was not empty silence, not lonely silence in the house. He was there, growing, eating, sleeping. He was there to be carried in her arms. She carried him in the spring to the woods and made him a bed upon soft old leaves and he lay in the warming sun while she found bloodroot and violets and she carried him into the orchard and saw him seraphic beneath the blossoms, his cheeks pink too, his hair a fluffed gold, his eyes blue. She must have him everywhere. When he was awake, she propped him in pillows near her while she worked. When he slept, she ran to see if he still breathed.

Nothing else was real. Bart was surly with her these days. "I'm still nursing him, Bart," she said steadily. "I'm not willing —not until I've finished nursing him anyway." Bart glanced at her often from underneath his thick red brows. He tried to catch hold of her awkwardly when she happened to pass him. But she made her body tense and cold against him and he let her go. Once his mother said to her, a faded pink in her cheeks and red staining the folds of her neck, "If you take care, you don't need to keep Bart waiting till the baby's done nursing." Joan was ironing one of Paul's little dresses and at the words she turned her head quickly back to her work. Bart had complained of her.

"I can tell you what you can do," the voice came again from beside the stove—halting, thick with embarrassment. "I can tell you what my own mother told me. She said to me the day I married Abram—'a man can always spit outside the pot'— that's what she told me."

Joan went on steadily . . . Now run the iron along that tiny tuck, now along the fine edge of lace. She folded the little dress and for a moment lifted her eyes to the window and gazed into the maple trees. They were summer green, the fresh young leaves now fully grown. A little wind moved among them and stirred the clear green shadows and the branches showed for a moment, dark and smooth. She knew the branch shape of every tree. On winter mornings she had lifted her gaze to them, bare against a gray sky, or standing noble under snow, statues in the storm. She did not answer. She could not answer with this sickness in her. Let her think of lovely things, of the ferns in the rocks of the wall, of the lilies growing under the trees. But what she saw against the inner curtain of her brain was a man's face, Roger Bair's face, thin and finely drawn upon her brain. And she knew she could never go back to Bart now. She picked up the pile of dresses and climbed the back stairs to the attic and put them away in the round-topped trunk, the smell of their newly ironed freshness warm in her nostrils. She went over to the crib and looked down at the child. He was lying awake and he looked back at her. "Paul," she whispered. "Paul." All her lonely being rushed out and laid hold upon this child. "Speak to me," she whispered, "your mother—"

He was nearly eight months old. She fell upon her knees and wrapped her arms about him and lifted his head in her hand. She forced a smile to her lips and nodded her head at him to draw his wandering eyes back to her face. They came wavering back to her at last, the great beautiful blue eyes. For a moment they met her eyes fully, for a moment before they slipped again. For that moment she looked down into their depths, caught and plumbed them and stared down into them. They were empty. He could not answer her because he did not know her. She held him rigidly a moment, terrified, and then laid him gently down. Something was wrong with Paul. It was as though when she laid him down he was gone away forever. She went to the window and stood there. She had a fantasy that somewhere a little boy had tiptoed away and closed the door and left her alone again.

It began to come to her in the early dawn that perhaps the real Paul had never been born at all. She sat holding him, holding his body to which she had given birth. She had sat holding him all night. She could not bear to lay him in his crib. She must have his warm body in her arms at least. It's like holding him dead, she thought. It's holding my dead child. Paul is dead.

In the early morning she heard Bart's footsteps on the stairs. He stumbled upon the threshold and caught himself. "Say, where did you put those blue shirts I had last summer? I've got to make hay today and I'll roast at best." He saw her face bent over the child. "Kid sick?" he asked. He came over and took the child's hand in his great hand. The small plump white hand lay there in his lined, grimy palm.

"Bart," she said, "there's something wrong with this child." She forced every word slowly.

But Bart grinned. "He looks all right—not fevered—hand's cool as a cucumber."

"He doesn't know me—he doesn't sit up alone."

"He's too little," Bart said.

"No, he's not. Rose says David sat up long before this."

"Kids aren't the same. You fuss too much, Jo. Sam was sort of slow, I remember, but he turned out all right. Give him time. Here, kid—" He put his thick finger under Paul's chin and tickled him. A slow vague smile came to the small lips. "Sure, you're all right, aren't you? Say, Jo, I wish you'd come and get me those shirts. Pop's yelling to start on the hay." -

"All right, Bart."

But then it was good to stir, to have to move and do something, to know the night was ended. She laid the child down upon the bed. After the shadows of night it was good to feel the stairs beneath her feet, to open drawers, to feel solid stuff in her hands, solid, coarse, everyday stuff.

She found the shirts and gave them to Bart. She went downstairs and busied herself about the kitchen. The sun was tipping the horizon and light spilled from it like shining water. In the barnyard across the road Sam was harnessing the horses, forcing them backward into the traces. Their great heads towered over him, snorting, protesting. The cows were coming in a solemn procession out of the gate and turning down the road to the pastures, lush with the full-grown grass. Behind them was Bart's father, his shoulders bent beneath the weight of a full milk bucket in each hand. She fetched a cup and went to meet him to dip up the new milk. The old man watched her, grudging, silent, and went on his way into the cellar.

She stood drinking the milk in the sunshine. Within her was the waiting darkness of the night, to which she must return. But just for this moment it was morning. The trees, the hills, the sky were real. She stood among them in the morning. The night was behind her and before her, but here was morning. She looked upward to the sky, quickly, searching. It was a habit now to search the sky. But it was empty, high, above her, serene and blue.

"When did Bart begin to talk?" she asked his mother, when Paul was well past a year old. For these many months she had spent her every moment watching Paul, measuring him, testing all his powers. Did he hear her when she called him? Yes, he turned his head slowly when she called. Did he see? Yes, his eyes followed the red flannel dog if she moved it slowly enough. Would he put out his hand to take it? Yes, he took it, but he let it fall. He did not remember that he had it.

Bart's mother stirred the sauce made from the sweet apples. She used sweet apples for sauce so that sugar could be spared. "There's enough sugar in food natural," she said. "Folks shouldn't want to keep eating sugar. It's a flesh pander."

Sam and Bart both bought cheap candy, secretly, like little boys, and ate it as men drink liquor, starved for sweetness. Bart's pockets were sticky with the stuff when Joan washed his garments.

"Bart?" said his mother vaguely. "Oh, I don't know—he was kind of late. He didn't really talk before he was five, I guess. I remember some pestering neighbor woman came in one day when he was three and said it was funny he didn't talk yet. But I always said he'd talk when he got ready to, and he did." She stirred and tasted the stuff. "Em had a girl who never did talk, though. She had a fall, they always said. She never was just right. They got her put away finally. Em couldn't do with her around when she was grown up—she'd act queer before folks."

On a spring morning she waited for Fanny under the oak tree around the bend and when they came, she took Frankie's hand and said, "Look at me, Frankie?" He looked up at her instantly, fully, his eyes directed into hers, knowing, intelligent.

"When did he talk, Fanny?"

"Who—him? That child? He talked as soon as he walked, I reckon—he wasn't a year old before he was talking."

"He's very quiet," she said.

"He talks when he wants to," Fanny said indifferently. "And can he sing! Sing, Frankie!"

He dropped her hand then, and clasping his hands behind him, he opened his mouth so wide she could see his rosy red tongue and small white teeth, and he began to sing. His voice came out clear and full and unchildlike. "I'm singing with a sword in my hand, O Lord," he sang fervently, swaying from side to side. She listened in silence until he finished. In the tree above them a bird began to twitter madly.

"Here," she said to Fanny, giving her the dollar she had now been giving her each week.

"Thank you," said Fanny. "Come on, Frankie, let's go."

But Joan did not wait. She was plodding down the road. And what sort of God was it of whom her father used to speak in such belief, who numbered the very hairs of their heads, who watched a sparrow lest it fall? So carelessly was a dark and nameless child born and gifted. But her child, her wanted child, had been given nothing.

Precious body of Paul! Let her keep his body sweet and

fresh—his perfect body which she had made. She went to Clarktown and bought recklessly fine soft linen, blue, yellow, and gay gingham printed with flowers, and made him little suits. Above the vivid stuff his rosy face glowed. It was a beautiful body, the body of a beautiful little boy, the shoulders square, the thighs full, the dimpled knees and feet. She held him all the time now, sleeping and awake. At night she put him beside her in the bed. In the day she sat him astride her hip and held him as she walked and worked. She must feel his body. She had this body.

On one August day she dressed him carefully and drove into Middlehope to Dr. Crabbe. She drove down the street, not seeing it. The buggy top was up. That was to shield the child from the sun—the child and her. From the shadow she need see no one. She would reach there at noon and Dr. Crabbe would be at his own house—and everybody else would be at dinner. She planned all the way what she would say. She would be very calm and matter-of-fact. "Dr. Crabbe, I am worried about Paul. He is slow about doing things. I want you to see him. I want to know the truth."

Yes, she must know the truth. She must press the cruel truth across her heart and know it whole. But she would be very calm and wait for him to see the truth and tell her. She had waited all these months, gathering herself to be strong, to be calm.

She went into his little dun-colored office and sat down, and his housekeeper, Nellie Byers, stuck her head in at the door. "That you, Joan? He's just eating his dinner. My, isn't that a cute baby you got? Yours, isn't it?"

"Yes, mine," said Joan. "I'll wait, Nellie."

She would be glad to wait, glad to have the chance to force down this hardness in her throat. But she had no chance. He was there at once. He wiped his lips with his napkin and threw it on the floor.

"Well, well, Joan!" Oh, his blessed hearty voice, his warm good voice!

"You came just in time. I was about to go and see Mrs. Mark—nothing urgent, poor soul, just going round to see how much more of her is dead. I try to get around once in a while, though she don't want me to come. Why, Joan, what's wrong?"

She was staring at him, sobbing, sobbing loudly. The sobs

came loud and dry, and she was helpless in their gasp. They seized her and shook her. Speechlessly she held out the child to him and he took the baby. She gasped through her terrible sobbing, "Something's—wrong. He doesn't—know me."

She gave her burden to him, and she was eased. She stopped sobbing. For the first moment in all these weary wakeful nights, these restless frightening days, she had rest from her burden. The long silence in her broke. Now she could not stop talking. She must talk on and on—"He lies so still—he's so awfully still—I can't tell you, Dr. Crabbe—it's him. No one ever says anything. They think it's wrong to talk—it's as though they had blighted him—" All the time she was talking, talking, and he was looking at the child, testing him, touching him here and there, moving his limbs. He took off the little clothes and held the child.

"Beautiful body," he said abruptly, breaking into her talk. "Got your fine body, Joan."

She was panting with her terror, her lips dry. Now let her seize the pain firm and hard with both her hands.

"Dr. Crabbe, where is his mind?"

The pain of waiting for birth was nothing to the pain of this waiting. All of life, all the world, stopped, faded, was nothing. In all the world there was nothing but this tiny room, this old man, this child, herself. But he did not answer for a long time. At last he began to put on the garments again, slowly, carefully, to fasten them expertly, securely. At last, when the child was dressed, he looked at Joan, his face a twist of wrinkles.

"His mind was never born, Joan—my dear child—"

She drove slowly through the leaf-shadowed street. Once someone called after her excitedly, and she saw, through the fog of her terror, Netta Weeks pushing a baby carriage. "Joan, Joan!" she screamed. "Wait. I haven't seen you in ages." She had to stop then, for a moment. "No, I won't get out, thank you, Netta. I must be getting home. Yes, this is my baby." Paul was asleep. He lay upon her lap, his head in her arm. He was so still she could manage the reins while she held him. She was glad he was asleep. He was beautiful in his sleep—all children lay quiet in sleep. She listened while Netta praised him.

"Why, he's a beauty, Joan! He favors you, doesn't he? My,

he looks grand and strong! You're lucky—I bet he's easy to look after. My Petie is a terror—into everything these days." She pulled back the hood of the carriage and disclosed a thin, sandy, lively-looking child. He was sitting upright, babbling over a toy duck which he was picking to pieces. Netta screamed at him. "Oh, my heavens—his granddad just gave him that down at the store! He's so mischievous—" She snatched the duck away and instantly he bellowed and she gave it back to him and winked at Joan. "Smart as a tack," she confided. "Your baby's a beauty, though," she added.

"He's a good baby," Joan said quietly. Paul stirred a little and she gathered up the reins quickly. She must go, lest he wake, lest he open his lovely wandering empty eyes. She could not bear the thought of Netta's gossip. "Joan Richards always held her head so high—but you ought to see her kid—"

"Come and see me, Joan," Netta cried after her.

"Yes," Joan called back. But she knew she never would. There was this pain in her, waiting for her, shutting her away from everyone. She had to seize it, to wrestle with it, to plumb it, to live it alone. She drove slowly back, holding Paul. But around them, beside them, like a separate presence, was the pain, waiting for her.

In the attic she laid him down upon the bed and took off his little hat and coat and she fetched a soft damp cloth and wiped his face and hands. Then she sat down beside him, and fed him. There were these things to be done for him, to comfort her. Though he had not cried, he was hungry. She studied his absorbed face. When he slept, when he ate thus, he looked like any other child. Dr. Crabbe was only an old man. Perhaps he was wrong. She reviewed the morning quickly. She had forgotten to tell him that Bart had not tried to talk until he was five. And Bart was all right now. Wasn't Bart all right?

Dr. Crabbe was so impetuous. He made up his mind so fast. . . . She still had nearly three hundred dollars. She could take Paul to a city doctor and see what he said. She could go to New York and look in the telephone book for a baby doctor and ask him to see Paul. Yes, she would do that. She was happier, suddenly, planning something to do. She would not say anything to anybody until she had done it.

Until she had done this she could push the waiting pain
away. It was like pushing away a solid substance with her
hands. She held it off.

"It's all a fuss over nothing," Bart declared.

Downstairs in the kitchen when he was washing up after
milking, she had told him. "Dr. Crabbe says Paul isn't right,
Bart."

"I don't hold with doctors," Bart's mother said. "I wish I
hadn't ever told you about Bart not talking till he was five. I
told you to ease you. Bart turned out all right."

She did not answer. It was always easier now not to
answer. She would go tomorrow. Perhaps when she knew,
she could sleep again—when she knew Paul really was all
right. She reckoned the day swiftly. It was Thursday. Fanny
would be waiting. She'd have to tell Sam to get word to her
to come on Saturday this week. She watched and made the
chance to meet him before he reached the kitchen door. He
was carrying the milk pails. But when she asked him, he
shook his head shortly.

"I don't see her any more," he said. "She's got married."

She was frightened for a moment, then it did not matter.
She could only fight one thing at a time. The fear of what
Fanny might do if she were disappointed must wait until
this waiting pain was fought off. She went back to the attic
and packed a small bag of garments for Paul.

She found a doctor easily. There was a woman at the
telephone booth waiting for a turn, and when she saw her
holding Paul in one arm and turning the pages of the book
with the other, she said, "Can I help you?"

"I want the name of the best baby doctor in New York,"
Joan said. Paul's head was slipping from her shoulder and
she put up her hand quickly to hold it.

"You'd better go to the Edmonds Clinic," the woman said.
She wore a bright red dress and her yellow hair stood out
from her round fat face. But her small blue eyes were kind,
and her full bright red lips were soft. "You can go and it
don't cost you anything if you say you haven't any money.
Just write down you haven't no support. My, he's heavy,
isn't he? What's wrong?" She was turning pages slowly,
moving her glittering pointed nail down the names. "Here it

is—see? You take the bus here at the corner uptown. What did you say was wrong?"

"He doesn't walk or talk," said Joan. There the pain was, as near as that. When she said the words, it flew at her, stabbing her. She pushed it back again.

"Don't he?" the woman said. She was about to go on when the door of the telephone booth opened and a man made to enter. She recalled herself. "Here, you!" she cried loudly. "I'm next in line!"

"Well, go on then," the man muttered. He was tired and sallow and middle-aged, and as he waited he sucked the handle of his umbrella. The door banged and the woman was shut behind it. She was screaming into the telephone, her face twisted and red.

Joan looked at the address. It stamped itself upon her mind instantly and she found it easily. People were very kind to her on the way. It was wonderful that people were kind to her as they passed, so much kinder than Bart was, or Bart's family. It was sweet to have a courteous word or touch. In the bus a white-haired man gave her his seat and smiled and touched his hat, and when she got out, someone held her arm when she stepped down.

"He's too heavy for you," a voice murmured, a gentle pleasant tenor voice. But when she turned to speak, she could not see who it was. It was only a voice in the crowd. But she was comforted. There were kind people, unknown and kind.

She looked out into the streets of New York as the bus ground its way along. And yet these hurrying people did not look kind. They were so distracted in their gaze. Once when the bus stopped in front of a store she saw some people who were not hurrying—a woman and two men in dingy clothing. They were sauntering back and forth, their hands folded in front of them, and carrying signs that read LOCKED OUT OF BRISK AND BRAM FOR DEMANDING HUMAN CONDITIONS. But no one looked or gave them any heed. The bus went on again and she reached the hospital and entered a door over which was painted, FREE CLINIC. She went in and sat down on one of the benches in the long hallway. The benches lined the walls and they were full of women with sick children—with children crying and moaning and lying in weary stupor. Beside her a young woman with a white narrow face and exhausted eyes held a little girl with a huge misshapen head. She looked at Paul enviously. He was asleep, as soundly as though he were in the crib in the attic.

"It doesn't seem as if anything could be wrong with such a lovely child."

"No, it doesn't, does it?" said Joan gratefully. It was true that among the sick children Paul looked sound and beautiful. She could not help being proud of him, a little. At least, sleeping, he was beautiful. The other woman's child began to cry fretfully.

"She gets so tired, the poor little thing," the woman said, trying to shift the weight of the huge head. "The doctor is late. They're always late. I wish I had back all the hours I've wasted waiting for doctors."

"Can't they do anything?" Joan asked. Under the bulging enormous forehead the little girl's face looked out, weazened, tiny, mouselike, twisted in old, old suffering.

"I don't give up hope," the mother said fervently. She bent and kissed the great forehead. "I keep hoping. You've got to hope."

They all had the same hope, Joan thought, looking at the women's faces. They looked eagerly at each other's children, relieved when their eyes fell on one worse than their own. They looked quickly away from Paul because he seemed so sound, and they stared at crippled, deformed children hopefully.

When the doctor came in, their faces turned to him together, their eyes following him, searching his face eagerly. He came in, a robust, middle-aged figure with a small square beard and very clear agate-gray eyes. He was talking loudly and positively to a younger man who was with him.

"I tell you, Proctor, the diagnosis is perfectly obvious in ninety percent of these cases. The congenital undeveloped mind is consistently different from the birth-injured case that is possibly mentally normal. I never confuse the two— Just look at these here—"

His eyes ran, cold, darting, analyzing, along the walls. He was directly in front of her. She could smell a strong clean perfume upon him. She could see the hairy underside of his chin, the sharp triangle of his nose, the cold agate gray gazing downward. They did not see her. They saw only Paul. He had waked and was lying quietly in her arms.

"I am his mother," she said steadily.

"You needn't wait, my good woman, unless you want to. I don't have anything more to say anyway. Take him home. When he gets too much for you, you'd better find a good institution."

He passed on, talking and talking. She had turned in agony to the young doctor. But he had not met her eyes. He was listening closely and with respect to the cold, intelligent, knowing voice. She rose, pressing Paul's little cap to his head.

Let her get home now, to the attic. She could fend off the pain until then. She would not examine the words until then. When she got home, under the close dark roof, she would take them out of her memory and comprehend them and let the waiting pain flow over her and cover her at last. Around her the patient women sat, not heeding. The door of the doctor's office opened and their faces turned to it. A nurse came out, white and brisk, "First case, please!" No one saw her as she slipped away.

Bart met her at the station in his car. She climbed in and sat in silence beside him. He clattered along the rocky country road. She knew he was showing off to her. He wanted her to say how well he drove the car. The speedometer crept up and she could feel him wanting her praise, and when it did not come, perversely driving too fast that he might force her to say something. He had no imagination and so he never sensed danger. He could climb the barn roof and laugh when she looked away, shuddering. But if they were all killed, it would be well. She said nothing and at last he slowed down, sullenly.

"What did the doctor say about the kid?"

She seized the blade of pain in both hands. "He says Paul will never be right."

She looked out over the fields. The corn was tasseling, and the summer was at its full. The forest green was deep and dark.

If Bart were a grown man, if he was really what his body seemed, she could turn and give Paul to him and rest her head upon his shoulder. There would be a bottom to this pain then. It would not go deeper and deeper, fathomless, endless, a black tunnel through which she must walk alone all her life, without light to guide her to the end.

"Shucks, you can't believe everything them city doctors say, Jo. He's healthy as can be."

"His body's all right."

"He'll turn out good," Bart repeated heartily. "You see if he don't."

She did not answer. The road was deep with dust. The sunset was flaming out of orange dust.

Bart cleared his throat. "Need rain," he remarked. "Good growing weather for the corn, though."

"Yes," she said.

The house was just around the turn. They were there. Now they were at the kitchen door. Bart's mother was at the stove, frying potatoes.

"Supper's ready," she said, without turning her head.

"I'll be down soon—don't wait," she answered. She carried Paul upstairs and washed him and fed him and laid him in his crib. He was tired and fell into effortless sleep. She fetched the small oil lamp from the box she used as a table and stood looking at him. These must be her moments of dreaming now, these moments at night when he was fast asleep. She could dream that he was like any other child. He had had a day of play, shouting, calling, chattering, crying, carrying out his busy little-boy plans, and now at the end of the day he was tired out. As his body grew she could pretend he was going to school, that he played baseball and rode a horse. When a young man's body lay asleep, she could dream he was going to college. Her imagination flew in agony down the years. This was the waiting pain. Now it was come—now it could no longer be put away. It was here. It would go with her night and day as long as she lived, walk with her wherever she went, wait in her awake or if she slept. It seemed now she would never sleep again.

She opened a drawer to put away Paul's cap. There lay the song she had begun to write on the day before he was born. The opening lines were there, the gay and triumphant beginning. But she had not known the ending. Today she knew. She took the paper and tore it into bits and went to the window and let them fly out into the deepening dark. Then she blew out the light and groped her way down the stairs.

At the table the food was dry in her mouth. She kept taking gulps of water to force it down. She must eat, of course. She must live now, as long as Paul lived. And his body had a long life to live.

"What did the doctor say?"

She looked up at Bart's mother out of solitary deeps of pain. The question came from a long way.

"He said Paul will never be like other children."

Over and over her life long she must be ready to say that. Wherever she went, people would say, "What is the matter with your baby?" After a while they would say, "What is the matter with your little boy?" They would say, "What is the matter with that young man?" Steadily, over and over, she must be ready to repeat, "He will never be like other children are—never as other young men are." She must not flinch.

"Pass the bread," Bart said. "I don't take any stock in it."

Sam passed the bread.

"It doesn't pay to listen to doctors," he said cheerfully. "I had a doctor tell me once I had a bone felon. But it was no more'n a boil."

"I wish I hadn't told you about Aunt Em's girl," said Bart's mother fretfully. "Now you'll get notions. They're not one bit the same. Em's girl was sickly from the time she got her fall. Paul's different in every way. He's just like Bart. Bart was an awful healthy baby, I said he'd talk when he got good and ready and he did. And Paul will, too."

"Get some more milk," Bart's father interrupted. "I have to get done early tonight. There's a meeting over at the church—a missionary from Africa's talking. The parson wants a crowd and spoke to me as superintendent. Sam, get your good clothes on and go, too. You'd better go, Minna. He's got lantern slides."

"I haven't planned," she exclaimed in distress. "You ought to have told me sooner, so I could plan the work after supper."

"I'll do everything," said Joan.

"Wouldn't you like to go though, maybe, Joan?" Bart's mother, about to agree, paused. "It would be interesting—your sister a missionary and all. I'll stay with Paul."

"I'm very tired," said Joan.

"Then maybe—" Bart's mother said, unwillingly pleased. Then she said quickly, "It isn't that I just want to see the pictures. I feel I ought to take an interest in the work the church is doing in heathen lands."

"Yes," said Joan. She turned to Bart. "Why don't you go, too, Bart? You'd like the pictures."

"Don't know but I will," said Bart.

So the house was emptied. There was only Paul and herself. The silence was complete. There was no sound of breathing or of footsteps. She washed the dishes and swept the crumbs away and set the table for breakfast and covered the table with the cloth. Then she bathed herself and brushed her hair and put on her nightgown. It was, she thought, as though she were laying herself down to die by her own hand. But she could not die, for Paul was alive. In the darkness she went to his crib and listened. He was breathing steadily, soundly. She felt his hand. It was warm and lax. She had done everything she could think of to do. She went and laid herself down in her bed and let agony fall upon her, unchecked at last.

But how could one live in agony day and night while a year passed, and then another and another? She would sleep a little and wake in the morning stifled, as one might wake in a dense smoke, or under a heavy weight. Before she was well awake, dragging her mind upward out of sleep, she knew something was wrong—terror waited. Then she was awake and there the terror was, fresh and sharp and new with the morning.

When she forgot, as sometimes she could forget, for a moment, for a moment of sunlight through shining leaves, for a moment of the phlox bed glowing under the noon sun, for a moment of dewy madonna lilies freshly blooming at twilight, the beauty of mists stealing up the hills from the valleys under the moon, the terror was there, new again, to be realized again and again. Better never to forget it than to have that continual new realization. "Oh, how lovely the hills are today under the moving shadows of the clouds!—Yes, but Paul will never be like other children."

And there was no edge so desperately keen as when he himself made her forget, the close dearness of the nape of his neck when his fair hair began to curl against the white skin, the lovely roundness of his body in the tub. She could laugh with her passionate tenderness, adoring his loveliness, forgetting for a moment's adoration, and feel her heart dissolve again in the eternal agony.

She longed to see other children. She plied Rose with questions of David. But Rose wrote unhappily that she was going to have another child. "I have so little time for the work now," she wrote.

"I don't know what she's talking about," Joan cried aloud to herself, fierce with envy. She thought of going to Netta, and shrank from it. Meeting Fanny under the oak tree beyond the bend of the road, she begged her, "Bring little Frank with you next time. I want to see him again. It's been so long."

"Surely," said Fanny. She had put on flesh in the past two years, and looked like a great dark poppy in a ruffled dress of scarlet lawn.

And the next week Joan could hardly listen to her for looking at the boy. There was some trouble. Fanny was in trouble, quarreling with her husband. She took pleasure in trouble and quarreling.

"Darling," said Joan to the little boy, kneeling in the dust to him, "you've grown so big. Are you going to go to school?"

The child stared at her, charmed, his great black eyes soft and fathomless.

"If Fanny'll let me—" he whispered.

"Don't you say mamma?"

"She doesn't like me to."

Fanny laughed richly. "No, I don't have any of them call me ma. It looks better. If I take him anywhere. I say he's my brother."

The child looked at her gravely as she laughed. Then he turned back to Joan and regarded her curiously and quietly with profound intelligence. That was the look Paul's eyes should have had, that comprehending aware look. Francis, for all his waywardness, used to have it, and their mother seeing it would seize him and hold him and murmur over him. Strange to see Francis looking at her now out of the jungle!

"What are you going to do with this child, Fanny?" she asked anxiously.

The girl shrugged her shoulders gaily. "He's all right, long as I don't decide to go away. Long as that man behaves, that is!" She frowned darkly. "Not many men been to my taste like Frank was, though, I declare. Sometimes when I get thinking about Frank, I just lose my taste for them all. Isn't he ever coming home? I wouldn't bother him—just show him the boy and say hello."

"No," said Joan quickly. "He's never coming back—he said so."

The girl sighed, a deep full sigh.

"Well, I've got to be going. Thank you for the dollar again—it sure does help. I keep Frankie the nicest of any of my children."

But she could not let him go. She felt the small body all over with her hands. It was firm and hard and shapely. She took his hand and it held to hers closely. The very feel of the body was different from Paul's heaviness, the cling of the hand so different from Paul's loose, varying clutch. She held the hand a moment and looked at it She could imagine the smooth fresh skin white. But underneath the blood ran dark.

"Is your little fellow all right?" asked Fanny. She was staring into a small mirror, rouging her already scarlet mouth.

Joan hesitated. Then she said firmly, "No, he's not all right—there's something wrong."

Fanny lowered her mirror. Her face warmed with pity. "That's too bad! My children's all healthy. But I know a girl with a puny baby. She took her to a gospel meeting, and the preacher put his hand on her and she's better—at least her ma says she's better. Come on, Frankie—Lem'll be mad, waiting for us!"

She had to let him go now. She rose and stood watching him walk sturdily through the dust. When she could see them no longer, she sat down beside the road, again desolate. Summer was passing, the corn was ripening, nothing was growing now. Summer after summer, before, she had left everything growing, pushing to bud and blossom and fruit, life full tilt with growing Now it was stopped, over the whole land, over forest and field. There was no more growing. There was only ripening and slow downward dying. Another autumn was near. She got up and went home to Paul.

She kept remembering what Fanny had told her. There was a woman with a puny baby who took her to a gospel meeting and she got better. In South End the people were very ignorant and full of superstitions Rose still wrote her long letters which Joan still sent to Mrs. Winters when she finished them, so that they could be read at missionary meeting. Rose said there were heathen women who went to temples if their children fell ill.

"In their blindness and ignorance," Rose wrote, "they go to their gods and promise new robes or new shoes if the child recovers. It is difficult to persuade them to give up this foolish and wicked practice."

On that first Sunday morning when she came home from college, it had not seemed necessary to think about God, because then she had taken everything for granted. God would take care of her. She had been told so often that God was good.

Here in this home night and morning she sat while Bart's father read "the Word of God." She had not needed to listen, since God was good.

But now there was no use in pretending that Paul grew any better. He was no better. She played with him every day, singing over and over to him with desperate grim patience the gay childish songs her mother had sung to them all. "Pat-a-cake, pat-a-cake, baker's man." Francis used to pat his baby hands together in solemn ecstasy. "Paul, Paul, see? Pat-a-cake, pat-a-cake—" She held his hands and patted them together day after day. Each day she waited to see his hands move a little upward of their own impulse. "Pat-a-cake, pat-a-cake—" Day after day she let his hands fall and got up quietly to busy herself at some other task. It took a long time to teach little children—a long, long time. Her mother used to cry, "It does seem to me I have to keep telling you children the same thing over and over." Every day she told Paul the same thing over and over.

Then one day when he was nearly five years old, she put his hands down. She went to the trunk and found a little box of toys she had made ready for his Christmas. Each year she had planned in happiness. "Next year, I'll have a tiny tree. He will be big enough surely to notice the candles and to laugh at toys."

She would not wait this time for Christmas. She lit the lamp and set it where he could see it. She opened the box and brought out a rattle she had bought, with bells on the handle, and she jangled it near him. She took his hand and curved the fingers about the handle and moved it gently. But when she took her hand away, the rattle dropped. She snatched up the lamp, sobbing, and held it above him. He did not recognize the light. His wandering eyes saw and slipped away.

"It is no use pretending anymore," she said aloud, fiercely. She set down the lamp and put all the toys back into the box and set the box into the trunk and closed it. There never would be Christmas in this house. She knew it now. She began her old sobbing again. "Oh, God," she said sobbing, "oh, help me, God!"

Her father used to teach them, saying, "Ask and you shall receive, for so we are taught."

She searched in the trunk for her mother's Bible. She and Rose had put it there. It had been years since she had read the

Bible for herself. On Sunday afternoons when she was a little girl they each had to read a chapter. And once for a while when she was a young girl she had read it of her own will, to delight in the swinging powerful words. There was the Song of Solomon. And then abruptly she had put it aside and read instead the poems of the Brownings, and Tennyson's "Princess," and any love stories she could find.

Once she had really prayed for her mother's life and her mother died. But then her mother was no longer young and there comes a time to die. Paul was only a child, and death was not for him—not for years upon years. She fell upon her knees by her bed, clenching her hands together, her eyes closed, her whole being pouring and concentrated. She felt a power sweeping up from her feet, through her limbs, her body, soaring upward to the cold starry sky, a shining shape of intense desire. "Oh, God, make Paul well!"

... She would give God time. She lived in a waiting intensity through days and nights. The work was to be done, in this house. There was so much work to be done, a routine of sweeping and polishing and cleaning. She worked at it doggedly. On Tuesdays she opened the dark unused parlor and wiped all the furniture and the pictures, all the curly carved surfaces. She knew every surface now without loving any. There was no meaning to any shape. She had never seen anyone sit on the chairs. The window shades were not lifted except on Tuesdays. On Wednesdays she cleaned the pantry. There were three heavy complete dinner sets on the shelves. "You shall have them when I'm gone," Bart's mother said often.

"Why don't you use them?" she answered heartily. "I'd rather you used them now."

"Use Mother's good wedding set every day?" Bart's mother cried in horror. "She never did, nor I. Besides, there's the trouble of washing them every day. I'd never get over it if some were broken." They ate from ten-cent-store dishes. She wiped the empty old-fashioned dishes savagely. If they were ever hers, she'd use them every day, every meal, and she'd slash them about in the dishpan.

"I always say," Bart's mother's voice came dolefully from the kitchen, hearing the dishes clatter, "if you break up your few good things, you don't know where you're going to look to for more."

She did not answer. She moved the dishes, wiping their edges. Nothing but things and things. This house was full of silent lifeless things, things to be taken care of. She'd like to walk straight out of it, walk away down the road, anywhere, never to return.

"I *must* be patient," she cried, terrified. "How can I expect God to do anything for me when I am so unruly?"

It was very hard to be patient so long. She waited, day after day, prayer seething in her constantly, fretful, desperate, importunate prayer. She nagged at God with her prayers, unbelieving. "There's nothing in it. Paul doesn't change a bit." Nagging desperately again. "There's no other hope—Oh God, help me—"

She brimmed with a dreadful energy. She polished the front stairs she never used. Living in this house she had come to feel it sacrilege to use them. Bart's mother's disapproval made rebellion worthless. "But it means more to clean," she said, hurt, to Joan's cry: "Why should we climb up those steep back stairs?" The intensity of hope deferred was making her ill-tempered. She was often angry with Bart's mother, furious at her large soft stupidity, her unwavering obstinacy ... "Oh, God, when—when—is Paul going to get better!"

"Yes," she answered violently to Bart's mother, "I did wipe each banister—Yes, I did move the little marble-top walnut table and I did wipe behind the mirror."

"Well, I'm sure," said Bart's mother, bewildered, "I was only asking—if you hadn't, I was going to—if you had—I'll begin picking over these windfalls to stew up."

All the time she was watching Paul, testing Paul, trying to arouse Paul. One day she took him into the parlor and opened the old crack-voiced piano and holding him on her lap, she took his lumpish hands and holding them touched the keys softly. It had rained all day, a dark long day. In the attic she had walked with him, played with him, until the close down-sloping roof shut her in and made her breathless. Against the window the rain had beaten in gusts so that to look out was to see the trees' indefinite cloudy green swimming in down-rushing water. She was as restless as a child, and taking Paul in her arms she had gone recklessly down the front stairs—"After all, I clean them!"—and to the piano. "Pat-a-cake pat-a-cake," she was chanting, drumming his fist softly upon the keys.

The door opened suddenly and she turned, Paul's head bobbing helplessly upon her breast, to Bart's mother. Her large vague face was violently distorted.

"Now, Joan, that's one thing I don't allow anyway. I've stood enough. I never did let one of my children touch that piano, and you can't start Paul doing it."

She walked heavily across the floor, wiping her hands on her apron, and closed the piano with a bang. Joan rose. Now she knew she hated this woman. She hated them all. No use pretending anymore—no use trying to pretend. She stared into the small yellowish-brown eyes, lost in her hatred. She was holding Paul so tightly he began to cry. She turned and ran from the room ... And all the time she knew she was herself hindering God. For how could God help her when she was so wicked and full of hate? In the attic she began to sob. "That old worthless piano—he's her own son's child—I don't want to hate her—" She put Paul in his crib and threw herself upon the bed, sobbing. She cried so much these days. Any little thing would start her to crying.

When she grew quieter she lay in the darkness, thinking. She must just begin again. There were things she ought to do which she had not done. It was very easy for the heathen mothers who promised God a coat or shoes. She rose up and lit the light and found her mother's Bible, poring over one of the pages heavily underscored. There was one verse blackly underscored: "He that cometh to God must first believe that He is—"

She had not been been believing enough. "I believe, I believe!" she whispered fiercely.

"I believe!" she cried in her heart every day, every hour, as she swept and washed and mended. "I believe!" she repeated, holding Paul. She gave up the singing now. Instead she murmured over him like a fierce litany, "I believe—I believe in God!"

She began to be meticulous with herself, to read the Bible and to pray a certain time each day as her father had done. In her youth, she remembered with terror, she had laughed at people who were like this. It used to be a joke in the village because Mrs. Parsons always prayed before she began writing on her novel every day. "I want God's blessing on all I write," she used to say. "If I have God's blessing on all I write, some day a publisher will take my book." They had laughed at her in the careless fullness of their youth. Prayer was for church or to be murmured before sleep. It was like brushing your hair a hundred times, or like keeping your bureau drawers neat—all nice people did such things. Prayer was a nice habit. But nothing ever came of it beyond the feeling of niceness it gave. But perhaps they were wrong. Perhaps there was something there, a power upon which she had not laid hold.

Pray, Rose, she wrote, distracted, *pray for Paul.*

"God," she cried to hills and sky, walking through the forests, green again with spring—incredible spring, coming year after year, just the same!—"God, help my little baby Paul!"

In this cunning to persuade God she whispered like a child to her dead mother. "If you are near God now, speak to Him of Paul!" She thought, if there is any way, she will find it and do it ... But Paul still did not know her. He ate and slept and grew heavier and she tended him as she always had. For all her crying there was no sign that she was heard.

"Bart," she said, "I have an idea I want to go to our old church. I want you to stay in the house with Paul once on Sunday." Perhaps in the familiar church she might recapture the childhood sense she remembered of God's being near and loving. They used to take it for granted that God loved them.

"You needn't do anything," she added to Bart. "Just be in the house—don't touch him unless he cries." She was jealous of Paul's immaculate body. She did not want Bart's great grimed hands touching him.

He spoke so heartily she looked up in surprise. He seldom spoke to her these days, and to him she did not speak unless she must. Between them there was that eternal wordless question-and-answer waiting. Whenever he opened his mouth, she drew up her resources ready for refusal. If she should speak to him, he might be led on to ask that question. Silence was safe. At first he had touched her hand often, and made awkward opportunity to brush against her as she passed. She learned to stay far from him, to come and go steadily, cold, never touching. "You'd think I was dirty or something!" he roared at her once. She looked away and did not answer. It was true—his flesh was like filth to her.

Then at last he made no more effort. He came and went from the fields, eating enormously, sleeping immediately after he had eaten at night. She ceased to feel the pressure in him. He was content to be silent toward her as he was to the others. They all lived in the round of silence. Sam was going with a girl now, a farmer's daughter five or six miles away. Each evening after milking he cleaned himself and ate his supper in solemn uneasiness. He gave up his coarse joking and gazing at her secretly. He was going to be married. He was settled, or soon would be. Bart's mother fretted a little. "They say Annie Beard is a real good cook, but she's so free with butter and sugar. I ate a piece of her cake at the church supper once, and it was so rich it was sickening. I don't care for anything but sponge, myself— more is flesh pander." She sighed. It was not decent to say more. Her sons were men, and she supposed they must behave like men. Since Bart was not complaining anymore, she guessed he and Joan must have fixed it up. After all, his room was right at the foot of the attic stairs, and she'd told Joan—

"You go right ahead," Bart said boisterously Sunday morning in the attic. "Paul's all right with his dad, aren't you, Paul?" He grimaced at the cradle.

She put on the white chip hat she had had before she was married. She had not worn it for so long that everybody would have forgotten it. Her white linen dress was old, too, but it was simple enough to wear without notice. She was thinner than she used to be and it hung a little on her hips. She had not for so long seen herself dressed like this. Her face was thinner, the lines of her bones clearly shaped, and her mouth was not so full as it once was. Her lips were restrained and set. But she had her clear skin and her mouth was still red.

She turned away from Bart. She knew she was still pretty enough so she did not want him to notice her. "I'll walk from the Corners," she said. "I can go in the surrey with them that far. Then it is only a little way,"

But Bart did not see her at all. He had thrown himself across her bed and was staring into the rafters.

She was a little late in church. They were all singing when she slipped into a back seat and sat down. She bent her head a moment and suddenly began to tremble. She was very tired. She had not realized how tired she was until she came to this familiar place. The singing went quietly on. The old folks sang gently:

> *"We may not climb the heavenly steeps*
> *To bring the Lord Christ down"*

The organ picked the notes out delicately, muted. The sunshine fell in bars as it used to fall through the closed windows, and lay upon the dying still air. All through her body little nerves began to relax and tremble. She wanted to cry again. She wanted to cry for herself, piteously and aloud: "I've had a hard time. I've really had a very lonely hard time."

The singing softened in an "Amen," and the people sat down. All their backs were to her, but she could recognize them. That was Miss Kinney's summer hat, the tan leghorn with the circle of red cherries. There sat Mr. and Mrs. Billings. He had grown fatter than ever, and Mrs. Billings was already nodding, bless her heart. But the boys were gone. In the organ loft she saw Martin Bradley's back, angular, as neat and spare as ever. His hair was almost white. He was moving his fingers over the silent notes as he always did during Scripture reading. Old Mr. Parker was dead. She had read that in the paper one day. He had died just before he was to retire on his savings, as he had feared he would. He had saved and saved for an annuity, going pinched all his days that he might be independent in age, and someone else was using it, someone who never cared for him, for he never married. "I have never made enough to warrant my inviting a lady to share my poor fortunes," he used to say. Once he had said it at a church supper—that was when Mrs. Mark still had her legs. "I have asked the Lord concerning a wife, but there was no answer. I fear I asked amiss." Mrs. Mark, cutting smartly into a huge white-iced cake, had shouted loudly, "That's it, Brother Parker—you never asked a miss!"

Everybody had roared, and Mr. Parker smiled painfully and went out of hearing. Mrs. Mark was known to be a little indelicate for a lady.

Joan sat, smiling, remembering, forgetting for the moment why she had come. There was so much to remember here in this place—her mother, Francis, Rose, herself. It hurt most of all to remember herself. It was like remembering someone else, a young ardent girl. The door of the vestry opened and she looked up quickly, remembering her father. But instead a youngish bald-headed man came out in a dark business suit. He began to speak in a sharp practical voice.

"Today's lesson is found in—"

He read quickly, plainly, without acknowledging any poetry in what he read, and sat down abruptly. A woman in the choir rose and sang in a sharp clear soprano. It was his wife. She remembered that definite high voice. "Is there only one bathroom in the manse? What sort of a kitchen stove do you have?"

She bent her head, waiting for the song to finish. When the congregation sang, she could go back to remembering. The soft murmuring of old voices, the muted organ—remembering, she might remember God. Her father could so invoke God in this place. Oh, that she might feel God true!

There was a short practical sermon, a few notices read. "There will be the usual meeting in the vestry after service. I shall discontinue the Wednesday prayer meeting while I am away on vacation during July." A strange young man passed the collection plate and she shook her head. She had forgotten to bring money.

Then suddenly when they rose to sing the last hymn she could not face them. She could not bear the pressing questions, "Joan, what's become of you?" "We never see you anymore." "It's nice to see you in the old home church again, Joan." She was at their mercy, because they had all known her so well. She could not hide herself. She turned and hurried out of the church and went down the street. After her came the soft sound of their peaceful aged singing. The singing made the noon unreal.

. . . "Was Paul all right?" she asked Bart.

"Sure he was," Bart answered. His voice sounded thick and queer, as though he had been drinking. But he could not have been drinking in this house. When a stranger asked Bart's father for a match even, he would not lend it if he knew it was to light a pipe or a cigarette. "That's flesh pander," he said. And to drink even cider was wicked.

She looked at him closely. But he did not look at her. His red hair was tumbled and he smoothed it roughly. "You've been asleep," she cried.

"Yeah," he muttered.

"Asleep when you were to take care of Paul!"

"Well, he's all right, isn't he?"

Suddenly gorge rose in her. She could not bear to look at Bart. She let it pass. It did not matter, so long as Paul was safe.

She importuned Rose to pray for her, while she hung her own prayers on God. And she so prayed that almost she prayed herself into believing that her prayers must drive through the walls around her and reach an ear beyond. But in the night it was hard to believe. In the night, alone in her attic with Paul, the round-topped trunk pushed against the door, in the darkness of the deep night she might doubt and did often doubt. ... "I must remember this is only because it is night and everything is so still, and because there is no one near me. I must remember that I believe in God and that the morning will come soon."

She thought humbly of Rose who was so good, so sure. Rose's prayers would count with God. In the night it was a comfort to think that far across the sea Rose was praying for her, too. And in the morning, when the sun came streaming through the treetops, it seemed to her that Rose's prayers must be answered.

But it was a long time since she had heard from Rose. She went out one late summer morning to the mailbox at the road. When she saw the mail carrier there in his old Ford, she ran out. He seldom stopped, scarcely more than once a week to deliver the *Sunday School Times* or a farm circular.

"Good morning, Mr. Moore!" she called gaily. It was one of the moments of forgetting. The morning was clear over the hills, the earth was throbbing with sun and heat. The air was still and fertile with warmth. She felt her feet sure and vigorous upon the rich grass. It was impossible not to hope this morning. Paul was so well, so placid, so good.

Mr. Moore grinned at her, his gums toothless. "Foreign letter for you," he said. He liked to bring her a foreign letter. "Makes your eyes shine!" he said, as he always did.

"Good!" she cried heartily. "I knew something nice would happen—it's one of those mornings!"

"It's not a bad day," Mr. Moore admitted. It was so warm he had taken off his coat and was in his brown vest and gray chambray shirt. He was a little embarrassed as she reached out her hand freely for the letter. "I might have kept on my coat if I'd known you were coming out," he apologized.

She took the letter and smiled at him warmly. It was Rose's letter, the address neatly typed. Rob had never written. Rob was so busy, Rose said—and he had his own parents to whom to write. Rob was opening a new field often, Rob was pushing northwest among the Mohammedan peoples, over the deserts, into the high barren plateaus near Tibet, where the men looked like Indians, lean and dark and fierce.

"Well, you'll be wanting to read your letter," Mr. Moore said. His car set up a fury of noise and stirred a rush of dust. He jerked it into movement and urged the motor with a clatter of gears, and the car, choking, was on its way.

She thrust the letter into her dress and went upstairs to the attic. It was midmorning, and there was a pause in the work. In a few moments she must go to the kitchen and peel potatoes. But these few moments were empty. Paul was asleep in a clothes basket under an apple tree. She was always happiest when he was asleep. He was just a little boy asleep. The attic was beginning to seem a room of her own. It was her uncontrollable instinct to make a room pretty. She had made little ruffled green curtains for the gable window and a cover for the box. Last winter she had sewed rags into a round rug. Bart's mother had showed her how. They were rags of colorless old work shirts too torn to wear, but she had dyed them green and brown. She sat down on a barrel chair she had found in the attic and had covered with the green curtain stuff. Now she tore open the letter.

It had always been a luxury to read Rose's letters over and over slowly, to extract from them every picture. Slowly through Rose's meager descriptions she had pieced the picture of a square mission house, dark servants coming and going, a garden thick with ferns and spotted lilies and quick-growing plants. "But, alas, there are snakes and centipedes," Rose had written. "We have to keep continual watch over David." David she saw clearly, a small, too thin, intrepid child. David was always running away. David was continually being sought for and found down by the riverside among the junkmen, or in the marketplace. Sometimes they found him first, but other times before they found him there would be knocking at the compound gate and a man would be there, a bare-legged farmer or a riksha coolie, holding the small boy firmly by the hand.

"He runs away in spite of everything," Rose wrote anxiously. "Nothing will keep him inside the compound walls."

She had read every letter absorbed, eager to see David, laughing at David, ten thousand miles away.

She tore open the thin Chinese envelope . . . But this was not true, not these words typed scantily here. A letter could not carry a message like this, a common letter! The lines ran together as her eyes read them. Now let her begin again carefully and quietly disentangle the words. The name of John Stuart— that was the doctor at the station—Rose had told her about John Stuart, a little. "He is a faithful worker," Rose had said, "a man of few words." Few words! In this handful of words he wrote, "And without warning bandits came into the town and forced the compound gates. Mr. and Mrs. Winters were killed almost immediately, we heard later from those who were watching in the crowd. The children were saved by their faithful nurse. The little girls was eleven days old. We escaped—" The lines were tangling and twisting again.

. . ."Rose, you are to stay here in bed and keep the children here and the amah with you. I shall go out to meet them. I shall speak to them quietly and tell them we are here only to help the people, to give them the true knowledge of God. You aren't afraid?"

"No, Rob." Rose was lying on the bed in the middle of the room, looking at him. She looked like a young girl again suddenly, smiling, her eyes shining. "I feel as though all my life had led up to this hour."

"God, in whom we have believed—" he said steadfastly, his hand on the door. There was a great roaring from the street.

"In whom we have believed," she repeated, her voice thrilling through the words. He opened the door quickly and went out. The silent little boy broke away from the Chinese woman's grasp and ran to the window. He screamed suddenly, loudly, "Mother, they hit—"

The door burst open and the men surged into the room. He was lost—his mother was lost. It was like water rushing into the door and drowning them. A hand reached out and pulled him . . .

"They were found, he upon the threshold," the letter said, "stabbed, and she, stripped and stabbed in the bedroom of their little house against the city wall. It was probably done very quickly. They were buried in the garden secretly at night by friends . . . I am bringing the children home."

She sat with the letter in her lap, trying to know that they were dead. She had been trusting Rose to pray for her, and Rose for weeks had been lying folded in her grave. She would have said that surely she must have known it, that her hope, flying through space, would have met a barrier and dropped, daunted. There had been no sign. She had not felt Rose dead. She had not known. But all the time Rose was dead.

Now, any day, following this letter, this man would come

bringing Rose's two children across the sea to her, to be hers. Under this roof she must somehow make a place for them, too. The attic stretched about her, down to the eaves. If she could put two small beds there at the south, away from the wind—

Through the glorious still day she moved in silence. She could not speak to anyone yet. She went in quiet dazed mourning, tears often in her eyes. Whatever she did, she saw Rose at some past moment—Rose, demure even when she was very small, decided, knowing always what she would do, sure of how to make her life. But she could not decide against death. As reasonless as idiocy was death. One could only accept.

She went the length of the day and of the next day, death a secret in her. It would mean nothing to them that Rose was dead. They had never seen Rose, Rose standing to receive the dress like a shower of summer flowers about her white shoulders, Rose moving about the house with her quiet beaming look.

Bart's father said fretfully, "All this government fuss and fidget with farming isn't going to do any good. Things are getting worse all the time. In my dad's day—"

Rose was lying now ten thousand miles away, on a low hill overlooking a Tibetan plain, in a garden beside a city wall. . . ."Apples won't sell more than a couple of dollars a barrel this fall," he continued. "Stew up as much as you can, Minna. We'll eat apples." And John Stuart was bringing two children to her, two more little children . . . "Don't see how Annie and I can live on the little I get," Sam was saying. He was afraid of his father and his face was redder than ever. "She's a good manager, but—"

"She'll have to be," his father said. He soaked a crust in his coffee and sucked it . . . The children could eat apples and bread and milk. She'd get food for them. She could find a job. But she had less than two hundred dollars left out of the five hundred. Week by week it had gone for little Frank.

"She can't manage what she hasn't got!" Sam cried, goaded.

"I don't know as I've any call to have to support my son's wives and children."

She spoke suddenly for them all. "We work, all of us," she said clearly. She was not afraid of him.

"Lot of women in the house," he muttered, his mouth full of dripping crusts.

"Not all the children can be as good as Paul is," said Bart's mother. "Anyway, he's not much trouble."

"No," Bart said, pausing in his chewing, "you're right, Ma. Paul isn't any trouble."

. . . No, she thought drearily, listening, only trouble enough to break his mother's heart. And David was coming across the sea, who was always running away. He would want to run away from this house. Walls could not hold David. She had less than two hundred dollars left, and there were three children— and Frankie—four children.

In the church on Sunday she sat anxiously, planning, thinking. Paul was still to be healed, but here were these two, coming. She could not pray. The church was not full of remembering, now. She could not sit thinking about the past, even about her mother and father. She had to plan for what was to come. The minister began to speak. "Today we are to pray for one of our members who is in sore affliction. God has seen fit to take to himself as martyrs Robert Winters, son of Mr. and Mrs. Winters, a missionary to China, and his wife. Eight years ago the young couple went out from this church, and today they lie in their graves. Let us pray for our friends, the bereaved parents, the motherless children—" He did not put her name among the bereaved. He did not know her.

His unctuous voice flowed on. The people bowed their heads. She felt the tears rush to her eyes and got up abruptly in the middle of the praying. Yes, but something had to be done. She had to do something. She left herself betrayed. While she had been praying . . . She walked swiftly down the street to the Winters' house. At a window next door she saw Mrs. Kinney's old withered head like a skeleton trembling at the window, but she did not call or make a sign of greeting—old Mrs. Kinney taking care of herself, living on and on, uselessly. She ran up the steps and rang the doorbell, and Mr. Winters came to the door. They had not gone to church today, but he wore his coat, because it was more decent in such sorrow. It was real sorrow. He choked a little when he saw her and said more loudly than he usually spoke, "It's been a long time since I saw you, Joan. Come on in. Mattie's lying down. She's terribly upset. It seems as though she blames Rob and Rose for it."

He followed her into the square neat sitting room. "I'll go and tell her." At the door he paused and looked back, his long pallid face melancholy. His voice broke in a sudden squeak and he pattered away, his bedroom slippers clacking.

She sat waiting. Once in this very room Rob had had a

birthday party and the cake had been on the square carved center table, and he had given the first piece to Rose, and Rose had eaten a little of it and tied the rest in her handkerchief and had taken it home. That was the difference between Rose and herself. Joan always ate her cake immediately. Rose said, "I knew there'd be ice cream and things I couldn't take home, so I saved the cake and two pieces of candy." But she couldn't think ahead like that. Rose had worn a pink dress, and she a yellow one.

Mrs. Winters came in suddenly. She looked older. She was thinner, much thinner. Her skin seemed loose on her, as though the flesh had melted away from under it. Although the day was warm she wore an old black cloth cape around her shoulders.

"Well, Joan," she said, "I'm sure—"

Joan rose quickly and put her arms about her and for a second Mrs. Winters leaned against her. Then she withdrew herself and sat down, dabbing her eyes quickly with her handkerchief. "If I'd been listened to," she said. Her full bluish lips trembled a little. "I was never listened to. Now this has happened—the two children—I'm not a bit well myself, and business has been dropping these two years in the store. If Rob had only listened to me and stayed home. What are Reds? I couldn't seem to understand."

Joan said quickly, "We can never understand. I'm to have the children."

Mrs. Winters looked at her dubiously. "But how are you fixed?" she said.

Joan smiled. In his room she had once eaten all the cake on her plate at once, not thinking of tomorrow. "I'm all right," she said sturdily. "I live on a farm. I have a little son of my own, you know. There's a big house—plenty of room in the house." She'd take the house and wrap it about the children, her children.

"I'm not real well," said Mrs. Winters at last, looking about the neat room. "Rob was such a good boy. He never upset a thing. What I say is, people have no right to go off to the ends of the earth and leave their children for other people to bring up. But I'll do my duty by my own son's children, of course."

Mr. Winters sat drooping, saying nothing.

"But I want them—they're Rose's children too," Joan cried. "I'll come to you sometimes and you can advise me and help me—"

Mrs. Winters shook her head sadly. "I'll do all I can, I'm sure," she said. "I always want to do all I can—and I do—"

"Of course you do," said Joan quietly. Mrs. Winters looked old and tired and bewildered, more completely bewildered than she had on the day when Rob and Rose were married. "Goodbye," said Joan. "Don't worry. I can manage." She went away quickly.

She strode through the street and down the road, her heart firm and sorrowful and exulting. She was to have the children. She went recklessly, her big body impetuous with generosity. She didn't know how to manage, but she would manage. She must write to Francis and tell him. He never wrote to her, but she kept on writing to him anyway, because her mother would have wanted her to.

And then there she was at Mrs. Mark's little stone house. She stopped short. She might go in, since she was early today. She hadn't heard anything of Mrs. Mark for a long time, and she had not gone to see her. She had not wanted Mrs. Mark's ruthlessness probing her—Mrs. Mark's disgusted voice, "What'd you go and marry in a hurry like that for? A lout—"

But today she could forestall Mrs. Mark. She did not matter today—nor what she had done. She opened the door and called and a small voice answered and she followed it. Mrs. Mark lay buried under a thick cotton quilt. Her face looked out at her with the withered waiting look of an aged and suffering monkey. "I'm glad you've come, Joan Richards," she said. "I've waited a mortal time for anybody to come. I been dead since yesterday noon from the waist down. I'll never stir out of my bed again."

"Oh, Mrs. Mark!"

She waited, groaning a little, while Joan heated soup she found congealed in a pot. She drank it slowly, and a thawed look came about her wrinkled mouth. "Wash me off," she commanded. "Hot or cold water, it doesn't matter from the waist down, but make it hot above. I like to feel as far as I can."

When she was cleaned and fed, Joan said anxiously, "I'll have to find someone to come and stay with you."

"I won't have a soul," said Mrs. Mark promptly. "You can put some bread and milk by me and the clean bedpan and come back in a day or so. I hate fuss. It isn't going to be but a week or two at most. An inch or so and it'll hit my heart."

"And maybe you'll be alone!" Joan cried.

"Everybody's alone," said Mrs. Mark.

"I'm glad I came by when I did," Joan answered.

But Mrs. Mark looked at her with suspicion. "Don't you go thinking I prayed and you came by. I don't pray. I lie here and take it, though it's not coming to me more than to another. It's chance—just as it was chance you came by. There wouldn't have happened anything different, no matter what—"

"I wouldn't leave you if it weren't for Paul," said Joan.

"Get along," said Mrs. Mark. Her eyes were small and sharp and dark with the never-dying tragedy of an ape's eyes. "Get along with you." She shut her eyes and waited for her to go.

"I'll go, but I'll be back tomorrow," said Joan. But Mrs. Mark would not answer and she went away.

She had stayed longer than she realized in Mrs. Mark's cottage. When she reached the Corners, the sun had swung over the zenith and was on its way downward. There was no sign of the surrey. She searched the deep dust of the road and saw the narrow rut of its wheels, double, coming and going. There was the slight wavering of the right hind wheel, slipping a little. It was loose on its axle. They had come and gone, then. They had not waited. There was no sign of restless horses' feet, stirring the dust.

She set her lips and struck out in long strides.

Paul would be hungry, and they would not feed him. No one had ever fed him except herself. It was not easy to feed him, not pleasant. It took a great deal of patience. She had to prepare his food and mash it soft and push it back into his mouth again and again when it ran out. They would let him lie hungry until she came. It never seemed to occur to any of them that Paul belonged to the family as much as Bart did or Sam. But she must not be bitter. It was easy not to be bitter about small things when all was well. But now sorrow stretched her soul.

She quickened her steps until she was half running through the hot dust. She took off her hat and let the sun beat down on her. Her thoughts marched to her feet. She must manage to get back to Mrs. Mark somehow tomorrow. She had put bread and milk and tea beside her and two tins of soup, and had filled the little spirit lamp freshly. If she could only find someone to go in every day—maybe Fanny would if she gave her a dollar more every week. She must get more money somehow. Maybe if she wrote to Francis he could send her a little.

Or maybe she could earn something somehow. She used

to think she'd write songs. But what could she sing now? She had no song to sing. Songs could not be made out of the sort of days she lived. She could not even sing to Paul. She was living in deepest silence now that she knew she would pray no more. She strode on under the hot blue sky.

She had not prayed these last two days since the letter came. There was no use in it. Everything was stopped in her, every voice—even her own voice. The sky was blue emptiness, deeply, endlessly empty and blue. She stopped a moment to hear the utter stillness of the sky. But it was not quite still. There was a faint steady approaching drum of noise. That must be the plane. She turned her face up quickly. Far above her the silver flight went past, out of the sky and into the sky again. The sun poured its heat down upon her and she stood abandoned to it, her face turned upward. The sky was not empty. The sky was a sea for that ship to sail upon. She smiled, forgetting—That could be a song if she went on with it. Then she remembered that Rose was dead and she began to hurry again.

When she turned the bend of the road by the big elm she heard the noise. She was so used to silence heavy about the house that she could not believe it came from the house. Someone was shouting, a man's voice, loud, hoarse, bellowing. She heard the crack of wooden furniture overturned. A woman's voice screamed—a strange voice she did not know. She began to run. Noise was coming out of the silent house. Something had happened to Paul. She ran faster, her mouth dry, the perspiration upon her body stopped. The surrey was still standing at the side of the road. The horses were kicking and tossing their head at the flies, and they whimpered when they saw her. She ran across the grass. She could hear the voices, Bart's father, Bart's sullen voice, Bart's mother begging, "Now, Father—" The strange voice crying and crying, Sam's complacent voice coaxing: "Let up, Pop—it's done, isn't it?" She ran into the open side door of the dining room, gasping. "Is Paul—is Paul—" and stopped.

Bart's father and Bart were struggling together, and Bart's mother and Sam were clinging to them and pulling at them. Sam was jerking at Bart, and his mother was hanging to the old man. Bart was standing, huge, stolid, warding off his father's stiff clumsy blows. At the sound of her voice they parted. They were ashamed before her.

"Sit down!" Bart's father roared.

Bart picked up the overturned chair and sat down sullenly. The old man sat, panting, and dusted off his clothes. Bart's mother dropped into a chair and leaned her elbow on the table. They had not eaten. The table was still covered and there was no smell of cooking food.

Then she saw the girl, that silly coarse girl, the daughter of the tenant farmer over the next hill. She knew her. They were shiftless and let their cows run dry and the girl came sometimes for milk, not to the house but to the barn where Bart was milking. There she sat. She had painted her face and the paint was all smeared with crying. Her arms were bare and her hands were thick and red, like Bart's hands. She did not look at Joan. None of them looked at her. But the noise stopped at the sound of her voice.

"Is Paul all right?" she asked again, sharply.

Bart's mother lifted her head. "That's all you think of!" she cried. "You don't think of nothing but that dumb child—" Her heavy pale face was spotted with red. "You've ruined Bart!"

The girl began to cry again, foolish loud crying.

"I don't know what you mean," said Joan. The girl was staring down at her big red hands clenched in the lap of her pink cotton dress. She had seen girls like that. There were many girls like that. They came to Mr. Winters' store on Saturday mornings to buy fifty-nine-cent dresses, pink and blue.

"I'll tell you what it means!" Bart's father shouted at her suddenly, turning in his chair at her. "It means we came home from church and found Bart out lying in the hay with this girl! You and your fine ways, thinking you're too fine for us—too fine to do your duty to Bart—you've driven him to it—he's as good as had no wife for years!"

She stared at Bart. He sat there, his heavy inert body, his hair awry, his face thick and red, his great hands dangling between his knees. Bart and this girl—she was sick suddenly, her stomach writhing in her with sickness. His horrible thick heavy body. . . . The girl was wailing on and on. She wiped her hand across her nose on the edge of her sleazy white petticoat.

"Is Bart in love with this girl?" she asked.

"I don't want any hifalutin talk!" Bart's father shouted. He was panting as though he were still fighting. "If you'd done your duty as a wife—" His voice broke. He drew his sleeve across his forehead. "It's an awful thing to happen in this house of a Godfearing churchgoing man," he whispered, panting.

"Bart's a good boy," Bart's mother began. "Bart's a real good boy. My boys have been raised to be good boys."

Bart coughed and wrapped his hands together and let them drop again. Sam tilted back on his chair. In his church clothes he looked neat and complacent beside Bart. Bart was in his old work shirt and trousers, his feet bare. But this morning when she went away he had on his blue Sunday suit.

Standing in the doorway, clinging to the door, she looked at them. They were waiting for her. They were all waiting for her, to see what she would do. But she did not know what to do. She looked around at them, and she was struck with their grief. They were grieving, this old man and woman. They were suffering, understanding no cause. They did not understand anything, not any more, really, than Paul did. But then, nobody understood why things happened to them. She could have touched their hands for the first time without repulsion and said, "Let's be patient with each other because none of us knows why—"

But it was true. She had been unjust to Bart. She had done wrong to them all. She had come into this house of simple people, good people. Bart was not bad—he was only stupid. Ah, Paul helped her to understand them all—Paul, who was born as he was and not to be blamed.

"Yes," she said. "You are right. I've done very wrong." They looked at her astonished. They had not expected her to be gentle. She was not by nature gentle. But Paul had taught her to be gentle—she had learned how to be infinitely gentle.

Bart began to mumble. "I'm not—"

"I don't blame you," she went on quickly. "Don't tell me, Bart. You— maybe this girl would have made you happy. I've injured you."

The girl stopped crying and listened, her look upon Joan's dusty shoes. Her coarse mouth was swollen and pouting, her small pale eyes were hidden behind their swollen lids. She looked like the girl who had come to the manse to be married, long ago—

"I won't have divorce in this house!" said Bart's father loudly. "That's worse still. What God's joined—"

"Bart and I aren't joined—we can't be—if we lived together all our lives we wouldn't be joined." They sat stupefied by her quiet voice. They were not able to understand. She turned from one bewildered face to the other. They understood meat, drink, work. But she went on. "I see how difficult I've been for you to bear." She hesitated and went on quickly, forcing herself to smile. She made her voice bright as one makes one's voice bright to speak pleasantly and resolutely to children. "I see it all so clearly. The only thing I can do for you is to go away. You can live as you did before I came. After a while you will forget I was ever here."

Without waiting for them to answer, she ran through the room and up the back stairs to the attic. She must go away at once. She must not wait for Bart to come to her, sheepish, sullen, wanting her back. She must not wait until they laid hold on her to keep her so people would not know. Paul was whimpering for food, but she paid no heed to him. She would go by the cellar and get him some milk as she went out. She began to pack with frantic speed.

Where could she go in the world? There was no door anywhere hers to open. Then she thought of Mrs. Mark. She could go and stay with her—take care of her. In a week or two she could find something elsewhere. She'd put their clothes into a bundle—it would be easier to carry than a bag. She opened the round topped trunk and found the sandalwood box and took out all her money. That was comfort—it was her own. She put everything she was not able to take into the trunk and locked it. She would send for it. Now she must get away before they knew it. They would not believe she could go so soon. They would not imagine she would go on foot, carrying Paul. But she had her strong good body for servant.

She put a cap on Paul, picked him up and slipped her arm through the bundle and went softly down the front stairs and out the open door. She went around the porch into the cellar and filled a cup for Paul and put it to his mouth. She listened. Bart's father was talking on and on. She held Paul to her and let him drink.

No one came after her. No one called. All about her was the rich silence of the lengthening autumn afternoon. She looked light. The sun was shining through the golden dusty air. An hour ago she had been walking this road, not dreaming of such a thing as she was doing. But now it was the one inevitable end ahead, into the sky. It was a deep empty bowl of pure blue to which life led her. She had been coming unaware down a long path alone and the path stopped at a gate, and she had opened the gate and closed it behind her forever, not knowing what was beyond.

She plodded steadily eastward. Paul slept again, content. By sunset she would be at Mrs. Mark's cottage, at least by twilight.

The sun would swing its way around the world to bring another day. No cry or prayer of hers could stay or hasten the measure of the day and night. She knew it now and accepted all that had been her life. What had happened to her, she accepted. What was to come, she had strength to accept. She went steadily on, in freedom and alone, carrying her own burden.

IV

SHE LIFTED THE LATCH VERY softly. The cottage was dark, a dark small solid shape in the faintly lighter surrounding darkness. Mrs. Mark must be asleep. But she was not. Her voice came cutting small and thin out of the darkness.

"Who's that?"

"It's only I—Joan—back again."

"What are you back for at this time of night?"

She heard Mrs. Mark fumbling for matches, and there was a scratch and a flaring light. In it Mrs. Mark's wizened face peered out, a jumble of lines.

"My soul, Joan, what have you got there?"

She stood holding Paul, her bundle on her arm. "I've left my —the house—the Pounders' house. I can't go back. If I can just stay the night with you—"

Mrs. Mark was lighting the candle beside her bed. "My soul and body," she was muttering, "my soul and body! There's no peace."

"He's a quiet child," said Joan quickly.

"I don't mean him," said Mrs. Mark. "Come on in. There are sheets in the bureau drawer and quilts in that old box. I don't know where you can sleep."

"I'll sleep in the other room, on that settee—I'll manage."

She was desperately tired. Paul was so heavy, always inert in her arms. She laid him down on the foot of the bed. Mrs. Mark peered at him.

"He's a big child to carry. What did he do—go to sleep?"

She had better speak at once, tell it definitely and clearly. "He'll never be right—he's born wrong."

"Oh, my soul," Mrs. Mark whispered. "Give him to me."

Joan lifted Paul and laid him across the dead legs. Mrs. Mark held him in her sticks of arms and stared at him with her small inscrutable eyes, muttering over and over, "Oh, my soul—my soul—" Her face was gathered into a knot of pity.

Joan sat down on the bed and suddenly the old sobbing began to rise in her, the old dry aching sobbing. But she held it in her throat, choking, dry. No use crying. There was really no use crying. She set her teeth. "Don't—don't feel sorry for me," she said. "I can just manage if you don't feel sorry for me."

"I'm not being sorry for you," Mrs. Mark answered. "What's the good? Well, get along and fix your bed. It's late. There ought to be milk and bread in the kitchen. I heard the delivery man leaving them tonight."

She lay back and Joan took Paul from her and undressed him for the night. She made the bed upon the couch in the small sitting room and laid him there. Then she went back to Mrs. Mark and took her scrawny yellow hand. "Shall I tell why I left that house? I feel as if I ought to tell you, coming here like this."

Mrs. Mark's hand was like a clutch of wires, thin, stiff, dry.

"It doesn't matter to me," she said. "I gave up wanting to know why long ago. What happens happens. You came away because you had to, I reckon."

"Yes, I had to," she said.

"It's why we all mostly do the way we do. Get along now. I'm ready for my sleep."

She blew out the candle and Joan felt her way out of the dark room.

When she woke in the morning it was light. She woke in light and the small stone house was full of a warm peace. She got up and bathed and dressed Paul freshly and fed him and then when she was dressed she opened the door quietly. But Mrs. Mark was not asleep. She had brushed her hair and tidied her sheets about her and put on her bedsack and was lying with her eyes fixed upon the door.

"I wasn't sure I hadn't dreamed it," she said in her high small voice. "These days I take to dreaming. There are times when I feel my old man in the house and my girl that died when she was six."

"I'm no dream," said Joan, smiling. No, this morning was real. The sun was streaming in the windows. She felt strong and actual, able for whatever was ahead. "Now your breakfast. I shall bring you hot water and when you've washed you shall have a tray. I'll not ask you what you want—I'll just bring it."

She straightened the bed and put the table to rights. Under the bed Mrs. Mark had had drawers put so that she could reach them, where she kept her things, the clothes she needed, her comb and brush.

"Not going to give me my choice, eh?" she grunted, her small sad eyes amiable.

"No," said Joan cheerfully. "You're always bossing other folks, you know."

She busied herself, fetching the water, turning her back while Mrs. Mark struggled. She heard her panting and dragging at her legs, and she could not bear it. "Why don't you let me help?" she said. "I took care of my mother so long."

"I guess I can still take care of my own two legs," said Mrs. Mark sharply.

"I'll get your tray ready then."

In the small kitchen she fed wood into the stove. She tried to realize that she was a woman who had left her husband the day before. Was this how such a woman felt? But she felt as one feels who has stepped out of stumbling through a darkly shadowed wood into a meadow in the morning light. The very sunshine was different. She had so often risen in the cold shadows of that house and gone downstairs into the cold silence. Bart was always there to overpower her spirit. She knew him for what he was, and daily she had determined to be as she would. Yet because he was never changed he could overpower her every mood. She could never be freely happy when he was near. If she was for a moment happy, he was there like the knowledge of Paul—a dark weight.

But Paul was still her baby. He did not ask anything of her, only to be fed and cared for. Her heart flew out of her in tenderness to Paul, who never asked anything of her, and she dropped the stove lid and ran to fetch him. She propped him with quilts in a corner of the kitchen and made laughter over him, talking to him. This morning she could not be sad. He was her little boy anyhow. The fire was crackling in the wood stove and the bottom of the kettle began to sizzle. The room was full of sunshine.

If I lived here I'd hang yellow curtains, she thought in the midst of everything. She loved this small, sparsely furnished house. Perhaps Mrs. Mark would let her stay. She could make a garden and buy a cow and then if she could make just a little money . . . Her mind, freed, was dancing about the house like a beam of light. She could do anything. She could find a way. She would write to Francis. No—she paused and stood still, the bread knife in her hand pressing into the loaf—she thought of Roger Bair. Even after all these years why shouldn't she write to Roger Bair and ask him how a woman with little children could make some money? She stopped again above the eggs she was frying, her spoon poised. She hadn't said a word to Mrs. Mark about Rose—about Rose's children. She was leaping ahead as she always did without thinking how she was going to do the thing she wanted, seeing it done. She was always seeing things done. She lifted the eggs and put them on a plate with the bacon and ran into the wasted garden and found a spray of small scarlet leaves from the top of a woodbine vine and laid it upon the white cloth of the tray and poured the coffee. It was all ready. "There!" she said, setting it before Mrs. Mark with delight.

Mrs. Mark looked up at her. She had made herself very neat in a clean high-necked nightgown. Her wrinkled face was like a triangle of cracked old ivory, her small black eyes peering deeply out. She looked at the tray and wet her withered bluish lips.

"My soul," she exclaimed, "I don't eat two eggs. You'd think I could walk ten miles! I'm not going to feed up legs like this that won't even heave theirselves to the other side of the bed."

But she began to eat.

"Good?" said Joan, watching her, smiling.

"The toast's a mite brown," said Mrs. Mark. She drank a little coffee. "You're not going away?"

"No," said Joan, "not if you will let me stay."

"Coffee's a mite strong," said Mrs. Mark, gulping it. "It makes my eyes water—I'm not used to it." Deep in her eyes were scanty tears.

"I'll get some hot water to thin it," said Joan gently.

It was not possible in this quiet free house to keep from telling Mrs. Mark everything.

She told her about Rose. "Rose is dead—my little sister."

"Don't tell me!" said Mrs. Mark. "That little thing! She pestered me so trying to be good to me, reading to me when I wanted to go to sleep—Oh, dear," she sighed, "and why should she die, a little kind-meaning young thing, and me like this?"

"She died far away in a city near Tibet—a Chinese city. I'm to have her two children. It's all I can do for her."

"What for?" said Mrs. Mark. "You're being put upon. That Winters woman's got a great big house and Winters has the store, and you have nothing."

"I want Rose's children," said Joan.

"How are you going to take care of them?"

"I'll find some way."

Mrs. Mark lay silent for a moment regarding her, her small black eyes winking lidlessly like a bird's eyes. She grunted at last. "Well, you're big enough to do what you want. I reckon nobody will gainsay a great thing like you—scared of you—I am myself. I didn't want those two eggs. But I was scared not to eat them before you."

She laughed a dry wheeze of laughter, and Joan let out her own great laugh and was startled by it. She had not laughed recklessly like that since before her mother died. Then she was shy, having laughed so loudly. They were talking about Rose and it was strange laughter. But there was some odd happiness in her, mixed with sorrow. Paul was standing by her knees, his head leaning against her. He raised his head a little and she remembered him.

"I believe he's really trying to walk alone," she said eagerly. They watched him, and laughter died between them. She said sadly, "But I don't believe he even knows me—see—Paul, Paul —Paul?"

But Mrs. Mark continued to stare steadily at Paul, watching him. "It doesn't matter," she said. "You know him, don't you? The value of him you've got—giving birth, feeding, tending. I think of that a lot with my dead girl. I birthed her and tended her. It was a life, though she died. Paul's life is a life, too, one kind of a life."

"Bart's mother wanted me to put him away somewhere," Joan said. Little by little all the bitterness was seeping out of her into words now.

"You can't ever put him away anywhere," said Mrs. Mark. "That's what folks don't understand. Putting his body away wouldn't help. You can't put your child away from your heart. Besides, you don't want to miss everything of him just because you haven't all of him. He's got his own ways. He's Paul. Don't measure him by other people. Just take him as he is. If he talks, those few words he'll say will mean more to you than anybody's."

She listened, drinking in the short words. Nobody had ever talked with her about Paul. It was a comfort to talk about him at last. A mother wanted to talk about her child. She had always shrunk from talking before the few she knew. She heard women in a store talking: "Johnnie's walking now—pulling himself up by anything." "My Mary Ellen starts school in the fall—" "Polly's first in her grade this month—" And by such words she was tortured. She held herself away from all mothers of children. Now through the morning she sat holding Paul, talking to Mrs. Mark about him, playing with his fingers, with his golden curls, weeping sometimes.

"Go on and cry," said Mrs. Mark calmly. "I used to cry. You pass the need, after a while. You can't keep it up."

She pointed out to Mrs. Mark the lovely perfection of his body, the shape of his head, the set of his shoulders, the sweetness of his flickering smile.

"I suppose it all makes no difference really," she said sadly.

"Nonsense," said Mrs. Mark. "It makes a difference to you, doesn't it? He's a handsome child, and be thankful he is. You get more fun out of tending him anyway than if he was homely. In the smallest drawer under my bed there's a little black money box, locked. Here's the key." She dragged up a string from her bosom. "I want you to buy a bed. You could have this one almost any day—I'll be done with it and soon. Still, I don't want to feel people are waiting for the bed I die in."

"Oh, no!" cried Joan. "I don't want you to give me anything."

"I'm not giving you anything," said Mrs. Mark irritably. "I'm making it so you can stay and take care of me while I finish dying. Don't be an interruption. I didn't pray God to have you come. I wouldn't demean myself to pray after what's happened to me. The politest thing I can do about God now is to say there isn't any under the circumstances. But I'm mortal glad not to die alone."

"There's Rose's children to come," said Joan.

"Pack them in if that Winters woman won't have them," said

Mrs. Mark, closing her eyes, "There's a room finished off in the garret. I was going to fix my girl a room there and Mr. Mark died that winter and she stayed with me. That Winters woman —well, she's a Christian, isn't she? Get along, Joan, I'm tired." She opened her eyes as Joan tiptoed away. "If that Bart Pounder comes around don't pay any attention to him. Fire and clay don't mix, and all the stirring in the world won't mix them. Get along now, for mercy's sake! I'm worn out."

In Bart's house where she had never belonged, everything had been a burden. To be free had seemed impossible, to write to Roger Bair would have been a task beyond her power to do. She lived submerged and overcome. Now by the simple processes of this small house wherein she was free, by the approval of this one old dying woman, by the desperate simplicity of crude sorrow, she thought easily, Why should I not write to Roger Bair? While Mrs. Mark slept and when she had made the house neat, she took Paul out into a sunny corner behind the house and set him in a nest of dried leaves and stretched herself beside him and planned the letter. It need only be very short. She could speak directly to him if ever they came to speech. She could write directly. She would begin, "Dear Roger Bair. . . ."

She lay in the warm sun, dreaming. It was so easy to think of him here. When she had thought of him in that house it was a hopeless thought. So might a mole think of a bird, so might a bird think of a star. When she remembered him, the thought of him fell back, like an arrow blunted and stopped too soon of its aim. But today, in the free loneliness, in this joyful loneliness, she saw him very clearly. Of course he was the one who could help her. She felt him instant and warm to help her. They had known each other that day without waiting. She would write and he would answer.

The day was full of the certainty. She lay with her face turned to the sun, her eyes closed that she might see inward the more clearly and remember him. Soon she would get up and write the letter. She put off the writing, planning. It would be sweet to take the pen and make the words, "Dear Roger Bair." Then she would write, "You have helped Francis so much, and now I need help too. I remember you." Or she might write . . . She paused, dreaming, and without knowing it, was swept on into warm dreaming sleep.

When she woke it was cold with sundown. A wind had risen out of the nearby wood. Paul was fretting among the leaves, struggling to get up. He certainly tried to get up alone now sometimes. She jumped to her feet and brushed the leaves from her skirt and out of her hair and picked him up and ran into the house with him.

"How I slept!" she called to Mrs. Mark in the other room while she tended him. But Mrs. Mark did not answer. She went to the door and cried merrily, "Still sleeping?" But Mrs. Mark did not answer. She found the matches and lit the candle quickly. The room felt strangely empty. When the candle was lit she saw Mrs. Mark lying in the dusk, her hands neatly folded upon her breast. She was dead.

She laid Paul safely in quilts upon the floor and locking the door upon the two of them, ran through the deepening twilight to find Dr. Crabbe. He was eating his supper of bread and milk and he leaped up when he saw her. But when she cried out her message he sat down again.

"I'll finish my supper," he said. "I learned a long time ago not to run if the patient was already dead. Run for the dying—but if it's too late, finish your supper—that's sense for a doctor." He dipped up the last mouthful. "Poor soul," he said heartily, "I've been expecting her to go off suddenly like this any time for months. I've been trying to get her to have somebody in, but she always said she hadn't had much of her own way in life, and she was going to die as she liked. How come you were there, Joan?"

Joan hesitated. Dr. Crabbe had taken her when she was born. She had begun her life naked in his hands. "I've left my husband," she said.

"You have!" said Dr. Crabbe. "You and your upbringing!" He put down his spoon and bellowed, "Nellie!" The housekeeper put her head in the door. "I'm going! Mrs. Mark has died at last."

"You've got rice pudding yet to eat," cried Nellie belligerently.

"I won't eat it," he shouted, struggling into a threadbare brown coat. She disappeared, muttering. "Come on," he said to Joan. He tramped ahead of her to his small rackety old car and started the engine with a roar. "Left Bart Pounder, eh?" he shouted. She nodded. The engine calmed and the car jumped down the road like a jackrabbit. "I never told you," he said, "I was married once."

"No!" she whispered, unbelieving.

"She ran away from me," he said abruptly, "ran away with a fellow—friend of mine—a fellow I knew in college. He came to visit us—decent chap, too. We'd talked some of being partners. I couldn't blame her. Smooth-skinned fellow—I've always been kind of hairy."

"She didn't run away for that," said Joan.

"How do I know what for? She ran away when we'd been married less than a year. Some women run and some stick it out, I reckon. Your mother stuck it."

"I couldn't," said Joan quickly.

"No. Well," said Dr. Crabbe, "some women do. It doesn't matter in the end. Lucille—that was her name—she's been happy. Every now and then she writes me, wants me to get married again. I say who to, for God's sake? There isn't anybody else. Get out that side, Joan. Not that I can do anything, if she's dead."

But he went in and washed Mrs. Mark's dead body carefully while Joan waited outside. He called Joan at last. There was a slip of paper in his hand. "She had this under the pillow—wrote it today, I reckon."

There were four lines sprawled upon the paper.

Joan Richards, married Pounder, is to have my house and everything in it. In the money box is one hundred and thirty-seven dollars. I write this in full and right mind.

ABBY MARK

"Has she anybody?" asked Joan in a whisper. Mrs. Mark lay stiff and still on the bed.

"Never heard of it," said Dr. Crabbe, washing his hands.

"It's not legal," she argued.

"No, but if anybody shows up and says it isn't, tell him to come and see me, and I'll sic Martin Bradley on him. Martin's beholden to me. I've kept him out of trouble for years, and there's never been anything to have him do back for me." He dried his hands and glanced at Mrs. Mark. "Are you scared to stay here till tomorrow with her?" he asked.

Joan looked at Mrs. Mark, neat and composed. "I can't imagine being afraid of her," she said.

"No," said Dr. Crabbe. "She's been as good as dead for years. Well, I'll go back and eat my rice pudding." He seized his dilapidated leather bag and trudged away.

So she had had no time to write the letter to Roger Bair. But in the night she woke, and the thought of it was sweet. It lay ahead of her, like a treat to a child, a pleasure to be fulfilled. Even if he never answered her, she would have written the letter and signed her name, Joan Richards. He need not know her life. She would simply be herself to him, Joan Richards. Behind the closed door Mrs. Mark lay dead, but she was not afraid. She would like to have gone in and thanked Mrs. Mark if she could. "Thank you for giving me a house, a home. You've made me safe." It seemed impossible to bear it if there was no way to thank Mrs. Mark in the power of her gratitude. But Mrs. Mark would have been the last person to endure thanks. She could imagine Mrs. Mark opening her small dead eyes to say, "Get along—don't bother me. Don't you see I'm dead?" and instantly closing them again. It was like Mrs. Mark to give her all she had and then die before she could be thanked. She drifted into sleep.

In the morning when Mr. Blum came with his two men she had everything ready. She had picked a bouquet of pale purple wild asters and goldenrod, and placed them by the bed, and she had opened the windows to sun and wind. There was no odor in the room. When she had opened the door she had half expected the remembered smell of death. But Mrs. Mark had not died suddenly in health and fullness. Her body was spare and dry, bone clean, withered without decay. She lay exactly as she was. Mr. Blum put on his gloves and his men set a long box beside the bed.

"Dr. Crabbe's given full directions," he said unctuously. "You are the sole mourner, ma'am, I understand?"

"She had no one," said Joan.

"Very nice, I'm sure," said Mr. Blum. "I remember your mother so well—beautiful in death, I said of her. I don't remember the name of the gentleman you married, Miss Richards."

She did not answer, and he forgot her. "Easy there, now, men, feet first—There she is, comfortable as a baby!"

He fitted the lid down exactly and took Mrs. Mark away.

It was impossible to feel sad. She was ashamed that she

could not feel sad. She was not sad even when she stood in the corner of the churchyard beside the grave. About the narrow hole stood a few old people—Mr. Pegler, Mr. and Mr. Billings, Miss Kinney, Dr. Crabbe and Mrs. Parsons. They stood listening to the new minister's quick abstracted voice. He had not known Mrs. Mark except as a rude old woman who pretended to be asleep when he went to see her, and now he made haste to bury her.

They stood about him in the bright afternoon, old and wrinkled and shabby. Only Dr. Crabbe looked sturdy, stocky and rough like a thick-trunked tree whose top had been early chopped away and the wound long healed. His curly white hair blew in the breeze as he held his hat in his hands. Miss Kinney stood a little away from them all, a wraith. She talked to herself, her lips moving, smiling. Catching Joan's eyes she waved her hand gaily across the grave and then remembered where she was and blushed an ashen pink. Her face was more than ever like a small withered flower at the end of a long stalk.

It was over very quickly. Mrs. Parsons sang, her voice rising feeble and shallow in the autumn air. "For all the saints who from their labors rest," she sang. Joan listened, gazing across the grass to where her mother and father lay. Mrs. Mark would have hated such singing "Don't call me a saint, for pity's sake," she would have snorted if she could.

Yes, it was soon over. The minister shook hands with them briskly and went away. The old people lingered. They spoke to her. "Well, Joan, we don't see much of you these days," and lingering they spoke together a moment. None of them had known Mrs. Mark very well. "She wasn't a woman you could know," said Mrs. Parsons gently, "but I am sure she was very good."

Mr. Pegler pondered, "I didn't make her a pair of shoes—let me see—not for twelve years, and then they were house shoes —slippers. She came to me that day, I remember, saying she was stiff in the legs. Well, we all have to go, one way or another, and soon it's all over with us. We've had all there is. There's nothing beyond."

They fell silent, these old people, looking at a new grave, troubled, frightened. No one contradicted Mr. Pegler, for once. Any day now, any one of them—Miss Kinney was staring down at the coffin, bewildered, as though she had not seen it before. The sexton was beginning to shovel in the earth.

"Why, we are all getting old, aren't we?" Miss Kinney cried.

She looked down upon them, one and another, her small face frightened.

"Come along now," said Dr. Crabbe, taking her fragile arm in his hand. "I'll take you home. Your mother will be wanting you."

"Yes, of course," said Miss Kinney. "I must go, of course. I can't leave Mother too long." She bobbed away beside Dr. Crabbe, a head taller than he, a wisp dropping over his thick rolling body.

Mr. and Mrs. Billings were waiting. They stood together, a little to one side, waiting for her. These two were not afraid. "Everything's got to die," Mr. Billings was saying respectfully. He said this often in his butcher shop. He had not sold Mrs. Mark any meat in years. But she was part of the village, so he had come to her funeral.

"Joan, honey," said Mrs. Billings. "How are you getting on?"

Now everyone was gone except the three of them. And she wanted to tell this plain old pair everything. They stood so honest in the sunshine, their big comfortable bodies, their red honest faces. "I've left my husband," she said. They stared at her. "I just couldn't go on," she said quickly.

Mr. Billings nodded. "I know the Pounders," he said very slowly. "They're honest folks—though queer. They keep to themselves. I buy a steer or two from them now and then."

Mrs. Billings patted her hand, sighing hoarsely, "Well, dear—"

"I'm living in Mrs. Mark's cottage," Joan said, hurrying on. "She left it to me. I'm to have Rose's children."

"That little pretty Rose," mourned Mrs. Billings. "It's hard to understand all that's took place—so much scattering and sorrow these last ten years. Yet it seems only yesterday that your mother went."

"Yes," said Joan. They stood in silence a moment. She felt them warmly near her, without condemnation, taking her as she was.

"Well," said Mr. Billings, clearing his throat, "with all them children you'll be like the old woman in the shoe. I better send you some meat to make 'em some broth."

He grinned at her cheerfully and she smiled and tears rushed to her eyes. "You're two of the best people in the world," she said.

Mr. Billings laughed. "We're most common," he said.

The sexton was shaping the grave carefully, patting down the sod. It was all over and they went away.

But still it was not possible to be sad. Waking next morning, in the little house, it was as though now for the first time she was really beginning to live. Mrs. Mark had given her a place where she could live and had gone quietly away, leaving nothing of herself.

She set the three rooms straight and neat, and put Mrs. Mark's clothes together. There was very little. Mrs. Mark had lived here without small possessions. She was not willing to be cluttered by many things. In the closet hung two black dresses. They were limp and the folds were faded from long hanging. She had not worn them in years. All the things scarcely filled a bushel basket. Joan packed them neatly and took them into the attic and found a corner under the eaves.

She had not been in the attic before. There was a room finished off in unpainted boards, a room never lived in, clean except for dust. That was David's room, she decided quickly. This house was now her own! Every room was hers to do with as she liked. There was no feeling of strangeness anywhere in it. It had been given to her and she had taken it. The other house to which she so foolishly had fled for shelter could never have been hers. It was shaped from the beginning by alien life. Though they had all died and left it to her, it would not have been hers and she could not have loved it. But this house sheltered her at once, warmly, closely. She felt as though she had already lived here a long time. She loved the deep walls, the many small windows the hues of brown and golden stone. There was an old fireplace Someone had taken the stones of the field, from his own land, and built this house and made a fireplace to warm him and his love. Surely, surely sometime this house had been made in love and lovers had planned it and Mrs. Mark had only kept it for her. And she would live here with all her children, gathering them together beneath this roof.

And warm in all she did, like a southern current through the sea, ran the thought of the letter to Roger Bair. It would be like bringing him, too, under this roof. She put off writing hour by hour—her heart needed its dream. She set the house neat and made the bed fresh, the mattress fresh with sun and wind, and she gathered flowers from the meadows, goldenrod and small starry purple asters and a bunch of scarlet leaves, and when the house was made wholly her own she sat down in the evening of a day of sweet loneliness, when she had seen no other face than Paul's, to write the letter at last. So how could she be sad?

"Dear Roger Bair—" she wrote. Then she stopped and over her at that instant flowed the meaning of his name. She loved him. All these years she had loved him. Whenever his name had been written in any letter of Francis', she had seen it above all other words upon the page. But not until now had she been free to know she loved him. Under the shadow of that silent house, love had stifled, alive but not known. Now in this free solitude it came forth, a lovely noble shape, full grown. It had been growing all this time. She sat staring down at the name she had written. To write it had been to open the door and he was there. He had always been there, ever since that morning she had seen him on the flying field. She put aside the pen and sat quietly in her little house, the shades drawn, alone in the lamplight. She could love him fully and freely, quite alone. She could love him and live in her love for him, asking nothing. It was filling her even now, an energy for life. She took up the pen again and began to write swiftly and clearly. *I need your help. I am not afraid to ask for it.*

When she had asked of him what she wanted she signed her name and sealed the letter and made ready for the night. She had early laid Paul in the bed and he was asleep. She stood in her nightgown, looking down at him as she always did before she put out the light. He lay quietly, his smooth child's face untroubled, his lips parted and rosy. He was getting tall. He was growing stronger and trying to get to his feet when she put him on the floor. She had watched him, the feeble brain dimly struggling to follow the strong beautiful undirected body, and daily her heart had broken by him. He was all she had and she had often wept to know it. But now looking at him it came to her that he was no longer everything. She had something more at last. Even weeping could not be the same now.

Under the speed of the days went the knowledge of this silver thread weaving between her and Roger Bair. His letter came back to her quickly, immediate, sure. She knew his handwriting, which she had never seen, small, clear, square letters, free of each other, each standing independent in its shape. It was a cool letter, a letter wary of feeling, ready to help her at a distance. He had talked with her brother, he wrote, as to what she was able to do. Her brother had remembered she used to write music, that she and Martin Bradley had worked at music together. He remembered Bradley as an uncommonly gifted fellow in that way. He had called Bradley at his office and got suggestions. Bradley said one could do music writing for a music publishing firm—make orchestrations, set in harmonies melodies others had made—hack stuff in a way, but she could do it at home. Bradley had given him the name of a firm and he had been to see them and they were sending some things for her to try out.

She read the letter. It was long and closely written, but all concerning his errand, all except the last line about Francis— "Your brother is a good flier."

But at that moment it did not matter about Francis. Francis was not between them. There was something else. She must sweep Martin Bradley away from between them. She made haste to write to him. "I do not want to accept anything from Martin Bradley—nothing at all. Do not mention my name to him. I will accept only from you."

She wrote to him freely, not caring what he thought. He must know her from the beginning as she was. If she were free, then she was free. She would be nothing but herself. His letter came back again, immediate. "It is I who am doing this for you. I have mentioned your name to no one."

So their letters came and went, a bright warp and woof beneath her days. Under all that she had to do was this silver weaving back and forth between her and Roger Bair, a strong bright fabric underlying her whole life.

She saw it there, silver as the meshed steel of armor. It spread under her and around her, to save her and to make her strong.

On the fourth of October, John Stuart was to bring Rose's children home. She was making yellow curtains. She had been restless without them, seeing them inevitable against the smoke-dark plaster walls of the kitchen until, feeling as guilty as though she were robbing a till, she took two dollars of her money and went to Mr. Winters' store. "I want the brightest yellow stuff you have," she said to Mr. Winters. He was behind the counter, his pencil over his ear. He had grown very thin and stooped and looked continually dazed. More than ever he forgot where things were.

"Let me see," he pondered. He ran his finger down a pile of bright ginghams.

"I see it—there!" she cried. His finger halted and he pulled out a bolt of gold and threw it before her. She watched him greedily as he measured it off, the precious stuff she had no right to buy, not with Fanny coming now to her door every Saturday, complaining, "Frankie's grown right out of himself now, Miss Joan. He's got to have a new suit of clothes." Fanny had accepted with placidity the change in meeting place. "Yes, lots of ladies just can't stand their men, I reckon. I get that way myself sometimes. Lem's awful to live with steady. I reckon every man is." No, she had no right to the yellow stuff, bought for beauty against a dark wall.

"The children come the fourth of October," said Mr. Winters abruptly, his scissors sliding down the cloth. "Seven o'clock train."

"I've been waiting to hear," she said. "I'm longing for them."

"If Mattie had her health," said Mr. Winters gloomily above the bright stuff, "Rob's children would be with his father and mother. I always wanted more children. But she didn't want to go through with it. After our girl died she said she wouldn't go through with it."

"I'm all ready for them," Joan said. "You shall see them often. You can come and see them. I'm living in Mrs. Mark's little house, you know."

"Are you, now?" he said. He was folding the stuff and she saw he did not know she was living alone and she did not tell him. Time enough for that when the moment came. Time enough when she must hear Mrs. Winters cry out, "But you're doing a sinful thing, Joan!" She must have the children first, safe under the roof.

Looking at Mr. Winters' thin gray face she was sorry for him. The rest of his life he would be living with his old wife in their little square house on the village street, quite alone. She must take the children there often. She was so rich in all her children. "I'm going to bring them up often to see you," she said.

But he did not smile. He shook his head, sighing. "It oughtn't ever to have been like this. It doesn't seem as if we deserve it—God-fearing people," he muttered.

"No," she agreed. "Well, anyway, there are the children."

"I set my heart on Rob from the day he was born," he said.

She touched his withering hand before she went away. The skin was hard and dry and cold.

She took the stuff back and cut it and hung it in strips of yellow light. Even Paul turned at it. He could really walk alone a little now—if she put him on his feet. He held his head up a moment, staring at the yellow curtains. His eyes slipped away, and came wandering back again to their brightness. It had been right to buy them, after all.

Then she had her own letter from John Stuart. She looked up over the table next morning when she was ironing Paul's clothes and there between the curtains she saw Bart coming down the path. Her heart stopped. He had found her, then. Of course she knew she would be found. She was frightened, for a moment. He looked huge and strong in his work clothes, standing outside the door. He rattled the latch and lifted it and stood there in the open doorway. She looked at him, her body calm and straight, imprisoning her frightened, flying heart.

"Well, Bart?" she said pleasantly, sturdily. She held hard to the hot iron. A hot iron was a good thing to hold, if she needed it.

"I knew a week ago you were here," he said sullenly. She ironed busily, meticulous about the small belt.

"I haven't hidden it," she said cheerfully.

He fumbled in his pocket. "Here are two letters that came for you."

"Put them there on the windowsill," she said. Her heart was quieting now, like a wild bird gaining hope. She need not be afraid of him. He did not know what to say to her, what to do with her. She was stronger than he.

"Aren't you coming back?" he asked, watching her iron. She began to fold the little garment, but the iron was there, ready, hot.

"No, Bart. I'm never coming back," she answered.

"We never did anything to you. We were good to you," he said after a moment.

"I don't complain, Bart," she said cheerfully.

He waited, his slow brain searching. "Ma means well," he said at last. "It's her way."

"I know," she said. She unrolled another garment and worked steadily on.

"I don't give anything for that—that Snade girl."

"That's all right, Bart," she said quickly. "Don't talk about her."

"If you'd come back," he said heavily, "I'd forget her easily. A fellow doesn't mean anything. She hung around the barn a lot."

"Don't," she said. "I don't care."

"You don't mind?"

"No."

He pondered, leaning against the doorway. She ironed, longing fiercely that he would go away. What was this power of shadow which one creature could cast over another, merely by his dull being? But she was not afraid anymore. She would not need the iron. She could set it away.

"You never did care about me, Jo. I'll never get over liking you—loving you."

"I did wrong to marry you, Bart. I see that. You would have been really happy with someone else—maybe with her. I'm going to set it right."

"I'd rather you came back. I liked it the way it was before the kid came. You acted happy enough then."

She did not answer. She was putting things away, setting the room straight. She fetched some carrots to cook for Paul's dinner and began washing them. She watched their color come clean and clear out of the water—a pure deep color. It was beautiful the way color came out everywhere, out of the mud of the earth. The carrot was a shape of color between her fingers, mysteriously made . . . He was standing there endlessly and she could not forget him. She was mad to have him gone and the doorway empty to the sky. She fixed her mind steadily upon the carrot, slicing it firmly.

"You're not coming back, sure enough, Jo?" he asked helplessly.

Now she knew, quite simply, that if she had again to lie beside his great body she would kill herself. Pain and hurt, right or wrong, there was something still beyond these. Her body could not again be subject when her mind, her heart, revolted. She would kill her body and set herself free. She began to tremble.

"No, never, Bart."

"Gee," he muttered, "Ma and Pop'll never get over it—never get over the talk."

"I can't live to save them from that, Bart."

"You sure?"

"So sure I'm going to ask you to bring the trunk with my things."

He spat in the dust by the door and wiped his enormous hand across his mouth. He was in deep distress, she could see. She was sorry for him. He was suffering in his way. But he had not mentioned Paul's name. He began to talk again sullenly, scuffing the thick toe of his shoe against the threshold. "You act so high and mighty. But Ma says the kid's your fault. Your old man was crazy—everybody knew he was—"

"Go home, Bart," she said, steadily. "I don't want you here. I'm happier when you are not here."

He looked at her bewildered. But now she was trembling very much. Her head whirled with giddiness.

"If you don't go away at once," she said clearly, "I shall take Paul and go where you can never find us. I'll do that even if it is at the bottom of some river."

"Gee," he muttered. "I'm not hurting you—"

"Go—go—" she said tensely, her eyes forcing him, her will pushing him. He stared at her, and went slowly down the path. Not until the gate slammed, not until the air was cleared where he had stood, could she quiet her trembling. Let her forget— let her think of lovely shapes and colors, growing out of the earth. Let her never remember Bart and those years—or anything he had ever said.

Through the open door she could see the long lovely flowing together of the undulating hills. The sky was cloudless and the breeze was stealing in about her, pure and mild as the water in a sunny stream, as cleansing.

After a while, when her body was still, she opened the letters. One was from John Stuart, telling her when he was coming. "Dear Madam," he began formally. David was well. But the baby, Mary, had been ill. The artificial food had not nourished her. He had done the best he could, but she cried incessantly. Yet when she ate, she was ill. It was difficult to understand God's purpose.

The other was from Francis, a few scratched lines. His handwriting was exactly what it had been when he was a boy in school, loose, nervous, irregular.

It's too bad about Rose and Rob. But I can hardly remember Rose, somehow. She was the only one of us that did what she wanted, but she got killed for it. That's life

for you. I'm going on regular flying as soon as there's a
vacancy.

She read the letters through and tore them up. Bart had
touched them, he had taken them from his pocket. She rose
and washed her hands. Then she went upstairs and planned.
Here there must be a bed for David. She must buy a table and
a chair. But she could take a little of her own money now.
Yesterday the score had come from the music publishers and it
was not too difficult to do. She dared to buy a bed for David
and a crib for Mary to lie beside her.

The future was warm about her again. Bart was walking
down the road, away from her, his figure smaller each moment
that she planned. She was making her life, shaping it about the
children. One had to take life and make it, gather it from here
and there—yellow curtains, carrots, a bed for a little boy, milk
for a sick baby, sheets of music to write, her unfinished child, a
house—out of such and everything she would make her life.
And underneath was the strong sustaining web of love unspoken. What if it were unspoken and unreturned? A phrase came
flying out of her childhood, her father, from the pulpit, reading, "And underneath us are the everlasting arms." She had
caught the phrase then because it was lovely, listening to him
idly in the careless fullness of her childhood. But now when all
childhood was gone she could take the beautiful words, like an
empty cup, and fill them to the brim with her own meaning,
her own secret meaning.

In the dusky October evening they stood waiting at the
train, she and Mr. and Mrs. Winters. She had forced herself to
learn to leave Paul alone sometimes. It was not very far, not
really. The house stood just beyond the village, and if she put
him on a quilt upon the floor and locked the door, he must be
safe. But even so, she left her heart behind to guard him, and
now she stood impatiently.

They were silent and somehow forlorn in the dusk, the three
of them. "If I'd been listened to at first," Mrs. Winters said now
and then, but Mr. Winters said nothing at all and Joan could
not talk for thinking of Rose. Rose had gone away so sure of
God's will. But she was not saved alive. The train came whistling and pounding in, and paused a second at the wayside
station. It was a great through train that did not commonly

op at a small place unless someone asked it, and that was
seldom. But it stopped to bring home from very far this tall
stooping gray-haired young man, holding in his arms a wailing
baby. Beside him, clinging to his coat, was a small thin boy in a
brown cloth suit, looking in steadfast silence at all he saw.
They stood far down upon the platform, their few worn bags
about them. Joan saw them first and went running.

"Oh, give me the precious little thing!"

She took her from him, this fragment from Rose, this child her
sister Rose had given her. It was unutterable comfort to hold
her close at last. "You're home, my darling," she murmured.
"David, my darling, you're home. Oh, how tired you all look!"

"To the bone," the man said. He gave her the baby but he
still clung to David's hand.

"Well, well," Mr. Winters was saying. "Well, here you are."

"My mother and father died," said David, "so they couldn't
come with us." His voice was sudden and clear out of the
darkness.

In the evening she sat listening to John Stuart. She had
brought the children home with her and bathed them and fed
them. It had been her sacrament, the bathing of their childish
flesh, the giving of the bread and milk. She had washed and
comforted the wailing baby and soothed her chafed limbs. She
had heated the creamy milk and fed it to her and watched her
small worn face settle into sleep. Across from her, David sat
watching. "My Uncle John doesn't know how to make Mary
stop crying."

"Uncles don't, so well," she said. She looked at him, waiting,
ready for worship of him. But she must not hurry him. His
mind was full of images she did not know. She must wait until
he showed himself.

"Are we going to live here?"

"Yes, David."

"There's no wall."

"No wall at all. You can run as far as you like. Only come
home to me at night."

He sighed deeply and freely. "I want to go to bed."

"Yes, your bed is all ready, a new bed specially for you."

"I can bathe myself. I haven't had my amah bathe me for a
long time now."

"You shall do everything for yourself."

He looked up from his bowl of bread and milk. "I know milk runs from a cow. Once my father told me that. But I haven't seen it."

"This ran fresh today for you and Mary and Paul."

He lay clean and fed between the sheets made fragrant by the sun, waiting for John Stuart. "I'd rather not go to sleep without saying my prayers to my Uncle John."

She was glad she had said to John Stuart, "You'd better come down the first evening." She heard his footsteps soon.

"David's waiting," she said. They went upstairs together. But he had not been able to wait after all. He was asleep, lying on his side, his thin little hand under his cheek. The man hesitated. "I won't wake him to say his prayers tonight."

"No," she said quietly. "Sleep will do more for him, after all."

Downstairs she and John Stuart sat by the fireplace and she lit the logs. He sat as though he were exhausted, making no move to help her. When the fire was blazing he looked about the small quiet room and brought his eyes to her as she sat waiting for him to speak.

"You don't know what this means," he said. "The quiet—the stillness about the house. I keep listening."

"For what?" she asked. That was the look on his face, the look of listening.

"For the cries of people," he answered. "For strange separate cries—screams which no one goes to still, a child crying so that I know it's in pain, people quarreling, the drone of priests, the angry mob. The sea dashing against the ship woke me so often in the night. It was like that roaring. When the bandits burst the city gates it was like that—a swelling roar—I saw them hew Rob down. He called out something to me. I couldn't hear it, in the noise. But I couldn't have gone to him. I was bound to a bamboo and they were carrying me away."

She stared at him, trying to see what he was telling her. He was talking in a quiet remote voice, gazing into the fire.

"But how did you escape?"

"I had a friend among them," he answered, "a man who had been in my hospital. He tied me himself, loosely, and whispered to me not to resist. So I let him tie me. They burned my hospital. I have to begin again from the bottom. Nothing's left. They tore everything to pieces."

She thought suddenly of the peach-colored satin nightgown she had given Rose. In its way it had been precious to her—a small delicate something that was precious. She had never had another so pretty. There had been no one to give her such things, and she could not afford them. But the crowd had torn it and thrown it away. It was wasted after all.

"You're not going back!" she said.

He was holding his hands to the fire and around the narrow wrists where his cuffs had slipped up she saw deep scarified marks, still purple, where ropes had ground away the flesh.

"Yes, I'm going back—the people there need a hospital. There's no hospital in a thousand miles." He smiled a little. "Maybe that's why I go back, because I seem important there. Here I'd be one of hundreds—a country doctor, maybe. There I'm specialist, surgeon and everything. It's become a mania with me to save lives. I don't know what for—"

"See what they did!" she whispered.

"It's a curious thing," he said slowly, almost faintly, "the fellow who saved me talked almost like a Christian. Do you know, he made me think of Rob. He was so young and so anxious to do good—you know, serve the common people. The odd thing was he thought they were right to kill. He had it all worked out. He wasn't crazy at all. He was good in his way. He thought he was doing his duty. He used to talk about it in the hospital. And it was through him that I found the children afterwards. The amah had taken them to her home in the village. They weren't hurt—they were there several days before I could get them out. She dressed them up like the village children. I don't believe David realizes much. She covered his face when—when they took his mother—and she got him right away."

She could not speak.

"Yes, I must go back," he said, sighing.

But for the moment they sat sheltered in this still small house in the center of the wild and noisy world. She asked him no more. When he rose to go she said quietly over their handclasp, "You will come again sometime? This is more than passing?"

But he put his hand to his forehead in a gesture she remembered from her father.

"I don't know," he said. "I can't tell—I never know—" He put her hand down. "Wait, I remember I had something to give you." He fumbled in his pocket and brought out a small torn book bound between stiff black cardboard covers. "They found this. It was your sister's diary."

He went away, and she did not see him again.

But after all, she thought, sitting alone by the fire, holding the little book, Rose would have chosen to die in martyrdom. Death must have come for her large and shining and swift. That would be Rose, dying purely for Christ's sake, dying with a lift of angel wings. She opened the book. Rose's hands had written here. This was the story of her life in that strange far country. She began to read eagerly, tenderly, half-shyly. There would be things here which Rose had not meant anyone to see, intimate, secret things which Rose would never tell.

But over and over it was the same thing—"We must thank God today for—" "We must endure hardship as brave soldiers of Christ." There was really nothing there at all, nothing about Rose.

She was ashamed to be so happy. But she could not keep from happiness. It was the bodily happiness of one who, after long illness, deprived of sleep and food, of the pleasure of the power to walk and move, feels sleep fall upon him gratefully again, knows afresh the taste of fruit and meat and bread, and feels his limbs once again his own, to come and go. She spent her days in simplest joy of cooking and mending and making clean for these three who were hers. She was aghast when she suddenly thought, watching David run across a meadow in the wind, "It is better that Rose died." But he was a flying ecstasy in the wind and falling leaves. He ran everywhere. He could not walk. In the ceaseless wonder of all there was to be seen, he ran all day. She let him go free knowing he was born to be free and so must be free. She waited for him at night to give him food and rest. She sat beside him as he ate, waiting for him to speak, watching his vivid narrow face move and change with his thinking.

"In the woods I saw a kind of animal. It had a tail straight up its back."

"That was a squirrel."

"It held a nut like a monkey does. There aren't monkeys in these woods. I've seen monkeys."

"Here there are only monkeys in a zoo."

"I haven't seen a zoo. But I will. I'll see everything. Am I going to school?"

"You shall go to school in the village where your mother and your Uncle Francis and I went to school when we were little."

"I want to see the boys here. I hope they aren't cowards. They were cowards there—in the place I came from. They'd yell names at me in the street because I was a foreigner, and when I went after them they ran and hid." He scowled, remembering. "Some day when I'm big I'm going to lead an army against them. I'm going to fight them with an army and guns. I hate cowards. I used to fill my pockets with stones and hunt them, but I couldn't find them. There were so many little winding streets and courts. And they'd run into the women's courts and hide. They'd hide among the women!" He looked at her to share his disgust.

His mind was full of memories she did not know. She must wait for them to fade, she must make other memories for him. "You will find brave boys here, some of them," she said quietly.

He ate on, pondering over his plate. "My father didn't want me to fight. He said it was wrong. When I grow up I won't be a preacher, so's I can fight."

"It's only wrong not to fight fairly," she said.

"Oh, sure—not to fight fair, that's wrong," he agreed heartily. He rose, having eaten mightily. He laughed, quickly, loudly. "Gee, you remember that first day I came I didn't know how milk came out of a cow? I thought it ran out!" He laughed, boasting, "I know better now—you have to pull it out! But I didn't know much about America then. A fellow ought to know about his own country, oughtn't he?"

"Yes," she agreed, smiling, adoring him. She wanted to seize his small lean eager body to her, but she would not. He could make it blade-tense against even her, if he were not willing. She must leave him alone. All she had to do was to set food upon the table for him to take, put books near—she must buy books—open the door to the fields and sky. He went stamping upstairs to bed. He was just learning to whistle and she heard the uncertain piping of his whistling in his own room. He was trying to whistle "Oh, say, can you see—" Soon he would shout and she could go to him; not until he called.

But sometimes when he called she saw the look of pondering upon his face, that look of remembering. Yet never once had he spoken of what he remembered. She saw him look like this, pausing before he bit into a piece of cake, or at night lingering before he went to bed. Once in the night when the wind howled he called her and she went to find him lying tensely wakeful. "I just wanted to ask you something," he said, his voice carefully casual. "In America, they don't ever come ir big crowd to kill people, do they?"

She took David's hand. It was cold and damp. "Would you like to come and sleep with me?" she said.

"Yes," he whispered.

In her bed she held him quietly, feeling his body relax and grow warm.

"You're safe here," she said. About him, about them all, she would build securely the walls of her own house. There were no other walls that could be trusted.

Yet even as she held him in his sleep, she knew that in the morning she must let him go free again. In the morning she must pretend he had not been afraid and that the night had never been.

But the baby Mary she could hold in her arms until she was appeased. Mary had stopped her wailing. She was beginning to grow. She lay content in Joan's arms, watching her out of dark merry comprehending eyes.

My face will be the first she knows, Joan thought, trembling with joy, gazing back into her eyes. She knew now the mystery of flesh, sweet to the touch and sentient with mind. This child's flesh was informed with her mind. The mind ran through the veins and muscles and made them flow and spring. This child's hands were quick and searching, instant to seek and explore, tenacious to cling. To hold her was to hold a springing eager life. She grew within days to be a merry willful gleeful creature, moving, reaching, wanting, laughing soon, stiffening instantly at refusal.

From these two Joan turned to Paul in silence. She had learned to live in David when it was his time, in Mary at her hour. Paul must have his hour, too. But she tended him in quiet. He could struggle to his feet now and walk in a fashion across a little space. But she could not be sure he knew her.

"Joan, Joan!" David's flying voice rang through the house a score of times a day. Mary laughed aloud to see her come. But Paul smiled at anything, at nothing, his heavy body struggling dully to movement. When she held him now she held him in silence, feeding him carefully, tending him closely. He was hers forever, and yet he would never be wholly hers. Alien earthy ancestors had entered into his making and had withheld him. She had tried to mingle parts forever separate. His very flesh was not all her own. She did not kiss his hands, his feet, as ace she had. They were taking on a look of Bart's hands, Bart's feet. She put the thought away steadfastly. She held him, crying in her heart, "You are my own child." But he was not quite her own. She knew now that only love could make an own child.

... "I have no children," Roger Bair wrote when she told him of her houseful. "My wife is not strong and we have had no children."

She read the words and put the letter down quickly. He had not told her he was married. He should have told her. She was desolate for the moment, knowing he was not free. She had never thought him otherwise than free by his very being. She remembered him always free, soaring to the sky, as she had seen him the one morning. Everything seemed to be taken from her. She had to make her life out of bits. Then her mother's sense in her cried out, "And did you ever tell him about yourself?" No, but he had seen her big with child. He had seen her so at first. She wrote him fully then, plainly, "I have left my husband. I want you to know." She told him everything. When this was done she was at peace again. The pain was over. He was himself, he was alive in her time in the world. It was enough. It was still strength enough to live upon. And that day where the meadow behind the house ran down to a small stream, she found blind gentians. They were bright blue. She had never found them so late before.

In and out of the house Rob's father came and went, restlessly, hungering for the children, but shy of them because they made him think of Rob and suffer. And he was not in David's passionate life of school and play, nor in Mary's life of daily growing. Mary turned away from his painful smile at her to laugh at Joan, because Joan laughed easily. She always made Joan laugh and knew she did.

"This granddaughter of yours is going to be a tease," she said.

"Is she?" he answered. "Yes . . . Mattie isn't so well," he said at last, "else I'd say bring the children to spend the day."

"I'm sorry," she murmured. But her eyes were watching Mary secretly. Mary was staring astonished at her own small hands, moving them this way and that. She tasted them suddenly, carefully and critically, and Joan laughed. She must not

miss a moment of Mary. Nothing really mattered except M ...
inquiring the universe of her two small hands.

Rob's father hesitated. "She says you oughtn't to take care o...
the children. It worries her."

"But I *am* caring for them." She forgot Mary and her hands.
She looked at Rob's father sharply. This was the moment she
knew must come. She waited for the words shaping on his
tongue.

"She—she thinks—you oughtn't to take care of them. She's
heard about your situation."

"Did you tell her?"

"No—she heard it in the village—gossip. She came home
from the missionary meeting and asked me. I told her I knew.
She blamed me some for not telling her."

She leaped to her feet. "I shall go to see her," she cried. She
wavered and sat down. "No, I won't. You're the one to decide,
Mr. Winters. Look at me! Am I fit to have the children?"

She was begging him at first. If he denied her, then she
would fight for them. The words stuck in her throat, a gorge.
She shook back her hair. "Do what you like for yourself, but
the children are mine," she said loudly. "I can work to feed
them—you mustn't think of money. They'll be happy here. Look
at David!"

They looked. He was flying in from school, his black hair
tumbling, his cheeks faintly red, beginning to round.

"I'm starving!" he shouted.

"There's bread and apple butter ready in the kitchen," she
cried.

"I want to do my duty by my son's children, Joan," said
Rob's father gently. "I am fond of them, especially as David
grows older."

She stared at him, thinking quickly. She must think of something to force him. He was talking on. "If Mattie should feel it
her duty we could find a respectable woman to help." He was
staring into the lighted lamp, talking.

"You don't understand, Mr. Winters," she cried. "They're
mine!"

She stopped, helpless before his stupidity. Oh, the stupidity
of these good stubborn people! Her body prickled with anger.
She got up and sat down again. David was coming back.

He appeared, a huge slice of bread in his hand, his mouth
full. She gloated over him. She had made the good food ready,

..wing this moment would come. Then she was tricky. She
..ok him by the shoulder and held his wiry body in her arms.
..le did not give himself to her. He was full of impatience to be
away.

"David, want to go live with your grandmother?"

They looked at each other. The boy forgot to chew in his
consternation. "I won't go," he said. She felt his body stiffen. "I
can't go. I'd have too far to walk to school next year. I'm going
to try for the junior baseball team."

"You've never played baseball," said Rob's father mildly.

"I've thrown a lot of rocks," said David hotly. "You don't
know how many rocks I've thrown at the people in Chito. I
throw good!"

She wanted to laugh, but she must not. She said gently,
releasing him, "You're not going. Go on out and play."

"I wouldn't go," he paused to tell them. "Because this is my
home."

"I don't know where David gets his temper. Rob was so
gentle," Mr. Winters said.

"Rose was stubborn as a mule," she answered in triumph.
"You'd better leave him to me."

They looked at each other. She kept her eyes on him, steadily, willing him. What a gentle good face he had! What troubled
serious blue eyes, innocent and stubborn in goodness! She was
not good, and she did not care. She would have what she
wanted now. She had to make a life.

"They'd be a great trouble to you and Mrs. Winters," she
said. "Mrs. Winters is so busy in the church. And she does so
much in the village. I remember how she used to do—"

"Doggone it!" he said suddenly, looking at her. She laughed.
Oh, it was good to laugh. He rose, his eyes twinkling. "I'm not
going to say you're a good woman," he protested. "You've run
away from your husband and you don't come to church and
you're as good as kidnapping my own son's children."

"Come in as often as you can," she begged him. "And tomorrow I'll dress the children up and bring them to see Mrs.
Winters—that is, if David doesn't have to play ball!"

He turned at the door to say, "Don't be afraid of Mattie—I'll
tend to her."

"I'm not afraid of anybody," she said tranquilly.

The year flowed on into deep autumn again and there
the first frost. In the field next to her meadow her neighbo
corn was shocked and pumpkins stood naked gold, waiting.

She lived day upon day, from end to end of every day,
abandoned to each day. Never did she get up from her bed in
the morning to plan, "Today I must do this and this," nor did
she ever at night say to herself, "Tomorrow . . ."

She lived as much a creature of the hour as any bird or beast.
The hour brought its need and she fulfilled it. The pressing
haste of wife and mother was not hers. She lived within no
circle. No one came to her door to urge her to the church or to a
meeting of the women. Because she was not in the beaten path
of living they let her be, shy of what they did not understand.
Neither was there anyone to cry her down, or if they did, she
did not hear it and did not care.

She came and went about her business in the village as
decently as any wife and they were puzzled by her decency
and let her be. Only she never went into the church. She could
not enter it anymore. Where God had been was now only
silence. Her spirit cried a truce with God.

One day there was a knock upon the door and she opened it
and saw the new minister. She asked him to come in, as she
asked anyone to come in who stood there, and waited for him
to tell his errand.

He began brightly and quickly. "You are in my parish, Mrs.
Pounder, and I have missed your face in the congregation."
She fixed her eyes on him fearlessly and strongly, and he began
again. "God is ready to forgive us if we come to him."

"Forgive?" she said clearly. "For what am I to be forgiven?"

"God . . ." he began, the sweat breaking out a little on his lip.

"If there were a God," she said quietly, "I could not forgive
Him." He looked at her bewildered and went away soon. She
watched him trudge down the road. I spoke exactly as Mrs.
Mark would have spoken, she thought, amused.

If it had been a generation earlier she could not have lived
thus freely. But the times had loosened everyone. The village
paper told of strange doings in the great towns, men and
women living anyhow, drunkenness and heedlessness. Automobiles began to be built in long flying lines of speed, open to the
winds. They raced through the village, full of young men and
women going so fast their faces could not be seen. They were
blurring lines of scarlet and green and yellow and kingfisher

, and their hair streamed behind their profiles, sharp
nst the sky.

One morning old Mrs. Kinney stepped from the curb. Sarah
Kinney had run back for a shawl and had been slow, and old
Mrs. Kinney had been provoked. She called shrilly, "Sarah, I'm
going on!"

She stepped off the curb to punish Sarah, and a car tore by at
her left side, threw her and went on. It was a long red car, and
all the young faces were turned straight ahead and it did not
stop. Miss Kinney, running out, saw no more. She screamed
and ran to her mother. Old Mrs. Kinney was lying on the road,
dying. But she paused long enough to say with impatience,
"You're always forgetting something."

"I declare I miss her," said Dr. Crabbe to Joan at the funeral.
"I feel downright cheated. I believe I could have kept her
going another ten years."

Behind her black-gloved hand Miss Kinney whispered excitedly, "I'm going back to Banpu as soon as I can brush up on
the language!"

But day after day passed and she did not go. "I shall begin
brushing up right away," she said gaily, and then she forgot
and played in the garden among the falling leaves. They made
her laugh, falling on her face, on her spraying white hair. She
shook her head at them, laughing.

So Joan's coming and going seemed gentle. Besides, she had
been a child there in Middlehope. The old were growing older
and they saw her still a child. "Joan will turn out all right in the
end," they said, seeing her still a small girl, wayward for a
moment. But she was a woman, making her life out of what she
had about her.

When she went into the store for food or clothes or shoes, the
clerks greeted her as smoothly as they did another. It was true
Ned Parsons was a little wary of her, kind but wary.

"What can I do for you?" He made her nameless. There was
no saying "Joan"—it seemed too close now that he had two
children. And Netta never quite forgot that he had once been
in love with Joan Richards, or very nearly in love. She talked at
night in bed against women who left their men.

"Nothing makes it right, I say," she cried. "I'd feel it my duty
to make the best of it." She hinted against Joan. "There's things
about her I've never told even you—her and Martin Bradley."

He said mildly, "I thought Martin was sweet on you once."

But she screamed at him out of the darkness. "Me? No, thank you! I wouldn't have married Martin Bradley if he was the last man on earth. I wouldn't touch him or let him touch me —he gives me the creeps—always did, too! I never did understand Joan Richards—"

But Netta talked against women. She'd talk against his own sister. "There's Emily—she's got a good job in the city, works on a newspaper. She hasn't anybody except herself. You'd think she'd send Petie something. She didn't even write when little Louise was born—People are so selfish."

He listened. Netta talked so much. He couldn't answer everything. He had stopped answering her years ago. His mother had been such a quiet woman, smiling and dreaming and writing her stories. They used to think her silly when they were growing up. He was glad now he had not been quite so impatient as Emily had been. Emily had said to her mother, "I don't see how you can expect any publisher to take such drivel as you write." But Emily was always on their father's side. She'd get angry when they came home from school and dinner wasn't ready and their father would be puttering distractedly about the stove, and their mother's voice would drift down from the attic, "I'll be right down." But very often she wasn't right down and Emily was angry and left home as soon as she could get a job. It seemed she was all the angrier because she herself secretly wanted to write stories and couldn't be happy at anything else, though she always made fun of it.

But his mother never seemed to know Emily was angry. She was always quiet, thinking and smiling to herself and saying, "I really think I've got it this time." A quiet woman was nice in the house . . .

"I'd like to see some clear blue gingham," said Joan's cheerful voice. Joan always had a lovely rushing voice.

"Let's see. Netta's just made some dresses for Louise out of this."

"You've never seen my Mary's eyes!" Joan's voice was like laughter. "There—that sky color!" She looked just as she used to, a little heavier maybe, but she was tall. Netta was growing thinner all the time. Netta boasted, "Joan Richards—there, I forget all the time she's married—Joan Pounder's hair's getting real gray. I haven't a gray hair myself. I take after my mother. She hasn't a gray hair at sixty!"

Joan's smooth rosy face under soft early-graying hair— He

tied up the bundle of blue gingham. "Here you are," he said abruptly. "Anything else?"

"No, thank you, Ned!" Her voice was like singing and she walked out of the store as though she were dancing.

Ned's getting bald, Joan thought, the blue gingham under her arm. He looks dyspeptic. I wonder if Netta's a good cook? She thought a little tenderly of Ned's pimpled young face, yearning at her over a guitar. It seemed very long ago. He would be ashamed now if he knew she remembered him thus. But so he had been and it made a small memory, precious, too, in its way. Everything in life that was her own now was precious. She had used to plan so much for the future, to want everything. Now she wanted only to sort out of the world that which was her own. She had only lived in Middlehope. She heard of strikes and ferment outside, of hunger marchers, of men jailed for discontent too freely spoken. A turn outward, at a moment, and she might have been one of them. But she had made the inward turn.

She was drawing near to the house and now she saw someone sitting on the stone steps of the little porch. She had left David at home to watch Mary and Paul, but this was not David. She came nearer and it was Frankie. He was sitting quietly and compactly, waiting for her, his hands in his pockets. The winter air was biting cold. She hurried toward him. "Why, Frankie!" She had not seen him in months. Fanny had come and gone irregularly. She had been away working, she said, and had taken Frank with her. She had not been to get her money for nearly a month. "Why didn't you go in, Frankie?"

"Your boy told me to, ma'am, but I thought I'd rather wait here."

He had grown a great deal. He was much taller than David, tall and strong, brown-skinned, dark eyes madly lashed. But his lips were like her father's lips, purely, coldly set into the round soft oval of his face. His body was not lean and angular as David's was. It was soft-limbed, lightly fleshed. She looked him over swiftly.

"I thought I gave Fanny money to get you some new clothes!" The boy was completely out of his clothes, his hands dangling out of his short sleeves, his trousers tight about his legs.

"I haven't seen her, ma'am—not in a mighty long time. She went away and left us."

"Where did she go?"

"She said she was going to New York to get a job. The factory's closed again, ma'am. There's a strike on again, and they aren't going to take back any colored hands. Lem stayed a week and a day or two and he went to get a job at the pants factory in Newville he heard was looking for help."

"Where have you been all this time?"-

"Waiting—waiting for her to come back. She told me to wait. But I finished up everything to eat in the house."

She stood looking at him, and he looked back at her trustfully, quietly, waiting for her. Did he know what she was to him? She could not tell.

"Where are her other children?"

"Willa's got a job at the chapel dancing—she's only fifteen but she looks grown up—and Roberta's got a fellow to feed her. Roberta's the oldest."

He stood looking at her patiently with his lovely mournful dark gaze.

"I don't know what to do with you," she said, distraught.

"No," he said. "I didn't expect you would. Fanny's always saying so, too."

He looked down and scuffed the dead grass a little. Then she saw he was barefoot.

"You haven't any shoes on," she cried.

"No." His voice was acquiescent, mild. "Fanny was going to get me some before snow, she said, but she hasn't come back."

He looked at her apologetically.

"I'll be all right in a year or two, ma'am, when I'm grown enough to get a job somewhere singing. It's only just now I haven't anywhere to go."

He was so uncomplaining, he so took for granted that he was homeless and that he was nowhere wanted, that her heart ached over him. And everywhere about him, like a visible aura, hung an air of Francis. No single feature was quite the same. Francis' brown hair was here blacker and curlier, his dark eyes were darker and more liquid, his head rounder and his face fuller. But there was the likeness in his look, in his pose, in the way he stood, his weight relaxed upon his right leg, his hands in his pockets. There was even a look of herself— She caught it, hauntingly, like a fleeting glimpse into a distant mirror.

"Come in with me," she said quietly. The old familiar need to do for her own flooded into her again. In the troubled world there were the few who were her own. She took Frankie into her house and closed the door against the cold.

Inside, David was lying upon the floor reading furiously, his face set as though for a fight, his hands clenched in his hair. Mary was sitting beside him, absorbed with a little doll. In his corner in a pen she had made for him Paul was clinging to the side. He was six now, and he still said not a word. To these three she said calmly and with resolution, "This is Frankie."

She went into the kitchen at once and quietly began to prepare the supper for them all.

She had not for a long time heard from Roger Bair—not, that is, for weeks. That was a long time. He had asked her to send him a picture of herself and she had none to send him. She had not had a picture taken since she left college. Instead she had written how she looked and what she did, and sent it to him. "Do you see me? Thirty-three years old, hair already a little gray and never cut. Height, five feet nine, weight to correspond, eyes green-blue, tending to be a little stern, maybe? There—I can't write of myself."

She also asked David. "David, write down how I look. Some-one wants my picture and I a haven't one." He stretched himself before the fire with pencil and pad and considered her seriously and wrote hard, for almost an hour, his tongue be-tween his lips, scratching out an occasional word. When it was done he folded it very small and gave it to her.

"Shall I read it?" she asked.

He blushed brilliantly. "I don't care," he muttered, and ran out of the house into the spring evening. But she did not read it, telling Roger she had not. "I told my boy David to write you a picture of me."

She had not heard from him since. She could not forget that she had not. It gnawed in her all day and she remembered at night with a feeling of emptiness that it was a long time since she had seen his handwriting. But she waited. She would wait and if the time went on she would ask Francis. But she read the newspaper carefully each day because she grew a little fright-ened. Among the headlines of stocks falling headlong and swarming runs upon banks she searched for a news item— PILOT CRASHES. But it was not there. It came at last to be almost enough that it was not there.

In her house her life was divided into the four children.

David was the warm vivid center about which they moved. He was the one who was always having something happen to him. Every particle of him was adventure. She could go all day with her heart in her mouth because in the afternoon his school team was playing the Clarkville team. He was so little but he would go wherever the big boys went. When he burst into the house shouting for her, shouting, "We beat 'em—we beat 'em!" her heart let down in instant relief. "Oh, David, I'm so glad!" "Yep," he boasted, "we beat 'em ten to nothing—to nothing, mind you, Joan!" He was strung so high, so fine, suffered in such an abyss of agony, he was so impaled by pain, joy such ecstasy, that the house vibrated with him. She was involved in all his being. He was shy with her for a while until he asked her, "Did you read what I wrote about you?" She shook her head, smiling. "I sent it off just as you folded it." He was relieved, his shyness fell off him like an awkward garment not his own. He was not naturally shy.

But after a while she saw he had something to say to her and she put herself quietly in his way, that he might speak. "You're a comfort to me, David. I don't know what I'd do without you." Remembering the rare precious praise her mother had given her, she was lavish with her own praise to them all. Even to Paul she gave praise. "That's just fine, Paul—now walk to me, here, Good boy, good boy—" He staggered his few steps industriously, clutching her hand, turning his empty face up to catch her praise.

The warmth in her voice freed David's tongue. "I just wanted to tell you," he said offhandedly, "that I only wrote good things about you." He was turned away from her, but she saw that his trim close-set ears were crimson. "Thank you, David," she said composedly, careful not to be tender. He turned over the pages of a book he was reading. "I said," he added, suffused, "I said I wished you were my real mother." She wanted to run to him and take him in her arms, to fondle him and adore him. But she knew him. She went on with her sewing. "You are like my own son," she said. She lifted her eyes and he met them and a deep look passed between them. "Guess I'll go out a while," he said quickly.

"Fresh cookies in the jar," she reminded him. So that was the picture he had given to Roger. It was easier to wait for Roger again.

She had been anxious until she knew what David would feel

of Frankie. She was silent while David watched Frankie, weighing him.

"Why is he so brown if he isn't Chinese?" he asked starkly before them all.

"Frank is American," she answered. "There are many Americans who are black. Frankie's mother was dark and his father was white. That's why he is brown and why his hair is curly and why he has his lovely voice."

"Sing," David commanded.

Frankie opened his mouth and began to sing. The song was abominable, musical claptrap, but his voice startled her again. It flowed out of him richly, largely, noble in its volume, dignifying the cheap tune. They listened, even Paul listening, his eyes wandering, searching for the source. Mary stretched out her arms, imperious to be taken and brought near.

"What else do you know?"

"I know a lot of things," said Frankie. He began to sing again. "Like a river, glorious, is God's perfect peace." She listened, remembering her father.

"Who taught you that?" she asked.

"I've heard 'em singing it down in South End," he answered. "Some of the old folks sing it. Fanny sings it sometimes when she's feeling good."

Well, she had found a peace, too. And David loved Frankie. "Sing something funny!" he would demand. And Frankie, his great eyes suddenly droll, sang a witty tune, "De farmer say to de weevil." David listened, laughing. He loved Frankie because Frankie could make him laugh. But Frankie, without knowing it, shaped himself to each one of them. He made David laugh, he fetched and carried for imperious Mary, he lifted Paul to his feet and urged him to stepping. "There now, 'atta boy!" And to Joan he was something she did not understand. But she knew that if she were to grow old and weak, David might be wandering beyond seas, and Mary would be having her own way, and Paul would be as he had been born, but Frankie would come back to see that she had food and shelter. There was faithfulness in him. She could feel it, deep and steadfast in his quiet lovely look.

David and Frankie grew together, sleeping in the same room, going to the same school. But Frankie was far below his grade. David came home one afternoon bleeding, blown with battle.

"Why, David!" cried Joan horrified, hastening for water &
bandages.

"Some of the fellows laughed at Frankie," he said furiously.
"They said he was dumb and they called him a nigger, and I
socked 'em. He's just dark, isn't he, Joan?"

She looked at Frankie and caught his look, full of deep
self-realization.

"Let me wash you, David," she said. "Turn around and let
me see you." He turned, not knowing in his anger that she had
not answered. When he had gone clattering upstairs to change
his bloody shirt, Frankie spoke to her.

"I know I'm a nigger, ma'am."

She looked back at him impulsively. But he might at this
moment have been Francis, cut in bronze! She leaned to him
and quickly kissed his forehead. "You are one of my children,"
she said.

He warmed and melted, wavering, longing. But he did not
dare to come too near her. He took her hand and held it against
his cheek. His cheek was hot and soft beneath her palm. Now
she felt this other flesh. It was as sweet, as sound, as any flesh,
not strange to her. "There," she said. "Run along and find
David. I'll spread you both some bread and jam."

But under this passage of the days there was a stillness. They
were very nearly enough, these children. Paul was nearly enough
of sorrow. He was there among the others, blind, stumbling, mumbling at his hands, seizing gluttonously upon his
food. His placid baby face was changing. The vacancy of his
mind was beginning to shape it inexorably and more swiftly
than wisdom might have shaped it. He was nearly sorrow
enough, but not quite. There might be, she was beginning to
know, a sorrow deeper than Paul, even as there was a joy
deeper than David's and Mary's growing, sweeter than Frankie's singing. They were not quite enough, all of them, for her
sorrow and her joy. Something bright had ceased to weave
beneath her, as though Roger were not living. Silence was
worse than death. She never could bear silence since she had
left Bart's house. To be alive and silent was more meaningful
than death. Day after day went past and he was silent. She
came to feel she was living on a far island, out of sight and
sound. Above her in the air, around her in the seas, people
came and went and moved and struggled. But she heard nothing. Fanny had not come back. Francis did not write. Even in

village there was silence. No one came near her, day after
y. Only Mrs. Winters had come twice, to look at the chil-
ren. "I want them to know their grandmother," she said. But
ooth times she had stared at Paul.

"My goodness, Joan, you can't keep a child like that here!"

Joan picked him up and wiped his drooling mouth and made
his garments neat. She bore the pain drearily. It must come
again and again, David asking sharply, "Why can't Paul walk?"
—Mary snatching Paul's toys, knowing already he was without
defense. Only Frankie was never surprised. "Yes'm, there's
quite a lot of babies in South End slow like Paul." He looked
out for Paul, always. He took Paul's toys gently away from
Mary and gave them back to him.

She said quietly to Mrs. Winters, "I think it just as well that
they grow used to children like Paul. They're part of life."

"If I'd had my health," said Mrs. Winters, "you'd never have
to. Mr. Winters used to be so delicate, and now he's heavier
than me." She held up her arm. "Remember what round white
arms I used to have, Joan?" She looked at her withered yellow
arm sadly.

Joan forgot what she had said of Paul. "Have you seen Dr.
Crabbe?" she asked.

"Him!" said Mrs. Winters. "I wouldn't go to him—I don't
put confidence in him—never did. He's always abetted Mr.
Winters against his egg-nog, anyway. Says it doesn't do any
good if he doesn't want it. It's contrary to religion, if nothing
else. We've all got to do what we don't want to—it's life."

Joan smiled. Mrs. Winters was old now. There was no use
contradicting the old, whose voices would so soon be stopped.
But she knew life only began when one did what one wanted to
do. She wanted to see Roger Bair—to speak to him. It was no
longer enough to write.

"Well, I'll be going," said Mrs. Winters. "David looks peakedy to me. He's too thin. I saw him on the street yesterday."

"He'll never be fat—he burns himself up." she answered.
"Look at Mary!"

They both looked at Mary. She was chewing a rubber doll
and when she saw them looking at her she dimpled madly,
murmuring. Mrs. Winters capitulated. "Yes, she's real heavy.
You've done well by her, Joan. Well, as I was saying—my
Ellen was just as healthy and in a week she was dead—pneu-

monia. You can't fix your heart, not on anything in this world" She turned away from Mary.

Joan did not answer. "I will fix my heart," she said silently. "What is the use of living if you do not fix your heart? It is not living, living only to avoid pain." And always she waited for Mrs. Winters to complain because she had left Bart.

But Mrs. Winters began, "I don't go to church anymore. I can't abide the minister's wife—a cold driving woman, laying down the law, especially in the missionary society. I told her, Haven't I got a son that was a missionary and my own daughter-in-law, lying out there martyrs? These children wouldn't have been motherless if I'd been listened to. Well"— she sighed—"you'd better start David in on cod-liver oil. And if I were you, and I don't mean to hurt you, Joan, but I'd put that child away. It isn't right. Now you listen to me."

She held Paul to her closely for a long time after Mrs. Winters was gone. One could not put sorrow away and have done with it. It lived on as long as one's heart could beat to feel it.

David burst into the room. "Hello, Joan!" he shouted, and darted toward the kitchen. In a moment Frank would be there. He came and followed David, smiling at her silently. Did he really look as much like his father as she thought? She was frightened sometimes lest someone in the village might see him and see how much he looked like Francis Richards. But who now would remember Francis? No one thought about Francis anymore, no one except herself.

Whether Roger reached her first or whether she saw the notice of Francis' death first, hardly seemed important. The notice was only a small paragraph, a plane had been lost in a curious manner by a man who had, it seemed, meant to lose it —a man named Francis Richards. She stood holding the paper in her hand, staring at the name. But Francis Richards was not a very common name. Still, it was common enough so that she must keep her head. She must telegraph. But the doorbell had rung at that moment and without waiting there was such a knocking that she put the paper down and ran to the door. He had telegraphed her first, of course. Roger—but it was he himself! She knew him instantly. She had not forgotten a line of his face, his body.

"Am I in time?" he asked quickly. She stared at him. "I mean —have you seen the morning paper?"

Then it was Francis!

"Yes, I've seen it," she answered. He came in as though the house were his own and sat down before her. He had come to tell her Francis was dead. After a while, very soon, it would matter that Francis was dead. But not yet.

"It is true?" He had put down his hat. Now he took off his coat. She had never seen him in ordinary clothes before. This was the sort of clothes he wore, this rough brownish stuff.

"I've got to tell you. I wish I had been there. He was such an odd fellow—never himself on the ground. People didn't like him. But in the air he was quite different." He was swallowing hard, wiping his forehead with a brownish linen handkerchief. "In the air something changed him. He was gay, you know— quite gay, as soon as we'd left the earth. I saw it happen again and again when we went up together."

He was telling her about Francis and she must listen. It was not right now to look at his eyes, his mouth, his hands.

"He'd been getting on very well—only nobody liked him. I don't think anybody ever had any proof that he had actually any part in the trouble we had over wages. But he was the sort you'd suspect of discontent. I hope I'm not hurting you?" He was looking at her kindly. She shook her head and he went on.

"I liked him—knowing how he was in the air, you know."

But he was talking to her at a distance, as though they had never written to each other, as though letters had not come and gone a hundred times.

"Don't—don't be sad," he begged her. He leaned forward and his face was near to hers—very near. She could see lines about his eyes. His skin was fine-grained, burned brown, his teeth strong and even. "No one will ever know exactly what happened. No one was near him—I mean he had no close friends. The men saw him coming to the field, walking along with a woman. She was telling him something, talking to him . . .

"Sweet boy, haven't I told you I can't get a job? Take me with you where you live. How did I find you? I have my ways. No, I'll tell you the truth—I asked a farm fellow—"

"Let me go. Take your hand off of my arm!"

But she would not loose him. She was there, still pretty. How did women like that stay pretty so long? God, if she'd only been fat—ugly—old! But she was pretty. Her breast was

against his arm. He could feel it. No white woman had s...
lovely breasts. She had pulled back her coat on purpose. Wh...
he knew what she did on purpose why couldn't he hate he...
But it only made him want her again. And when he wanted he...
he thought of his mother, and he couldn't take her—not to glut
himself. If once he could glut himself, he might get it out of
him forever.

He used to sit in church beside his mother. He could sit still
a long time feeling her warmth, catching the smell of her, the
organ, the sound of his father's high intense voice, playing
intensely upon him.

"Get away!" he shouted. He began to walk quickly, as fast
as he could. But she was saying something, hanging to him,
never letting him go. There was a smell about her, warm, close.
He began to run. But she was saying something.

"And your boy, Frank—there's Frankie—"

He stopped. "Who?"

"Didn't Miss Joan tell you? You put a boy in me, Frank—
he's almost as big as me now."

"Joan?"

"She's been helping me with him this long time."

"You're lying!"

"Come home and look at him! Spittin' image of you, Frank.
Your sister knows it—everybody knows it if they see him—"

Now he could shake her off. Now he must shake her off. He
ran through the station and into the field. There the plane was
waiting, the little plane in which he had learned to fly. Some-
one was getting into it, someone else who was learning. He
pushed the boy aside.

"I've got to," he gasped, and leaped into the seat and seized
the stick. That was the engine roaring. Now, now he was off
the ground. There—up . . . up . . . up—as high as he could go,
into the sky!

. . . Roger was holding her two hands. "The plane dropped
like a shot bird, wheeling, over and over. No one will know
what happened. He was burned to death."

The room was so still. The two boys were at school, the two
babies were asleep. She was ashamed of her hands, rough from
gardening. He would feel her hands rough in his. Francis
burned to death—that was because Fanny had found him. She
had tried so desperately to keep them apart. If Fanny ever

back she would say, "I never can see you again. I have
the child. Now let me never see or hear of you again."

"Don't grieve so silently—speak to me—ease yourself to
me." He was caressing her hands. She must draw them away.

"My hands are so—so rough," she said indistinctly.

"Why should they be so rough?" He was looking at them,
tenderly.

"I raise a good many of our own vegetables. The children eat
a lot."

"You don't make enough at that music?"

"Oh, yes," she said quickly. "It really mounts up. I work at it
several hours every day. But it all helps. Besides, I like gardening. It's good soil."

He was still looking at her hands. Now he dropped them as
though he had thought of something. He began to feel in his
pockets for his pipe. He began to speak as he had before he
took her hands. "Well—did your brother help you in any way
—financially, I mean?"

"No," she replied. "No. Francis never helped me in any way.
He wasn't really able to."

He lit his pipe and began smoking it. He looked around the
room and at her. "This is where you live," he said. "I've wondered what a room would be like where you live—you and all
your children!"

"It is really where I live," she said. She must look at him
carefully, at every line of his body, his hands, his hair and
head, the shape of his mouth, the color of his eyes. This was he.
She put aside Francis. Francis must wait now, being dead. He
must wait upon this moment of life. Soon Roger would be
going. . . . But he was going even now, standing up, putting on
his coat, his hat in his hand.

"Now, I must go. You will not grieve too much?"

She shook her head, not smiling, her eyes steady. "I am too
used to sorrow. But it will be sorrow. I remember him a little
boy—"

"I must come back," he said abruptly. He had a very kind
quiet voice, the voice of one habitually kind.

"You will come back?" she cried, smiling at him.

"Yes," he said, "I must come back—to see how you do. You
are very solitary here."

She shook her head, speechless, and he went away.

•   •   •

Now their letters began again, now without pretense.

"I am used to seeing women helpless, leaning upon men. 1 live on that solitary hillside and are not afraid . . . "

" . . . Don't you see I am not solitary? I have everything."

He began to write of his wife—quietly, without apology that he had said so little about her. "She is a delicate creature—you would make two of her—a small creature looking like a child until one sees her face. It's always been like living with a small child."

She put the letter away. Let her remember Francis—let her remember she had a fresh sorrow over which to mourn. His clothes had come home to this house he had never entered, but it was his home because she was here, because she was the only one to know if he lived or died. She sorted them, his few clothes, his books. She looked at them. There were two little books about revolution, a copy of a book by Marx—she remembered hearing of Marx in college, long ago—a book about communism in Russia. Yes, the papers talked a good deal about Russia. It was all so confusing. Nothing was clear except the days of her life, beginning each morning and ending with the night. She found a picture of his mother among the books. But nothing else—no letter, no trace of how he had lived. His clothes were cheap and old, except his extra flying clothes. Those he had bought of good quality. He had paid well for those.

Strange how agony went out of pain when youth was gone! Sharpness of pain was gone, frantic pain was gone, sorrow was only an ache now, a deep swelling ache. Or was it that having suffered so vividly over Paul she had filled her capacity for suffering, so that now nothing could stab her again? Death seemed not sorrowful anymore, no more since she had come to think of death to free Paul. There was no other healing for Paul. So the sting was gone from any dying. When people died, they were set free. Francis was free, free of Fanny at last, free of himself. No, death could no longer wound her . . .

" . . . You understand how I could never leave my wife," Roger wrote. "She is so defenseless—a helpless creature. You are so strong you are able to bear life as it is."

She put his letter down and began to weep. She wept aloud, in the middle of a shining morning, in the midst of spring. For now she was mortally wounded. Because she was strong she must bear to the uttermost. Because she was strong, he said, she must again give up what she wanted. She wrote back to wildly, out of her intolerable hurt. He answered, "I cannot ᵤke her suffer. Shall the deer suffer because it is the deer, ᵤcause it is not born the lion?"

She was silent in her agony—shaking and trembling, feeding the children blindly, going blindly about the house. "Joan, you don't laugh!" David cried. "I wish you'd laugh again about something!" Frankie was silent, watching her with great melancholy eyes.

She flung back at Roger, "And shall the lion suffer because it is the lion? It suffers the more being strong also to suffer . . . Let us not write anymore. You are not free. I can see it."

She would end it. She sealed the letter and mailed it in hot hurry. Let it all be over. She was wounded to the core. He could wound her as death could not wound her, as even Paul had not the power to wound her. She walked back into her house. Let her be content with what she had. She had so much. She would stretch it to be enough.

She put a smile upon her face resolutely. Paul was walking, clinging from chair to chair, turning himself about the leg of the table, panting with his struggle to walk. Mary was already on her feet, a small nimble thing. They were all there in her house. David was frowning over his arithmetic. In the kitchen she heard Frankie moving about quietly, getting supper for her. In his delicate way he held himself aloof from the others, never quite like them, knowing himself, serving them in small ways unasked, shy of sitting down with them.

"Sit down, Frankie," she said every day.

"Yes'm, I'm nearly ready to." But he delayed if he could.

Then as she stood among them, Paul saw her. For the first time in his life he really saw. He looked up at the sound of her coming, and he staggered toward her, three steps, and caught her around the knees and looked up at her. Out of his dim gaze something focused in his mind for a moment and he spoke— "Mamma?"

It was his first word. She stared, incredulous with joy, into his upturned face. Why, he knew her—Paul knew his mother! She fell to her knees and seized him and began to laugh and to sob. "Children, David, Frankie, did you hear Paul? He called me!"

He pulled at the blue beads about her throat, the beads Mr. Winters had given her long ago. She had put them on this morning because of her blue dress.

They came running around her, David shouting, Mary clam-

oring with glee at the noise, Frankie smiling. "Say it aga
Paul!" cried David.

"Say it, darling," she urged. "Once more—Mamma—Mamma—say it, Paul!" She was avid to hear the word again, to
repeat the moment.

But Paul had slipped to the floor and was staring at the beads,
spreading them over his hands, as though he could not hear
her. The moment had gone. "But anyway he spoke once," she
said fiercely, getting up from her knees. "I've heard his voice
once, even if he never speaks again."

He was mumbling over the beads. She turned away quickly.

"Now, David, do you need help with your arithmetic? Yes,
Frankie, toast the bread—we'll have toast and milk for supper,
all of us."

But Paul really had spoken to her. In the great desolation—
"I have ended what was between Roger and me"—there was
the little taper burning. Once Paul had spoken to her.

"Did you think I was going to let you get away from me like
that?" Roger was there. She opened the door in the morning
and he was there. "Your letter came last night. She and I were
there alone. I saw her as I've always known she was—always in
my heart she was—never wanting to see. You made me see
her—"

He clenched his hands upon her shoulders. Across the room
Mary was pausing, astonished. She saw Mary's eyes, staring,
astonished, at this stranger bursting into the house.

"Roger, it isn't so easy—"

"No, it isn't so easy—It's so hard you've got to help me know
what to do. She's here. I brought her."

"Roger!" she cried at him in consternation. "What have you
told her?"

"Nothing at all except that you were the sister of one of my
best men who was killed, and I wanted to see how things were.
Come," he said brusquely.

She followed him down the narrow grassy path to the picket
gate. There in the road was a small low car. Roger's wife sat
there.

"Millicent, this is Francis Richards' sister. You know I told
you . . ."

She put out her hand and felt a cool slight touch upon it.
"How do you do?" It was a light, pretty voice. She lifted her

s to the face. "Will you come in?" she said quietly. This was e face Roger had once loved very much. He had said, "I was nce very much in love. I was very young." Yes, this was a helpless creature. The pretty, aging face turned to Roger, questioning, helpless.

"Yes, get out and come in," he said. He opened the door and helped her out. She went up the path in her dainty high-heeled shoes, clinging to his arm. Behind them Joan walked, alone. She had never in all her life clung to anyone as this woman was doing, never once.

In the house they sat down, the three of them. Instinctively she drew up for this woman the comfortable chair. "Will you sit here?" She made her voice quiet, hospitable. This was her house and these were her guests. Casually the slender figure in the girlish blue suit settled into the chintz-covered chair which was her own. She sat down on a straight chair, feeling herself huge, untidy, beside this minute perfection. Roger had loved this porcelain creature. Roger's deep passion had been poured upon this childish woman. She glanced at him. He was sitting there, gloomy, waiting.

The little creature was looking at him with pale anxiety. "I don't believe you feel well, Roger. He hasn't seemed well since last night." She was gazing at him out of her pretty, china-blue eyes. "I didn't want him to come this morning, but he would come." She laughed with aging coquetry. "I have to fuss over him a little. I've never had any children, Mrs. . . . . Mrs. . . . . "

She did not supply a name for herself. It did not matter what her name was.

"It is right for you to take care of him," she said gravely. Of course Roger could never leave this little creature, this little defenseless creature. The strong, the strong must suffer. "I have my four children," she said suddenly.

"Such a comfort, I know," the cool high voice was murmuring.

But Roger had said nothing at all. He was sitting there in his brown tweed overcoat, silent, his hat between his fingers. It was true he did not look well. There were deep circles under his eyes and his dark skin was sullen. "Beloved!" she cried to him in her heart. As though she had spoken he lifted his head and they looked at each other fully.

"He doesn't look well, does he?" the chattering childish voice was saying.

"Let's go, Millie," he said suddenly. He took her arm and

went toward the door. He turned his head to say to her. "I'd like to see those four children sometime." They were going toward the car, across the grass. "I'm coming back to see them. Careful, Millicent—your dress is caught on the door." He disengaged her skirt carefully and helped her in.

"Good-bye," said Joan quietly. She turned and went back into her house and shut the door. She sat down in a straight-backed chair and waited to hear the sound of the motor begin. But it did not begin.

The door opened and he was back. He had shut the door and he was at her feet, kneeling, his head on her knees. But no, she would not touch his head, his shoulders. She held herself by the arms, away from him. She was thinking over and over again, No one has ever taken care of me. I wish I were a small thing so someone would call me "little girl"—That was how silly she could be, she cried furiously in her heart, dreaming that anyone could call a great creature like her "little girl"!

"I understand," she was saying aloud. "Of course I understand how you cannot leave a little thing like that—" She had begun so patiently and quietly, understanding. For Roger to leave Millicent would be as though she were to leave Paul. She could understand that. Then why was all this bitterness welling up in her? It lay upon her tongue, like bitter gall. "What a pity," she was saying dryly, bitterly, "what a pity women are not all born small and pretty and weak! Women don't need anything except little weak pretty hands and faces, little slender bodies."

"I don't know what you mean," he said. He lifted up his head to stare at her.

She laughed, holding herself away from him. "I mean, go back to taking care of her!"

But he was looking at her as one of the children might have looked at her if she had turned suddenly harsh, who had never been harsh. He was frightened because she was pushing him away.

"But I came back to tell you I couldn't bear it not to see you anymore. There isn't any life for me away from you."

His long body was folded absurdly at her knees. His hair was gray at the temples, as gray as her own. But she loved him. He could come here into this house as the children had come. Some day he might so come, if she did not send him away now, if step by step he came his own way.

"I need you," he cried out at her. Then she let herself go. She released herself and took his head into her hands and pressed it against her bosom. It was right, this head against her bosom. This was right—this deep relief.

"Oh, how I've needed you, your strength. I've been so tired," he said brokenly.

"Yes, I know—I understand . . . Hush—I know—"

He sighed, like a child giving itself to sleep. She looked down upon his face. He had closed his eyes. The lines were gone out of his face now, for this moment. He was at rest in her, leaning on her.

" . . . Roger!" Millicent's voice came crying from the car.

He sprang to his feet at the sound. The lines sprang back again about his mouth, his eyes.

"I've got to go."

"Yes, go," she said.

"Roger, are you coming?"

He put the voice away. She could see him putting it away from between them. He took her hands.

"This isn't the end, you know. It's the beginning. I don't know what the end will be. But I'll go on until I find it. I'm coming back." He had her hands still. She nodded, smiling. He laid her hands down gently and she let them lie in her lap as he had laid them. He was gone. She had now only the moment of his head against her bosom. She felt still the touch of his head upon her bosom, his face there, the stigmata of love. He needed her. It was enough for love's beginning, whatever was the end.

She heard Paul whimpering, awake from sleep, and at his voice she rose and went back to him. The boys would be coming home from school, too. Yes, she could hear Frankie now, his voice calling down the road, "Singin' wid a sword in mah hand, O Lord—singin' wid a sword in mah han'. "

She looked out of the door as she passed. The car was gone. And down the road marched the two boys, hand in hand, to the tune of Frankie's singing. He had taken off his shoes and stockings and was walking barefoot. The spring sunshine poured down upon them. She paused on her way to the kitchen and began to sing with them as they drew near, her voice big and fresh, "Singin' wid a sword in mah hand, O Lord—"

After all, she need not hurry. The day was still at noon.